Praise for
The Confidential Life of Eugenia Cooper

"Kathleen Y'Barbo's *The Confidential Life of Eugenia Cooper* is a fast-paced story full of fun, action, drama, and love."
—MARY CONNEALY, author of *Calico Canyon*, *Petticoat Ranch*, and *Gingham Mountain*

"A fun read. Delightful, engaging, charming, and yes, funny. Humor in the characters, especially Miss Eugenia Cooper, humor in the events, as she dreams of and heads on an adventure in the West. I thoroughly enjoyed this romp of a read. If you loved Cathy Marie Hake, give yourself a treat with *The Confidential Life of Eugenia Cooper*."
—LAURAINE SNELLING, author of the Red River Series, Daughters of Blessing series, and *One Perfect Day*

"Take one spirited young woman seeking adventure—with a dime novel heroine as her role model—and add a lonely man determined not to lose his heart again. Stir in the excitement of an Old West setting, and you have a recipe for success. *The Confidential Life of Eugenia Cooper* is an absolute delight! Kathleen Y'Barbo's writing sparkles like the clear, blue Colorado skies."
—CAROL COX, author of *A Bride So Fair* and *A Test of Faith*

"Eugenia Flora Cooper has her Mae Winslow, but Kathleen Y'Barbo is my Woman of the West. In *The Confidential Life of Eugenia Cooper*, Kathleen takes you by the hand on the first page and draws you into a chase every bit as merry as any Mae Winslow adventure story. Before you realize it's happening, you find yourself in places you're reluctant to leave, among characters so genuine they only lack flesh to be real."

—MARCIA GRUVER, author of the Texas Fortunes series

"The gap between fiction and reality turns out to be much smaller than Eugenia Cooper realizes when she makes a last minute, ill-planned decision to hop a train to Denver in 1880. With excitement, romance, and humor, Kathleen Y'Barbo spins a tale that captures your mind. The author's enthusiasm for writing spills out of every scene, creating, as it should, enthusiastic readers."

—STEPHEN BLY, award-winning western author of more than one hundred books, including *One Step Over the Border,* *Paperback Writer,* and *Wish I'd Known You Tears Ago*

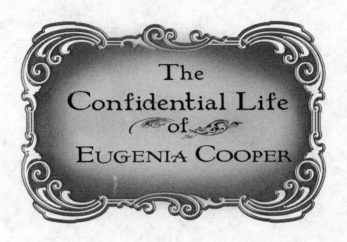

The
Confidential Life
of
EUGENIA COOPER

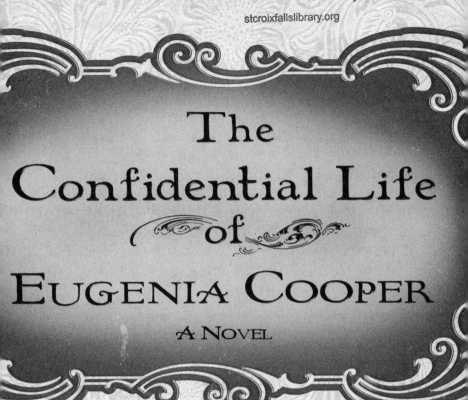

The Confidential Life of Eugenia Cooper

A Novel

Kathleen Y'Barbo

WaterBrook
PRESS

THE CONFIDENTIAL LIFE OF EUGENIA COOPER
PUBLISHED BY WATERBROOK PRESS
12265 Oracle Boulevard, Suite 200
Colorado Springs, Colorado 80921

Scripture quotations, unless otherwise indicated, are taken from the King James
Version.

This is a work of fiction. Apart from well-known actual people, events, and locales
that figure into the narrative, all names, characters, places, and incidents are the
author's imagination or are used fictitiously. Any resemblance to current events or
locales, or to living persons, is entirely coincidental.

ISBN 978-0-30744-474-5
ISBN 978-0-307-45792-9 (electronic)

Published in the United States by WaterBrook Multnomah, an imprint of The
Doubleday Publishing Group, a division of Random House Inc., New York.

WATERBROOK and its deer colophon are registered trademarks of Random House
Inc.

Library of Congress Cataloging-in-Publication Data
Y'Barbo, Kathleen.
    The confidential life of Eugenia Cooper : a novel / Kathleen Y'Barbo. — 1st ed.
        p. cm.
    ISBN 978-0-307-44474-5 — ISBN 978-0-307-45792-9 (electronic)
    I. Title.
    PS3625.B37C66 2009
    813'.6—dc22

                                                                            2009007465

Printed in the United States of America
2009—First Edition

10 9 8 7 6 5 4 3 2 1

❧

To Josh, Andrew, Jacob, and Hannah
My life, my loves, my world…I'm so proud of you!

And to Wendy Lawton, Shannon Marchese, and Jessica Barnes.
Without you and the wonderful team at WaterBrook,
Gennie would be back in Manhattan still reading under the covers.

"Sometimes what a person wishes
for is neither what they really want nor
what they need. Sometimes,
it's the wishing that's the best part."
—*Mae Winslow, Woman of the West*

1

The warning came too late.

Mae Winslow's finely tuned senses jumped as the fire bell rang, setting the populace into a motion akin to the stirring of a nest of hornets, and sending Mae into a fit of the vapors.

Before the sounding of the alarm, the only stings fair Mae felt in the bleak light of dawn were from her heart and her conscience. She had disappointed dear Henry once again, allowing the calamity that dogged her steps to set her on yet another path leading away from the home and hearth he so freely offered. Surely the long-suffering Henry understood that beneath her buckskin-clad exterior beat a heart that held nothing but love for him despite the vagabond life she must lead.

At the moment, however, her mind must turn from the excess of emotional thoughts that Henry Darling brought and toward the situation at hand. With the practiced eye of one far too well-trained in the ways of desperate outlaws and lowly curs, she lifted the sash of the boardinghouse window and lowered her gaze to the street below. With the fresh wind came the bitter scent of smoke. Alas, the odor did not emit from below or from beyond the bounds of the quaint structure, but rather swirled from behind, as if seeping beneath the slightly crooked bedroom door.

Mae made to turn when a shot rang out. A bullet chipped away several layers of paint on the sill and sent her scrambling to the floor. There, with her breath coming a bit freer, she crawled toward the bed, where her pistols hung on the bedpost.

"So," the fair jewel breathed as she wrapped her small fingers around the cold metal that had saved her life more times than she could count, "they've found me."

♋

New York City, July 5, 1880

Something tickled her nose. Eugenia Flora Cooper batted at the offending object, then opened her eyes to see that she'd tossed a fringed pillow onto her bedroom floor. A thud told her the book she'd been reading last night had gone flying as well.

The book, a brand-new episode of Mae Winslow, Woman of the West. Gennie sighed and pulled the silk and velvet coverlet over her head as she snuggled down into the soft feather mattress. Despite the fact she was required to attend a post–Independence Day breakfast with the Vanowens this morning, then catch a train to Boston at noon, she'd devoured every word of the dime novel last evening, staying awake late into the night.

After completing Mae's latest adventure, Gennie reluctantly closed her eyes. Even then, the story continued, this time with Gennie as the subject. She'd been running alongside a moving train full of stolen gold, her borrowed cowboy boots dangerously close to tripping her, when the dream abruptly ended. And, like Mae, she'd been fleeing the bonds of a man bent on prematurely tying her to home and hearth.

Gennie, like Mae, could admit no real aversion to marriage and family. In fact, she welcomed the idea of a life spent in such a way.

Just not yet.

Like Mae.

Perhaps that was what drew her to Mae's stories over other novels.

It seemed Mae was the only woman whose books never quite ended with a happily ever after. Each one promised it could—even should— and then the adventure took a turn, and so did Mae. By the end of the book, the bad guys were caught but Mae was not.

Someday, if Gennie ever had the nerve, she'd just head west down Fifth Avenue and keep walking until she reached South Dakota or Wyoming. Colorado, maybe, where she could pan for gold or dig for silver. Maybe save some hapless child or even a whole town from whatever evil preyed upon it.

Gennie smiled. Wouldn't *that* be an adventure?

Of course, Mama and Papa would miss her, but what a time she'd have riding runaway horses and fending off savage beasts with nothing but a broom and three wet matches. It would certainly be more interesting than painting flowers on china plates or embroidering her initials on handkerchiefs. Mama always had despaired of her stitching.

At the thought of her mother, Gennie bolted upright. It would never do for her choice of reading material to become common knowledge, even though she'd never understood the condemnation dime novels drew among her social set. Mae's adventures were tame compared to stories she read in the Bible. Surely the Lord smiled equally on the authors of such wholesome entertainment and on those who wrote more scholarly works.

Still, she should probably fetch the book and hide it with the others before the new chambermaid came in to open the drapes and draw her bath. Her secret had been safe with her previous maid, Mary. The dear Irishwoman carried off the books once Gennie read them. She claimed to be tossing them into a trash bin, but Gennie knew better. At least Mary hadn't informed Simmons, who would have told her parents at the first opportunity. Anything Simmons knew was destined for Papa's ear before the day ended, which was why Papa paid the elderly house-man so well.

But then Mama and Papa, along with fourteen-year-old Connor, were safely aboard a ship heading for their silver anniversary tour of the Continent. Gennie smiled and sank back into her cocoon of blankets. Surely a maid stumbling over a dime novel was beyond their concern. Perhaps she'd read the next dime novel in the drawing room instead of under her covers.

Opening one eye, she peered across the pile of pillows and through the bed drapes to see only the faintest glow of daylight at the edge of the curtains. "Still early," she muttered. "Just a few more minutes and I'll…"

She snuggled deeper into her pillow and closed her eyes.

"Miss Cooper, you've fallen back to sleep. Do wake up."

A blinding shaft of light intruded on her slumber, and Gennie fumbled for a pillow to cover her face. Finding none within reach, she struggled into a sitting position.

"I'm sorry, miss," the maid said, "but it's half past ten."

"Half past ten?" Gennie sputtered, suddenly alert. "How in the world will I explain to Mrs. Vanowen why I missed such an important event as her post–Independence Day breakfast?"

Gennie fought her way through the bed curtains and reached for her robe. As she tied the sash, she began to pace, carefully avoiding the pillows strewn across the Aubusson carpet. She'd also have to explain her absence to Chandler Dodd, although that prospect didn't upset her nearly as much as disappointing her father.

"Papa will be most upset," she said as she drifted toward the east-ernmost window and glanced at the midmorning rush on Fifth Avenue three stories below. "He so coveted a place on Mrs. Vanowens's list for Mama, and with this snub, she'll certainly be overlooked next time."

Mae Winslow, on the other hand, cared little for such frippery. *If only...*

"So sorry, miss." The hapless maid, Mary's replacement, ducked her head and inched forward, the silver tray she held wobbling with each step. "You see, there's been a most upsetting problem with my sister's departure, and I—"

"Never mind." Gennie gave the tray a cursory glance, then pointed to the dressing table nearest the window overlooking the park. "Perhaps you'd like to tell all of this to our neighbor." She paused as the maid's eyes filled with tears. Gennie sighed. "Forgive me. I'm being awful. I'm exhausted because I stayed up too late." Her heart sank. This was no way to begin with a new employee. "What's your name?"

The dark-haired girl fixed her attention on her shoes. "Fiona, miss. Fiona McTaggart."

"Perhaps there's no harm done, Fiona." Gennie seated herself at the writing desk and pulled a sheet of paper from the drawer.

Crafting two notes of regret that included only vague mentions of any specifics of her condition, she dried the ink, folded the paper, and then set her seal on the edge. When the wax hardened, she held the notes out to Fiona.

"Have Simmons send someone to deliver these, please." She paused to set her tone in what she hoped was a mix of understanding and firmness. "And then perhaps we will both be forgiven for our transgressions."

The girl grinned, then quickly seemed to remember her place. "You're every bit as nice as Mr. Simmons said you'd be. Oh!" She stifled a gasp. "Begging your pardon, miss, but I'd be ever so grateful if you'd not mention I forgot to wake you. I'm afraid I'd be out on my ear after my first day, and with my sister's leaving us this afternoon, I don't know how I'd take care of my mama and my ailing papa."

"Of course, I won't mention it. There'd be no purpose to it."

As Fiona scurried out, Gennie rose and turned her attention back to the scene unfolding on the street below. Several drivers had arrived with carriages, and liveried attendants milled about beneath a brilliant blue sky.

She let her gaze drift across the street and up the marble steps of the imposing mansion that sat on the corner like a wedding cake. The Vanowens' third floor ballroom stood at eye level, floor-to-ceiling windows open to the fresh July breeze. A lone figure swept the marble floor where, as a child, Gennie and her friend Hester Vanowen pretended to ice skate across the polished marble in their stocking feet.

Gennie's family returned the favor when Hester accompanied them to their house in Newport, where the long upstairs hallway opened onto a balcony that overlooked the lawn and the ocean beyond. Little imagination was required to believe that with just a bit of extra effort, one might be able to launch over the balcony's edge and soar into the clouds.

Hester only attempted it once, and thankfully the thick foliage broke her fall. Even better, Mama and Papa were away at the time.

"May the Lord bless you, miss. Perhaps you'd like me to pour your coffee now?"

Gennie turned to see the door close behind the maid. "Yes, Fiona. Please do."

A flurry of activity across the street again caught her attention. Gennie shrank back from the window and peered around the heavy drapes as a cluster of guests emerged from the Vanowen home. Among them was the tall figure of Chandler Dodd. Clad in his usual top hat and ascot, he looked every bit the banker he was. As Papa reminded her often, a life spent as Chandler Dodd's wife would be most comfortable.

Gennie sighed. Chandler was not an unpleasant sort. Far from it. He could even make her laugh if he put his mind to the task. But a husband? She hadn't decided what that would be like, although if Papa insisted, she'd do as he said.

Still, she'd wondered on more than one occasion whether Chandler would prefer a brownstone over a home in the country, what opinion he held of dime novels, and what he might think of a wife who wanted nothing more than a honeymoon in Deadwood or Denver instead of Rome or Athens.

One of her father's footmen dodged buggies and people to cross the street just as Chandler ducked into his carriage. Knowing the banker's first inclination would be to look up at the spot where Gennie now stood, she let the drape fall into place and turned her back on the window.

Thus far, she'd managed to escape any sort of private audience with Chandler, keeping their meetings to public gatherings. Soon enough he'd come calling; today, however, was not the day for it. Not when her mind was occupied with thoughts of her month ahead in Boston. Papa's Boston family was nice enough, but a month spent with them was a bit long, especially when she'd lack the comfort of escaping with Mama when discussions of politics became too tedious.

Still, it would be better than a month spent alone in Manhattan, although if she had a choice, she'd prefer to be headed west for adventure.

Fiona, who had set out the breakfast and poured the coffee, waited with a linen napkin in her hand. Obliging her, Gennie sat and accepted the napkin. Fiona lifted the silver cover and revealed enough scrambled eggs, bacon, and toast to feed three hungry men.

"You've been a bit generous with the portions," Gennie said. "Perhaps when I return from Boston we might sit down together and discuss my preferences." She paused to stab at the eggs. "Has Simmons given you my schedule?"

The maid pulled a piece of paper from her apron pocket and unfolded it. "You're to be delivered to the train station at half past eleven this morning, and Simmons will send a man to retrieve you on August 7 at exactly three in the afternoon. Any correspondence you receive is to be bundled weekly and delivered to you in care of the Eddington Cooper family, Lake Street, Boston."

Gennie scooped up a slice of bacon and situated it across her toast, then indicated for Fiona to sit. "Correct." A thought occurred to her. "What will you do while I'm gone? Mary used to take the month to visit family along with me. She was from Boston."

Fiona shrugged as she perched on the edge of the settee. "After I accompany you to Boston, I'm to come back here and busy myself about the house until you return."

Gennie set the napkin atop her plate as an idea formed. "You know, Fiona, I believe I'll make this trip on my own." She met the maid's gaze. "Have you ever had an adventure?"

"An adventure?" Fiona seemed to consider the question a moment. "No, I don't suppose I have. I'm not nearly as brave as my sister."

"Tell me about your sister," Gennie said.

"My sister?" Fiona's eyes widened. "Oh, miss, she's the bravest thing you'd ever want to know, that one. I shall miss her terribly." She hung her head. "'Tis a pity."

"A pity?" Gennie took a sip of coffee. "Whatever do you mean?"

"We have a cousin, Katie, who's a governess. Well, she *was* a governess until she agreed to marry Angus. But she couldn't just run off and leave the girl without guidance, what with the men she lived with, so a promise was made. Either my sister or I would go and take her place so she could marry Angus. I couldn't imagine it, being so far away, but my sister, she's the brave one. Then she met a young man too. Now she's leaving him to go out and take care of Charlotte." Fiona shrugged. "There's nothing to be done about it, really."

Gennie shook her head. "Fiona, I'm confused. Start over. Something about your sister Charlotte, a girl named Katie, and her fellow Angus."

"No, miss. My cousin Katie married Angus last month. When she left her job caring for Charlotte, she promised Mr. Beck—that's Charlotte's father—she would send someone to replace her. My sister leaves on the afternoon train."

"Ah, so your sister's going on an adventure. How exciting."

Fiona shook her head. "No, you don't understand. My sister's met someone. In order to keep her promise to Katie, she has to leave behind the man she loves."

"And he can't go with her?"

"No, miss. He can't leave so soon. If only someone could mind the child until my sister and he are wed. It would only be a few weeks, a month perhaps." She met Gennie's gaze as if asking for a solution.

Gennie was the last person from whom a solution could be received. She had her own dilemma: a need for an adventure of her own, a Mae Winslow–sized adventure. But would she be brave enough to grasp the chance if it were presented to her?

If You bring the opportunity, Lord, she vowed.

"I see." Gennie toyed with the gilt edge of the saucer. "And you are not up to taking that trip?"

Again Fiona's eyes told the story. "I'm...afraid."

"Afraid? Of what?"

"Well, it's far. Very far. And me, I've never even been to New Jersey."

Gennie moved the tray aside. "Where is this awful place? Shanghai? Siam?"

"No, miss." Fiona shuddered. "Denver."

"Denver, Colorado?" When Fiona nodded, Gennie rose and sucked in a quick breath. *If You bring the opportunity, I will go.* Had her prayers been answered so soon? "Tell me again why your sister isn't keen on this opportunity. Is this child naughty?"

Fiona jumped to her feet. "Oh, no, she's a sweet one, so I've been told, though I understand she can be quite the challenge. My cousin cried when she left the family. That's why she was so particular about sending for one of us to take her place."

"I see." A plan began to hatch and with it came more pacing. "I'm going to ask you a question, and I want you to think carefully before you answer. If your sister were offered the chance, would she give her ticket to someone else?"

A puzzled look crossed Fiona's face. "You mean would she sell her ticket? I don't think so. But if there was someone suitable to take her place as governess to that little girl, well, I think she'd be glad to hand her ticket over." She paused. "Begging your pardon, miss, but I feel I ought to remind you that you've got a train to catch shortly."

"Yes," Gennie said slowly, "but first, I need to write a letter to my Boston cousins."

"A letter to your cousins?" Fiona shook her head. "I don't understand."

Gennie kicked a pillow out of the way and settled at the writing table. "You'll understand soon enough. Grab your coat, Fiona, and tell Simmons to send the carriage around. This will only take a moment."

2

Dire circumstances seemed the order of the day for Mae Winslow, and yet never had she failed to have a plan. To panic would mean certain death, so Mae lifted the delicate lace handkerchief to her nose and raised her eyes heavenward. Her prayers completed, she sprang into action.

Through the haze of smoke, Mae found her boots and then her hat. What remained was to see whether the carefully devised scheme would actually work.

"Oh, miss, this will never work."

Gennie shook her head and pressed a gloved finger against her lips. "Quiet now, Fiona. We don't want our plan to be discovered until…" She paused to wait for the front doors of the house to close behind them. A fresh north wind whipped down Fifth Avenue and chased up her spine. "In order for this to work, we've got to stick to the plan."

The maid looked doubtful. "Are you certain? I know my sister will be ever so grateful for you to take her place, but I do worry what the child's father will say when he realizes he hasn't got a governess after all."

"Ah, but that's the beauty of it." Gennie nodded at a pair of matrons passing on the sidewalk. "He *will* have a governess. I plan to stay and assist the poor fellow in the caring of this child, at least until your sister and her new husband can cash in my ticket for two lesser fares and join me in Denver. By that time, I will be thoroughly satisfied with my adventures in the Wild West and ready to return home." She beamed and gathered her traveling cloak around her as Papa's carriage turned the corner. "If all goes well, Mama and Papa never have to know."

Fiona leaned close as the carriage pulled up to the curb. "But, Miss Cooper, you're *not* a governess."

"Well, of course she's not a governess, girl. Who would ever consider such a ridiculous thing?" Chandler Dodd grinned as he stepped out of the carriage.

"Mr. Dodd!" Gennie stepped back in surprise. Why was Chandler in her father's carriage?

"Good morning, Miss Cooper. My, you look fetching."

As did he. But then Chandler Dodd always cut a dashing figure. It almost made up for the fact that his dinner conversation, generally discussions of a financial nature, was usually so bland it was all Gennie could do not to fall into the soup in a dead slumber.

Chandler lifted her hand to his lips, then began the business of ordering the help about. Rendered temporarily mute, Gennie could only watch as her trunks appeared and were loaded. By the time she found her voice, the luggage was settled and she'd been handed into the carriage to sit beside the banker. A surprised squeak let her know Fiona had been loaded as well, most likely up beside the driver.

This certainly complicated her plan and left her with a difficult choice. Should she make a scene like Mae Winslow would have done, or give up her plan? Gennie decided to try a third option: using her rusty feminine wiles.

"Really, Mr. Dodd," she finally managed. "This isn't necessary. You're a busy and important man, and the train station will be crawling with persons of unknown ilk. Besides, the driver is here to assist us." She started to rise, but the carriage bolted forward, sending her tumbling back onto the seat. "Oh my," she squeaked.

"I insist." The banker's smile didn't quite reach his eyes as he tipped his hat. "I promised your father I would look after you in his absence. In fact, it was for that very reason Simmons suggested I accompany you to the train station."

Gennie grasped the seat to keep herself in place when the carriage turned the corner. "Yes, well, honestly, Mr. Dodd, I really don't mind tending to myself today. I've been looking forward to visiting my destination for some time now. In fact—"

"And speaking of absences," Chandler said as if he hadn't heard a word except his own, "you were missed this morning at the Vanowen party." His dark brows gathered above his nose. "Are you unwell? Your note was a bit vague."

"Vague." She stared out at the passing scenery until her stomach complained. "I didn't want to burden you with a woman's silliness."

"Nonsense. I adore you, Eugenia. You know your father and I have spoken on more than one occasion of the great possibility that I might—"

Gennie lurched forward and began to cough, hoping to distract him. When she felt she'd accomplished her goal, she leaned back and covered the lower half of her face with her cloak.

"Forgive me," she said through the muffling layers. "I'm so looking forward to fresh air and open spaces."

He arched a dark brow. "In Boston?"

She was saved by a commotion outside the carriage, which temporarily directed his attention away from her. When he looked back at her, she lowered her lashes. "Forgive me," she said again, "but would you mind terribly if I rested my eyes a moment? I'm awfully tired."

"Of course." He shifted positions to face her. "Rest while you can. The trip ahead is a long one."

He had no idea.

The carriage soon arrived at the edge of what could only be called a mob scene. While the mass of people seemed intimidating, Gennie felt her courage soar. The train for Denver awaited.

"That settles it," Chandler said. "A lady of your caliber has no place among this. There's nothing to be done about it. You'll just have to postpone the trip until Father can make arrangements for his rail car to be brought up."

"No!" The force with which she made the statement stunned them both. She offered a smile and lowered her lashes again. "That is, I couldn't bear to think of departing at a later date. That would mean our reunion would take place later rather than sooner." She lifted her gaze and one corner of her mouth, hoping for a shy, demure expression. "And I couldn't bear that either, Mr. Dodd."

"Do you mean it?"

The look in Chandler's eyes took her off guard. Had her ruse worked too well? Perhaps a bit of backtracking was in order. "I...well, that is—"

"Say no more, Miss Cooper." He leaned forward to envelop her in an embrace and then, to her astonishment, kissed her.

Gennie blinked hard as the world tilted, then righted itself once more. "Oh my," she managed through greatly shortened breath. "That was unexpected."

She spoke to an empty carriage, however, for Chandler had already jumped out and busied himself with her trunks. Gennie suspected the flush in his cheeks was not from the exertion of hauling her luggage.

By the time she climbed out of the carriage, her trunk sat atop a pile of luggage beside a Boston-bound train, and Chandler Dodd stood beside the porter with his money clip in hand. She pushed her way inside the train station. Fewer people populated the building than the platforms, and they moved about in a more orderly fashion. Still, the sounds and smells competed with the occasional roar of a train whistle to make Gennie feel genuinely less than well.

And then there was the kiss. She touched her lips with her gloved hand and closed her eyes. Chandler Dodd had certainly given her something to think about on her trip west. He'd also given her a good reason to come home once her adventure ended.

"Take care of her," she heard the banker say. He was moving her direction.

Gennie opened her eyes. Fiona cowered at her side, her face a mask of fear. "It's going to be fine," Gennie whispered. "Do you see your sister?"

The maid nodded. "Over there, miss." She pointed through the crowd. Any of several women could have been Fiona's sister. Under the circumstances, Gennie decided not to ask which one.

She leaned toward the maid. "Go tell her what is about to happen, then wait for my signal. I'll handle Mr. Dodd."

Fiona's eyes went wide. "Are you certain?"

"Go."

Gennie watched the maid weave through the crowd and embrace a slender woman, then point in her direction. She forced her attention back on Chandler and the trunks she must retrieve once he left. He stopped by her side, the porter on his heels.

"Oh, yes sir." The porter folded a thick wad of cash and stuffed it into his vest pocket. "Glad to do it, sir. I'd best get her seated before the train leaves without us both."

"I've paid you enough to see that I get a few moments alone with Miss Cooper." Chandler reached for Gennie's elbow but did not quite meet her gaze. "If you'll excuse us."

The porter grinned and nodded as he headed for her trunks.

"Wait," Gennie called. "Don't take them yet."

"But…" He looked at Chandler, who nodded. "Yes ma'am."

Gennie allowed the banker to lead her to a quiet corner, if anything in that madhouse could be called quiet. When she saw Chandler's face, Gennie's fear at the possibility he might kiss her again was quickly replaced by the thought he might not.

"Something wrong?" she asked. "You're wearing a frightful expression."

"Am I?" He shook his head, concern etching his brow, then began to pace, a difficult prospect considering the people streaming past. Finally, he stopped and stood before her. "I've let your father down."

The statement stunned her, but the emotion Chandler showed surprised her more. "Whatever are you talking about, Mr. Dodd?" Out of the corner of her eye, she saw Fiona and her sister watching them. "You've seen me safely to the train station. I understand completely that you must leave. You're a busy—"

"No, you don't understand." Chandler grasped her shoulders and turned her toward him. "I failed to keep you safe…from myself. My behavior in the carriage was reprehensible." He hung his head. "I don't know what happens when I'm near you, Miss Cooper. It's as if I take leave of my senses."

She might have laughed had the banker not looked so distraught. Instead, she offered a genuine smile. "I assure you I have never felt as safe as I do at this moment. And if it is the kiss to which you are referring, I must warn you that offering your regrets would offend me. You're not about to do that, are you?"

Chandler's worried look quickly shifted to a smile as he leaned closer. "I would rather die than offend a beautiful woman such as yourself. In fact, were we not in such a public forum, I might risk stealing another."

Gennie touched a hand to her throat while warmth crept into her cheeks. Where had this side of the staid banker been hiding? "Why, Mr. Dodd, this is all quite unexpected."

A train whistle blew, and the porter called for stragglers to board. Chandler loosened his grip on her shoulders and grasped her hand. "Perhaps, but I vow I shall write you daily, and until you return, I will be a miserable wretch."

Write daily? She hadn't considered that when making her plans. "Oh dear," she said. "Perhaps that's not such a good idea."

"No?"

"No." She inched toward the train, glancing over to indicate that Fiona should do the same. "With each letter, I'd only be reminded of what I left behind."

He took her elbow and led her toward the porter. "Yes, but what else shall we do?"

An idea occurred, at once brilliant and devious. Surely an innocent trip to Denver would never come between them.

She paused to look up into eyes the color of freshly brewed coffee. "I propose we keep a diary of the things we do each day. When I return, we can meet again and share them together."

Chandler looked skeptical. "You want me to write down what I do?"

"If you like." Fiona appeared through the crowd, her sister a discreet distance behind. Gennie nodded to her maid, then returned her attention to Chandler. "Of course, if you'd rather write, I cannot stop you, but I must say that receiving your letters would cause me great distress."

The confused look returned. "I cannot understand why. I certainly would not write of things that would upset you."

"And yet our parting upsets me." She nodded toward the train. "It's time for me to go. I hope you understand if I prefer to say our good-byes here."

"But I'd hoped to see you to the train."

Gennie rested her hand atop his. "I'm asking two things of you, Mr. Dodd. Keep your journal, and let me go to the train alone."

The banker sighed. "These are your wishes?"

"They are."

She held her breath while he considered the statement. Fiona stopped beside Gennie's trunks, the only luggage near a train set to leave any moment. A fair distance away, Fiona's sister stood watching.

A smile dawned on Chandler's face. "Then it will be my pleasure to do as you ask."

Relief flooded her, but Gennie was careful not to let the emotion show on her face. "Then, since you are in a mood to do as I ask, per-haps I could make one more request."

"Anything."

Gennie rose up on tiptoe and embraced Chandler. "Could I beg one last kiss?" she whispered.

"Miss Cooper, it is I who is reduced to begging in your presence." He lowered his hat to shield their faces. "But I cannot think of any request I would enjoy fulfilling more than this one."

This kiss, while not taking her by surprise, still stunned her. How in all the years she'd known Chandler Dodd had she missed this side of him? The answer came to her as he offered one last embrace and turned to walk away.

She'd missed it because she hadn't been looking.

Gennie waited until Chandler's top hat disappeared around the corner, then hurried to her trunks. The porter, considerably less enthusiastic about her delay now that the train whistle had blown, reached for the handle.

"Don't touch that," she called. "Whatever he paid you, I will double it if you see that this trunk gets to…" She turned to Fiona and her sister. "Tell him which train you're—or rather, I'm on."

Fiona did, and the porter shook his head and checked his schedule. "But that train's not going to Boston. It's headed for Denver."

"Exactly." Gennie reached for the velvet reticule hanging from her wrist. "Now, how much did he pay you?"

The porter waived away her offer. "Your gentleman told me to see you got safely to where you're going. I figure if you say you're going to Denver instead of Boston, then that's none of my business. Just give me a minute to locate a man to get your trunks over to the right train. According to my schedule, you've got nearly an hour before that one leaves."

As the porter scurried off, Fiona introduced Gennie to her sister.

"I don't know how to tell you how grateful I am that you've offered to take my place until my man and I can marry up and head west." Fiona's sister paused. "You're certain this is what you want to do, Miss Cooper?"

"Yes, absolutely certain." Gennie retrieved her ticket to Boston from her reticule and exchanged it with the one Fiona's sister held for Denver. "If I don't take this chance, I might never get another one." She smiled at Fiona. "Enjoy yourself the next three days, and don't let on to Simmons where I've gone when you return to work."

"Of course. Thank you again, miss, for letting me have time with my sister. I know it's a sacrifice, seeing as how you'll have to travel alone."

Strange how a trip to Boston had always required an escort, and yet she felt no such need on her excursion to Denver. Perhaps she was more like Mae Winslow than she thought.

Fiona's sister's voice penetrated her thoughts. "And you're going to take good care of Mr. Beck's girl until I get there?"

"Mr. Beck," Gennie repeated. "Yes, of course. Tell me again how I will know who he is."

3

"Nothing is as I expected," Mae muttered as she pressed against the door of the claustrophobic room and found it hot to the touch. "Neither the fire nor whatever form of ruffian favored me with a bullet shall dissuade me."

She pressed forward until her fingers wrapped around the sill. Giving a great heave, she slipped over the edge and, under the cover of thick smoke, landed in the soft and forgiving mud a story below. She rose unharmed but coated in mucky mire. What mattered, however, was that she would live to ride another day.

And ride she would.

ᛞᚷ

Gennie stepped into the railway car and stopped short. She'd done it.

She'd really done it.

No, she'd done nothing until the train left the station. This lunacy could be stopped with a backward motion and a race for home.

She could be dining with Chandler Dodd come dinnertime should she take that one step now and forget any idea of a great western adventure. Surely if Mae Winslow had been kissed as well as Gennie had been moments ago, she'd be happy to face marriage and a babe or two in the cradle.

Her gloved fingers found her lips. Chandler had captured the element of surprise in their kiss. Had he also captured her heart?

Close this door, Lord, if it is not one You wish me to walk through. I'll forget this adventure and go home if You disapprove.

A rough shove against Gennie's back moved her into the aisle against her own volition. Rather than look back at whatever uncouth clod stood behind her, she allowed her gaze to skip across those who had arrived before her.

Vast numbers of unwashed bodies huddled on benches that looked barely able to support their weight. In the air hung a decidedly unappetizing aroma she dared not contemplate. She reached for her handkerchief and held it against her nose in an attempt to deflect the odor.

The call to adventure no longer beckoned so loudly. Perhaps she'd made a mistake.

A child skittered past, and two more followed, all three tromping on her skirt and marring her reticule with what she hoped was only some form of melted chocolate. As she stopped to swipe at the stain with her handkerchief, she felt the push again.

"Now see here," she said, dabbing at the brown mark even as she tried to hold her breath. "I'll find my way soon enough."

"You'll find it now, miss, or else I'll have the reason why," a gruff voice said so near her ear that she jumped. "Where's your ticket?"

Gennie turned to see a pale-faced man in some sort of official-looking uniform that had been patched in several places and needed further attention in others. His narrowed eyes, squinting beneath a cap that proclaimed his position with the rail line, seemed to hold little empathy for her situation.

Nor did he seem to recognize her station, as he once again gave her a push. "Move along, miss," he said. "I'm the conductor, and if you're without a ticket, I suggest you march right out the other exit. I'll have no stowaways on my train."

"Stowaway? Well, of all the nerve." Gennie almost told him her father could have purchased this awful train had he the interest to do so, almost told him she'd rather be hung upside-down from her toes than find a seat in this railway car, almost told him she'd not subject an alley cat to such an awful journey, let alone a human.

But she didn't.

Surely the Lord would chastise her for such imperious thoughts. Mama certainly would.

Rather, she did as she'd been taught and offered her best receiving-line smile, then murmured the appropriate words of apology while she fumbled in her stained reticule for her ticket. The object found, she presented it to the conductor.

"So terribly sorry to inconvenience you," she said, eyes downcast. "Perhaps you might do me the honor of escorting me to my seat." Gennie lifted her gaze to find him blushing a most peculiar shade of pink. "I'm most unfamiliar with your railway car."

"Well, now," he managed as he beheld the ticket and then, by degrees, her. His expression softened, and he ushered her with great fanfare to her place near the back of the car.

Two fellows of dubious lineage stared sullenly out a window that could barely be called transparent. Their companion, a sleepy woman of middle age, sat with her chin resting on her ample bosom, lifting her head only when the conductor ordered her to remove her chicken from Gennie's seat.

Chicken? Gennie tore her gaze from the woman and looked at the opposite bench and the cage that indeed held a prize example of poultry. From the way it flapped and squawked, disgruntled poultry.

Removing a tobacco-stained bandana from his pocket, the conductor made a show of dusting off the seat. "There," he said as he swiped at his forehead, then stuffed the fabric back into his pants. "Fit for a lady, it is."

"Indeed," she said, managing a few words of thanks. Still, she did not move. Could not move.

"Miss?"

Gennie glanced at the conductor as the urge to flee rose. Surely this Mr. Beck would manage without her. But would she manage as a wife to Chandler Dodd without this one last adventure?

"Miss?"

Gennie straightened her shoulders and slipped past the sullen woman to settle carefully across from her companions, her reticule carefully placed with the stained side away from her traveling skirt.

"Good afternoon," she said to her traveling companions. "Lovely day for an adventure, isn't it?"

Those on either end looked away, but the bland expression of the man in the middle shifted to a smirk. "Lovely," he said in a voice that so closely approximated her own that Gennie wondered whether he was responding or mocking.

She clutched her bag tighter as a ruckus arose at the opposite end of the railway car.

"I must get past," a familiar voice shouted above the din. "Do move so I might warn the lady."

Gennie rose. "Fiona?"

The crowd in the aisle parted, and Gennie's maid raced forward. "Miss," she called. "Oh, a terrible thing's happened. It's Mr. Dodd."

Gennie climbed over the caged chicken and her seatmates' feet to meet the terrified maid in the aisle. "Chandler?" she asked, grasping Fiona's shaking hands. "What's happened?"

Bent over and breathless, the woman pulled one hand away to gesture toward the window. "Out there," she gasped. "With the porter." Another gasp, and Fiona straightened. "Your trunk. He spied it."

"Slow down," Gennie said. "You're making no sense. Mr. Dodd can't be with the porter. I watched him leave."

"Well, he returned," Fiona said, again pointing to the windows, "and he's bent on seeing the porter arrested for stealing. Said that's the only way your trunk could possibly be on this train."

Understanding dawned by degrees, as did the sinking feeling in Gennie's stomach. Not even out of the station yet and the call to adventure was about to be silenced.

Gennie moved toward the window, heedless of the many obstacles in her path. Through the sooty haze, she made out the broad back of her soon-to-be fiancé as he leaned toward the piteous porter. Joining the fray were two of New York's finest, both seemingly eager to believe whatever Chandler told them.

"Oh no," she whispered.

At that moment, Chandler whirled around and seemed to looked directly at her. Gennie ducked, landing between the squawking chicken and the smirking man.

Her heart pounding, she searched for Fiona, then grabbed her wrist and dragged her down as well. "Careful, else he'll see you."

"Oh, he knows I'm on the train," Fiona said. "He sent me, actually."

"Sent you?" Gennie shook her head. "So he knows I'm aboard." A sigh slipped out as she buried her face in her hands. "And it was going to be such a grand adventure."

"Oh, no, miss," Fiona said. "He asked me to see if I might find any more of your things aboard the train. He seems to think that poor fellow had a partner in crime." The maid winked. "I'll not mention I found *you* instead."

Gennie leaned back against the seat and tried to ignore the chicken, the awful man, and whatever caused her traveling dress to stick to the floor. "But there's still the matter of my trunk."

Fiona shrugged. "Perhaps I could offer to fetch it to you."

"Fetch it to me?" Gennie tapped her finger against her temple and tried to reason out the idea. "You know, it just might work."

"Except that I can't possibly travel to Denver with the trunk. Simmons expects me back at the mansion in a few days' time."

"True. Let me think," Gennie said.

"Beggin' your pardon, miss," Fiona said, "but there's not much time for thinking."

An idea dawned, and Gennie scrambled to her feet, careful to keep her back to the window. "I've got it. You'll make the offer to Chandler to see to the proper care of the trunk."

Fiona looked doubtful, even as she said, "All right."

"But rather than fetch it to me in Denver, you will hold the trunk for me until I return." Gennie paused. "Do you have someone who might come for the trunk and keep it safe for me?"

Fiona thought a moment. "I'm sure my sister's beau would see to it," she finally said. "But how will you manage without your things?"

"Whatever I need, I can purchase in Denver," Gennie said with as much dignity as she could manage, straightening her skirts.

The maid looked worried but merely nodded as she too rose. Gennie settled back in her assigned seat and glanced out the window, her reticule over her face, carefully covering all but her eyes.

Chandler stood alone with the officers, the porter gone. Gennie turned to Fiona and grasped her hands. They were cold, and her fingers shook.

"It will be fine," Gennie said, pushing her own doubts aside. "I'll not ask you to lie, of course, but unless it becomes absolutely necessary, I would repeat my request that you not speak to anyone of my whereabouts."

"No, miss," Fiona said. "I'll not say a word. And my future brother-in-law, he's as good as his word too." She smiled. "In fact, I'm sure he'll be glad to repay the favor of allowing him his bride."

"Perfect." Gennie managed a smile. "Please tell him he will be handsomely rewarded with a lovely wedding gift upon my return."

"I will." Fiona's grin was a bit smaller than Gennie's. "Are you absolutely certain this is what you should be doing? I'd be lying if I didn't tell you I've got my concerns."

As would I, Gennie thought. *Close this door if You do not intend me to walk through it, Lord.*

"I ask your prayers and your cooperation, Fiona." This time her smile was genuine. "It'll be a glorious adventure," she continued, "but I'll likely return quite ready to settle down."

"Oh, miss, you've had my prayers since I first heard about this adventure of yours."

"Good, then." From the corner of her eye, Gennie watched the conductor make his way toward them. "It appears you are about to be shooed from the railway car." She squeezed Fiona's fingers, then released her. "I owe you a debt of gratitude, and I shall be quite generous with my repayment."

"Are you certain? Truly certain, I mean?" Fiona stepped into the aisle. "You've not had to manage without help, and now you'll be alone without so much as a change of clothing."

"I'll be fine."

Fiona looked as doubtful as Gennie felt. "Are you certain?"

"No," she said honestly, "but I'm going to give it a go." She pointed to the conductor, who had spied Fiona. "Now, off with you before that fellow causes as much of a stir inside the train as it appears Mr. Dodd has caused out there."

Fiona hesitated only long enough to reach once again for Gennie's hand and give it a squeeze. "I'll not give away your secret."

"Thank you, Fiona. Truly."

She paused to grin. "Just like Mae Winslow, you are. If I were as brave as you, I'd be going along."

Gennie laughed.

"May the Lord protect you and bring you home safely, miss."

With that, Fiona slipped away through the crowded aisle. A moment later, she emerged to join a red-faced and pacing Chandler on the platform. A moment's conversation, and the banker was barking orders at some hapless porter.

Peering from behind her reticule, Gennie watched her trunk be offloaded and deposited at Fiona's feet. To her credit, the maid neither looked back toward the train nor seemed particularly distraught. Rather, she nodded several times, then placed her hand on the trunk while Chandler pulled the thick money clip from his pocket. A brief conversation ensued, with Chandler speaking and Fiona shaking her head. Finally, the banker put away his money and smiled.

"He your fella?"

Gennie started at the question, then glanced at her seatmate. It appeared the smirking fellow in the middle had taken an interest in the goings-on outside. The other two, thankfully, had slipped into slumber. Even the chicken had gone blessedly silent.

Perhaps if she ignored the man, he too would close his eyes. As if to offer inspiration, Gennie clutched her reticule to her chest and rested her head against the rough wood, angling her body so that anyone peering in from outside would only see her back. This had the dual advantage of hiding her from Chandler and keeping her line of vision away from the potential troublemaker.

"Maybe I oughta go and tell him his lady's runnin' off."

She gave the man a sideways look but continued to maintain her silence.

He sat straighter and made a show of leaning toward the window. "Fine fella like that surely would pay well for the return of his woman."

Gennie's heart had begun to pound. One word from this ruffian and she'd be found out. In all likelihood, she'd be summarily hauled from the train. Depending on whether Gennie could convince him otherwise, Chandler might also tell her father.

She sighed. Though she'd asked the Lord to close this door if it was not one He wanted her to walk through, Gennie had never considered He might actually do so.

The vile man leaned toward the window, then glanced over at her and smiled. The twin emotions of fear and loathing battled as she tapped on his arm.

"Look here, sir," she said. Then the whistle blew and the train jerked forward, knocking the ruffian back in his seat. "A pity." Gennie settled back for the ride. "We'll never know what might have happened, will we?"

Somewhere between Buck Springs and Deadwood, Mae caught up to the horse thief who'd taken her prize mare. Negotiations broke down when the distressed damsel attempted to take back what was rightfully hers. She lost a day and a night languishing in the jailhouse—they both did—until finally some man figured out you couldn't steal what was yours.

She could've complained, maybe even found fault enough to call the governor—an old friend who'd surely listen—but a woman of the West had no time for such trifling matters. Though, in a backward manner, she had done her job and seen the thief captured.

And so Mae, reunited with her steed, rode off into the sunset. It was only when she reached the horizon that she realized she'd ridden into a trap.

&c

Denver, Colorado

Today was shaping up to be the best day he'd had in ages. Daniel Beck pushed back from his desk and walked to the window. Today the white-capped Rockies appeared deep purple against the brilliant blue of the July sky, putting him in mind of Scafell Pike near the Beck ancestral home in Britain.

Recollections of feeble childhood attempts at scaling the mountain, along with later successful endeavors, were among the rare good memories of time spent with his younger brother, Edwin. Three years and thousands of miles separated them now, as did one lovely, green-eyed female.

Two, actually.

Daniel stepped away from the window. He wouldn't let ancient history wreak havoc on a perfect, if unseasonably cool, day.

Shifting his thoughts, Daniel reached for the telegram from his man in Chicago. It contained good news—a solution was on the way to a problem more troubling than any of his business ventures could produce. It was a very good day.

Though his office was of considerable size, today it would not hold him. He longed to be outdoors. He scooped up his hat and strode out the door.

His assistant found him on the stairs, just a few steps from freedom.

"You've a note, sir, just delivered, and these letters too, all marked urgent," Hiram called.

Daniel briefly considered the possibility that news of the aftereffects of the Leadville miners's strike might be contained in any or all of the correspondence. While Beck Mines had come through the disruption without suffering permanent harm, many others had not. Too often the mail delivery contained more unofficial pleas for help than anything else.

He could deal with that tomorrow.

"Leave them in my office, Hiram." Daniel took the stairs two at a time, bypassing the formality of speaking to the cluster of banker types crowding the building's palatial lobby. Several called his name, but Daniel kept walking.

"But, sir," echoed above the other voices as Daniel weaved through the crowd and out into the midmorning sunshine.

Denver smelled like mud and horse manure, a beautiful scent to a man whose greatest displeasure had always been being cooped up indoors.

His driver met him at the door, but Daniel waved him away. "Go on home, Isak. I'm of a mind to ride today."

Daniel turned toward the livery, intending to saddle the spirited bay mare he kept in town for days like today. Yanking at the starched collar that threatened to strangle him, he waited for a streetcar to pass, then set out across the busy thoroughfare.

"Sir, begging your pardon," came the persistent voice of Hiram Nettles.

Daniel stopped short and let a buggy full of females pass, keeping his attention focused on the livery and not the enticement a quartet of finely dressed women offered. By necessity, his was a solitary life, and one of the reasons for that rode in the back of the buggy beside the mayor's daughter.

"Lovely morning, isn't it, Mr. Beck?" Anna Finch called.

Daniel tipped his hat at Barnaby Finch's youngest daughter and her companions. "Indeed it is, Miss Finch. Ladies."

Anna leaned forward, holding on to her absurd creation of a hat with both hands. "Will I see you at the Miller soiree this evening?"

Daniel took a deep breath and let it out slowly. At best, the Miller soiree would be an evening of pointless and below-average conversation. At worst, the occasion would be another in a seemingly endless parade of political events disguised as parlor entertainment. In either case, he'd rather be horsewhipped than attend.

Unfortunately, Anna Finch took his silent no for a yes.

"I look forward to renewing our acquaintance then, Mr. Beck," she called as the buggy turned and mercifully disappeared around the corner.

Barnaby Finch, Daniel's neighbor, had been trying to pawn Anna off on him since she returned from her East Coast school last summer. For her part, Anna seemed a more-than-willing participant in the scheme. Obviously Finch figured he owned half of Colorado, so buying a husband for his youngest shouldn't be an issue. He'd certainly had no trouble betrothing the other four in a similar fashion.

But Daniel Beck could not be bought. Better men than Barnaby Finch had tried and failed.

Daniel jerked off his collar and tossed it behind him while he waited for a team of slow moving mules to pass. The delay allowed his assistant to catch up. Rather than fall in step beside Daniel, the young man planted himself squarely in his path. In one hand he held Daniel's muddied collar; in the other was a fistful of papers.

Daniel gave Hiram a look that had caused many a grown man to shrink back in fear. His assistant, however, merely pressed on with his cause.

"I would be remiss in my duties if I let you leave without calling your attention to the importance of these." He thrust the papers toward Daniel. "Mr. Beck, I must insist."

"You must insist, Hiram?" Daniel tempered his urge to laugh. "Very well."

He folded the documents in half and stuffed them into his pocket, then pressed past a buckboard filled with mining equipment to reach the front of the livery. The rush of activity inside let Daniel know his presence had been noted and his horse was being prepared.

"Are you finished, Hiram?"

While his assistant nodded, a boy hurried toward Daniel with boots and riding attire.

"Excellent," Daniel said. "Your work here is done. I suggest you return to the office." He turned to enter the livery, then thought better of his abrupt dismissal. "Hiram," he called, and the young man trotted back toward him. "Please understand I appreciate your efforts." He patted his pocket. "And rest assured I will read these today."

An hour later, with a bracing wind cutting across his face and the city of Denver at his back, Daniel decided he might not read anything work related today. Maybe not even tomorrow, as he had a bedroll in his saddlebag.

Then he thought of Charlotte. So like her late mother, and so unlike the Beck family whose heritage she shared. *Thank You, Lord, for that dual blessing.*

Just this morning, the imp had yanked on his coattails as he headed for the door and asked, "Are you leaving me again, Papa? Won't you be home tonight to play charades?"

Daniel halted the mare beside a gurgling stream. Charlotte was a Beck in one way: what she wanted, she generally got. He smiled. And what she stated with firmness that morning was that she required her papa to tuck her into bed tonight.

"So be it." Daniel glanced at the sun overhead, then jumped down to water the horse. A stiff breeze whipped past and caught the papers in his pocket, sending them flying. He retrieved the ones he could, then climbed into the saddle and chased down the last. When his fingers finally closed around the fleeing envelope, his eyes took in the distinctly British stamps.

A letter from Beck Manor.

His heart sank. How had they found him? Moreover, why?

He turned the letter over and stared at the handwriting as if it might hold the key. Unless he missed his guess, his father's hand and not Edwin's wrote this.

Not that it mattered. He hadn't wanted either to find him, much less send a letter as if he were still a member of the Beck clan.

Daniel shoved the letter back into his pocket, out of sight, and dug in his heels, urging the mare toward home.

When he arrived, Charlotte met him at the barn with a laugh more like his brother's than her mother's. He thought of the letter in his pocket, and for a second, his temper flared.

"Ride me twice around the barn," she called.

Daniel reached down and scooped the girl into the saddle ahead of him. The great antidote to any anger was his daughter, he remembered, as they flew at high speed in a circle so familiar the poor horse could likely run the path in her sleep.

After two laps, Charlotte was content to sail off the horse into his arms, then float to the ground in a swirl of arms, legs, and braids. Again she laughed, and this time it stabbed his heart even as it made him smile.

As was their custom, Charlotte led him around the front of the house, and then, as if she were a lady coming to call, he opened the gate for her with a sweeping bow. Any passerby would think him daft for knocking at the door of his own home, but Charlotte loved to make a grand entrance.

The door swung open on well-oiled hinges, revealing Elias Howe, who today wore the colors of his former Confederate regiment as well as a smart cap of dark wool that covered most of his gray curls. "Fancy meeting you here, miss. Top of the evening," he said as if he hadn't performed this routine for Charlotte almost daily since she came to live with them.

Had it been five years already?

"Charmed, Mr. Howe," the ten-year-old said with mock formality, tugging on the strap of her overalls. "Has my lady-in-waiting departed for the evening?" she asked in an awful attempt at Daniel's British accent.

"Indeed she has," Elias said. "Tova's done headed home for the night. A day of cleaning up after the likes of you has exhausted her." Elias smiled at Daniel over Charlotte's head. "Evenin', Daniel."

Daniel responded in kind, but his attention was fully on Charlotte. He was besotted with the child, as was Elias, the old ship's cook, who bent his creaking bones into a formal bow that would have passed as appropriate in Queen Victoria's drawing room.

The thought reminded him of the letter in his pocket, likely from a man duly knighted, who had taken tea in Her Majesty's drawing room more than once.

Daniel's fingers worried the edge of the letter, then abruptly withdrew from his pocket. The earl would probably like nothing better than to cast a pall on his evening with Charlotte. The letter would have to wait.

"Go wash up, Charlotte," he said, repeating the command twice before the princess-in-training deemed it worthy of a response.

"You know I prefer Charlie."

"And *I* prefer a daughter who does not speak in an unladylike manner to her father, *Charlotte.*" He paused to put on his sternest look, a difficult feat given the grin on the girl's face. "Surely Miss McTaggart taught you the proper way to converse with your elders."

The face she made nearly caused him to believe the argument was over. "Miss McTaggart had too many rules," she said, turning a perfectly sweet expression into a pout.

"Good rules, I warrant," he replied, "and I shall see that the new Nanny McTaggart also upholds these rules."

"I like Tova better."

Daniel sighed. "Tova is a housekeeper, Buttercup. And while she's invaluable to us, she hasn't the time or the ability to teach you the skills needed to be a proper lady. That's the job of your governess."

"Papa, I told you I'm old enough not to—"

"Not to argue with your father?" He paused for effect. "Indeed, you are that. Now go and prepare for dinner before I lose my patience."

The little charmer grinned. For all her ability to push against his authority, Charlotte certainly knew when to cut her losses and run. She hugged him, eyes wide, and kissed his cheek. "Yes, Papa," she said as she skipped off, he hoped, toward soap and water.

Elias took his hat and coat, chuckling. "She's a handful, that one."

Daniel followed him into the dining room, where a bountiful feast had been laid. "Elias, you've done it again. Unless Tova and Isak are joining us, you only needed to feed three."

"It's only us tonight," Elias said, "but none of us shall leave the table hungry."

Daniel reached for a slice of bread and tore off a corner. "Should we eat even half of this, none of us could leave the table at all."

"You know I've only one set of recipes, and they're for a shipload. If you don't like it, hire a real cook."

"What would I do with a real cook? I keep you here for entertainment value, not your cooking." The statement was patently false, as evidenced by the bite of rye bread Daniel popped into his mouth.

"Try to complain now, lad. I baked your favorite." Elias's laughter trailed behind him as he disappeared into the kitchen.

Rather than follow, Daniel moved to the window that filled one end of the room. Clouds gathering above the distant peaks foretold of rain. Likely the mines were already being soaked.

Though the strike that crippled the mines in May and June had been halted and their leader finally captured and placed under arrest, the underlying issues still remained. The men wanted better working conditions and a bigger share of what was quickly becoming a substantial pie, and now they'd had a taste of what striking might accomplish. A storm would do nothing to improve their temperaments.

One more thing to deal with upon his arrival.

An off-key version of a familiar sailing song drifted under the kitchen door. Daniel smiled. For all the grief that awaited him in Leadville and, likely, the trouble that would come with the opening of his father's letter, still he could find a haven here.

Trouble could not touch him inside his home.

Through dinner with Charlotte, charades, and a bedtime routine that included two trips to the library for just the right book, Daniel tried to ignore the letter in his pocket. Coffee and a game of chess with Elias followed, and still he postponed reading the documents.

"Something bothering you, lad?" Elias asked.

"Bothering me?" He moved his queen into position to take Elias's king, then looked up. "Check."

"You sure?"

Daniel nodded as his opponent countered and called checkmate.

He sat back and frowned. He'd missed the obvious.

"I'll not ask why you let me win," Elias said, "though I will inquire whether I might be of service in whatever problem you're contemplating."

Daniel thought only a second before pulling the letter from his coat pocket and setting it on the chessboard.

Elias glanced down, then looked at him with narrowed eyes. "So the old man's found you."

A statement, not a question. Interesting that Elias, too, never considered the letter could be from Edwin rather than his father. Edwin would never write. He was too much of a coward. Only the earl would send a letter to a son he'd declared as good as dead ten years ago. Likely Edwin was still too busy celebrating the victory.

"It appears so," Daniel said as he returned the letter to his pocket.

"What does your pa want from you?" Elias gasped. "Not her?"

Daniel shook his head. "I don't know. I haven't opened it."

"I see." Elias rose and yawned with more enthusiasm than necessary. "Besting you at chess sure has made me sleepy. I believe I'll turn in and leave the supper dishes for Tova. She always loves it when I do that."

Daniel mustered a smile. "I think you're harboring a secret crush for our housekeeper, Elias."

"Why would you say something as foolish as that?" Elias stepped over Daniel's outstretched legs to walk away. "You know I never did like a bossy woman. Why, that Tova, she's about the bossiest of all the..."

His voice trailed off as the old seaman disappeared down the hallway toward his bedchamber. A slamming door punctuated the sentiment.

"Methinks thou dost protest too much, dear friend." Daniel reached for his lukewarm coffee and smiled, until he felt the letter shift in his pocket. He touched it, then once again placed it atop the chessboard.

"What do you want from me after all these years, old man?" he whispered.

Daniel held the envelope up to the light, then turned and extinguished the lamp. Alone in the darkness, he crumpled the letter and stuffed it into his pocket, then walked upstairs to his room, feeling older than the person who penned the words he dreaded reading.

He settled heavily into the old leather chair by the fire; the chair Georgiana had only tolerated because it was his favorite. Closing his eyes, Daniel let the image of a golden-haired woman heavy with child, her skirts lifted just above the gurgling water of a mountain-fed stream, sneak into his mind. With it came the rage.

"Papa?"

Daniel opened his eyes to find Charlotte peering around the door. "You should be sleeping, Buttercup."

Bare feet pattered across the floor, and Charlotte launched herself into the chair with him. He caught the imp and tucked her into his lap, the top of her head nestled beneath his chin.

Legs that had grown long and coltish tangled around his, evoking memories of Charlotte at five. Newly arrived and shy, she'd kept her distance, preferring her mother to the man she refused to call Papa.

Where had the time gone? In the blink of an eye, the reticent five-year-old had stolen his heart and, upon her mother's death, filled the abyss of grief with rays of brilliant green-eyed sunshine. Contemplating where he would be without Charlotte was impossible.

"My new nanny is coming soon, isn't she?"

Daniel hauled his mind back to the present and thought carefully before answering. "Yes, the new Miss McTaggart's to arrive in two days, I believe."

"I was thinking, Papa." She peered up at him with her mother's eyes. "Maybe I don't need a nanny. I'll be eleven soon. That's practically grown-up. I think I can manage just fine."

"Eleven is eleven, Buttercup. Twenty, now that's grown-up." He gathered her back into his arms and held her, as outside, the night sounds rose. "And for the record, you only just turned ten."

Charlotte yawned. "Can I fall asleep here?"

"Of course." His heart lurched again. How many more years did he have before his little girl cared less for her papa than she did for her friends or, worse yet, gentleman callers?

The only sounds came from outside the open window. He patted her curls, the one visible feature she'd inherited from the Becks, and closed his eyes.

"Papa?"

"Shh."

He let out a sigh he hoped his daughter would take as exasperation. In truth, it spoke of pure contentment. Was there anything better than sitting in a comfortable chair on a cool evening with a cherub in your arms?

If only things could be managed in his absence, but Daniel knew running a business in Leadville meant he must attend to things there. Nothing was more difficult than leaving his daughter, especially now that her protests had become more vocal. His absences might perturb her now, but she was just a child. Someday she would know that his work was done with only her in mind.

Until that time, she needed a firm hand and a feminine influence. Hopefully the new Nanny McTaggart would provide that. Her predecessor had only been gone a month, and already he saw signs that what little the dear woman had managed to do in the way of civilizing Charlotte was coming undone. Just yesterday, Hiram had come to him with the distressing story that he thought he'd seen Charlotte among a group of youthful troublemakers tipping the spittoon in a nearby saloon, then pocketing money off the card tables in the ensuing melee. Then there was the neighbor who'd come to Tova, complaining of a pie with half its filling missing. Only Charlotte had been seen in the vicinity.

He'd expressed doubt to Tova about the girl's involvement, but in his heart Daniel wondered. She was a bit high-spirited. Adventurous, even. But petty crime? Not his Charlotte.

5

"Got you this time," One-Eyed Ed said. "For whatsoever you do, it will come back in the same measure."

"Since when do you talk like that, Ed?" Mae needed to keep the man talking, to force his attention anywhere but on the hands she was about to free from the ropes he'd tied around her wrists. In the meantime she talked, discussing meaningless things like the price of cotton and the fact the skies were an interesting shade of blue today.

Feigning sleep was easy, as she'd gone without it for a full day and part of another. Keeping awake was the endeavor fraught with peril, yet she managed until the outlaw left her to ply his trade, seemingly safe in the knowledge his captive would be waiting when he returned.

Which, of course, she would not. Mae slipped the loosened rope from her hands, then saved it to use when she found the sorry thief.

☙❧

"Miss?"

Gennie pushed away the maid's attempts to wake her. "Tell Mrs. Vanowen I shan't be attending the breakfast today."

"Miss?"

Again came the interruption, this time in the form of rough shaking. "Truly this is most inappro—" Her eyes opened to reveal a mousy couple staring at her. Mr. Mouse gestured toward the aisle, and Gennie's gaze followed his hand.

The conductor stood over her, his smile gone. "You're Denver."

"No." Gennie sat up and straightened her traveling hat, then sur-reptitiously swiped at her cheek. "I am..." She paused to consider the implications of giving her name.

"I don't care if you're Queen Victoria," he said. "This is Union Sta-tion. Your stop. Time to get off."

Realization dawned on her as the conductor moved on. Denver. Fatigue drained away as she leaned forward. Ash and soot covered the pane, making the city look as if it wore a coat of dull gray. A closer look revealed the slightest outline of snowcapped peaks.

"The Rockies," she whispered. "Oh my."

It was a beautiful sight. She, however, was not.

"I'll need to freshen up," she said to the conductor as she gathered her reticule and hung it from her wrist. "Then I'll be happy to accom-modate your request."

The man offered an inelegant snort, then pointed to the exit. "Denver. Union Station," he repeated. "Freshen up all you want once you're on the platform, but unless you want to pay to go farther, you've got to leave the train."

Gennie forced herself to exhale. Wouldn't Papa be surprised she'd taken such a risk? Mama, of course, would be appalled. She stood a notch straighter at the thought of her mother.

"Miss?" The conductor punctuated his irritation with a sweep of his hand. "Might I escort my lady to the exit?" he asked in a sarcastic tone.

With a quick nod to her frowning seatmates, Gennie rose. "Not necessary."

Her legs felt like they'd been encased in lead, but somehow she man-aged to move toward the nearest exit where all of Denver—playground of Mae Winslow and her frontier friends—awaited her discovery.

But first there was the matter of Mr. Beck, who must be told his permanent governess would be delayed by exactly one month.

Gennie pressed past the conductor into the aisle, then tried to smooth the wrinkles in her traveling coat, succeeding instead in smearing the ash and grime farther into the once-lovely fabric. No matter. A thorough cleaning and the ensemble would be as good as new.

She stepped out onto the platform and paused to look around. Denver. Or as much as she could see beyond the trains, people, and imposing structure of the rail station.

While the mass of men, women, and children could have represented travelers from anywhere, the snowcapped Rocky Mountains in the distance could not. She knew the air would be clean and bracing, and the skies so clear and deep blue it hurt to look at them. The only disappointment was in Union Station itself. She'd expected some sort of rough-hewn affair with logs and chinks of plaster holding the wind at bay.

Somewhere beyond this thoroughly modern train station was a wilderness waiting to be tamed by the likes of Mae Winslow. A giggle bubbled up, and Gennie covered her lips to keep from laughing aloud.

Now to search the milling throng for Daniel Beck. Having forgotten to ask for a description, she quickly realized any one of the men openly staring at her were likely candidates. Gennie took a step forward.

Someone bumped her, and Gennie stumbled. A man of middle age and poor taste in suits caught her and, with a modicum of movement, righted her.

"I'm terribly sorry," she said as she adjusted the ribbon on her hat.

He offered neither a response nor a moment more of his time. He merely tipped his tattered cap and disappeared into the crowd. A moment later, she realized her reticule had gone with him.

Shrieking like a banshee did not come naturally to Gennie, but shriek she did as she pressed through the crowd in the direction of the thief. The crisp air burned her lungs, as did the unaccustomed shouting, but the noise did its job as travelers parted to allow her a wide berth.

Spotting the tattered cap ahead, Gennie did the unthinkable and lifted her skirts to give chase. The wide berth became wider, and stunned faces gave way to a few smiles. And then she saw him, the scalawag who dared rob her of the last thing she'd brought from New York other than herself.

The fellow had the audacity to turn on his heels and face her. For a brief moment, Gennie thought he might have found his conscience, but then he laughed and darted away.

"You there," she called, her temper as fiery as the burning in her lungs, "I'll not lose my reticule to a thief!"

At the word *thief*, things around her changed.

A menacing fellow of larger-than-average size caught up to her. "Did you say 'thief'?"

She nodded and pointed, another breach of her mother's strict rules of politeness. "Him," she managed as the last of the air escaped her lungs.

"Get 'im, boys," Gennie heard as spots danced before her eyes.

Just like a scene from one of Mae Winslow's adventures, a collection of buckskin-clad men with weapons slung over broad shoulders swarmed the man in the tattered hat. Before she could blink twice, the criminal hung between two sets of strong arms and was being carried toward the street.

A third man, oddly dressed in some sort of jumbled military costume, parted company with them to present her with the reticule. "This yours?" he asked.

Gennie snatched it from his outstretched arms, her breath returning in gasps as she doubled over. "Thank you," she managed as she held the bag to her chest.

"The air's a mite thin here," the man said, "so take care that you don't become winded. And guard your personal items. There are scoundrels about."

Gennie peered up, intent on a sarcastic retort, until she saw his sincere expression. "Thank you," she repeated. A lad sidled up to the old man. "Well, hello there," Gennie said.

The boy eyed her from beneath his tweed cap, then skittered behind the uniform-clad man.

"Charlie's a bit shy," the man offered, "and also in trouble for not staying in the buggy."

Gennie suppressed a smile when Charlie, who couldn't have been a day over eleven, peered around the man's coattails, eyes wide.

"That's a lovely bag, miss."

She smiled down at the little fellow. "Why, thank you."

"Might I have a look at it?"

With a nod, Gennie complied, then turned her attention to the elderly soldier. "Perhaps you might assist me," she said. "I've a fellow to find by the name of—"

"Here, miss."

The lad thrust the reticule toward her. Gennie accepted it with a smile. "Thank you." She tightened the sash and slipped it over her wrist.

"Interruptin' your elders is rude," the old soldier said, pointing at the lad. "Apologize."

The boy turned wide eyes toward the older man.

"Don't try that face on me. It might work on your pa, but I'm onto your antics." The man swung his attention back to Gennie. "Forgive

the child's misbehavior, please, and 'scuse us, miss. We're meetin' someone and likely she's wondering where we are."

"Yes, of course. As am I, actually," Gennie said, "though I'm at a
loss as to what he looks like."

"Is that right?" He pressed his cap back off his forehead, revealing
a mass of iron gray curls. "I fear we're in the same boat."

"Say, I wonder if you might tell me where a lady of quality could
find lodging." The boy snickered. Gennie ignored him. "I fear I'll not
find the party and be left in the station."

The man looked much more sympathetic than the child. "Yes'm,"
he said, "we got a fine new hotel called the Windsor. Just opened some
two weeks ago over at Larimer and Eighteenth. Quite a fancy place,
with a pharmacy and all sorts of things." He paused and seemed to have
trouble keeping his smile under control. "Even if Mr. Duff's a friend of
ours, I reckon it's more than fit for a lady of quality."

"The Windsor at Larimer and Eighteenth." She reached out to
shake his hand. "Thank you. Best of luck to you."

"Hold tight to that bag, now, miss," the old fellow said. He snagged
one of the child's overall straps before turning to walk away. "Off with
you, Charlie. I'll not hear of any further disobedience, else I'll have to
tell your pa." His words blended into the hum of voices and the rum-
ble of train engines that filled the busy station.

Their departure, odd as the pair was, made Gennie feel instantly
alone in the crowd. Shaking off the silly feeling, she once again looked
for a man who might be seeking his daughter's governess. While she
searched, she also began to plan her speech. Once found, Mr. Beck
would have to be informed of the temporary nature of her employment.

A porter rushed past, pushing a cart overloaded with luggage,
reminding Gennie of her lack thereof. She sighed and aimed her steps

away from the train tracks, her reticule safely dangling from her wrist. At least she still had it and the traveling money she'd tucked inside.

It wasn't much, but surely the funds would purchase a serviceable wardrobe for her visit to the Wild West. Perhaps she'd find a store selling buckskin clothing in her size.

Wouldn't Chandler Dodd be surprised if she returned from what he thought was a trip to Boston outfitted for a home on the range? The corners of her lips tilted into a smile. Perhaps she'd purchase a set for Mr. Dodd as well.

The idea of him dressed in buckskins astride a racing pony caused her heart to flutter. Indeed, a full set of western gear might be in order for a wedding gift.

Who am I kidding? Chandler Dodd would think me a lunatic if I offered such a gift.

"A pity," she whispered as her mind returned to the kiss and the banker who'd surprised her with it.

Something small and swift collided with her. She felt a tug at her wrist, and her reticule slipped away.

The child.

Gennie lunged for the urchin and snagged an overall strap, hauling the criminal backward. Wide eyes regarded her with either fear or frustration.

"So that's how it is," Gennie said. "You're in this together. I should have known."

Ignoring the child's protests, Gennie retrieved her reticule and tightened her grip on his strap. A quick shake of the handbag told her it was empty.

"My money," she demanded, but the child only stared. "Now, or else I'll be forced to call the authorities."

That caused only the slightest reaction, and even then, Gennie wasn't certain she hadn't imagined it. Then she realized the criminal might not have her money, not if the child didn't act alone.

It only took her a moment to spy the odd, gray-haired fellow. He watched them with great interest.

"You there." She pointed at him. "There is nothing worse than using a child to commit a crime." Gennie glanced over her shoulder and found a porter. "I demand you hold these two until the authorities arrive. I believe you will find on their persons ample proof."

"What in tarnation are you talking about?" The older man looked past her, likely to signal his accomplice.

"You, sir," she repeated, "are a thief who has stolen from the wrong woman. I demand you return my money, or I shall be forced to prosecute."

He knelt on popping bones and met the little criminal eye to eye. "Got anything to say to the lady, Charlie?" When there was no response, he rose with obvious difficulty and turned his attention to Gennie. "I reckon you ought to go ahead and call the law, then. You've gone and caught her red-handed." The old man placed his palm square between the child's shoulders and gave a nudge toward Gennie. "I believe if you'll check, you'll find whatever you lost in the front pocket of her overalls. That's usually where she hides her ill-gotten gains."

Her? Charlie was a girl? Big crocodile tears started to fall as the child protested her innocence. When that didn't work on either Gennie or her guardian, she reached into her pocket and extracted a wad of bills, then slowly held out her hand.

Gennie returned the money to her reticule, then reached into her coat to pull out her handkerchief. After she finished dabbing the girl's tears, she thrust the damp cloth into her fist. "Likely you'll need this when your father is informed." She glanced up at the old man. "Unless, of course, you're the child's father."

"Me?" He shook his head. "Hardly. I'm the..." He paused. "I'm Elias." Elias reached out to shake Gennie's hand. "I see to things when the imp's pa ain't home."

"And right now he ain't home," Charlie said, her voice much less brazen than before.

Gennie glanced at the porter once more, giving him a nod of dismissal, then returned her attention to the older man. She'd done as she hoped and retrieved her missing money, but perhaps a stern reprimand from the child's father would prevent the girl from further stealing. Or, Gennie decided, perhaps she should have a conversation with him herself.

"All right," she said, "I'm willing to forgive this act of theft, but only if I am given the name of this child's parents so I might have a conversation with them."

"Him, ma'am," Elias said. "It's just her pa still living."

Practically an orphan. Gennie squared her shoulders. Pity would do the child no good. "All right, her father. I'll have his name and address."

Elias nodded. "That'd be Daniel Beck."

Gennie froze. "Did you say 'Daniel Beck'?"

6

As witnessed by his lax supervision of Mae, One-Eyed Ed wasn't the smartest outlaw on the trail. Thus far, however, he'd been one of the luckiest. With all the stages plying the east-west and north-south lines, Ed had rarely come across one that wasn't worth the trouble of stopping to steal whatever was aboard.

Mae lay in wait. When Ed made his move, she would be ready.

The plains stretched endlessly in all directions. To the north lay the Indian lands with their own dangers. East meant civilization and dear Henry, who she hoped still waited in Deadwood for her to come to her senses and take him up on his offer of marriage.

And marry she would—someday. Today she'd not be allowed that luxury. With One-Eyed Ed on the prowl, none were safe. And for all those on the right side of the law who'd tried and failed to take the reward that his capture would bring, there were a dozen more still trying.

Mae would never quit trying.

ᏻᏭ

Leadville

"Hiram, I need to see you, please."

Daniel stepped back to let his right-hand man through the door, then closed it, trading the smell of smoke and cheap liquor for the heavy odor of tobacco that hadn't left with the room's previous occupant.

While taking an office next door to one of Leadville's many drinking establishments was not his first choice, neither was being choosy. With his time divided between Denver and Leadville, he preferred to leave the mine boss at the site and take his work into town. It was as much a matter of security in these poststrike days as a matter of convenience, since the bulk of his time was spent outside the mine shafts and inside offices, boardrooms, and the occasional opera hall or ballroom.

In the three years since he'd come to think of the small mining town as a second home, the population had burst the bounds of available accommodation, leaving little for decent office space. With stories plastered in papers from the East Coast to the West of miners turning grubstakes into fortunes, Leadville had become known as the place where a man could arrive with nothing and leave a king.

The reality, however, was much different. Too many arrived, and too few found the rich silver veins they sought. Given the fact there were almost as many saloon girls as claim jumpers, fewer still kept what they found.

Daniel often thanked the Lord for His grace in allowing him to be one of those who managed to keep what he'd been blessed with. Today, however, he'd spent time with God on another matter before calling Hiram in.

Trouble at Beck Mines came in a variety of ways. Today, it arrived in the form of Jeb Sanders, an employee who never missed a day of work nor a night at the saloon. In between, he could be found holed up with two cousins, neither of whom appeared to be worth the gunpowder it would take to shoot them.

The three of them had participated in the strike that ended last month, as had many of the employees. But while the others returned when the strike ended, Jeb had been the only Sanders to come back to his job. His cousins remained in town, which concerned Daniel. The Sanders family might be intending to settle some lingering issues with Beck Mines by less-than-legal means.

Thus his decision to assign Hiram to investigate the Sanders brothers, rather than Jim Carlson, the current mine boss. Carlson was a good man, but Daniel wanted someone outside the mine to see what went on inside. The better to see what might otherwise be missed.

Daniel paced as Hiram settled himself in the only chair that would hold his weight. "What's the news?" he asked his employee.

The chair creaked as Hiram shifted positions. "It's as you expected, sir. The pair who bought up the Finn's Creek property didn't exactly ask the owner if he wanted to sell. Got it on good authority it was the Sanders brothers."

"So Ben and Cole are claim jumping again," he said. "I shouldn't be surprised. I didn't figure they'd give up on the strike so easily."

"According to the law, they're not jumping." Hiram shrugged. "For every claim they register, they've got proof they paid for it."

Daniel's snort said what he thought of the idea. Downstairs a sporting girl's crass laughter punctuated the ensuing silence.

"I know," his second-in-command said, "but the law's the law."

Stopping at the window, Daniel surveyed the scene a floor below on Harrison Street, where good men plied their trades in everything from shoeing horses to selling foodstuffs. The real fortunes, however, were earned either below ground in the mines, or beyond the reach of the law in extortion or outright murder. Then there were those who orchestrated distrust and fanned the flames of discontent among the workers. It usually started small—an accident or two combined with rumors and false reports. Then came the work stoppages and, finally, the walkout. A mine without workers was as useless as a claim with no silver at all.

Two months ago, the chain of events had begun with a partial cave-in rumored to be caused by sabotage. Then came the complaints, first that pay was too low, and then that working conditions needed improvement. At the heart of each protest was Jeb Sanders, seemingly the self-appointed leader of the workers at the Beck mine. What Daniel couldn't figure out was whether Sanders was out for himself alone or for the good of the men.

Daniel frowned. "What landed the brothers in jail?"

"Bar fight," Hiram said.

Daniel turned to see his own expression of disbelief echoed on Hiram's face. "If they arrested every man who got into a bar fight in Leadville, I'd have no one on the payroll except you, Hiram. What about Jeb?"

"Still free."

"I see." Daniel turned back to the window. "And is he free because there is no evidence to hold him or because he's not under suspicion?"

"Could be either," Hiram said. "The deputy wouldn't say."

"What's Carlson's take on it?"

"He said he's the mine boss, but you're the owner. He's bowing to you on this one."

"All right, then." Daniel didn't have to think long in order to decide what to do. "Until Jeb Sanders is arrested or cleared, he will remain in the employ of the Beck mine. I'd rather have him where I can watch him than fire him and offer reason for retaliation. Besides, the strike didn't turn out like the men expected, so I doubt anyone's going to try something so soon after such a spectacular failure."

"That's good business," Hiram said.

It was, though everything in Daniel made him want to seek out the

Sanders fellow and extract a pound of flesh for every wrong the trio had done to hard-working miners seeking nothing but their grubstakes and a few coins to send back to wherever they called home.

Daniel turned and caught his assistant checking his watch. "Have an appointment elsewhere, Hiram?"

"No sir," he said quickly, slapping on a repentant look. "I just don't want you to miss yours."

"With?"

Hiram reached for the ledger perched precariously on the edge of the desk and thumbed through the pages. "You've committed to a meeting of the Greater Leadville Beautification and Improvement Society." He swung his gaze in Daniel's direction and offered a blank stare. "A note states that Horace Tabor himself requested your attendance."

"Indeed?" Daniel resisted the temptation to roll his eyes at the mention of the town's wealthiest citizen. "Thank you, Hiram. Refresh my memory. What is the topic for this month's gathering? Are we discussing tidying up around the mine shafts, or will this be something of greater social and political importance?"

His assistant cleared his throat. "The stated agenda is this." He consulted the ledger a second time. "'Solutions to the pervasive attitude of dissipation and lax morals among citizens and temporary residents of Leadville.'"

"While I welcome a solution to dissipation and lax morals, I fail to see how a meeting of the civic committee will solve what even the marshal and his men seem unable to do." Daniel shook his head. "And yet if Mr. Tabor has requested my attendance, how can I disappoint him?"

"Indeed. You're expected in ten minutes."

"Fine," Daniel said, "but we need to handle a few items first."

Half an hour later, Daniel slipped into the back row of the Tabor Opera House, hoping his late arrival would not be noticed. He had to learn to better budget his limited time in Leadville.

With all the work he had to do here, there was little time left for frivolity. The Greater Leadville committee certainly ranked as such, but when Horace Tabor beckoned, any Leadville businessman with good sense came running. For any lesser mortal, Daniel would have tossed the invitation in the trash.

Daniel looked up to find all eyes in the room directed at him. The speaker, an odious fellow named Pratt whose stay in Leadville was financed by the railroad, peered over wire-rimmed spectacles that had no lenses.

"Thank you for gifting us with your presence, Mr. Beck. I was just going over the particulars of a proposition I would like to see adopted by the city before I take my leave and return to Pittsburgh next week."

There was nothing to do but rise and tip his hat to the quartet of ladies and trio of gentlemen seated at a table center stage. "Forgive the lateness of my arrival," Daniel said, hating the requisite kowtowing. "I was otherwise detained. Please do not let me interrupt these important proceedings."

Only the marshal met his stare. From the lawman's expression, he wasn't thrilled to be here either.

As he returned to his seat, Daniel discreetly searched the room for Tabor. Horace, Colorado's lieutenant governor, was well known in Leadville as a patron of the arts and a shrewd businessman. Today, however, he was absent from the proceedings. Absent as well was any interest Daniel might have had in the discussion of how to improve the morals of Leadville's citizenry. While he tried as hard as the next fellow to live right and appreciate what the Lord had given him, turning that into a set of rules to impose on others chafed at him. Perhaps it felt too much like the life he'd left behind.

Or worse, the one he'd found, then lost.

"So, Mr. Beck, can we count on your support with this measure?"

Daniel jolted to attention. Again, all eyes were on him. Again, he rose. "I'd need to know more before I could say."

Like what I missed.

"What more is there to know?" Minnie Strong, wife of the livery owner, asked.

"You do realize I'm only a part-time resident of Leadville. My home and family are in Denver."

"What does that matter?" Mrs. Strong's eyes narrowed. "Somebody's got to start acting right, else we'll all fall to ruin."

He offered his best smile to the elderly woman. "Indeed," he said, "and on that, you can count on my full support. Now if you'll excuse me, I've another appointment."

In truth, he'd just decided his appointment was with a train headed to Denver. A quick visit, and he'd return in better humor. In the meantime, there was nothing here in Leadville that Hiram couldn't handle. Unfortunately, he returned to his office to find his hopes of leaving Leadville anytime soon dashed.

Not only had there been a flood in the eastern shaft that nearly cost him half a dozen men, but in the ensuing chaos, a wagonload of firewood had gone careening downhill when the mules pulling it got spooked.

Daniel took a deep breath and blew it out slowly. "Tell me, Hiram, how long was I away?"

His second-in-command shrugged. "Half hour, forty-five minutes, maybe."

"And all of this..."

He walked to the window and looked past the traffic on Leadville's main thoroughfare to the mines situated on the easternmost range. Smoke billowed from chimneys, touching the low-hanging clouds, and the smelters belched enough foul scent to cover the town. To all outward appearances, there was nothing out of the ordinary happening at Beck Mines.

A commotion across the way caught Daniel's eye. From saloons on either side of the narrow frame building, men swarmed into the street. "What's going on over at the jailhouse?"

"I'll go see," Hiram said, his chair scraping against the already-worn wooden planks.

Barely nodding, Daniel turned back to his work. While Denver called, so did the Beck Mines.

A few minutes later, Hiram bolted through the door. "Someone let the Sanders brothers out of jail, and it wasn't the deputy," he said, struggling to catch his breath.

Daniel let a production report fall to the desktop. "How do you know this?"

"The sheriff found him heels up next to the empty cell." Hiram let out a long breath. "A single bullet sent him on to glory. Looks like he never saw it coming."

"And Jeb?" Daniel asked.

Hiram shrugged. "Jumped aboard the firewood wagon up at the mine and kept it from going over the edge. Got banged up a bit but nothing permanent. That's all I know."

"So unless he somehow slipped away during the excitement, it's likely these boys had someone else helping them."

Hiram dropped into the chair across from him. "It appears so."

Considering Daniel didn't know Jeb Sanders except by name, the relief he felt seemed misplaced. But knowing one of his men didn't cause the death of a deputy did matter.

"It's the eighteen eighties, for crying out loud. Things ought to be civilized by now," Hiram commented.

"I suppose," Daniel said. "Maybe the committee is onto something with their campaign to rid the city of its more unsavory element."

Now that the trains between Denver and Leadville shortened the trip significantly, he'd like nothing better than to have Charlotte with him when he made his visits to the mine. Even with Elias and the new governess for supervision, Daniel had his doubts as to how much longer Charlotte could be trusted with the friends she'd made in Denver without his presence.

But until the day Leadville proved safe enough, Daniel would have to rely on the new Miss McTaggart to take Charlotte in hand and teach her what it meant to be a proper young lady.

As Hiram slipped out of the office, Daniel's thoughts drifted to the letter that had ruined his last day in Denver. The one from his father, which he'd finally read.

The earl had put Daniel on notice of his impending visit to the States, and had specifically demanded that Charlotte be brought for an audience.

He would expect the child to be a lady. To bring an overall-clad imp would risk his rejecting Charlotte. And while the old man's opinions weren't worth spit to Daniel, the ten-year-old had lived through too many losses to add her grandfather to the list.

He'd have to figure out a way around it. Perhaps a letter begging the girl's age as a reason for not traveling east with her. It might work, except that her mother had brought her all the way from England with no permanent harm done.

Then it came to him. "Of course," he said softly as he reached for pen and paper. She was his child, and he didn't have to respond to the demands of a bitter old man.

Try as he might, however, Daniel could not write the words his thoughts demanded. Instead, he penned a perfunctory note of acceptance, allowing for the fact the old man might change his mind.

Praying for it.

While she waited, Mae gave some thought to what life in the big city of Deadwood would be like. Hot meals and soft beds, warm fires and cool evening breezes. Likely she'd find no further need to run or be her own protector. No, she thought as she checked the number of bullets in each of her three weapons, she'd be safe as a bug in a rug.

It sounded just awful.

She sighted down her pistol. Sometimes what a person wishes for is neither what they really want nor what they need.

Sometimes, it's the wishing that's the best part.

And right now, with her target coming into range, Mae wished for Henry.

☙❧

Gennie perched on the edge of the buggy's seat as much to get a better look at the scene unfolding before her as to be ready to jump and run if need be. Several seemingly upstanding citizens and two officers of the law had vouched for the identity of the man who called himself Elias Howe and the urchin known as Charlie Beck.

As to her identity, Gennie was not proud to admit she'd allowed them to believe she was the newest McTaggart in the household. There would be time enough to tell the truth, but Daniel Beck must be informed first. He could tell the child and his staff members. This, after all, was his purview, not hers.

Glancing to her left, Gennie noted the child's pout and decided that whoever was in charge of the imp would have to form an immunity to the expression, lest she be taken in. Wide eyes and a tiny, upturned nose completed the profile of what could have been an angel had Gennie not known the truth.

She moved her attention to the straight back of the older man in odd clothing. A dress coat that appeared to be a neatly pressed yet greatly patched Confederate uniform offered an interesting contrast to the formal hat perched atop gray curls. Were he not seated next to the driver in a coach of some expense, Gennie might have pegged Elias Howe for one without a home or means of his own.

As if he felt her gaze on him, Elias Howe swiveled in his seat. "This here's Lawrence Street, Miss McTaggart," he said. "It's not New York City, but we've got plenty of modern conveniences."

Gennie noted such illustrious establishments as the Denver Fur Company and Joslin's Dry Goods wedged among the numerous storefronts of the mud-filled thoroughfare. "Are those telegraph poles?" She resisted the urge to point. "And there, are those streetlights?"

Mr. Howe chuckled. "You sound surprised we have such a thing." He winked. "Been ten years almost since that was news."

"I see."

Before her was a scene that could have taken place in any city. A solid-looking bank dominated the block, competing for space among the other surprisingly civilized establishments. Women and men wearing clothing that could have come from the better stores in Manhattan strolled along sidewalks and picked their way across the wide street. Coming and going on both sides of the street were horse-drawn streetcars filled to capacity with well-dressed city folk.

Mae Winslow would stick out like a sore thumb on these civilized streets. It was terribly disheartening.

"Won't be long now," Elias said over his shoulder. "I reckon you'll find Mr. Beck's place comfortable enough."

Gennie bit back a quip about how short her stay would be and settled for a curt nod. Soon the true nanny would arrive and she'd be free to roam the wilderness, such as it was. Surely someone could offer insight into how she might find whatever remained of Mae Winslow's Wild West before Gennie had to board the train for her return trip to New York.

"You smell funny."

She looked down to see the child staring up from beneath the brim of her hat, two grimy fingers pinching her nose. Gennie likely did smell, given that she'd donned this outfit in the privacy of her dressing room back in Manhattan.

The girl awaited her response, but Gennie decided to let the moment pass. Correcting the child would be best left to the poor woman who would take on the permanent job of raising her.

The carriage veered to the right, and the commercial buildings gave way to broad lawns tucked behind tall iron fences. Homes of the latest fashion sat among gardens that rivaled anything she'd seen in her travels. The driver pulled at the reins, and the carriage slowed in front of an oversized Italianate villa.

Gennie shook her head. This wasn't the Wild West at all.

"Deep in thought, miss?"

She looked up to find Elias Howe watching her.

"We're here," he said with a sweep of his hand. "This is the home of Mr. Beck and Charlotte."

Gennie held tight to the side of the carriage as it turned through the massive gates and headed toward the Beck mansion. Elias and the girl piled out, but Gennie waited for the groomsman to assist her from the carriage. Before her feet could touch the ground, the child was tugging her coattails.

"I told my papa I didn't need a governess, and I surely don't want you."

"Enough of that," Elias said as he stepped behind the girl and tugged on her hat. "You'll apologize at once, Charlotte Beck, or I'll know the reason why."

As the hat came off, golden curls fell about the child's shoulders. In an instant, the urchin became quite a fetching girl. Except for the scowl, which left Gennie wondering whether it might be a permanent fixture on an otherwise lovely face.

When she refused to speak, Elias placed his hands on the girl's shoulders and turned her toward what appeared to be a back entrance to the home. "To your room, Charlotte Beck. And you'll stay there until you can tell Miss McTaggart you're sorry." He glanced up at Gennie. "Forgive the child's inhospitable nature. She misses her papa."

"Do not," the girl said, trudging toward the back of the house. "He's gone all the time, anyway."

The oddly dressed man shifted positions but did not move away from the carriage. Elias Howe seemed in need of further conversation but in want of words.

"A lovely child," Gennie offered, unsure as to any other topic that might be appropriate. "With proper instruction, she will likely grow into quite a young woman."

"And many prayers too." Mr. Howe let out a long breath. "She's a good girl," he said in a tone that made Gennie wonder whom he was trying to convince.

"I'm sure she is," Gennie said. "Perhaps a bit misguided?"

"Misguided." The old man's chuckle held no humor. "Indeed she is. Imagine a child with all this wanting to steal money off a governess. Then there's the incident down at the saloon, and at the post office. Well, I never did confirm that one, but..."

As his voice trailed off, his look implored a response. Gennie found none to offer. She clutched her reticule and pondered her options. The gate had not yet shut on her adventure at Beck Mansion. Though it would mean compromising her upbringing, Gennie had no doubt she could pick up her soot-covered skirts and run away faster than the old man could possibly catch her.

She sighed. Any governess who would contemplate such audacious behavior was not fit to tame a child.

Gennie looked up at the second floor, where an oddly shaped white curtain blew through an open window. On second glance, she realized the object was not a curtain at all.

"Sir?" She diverted her eyes and gestured toward the home. "Might that be someone's unmentionables?"

Elias Howe turned in time to see what was likely, from the size of it, his own union suit go flying from the window and land in a pine tree. Rather than chase after the garment or the child now laughing with great vigor, he turned his back on the scene to address Gennie.

"Miss, there are more good reasons than I can count for you to demand a return trip to Union Station without ever stepping through the door of Mr. Beck's house. Chief among them being the child herself." He paused to remove his hat, revealing a wild mass of curls that darted in all directions. "I can offer only one reason for you staying put and sticking it out with her. With us."

Gennie watched the girl disappear inside the window, her giggles a soft song carried by the brisk north wind. With difficulty, she removed her attention from the pine tree and its unusual decoration.

"And what would that be, Mr. Howe?"

"We need you."

Somehow that simple three-word phrase silenced every objection but one.

"Time is short," Gennie said, though she knew Elias Howe had no idea how very short her visit would be.

"It is," he said, nodding toward the house. "Perhaps you'd like to get settled before meeting the staff. Not that there's many of us."

In a home this size? What might her duties be, then? She caught him staring and elected not to ask.

"Just Tova and me in the house." He gestured to the fair-haired driver. "And Tova's boy, Isak, who drove us. He also takes care of the handiwork and the gardening."

"I see." She paused, unsure of the protocol in situations such as this. "Might I inquire as to my accommodations? I need to freshen up, though I fear I'm a bit meagerly prepared. Until I can purchase suitable attire, I've only what I'm wearing."

Elias looked her over and shrugged. "You're no bigger than a minute. We can fetch something that'll make do until Tova can wash that getup of yours. She's the day help. Cleans and such."

"I see." Gennie followed Elias to the rear entrance, where a tall, sturdy, and stern-looking woman of obvious Scandinavian descent stood, arms crossed.

"Tova, this is the new girl. She needs a tub of hot water and something to put on," Elias said as he skittered past the fair-haired woman with the agility of a much younger man.

Tova stepped between Gennie and the door. For a moment, nothing happened.

"Pleased to meet you," Gennie said as she stared into blue eyes that seemed unable to blink. "Thank you for your kindness in helping me settle in."

Again, nothing.

"Tova?" Mr. Howe called from somewhere inside. "I'd be obliged if you'd go on over to the Fisher's Dry Goods Store and fetch the lady a new dress and whatever she needs to go along with it." He appeared beside Tova and looked Gennie over. "Appears she'll need everything, head to toe."

At the housekeeper's raised eyebrows, Mr. Howe scrambled to explain. "What I mean to say is, likely she's got road dust on every layer." A brisk red climbed into his cheeks. "That didn't come out right. See—oh, never mind."

Elias mumbled something about womenfolk and the Confederacy and disappeared inside. With him gone, Gennie was left in Tova's sights. It was, to say the least, an uncomfortable feeling.

But she was not unaccustomed to dealing with the help. She needed to diffuse the situation with a gesture. A grand gesture.

Gennie fumbled with the strings of her reticule. "Here," she said as her fingers wrapped around the wad of cash she'd nearly lost. "I can pay." As soon as she made the offer, Gennie realized she had no idea what the price of such a purchase would be. "How much would a dress and some underthings cost?"

The housekeeper didn't respond, nor did she move.

"I'm sorry," Gennie said as she peeled off a few bills, then, when Tova lifted a pale brow, added a few more. "Generally I have my dresses made by this wonderful seamstress in a shop near the Seine, so I've no idea what size I wear. That is, I've never purchased a dress from a department store before."

The brow went higher.

Two more bills went into the stack, and then, for good measure, Gennie added one more. A glance at the remaining funds told her she'd spent half at least, possibly more. The remainder she would count in the privacy of her chambers.

"Please, take it," she said, thrusting her hand toward the imperious woman. "I'm ever so tired and grateful for your kindness." Gennie paused. "You're a true blessing and an answer to prayer."

At this, both brows went up. "You pray?" Tova asked in surprisingly unaccented English.

"Yes, of course," Gennie said. "More so, lately."

Tova relaxed her expression but not her posture. "Then we shall have an understanding, you and I."

"All right," Gennie said, lowering her hand to her side, the money still tight in her fist.

"You shall look after the child," Tova said, "and you will leave the care of Mr. Howe and Mr. Beck to me. When you are not looking after the child, you're mine, and I will use you to help with the cleaning. Is that understood?"

As Gennie nodded, another type of understanding dawned. No wonder the former governess left in such a hurry to become a bride. This Scandinavian housekeeper had a territory to protect, and young unmarried women were obviously not welcome.

Gennie thought back to the last time she'd encountered such a woman. Before her came the image of Mrs. Vanowen in all her glory, wearing a frown not unlike the one on Tova's face. Gennie had taken the old dowager into her confidence by offering up a choice tidbit on a favorite but quite exclusive dressmaker in Paris, one Mrs. Vanowen would surely want to share with her friends on their upcoming visit to the Continent. Perhaps that tactic, applied in a slightly different manner, might work now.

Gennie cast a glance to the right and then to the left before leaning toward the housekeeper. "I've a secret."

"Oh?" Tova's stoic expression remained in place, though Gennie thought she saw the beginnings of a spark of interest. A woman was a woman, whether in Manhattan or Denver.

"Yes," she said in a loud whisper. "You see, there's a fellow back home who I think will soon be declaring his intentions to my father."

"Is that so?" Tova's mouth relaxed slightly, her lips turned up a bit at the edges. "Then why are you here?"

Funny how the truth seemed the only good answer. "One last adventure."

Tova actually smiled. "Then you'll find caring for the Beck child exactly what you came for." She paused to glance at the union suit still caught in the tree. "Top of the stairs, turn right. Yours is the first room on the left. It adjoins the nursery. I'll have Isak bring your bath."

"Thank you." Gennie made to enter the house, only to feel Tova's iron grip on her arm.

The housekeeper pointed to the cash still in Gennie's hand. Nodding, Gennie handed over a large portion of her funds, then watched as Tova tucked it into the pocket of her heavily starched apron. "And see that you remember that fellow of yours back home when you're tempted to give my Elias a second look."

8

Mae waited until the last second, her finger all but squeezing the trigger of her favorite Colt pistol. The dust cloud drew nearer.

She dared not even scratch the itch at the tip of her nose. To do so would be to risk being caught, and being caught meant taking a bullet, for One-Eyed Ed rarely missed his aim.

Mae rested her fist on the rock and settled the Colt atop it. She'd get one shot, maybe two, before Ed returned fire. She had to make it good. With a prayer for good aim and safe travel home, Mae tightened her grip on the Colt and counted to five.

ᴏᴏ

Gennie tossed her traveling clothes into a pile and padded across the marble tiles to test the water's temperature. Warm. She sighed. How long had it been since she'd enjoyed a proper soak?

Too long.

Ignoring the twinge of combined regret and excitement, Gennie sank to her shoulders beneath the fragrant water. The tub, crafted in a generous length and width from the same marble as the floor, seemed out of place in such humble surroundings. Gennie recognized the soap as the same French-milled variety Mama had shipped in from Paris.

How did a common governess's room come to boast such a luxury? In Manhattan, the help had to make do with garden variety Pears soap, and their bathtub was a glorified bucket that could be moved nearer the stove in cold weather.

Slathering scented bubbles over skin that begged for a good scrubbing, Gennie leaned back against the edge of the tub and felt the heaviness of exhaustion tug at her eyelids. Sleep would be best, but the sun still shone on the snowcapped Rockies. Dare she hope her temporary duties as governess to the Beck child might begin tomorrow rather than today?

Until Gennie left the solitude of the bath, at least, she was responsible for nothing more than finding clean skin beneath the layers of ash and soot courtesy of the railroad.

After much effort, her skin glowed pink as, likely, did her scalp. The only thing that remained was to wash off the soap. Gennie preferred to sink beneath the water as if she were a mermaid, a habit she'd begun well before Mama disapproved. She slid beneath the water and held her breath until her lungs protested, then bobbed up and swiped at her eyes.

"I never seen a grownup do that."

Gennie squealed. The last of the water departed her eyes, and Charlotte Beck came into view. "What are you doing in my bathing closet?" she asked, sinking beneath a protective layer of soapy water and peering at the impudent child.

"Did I hear someone scream?" Elias called.

"No," Gennie said, but Charlotte responded with an emphatic yes.

Footsteps thudded toward her.

"Halt, sir!" Gennie called.

Charlotte giggled as she settled onto the edge of the tub and dipped her palm into the water. "You talk funny."

At least she no longer smelled funny.

The footsteps halted outside the bedroom door, and the resulting silence was filled by the splashing of water at the hands of the Beck girl.

"Stop it," Gennie snapped. The girl drew back, but only slightly. "You will take your leave now, Miss Beck. And in the future you will knock before entering a closed door. Do you understand?"

The girl's expression went curiously penitent. Gennie didn't buy it for a moment. "What time is dinner, Miss Beck?"

"That'd be six o'clock, miss," Elias Howe called from the other room. "My apologies for the girl," he added. "Were I a blind man, I'd come fetch her, but as I'm not, I'm forced to wait for the imp. I'm sure you understand."

"Yes, thank you, Mr. Howe." Gennie tamed her grin and turned to Charlotte. "We shall continue our conversation regarding proper deportment for young ladies at promptly six o'clock." Gennie narrowed her eyes. "Now depart this room immediately and never entertain the thought of returning, unless this tub is unoccupied."

When Charlotte did not move, Gennie leaned forward, careful to keep the soap bubbles and her arms well placed to preserve her modesty.

"You smell funny," she said to the wide-eyed girl. "When's the last time you had a bath, Charlotte Beck?"

Charlotte took a step backward. As Gennie suspected, the little heathen's love of adventure did not extend to a tangle with soap and water.

Gennie smiled. "Mr. Howe, are you still nearby?"

"I am," he said, "though I swear on the life of my dear departed mother that I've seen nothing, nor have I made the attempt." He cleared his throat. "I'm still figuring how to help, though."

"Might you be able to fetch a change of clothes for the girl?" she called. "A dress if she has one." She suppressed a giggle at the girl's expression. "Just leave them outside the door."

"Yes, miss," he replied without bothering to disguise his humor.

As the footsteps faded, Gennie reached for her wrapper. "Turn around, Charlotte. I'll not have my modesty compromised."

Turn the girl did, gathering up Gennie's puddle of clothing and scampering toward the door. In an instant, she and the only clothes Gennie had were gone. An outrageous situation, but what could be done about it? Screaming certainly wouldn't bring the desired result.

Gennie dried quickly, this time with the door locked, and donned her wrapper. Outside, the sun still hung above the Rockies, but Gennie felt the clock should read half past midnight.

Manhattan and her home on Fifth Avenue suddenly seemed very far away. The realization made her want to laugh and cry in equal measure. Somehow she'd become a woman capable of boarding a train for the Wild West with nothing but her reticule and a prayer, arriving in Denver with only her pluck and poise to get her through.

A stab of loneliness jabbed her heart, and tears blurred her vision. "Stop that, you ninny," she said as she furiously swiped at her eyes. "You asked for this adventure, and you're going to appreciate every single minute of it."

Gennie leaned against the fireplace mantel, a lovely piece carved from the same marble as the tub, and placed her forehead against the cool stone. *Father, is this the end of my adventure or merely the beginning? Gift me with discernment.*

A movement outside her window caught Gennie's attention, and she strolled over in time to see Isak shinnying down the pine tree, the union suit draped over one shoulder.

And, please, she added as she turned away from the window and walked toward the feather bed, *an extra measure of patience.*

She couldn't leave the room until Tova returned with her newly purchased clothing. Surely snatching a few moments of rest while she waited wouldn't hurt.

The feather mattress cushioned her, while a pile of pillows in various sizes provided just the right position for her to recline in comfort.

The bed coverings were a decent silk, and the sheets felt nearly as soft as the ones on her bed at home.

With the sun streaming through the pines, the room took on a pleasant, soothing atmosphere. All that remained was a good-night from her parents and a practical joke of some kind from Connor, and she'd feel right at home. Gennie settled back into the pillows and let her eyes drift shut.

Moments later, she opened her eyes and noted two things: her new clothing had been delivered, and she'd missed dinner by an hour. If the mantel clock were to be believed, she'd slept until a few minutes before seven.

Gennie scrambled to her feet and stumbled toward the dress, then froze.

The garment was absolutely hideous. She touched the fabric, then jumped back in horror. She wouldn't dream of asking her own maids to wear something this horrid.

Constructed of some poor version of homespun that would likely cause a rash, the garish, saffron-colored day dress, with its random sprigging of scarlet rosebuds and green leaves, would do nothing for her complexion or, likely, her figure. A matronly set of undergarments of the same rough-hewn fabric lay folded on the chair. A pair of service-able lace-up boots and heavy woolen stockings, both in dull black, com-pleted the ensemble.

Then she saw the hat. More suited to a prairie schooner than any possible city venue, the poke bonnet had been chosen, presumably, for its matching red roses, though the background of the chapeau was a sickly blue green.

"An absolute nightmare," Gennie muttered.

Casting about for her traveling garments, she sighed. Either they were hanging in a tree somewhere, or Tova had not yet completed laundering them.

There was nothing to do but don the newly purchased frock and make the best of things. She stepped out of her wrapper and into the dress.

A long line of buttons was the only way to close the gaping back. By putting the dress on backwards, she was able to button the skirt and a portion of the waistband, and reaching behind her took care of a few of the top buttons. The middle of her back proved a bit trickier, however.

After several more attempts to close the gap, Gennie gave up. Grabbing the cloth from the bedside table, she draped it over her shoulders like a shawl and headed downstairs to make her apologies for the lateness of the hour.

She found Elias in the kitchen, stirring something that smelled delicious. Before she could greet him, the older man turned around and grinned.

"I wondered if you'd climbed down the drainpipe and run off. Not that I'd have blamed you." He used the knuckle of his forefinger to straighten his cap, then went back to stirring. "Sit yourself down. The others have already eaten and gone."

So she had missed the meal. How odd that he would still be cooking.

"I'm terribly sorry," she offered. "I had no idea I was so tired."

"Sit," he repeated. "You've had a long trip. We'll not let a little thing like oversleeping cause you to be fired on your first day."

Only when he punctuated the statement with a chuckle did Gennie relax. She pulled a chair away from the table and sat, mindful of the fact that she'd never taken a meal in a kitchen in her life. Unlike the dining rooms she was accustomed to, the scent of food cooking and the warmth of the big stove gave the kitchen an informal air. Dining with the servants felt odd, but for now, at least, she was exactly that: a servant.

As this realization sunk in, her makeshift shawl slipped. Gennie hurriedly straightened it. Should the former tablecloth fail to cover her faux pas, bare skin would show, and so would her inability to do the simplest dressing of herself.

Gennie sat straighter in her chair and tried not to think of such things. Pots and pans clanged, and the cook seemed in perpetual motion. For a man of advanced years, the old soldier obviously still had plenty of energy.

"So," Gennie said to Elias Howe's back, "when exactly is Mr. Beck expected to return?"

"It's easier asking when the wind will stop blowing." The man's chuckle rumbled toward her. "No one knows for sure, though it always happens."

Despite having no interest whatsoever in staying with the Becks, Gennie felt her temper rise. "So he comes and goes without concern for what happens to his daughter?"

Elias froze, then slowly set his utensils aside and turned to face her. Gennie watched in stunned silence as the old man's genial expression turned sour.

"I don't believe you should judge Daniel until you know him." He reached for a corner of the apron he'd thrown on over his customary Confederate suit coat and mopped his forehead. "He does what he thinks is best for Charlotte and leaves it to the rest of us to honor that and not question it. You're here to take up where the girl's ma left off, so I'd advise you to hold your questions until you can ask them of Daniel himself. The raising of that child is important to him, especially now."

Elias suddenly looked as if he'd said too much, which intrigued Gennie.

"I'm sorry," she said. She rose and reached for one of the aprons still hanging on the pegboard. "Might I help with whatever you're preparing?"

Gennie's quick change of topic did its job, and soon Elias seemed to have forgotten her foray into dangerous territory. Gennie, however, did not.

She handed him three eggs and watched him crack them into what appeared to be some sort of cooked meat. "You mentioned Charlotte's mother. Might I ask what sort of calamity befell her that she's no longer raising her daughter? Just so I might be prepared should Charlotte speak of it, you understand," she hastened to add.

Elias paused in his work to give her a sideways look. Gennie put on her most innocent face. Gossip was wrong, but being informed seemed anything but. And with the child in question, any weapon was worth the attempt.

"A sad tale, that one," he finally said, going back to his work. "Hand me another egg. That one there."

Gennie complied, then knotted the tablecloth across her bosom to keep the fabric from slipping. Rather than probe further, she elected to remain silent. Men often spoke more when nothing impeded the conversation. This she'd learned in finishing school, though she'd not retained much more than that.

Of course, the school really intended to teach how to catch a husband. In that, she'd likely be called a success soon.

What would Chandler Dodd think if he were to walk in and catch her dressed in this garish ensemble helping a quirky fellow break eggs into a frying pan? Gennie couldn't muster up even the slightest image, though when considering what Mae Winslow might do in the same situation, she had no problem.

Mae would ask for the recipe, then fetch her pistols and be gone. How Gennie envied that fictional female.

"She was a pretty thing," Elias said, his voice soft enough to make Gennie wonder whether he spoke aloud on purpose or merely mused for his own benefit. "Too pretty for her own good. I told Daniel as much, but a man in love won't be warned."

He looked to Gennie as if he expected a response, so she nodded. "Indeed."

"And that younger brother of his, well, Edwin never struck me as anything other than a fellow who wanted what Daniel had." Elias stirred the last of the eggs into the mixture, then turned the whole thing into a baking dish and stepped away from the stove. "I've said too much. Fetch yourself a plate and mug off the drainboard and go sit down."

Gennie held her tongue and did what he asked. Before she could settle in the chair, Elias placed before her the iron skillet filled with the delicious smelling concoction, along with a pot of coffee.

"There," he said as he joined her, "that ought to do for a passable breakfast."

She paused, the fork poised at her lips. "Breakfast? I thought this was dinner."

Elias shook his head, then adjusted his cap. "No, you slept through that meal. This here's breakfast." He pulled a gold watch from his pocket and consulted it before offering it to her. "See there? It's nearly eight."

"Eight in the morning?" She placed her fork on the plate, the bite untouched. "I slept since yesterday afternoon?"

"You did, and it's a miracle that child didn't wake you." He reached over to spoon a generous helping of the concoction onto his plate. "I threatened her with the worst thing I could think of if she so much as tiptoed past your door."

"And what was that?"

He leaned toward her. "I told her I'd see that Tova threw out all her overalls and made her wear a dress to school." Elias leaned back and slapped his palms on the table, sending the silverware clanging together. "That put the fear of the Lord into her."

Gennie tried not to let her appalled state show. She reached once more for her fork. "How old is Charlotte, exactly?"

"She's ten," Elias said between bites. "I remember, because it was five years ago last winter when I first laid eyes on her and knew who she belonged to. It took Daniel a bit longer, but a man's blind when he's looking at the woman he loves. That's what I say, anyway."

"Speaking of me, were you, Elias?" Tova said from the doorway.

The old soldier's ears reddened as he leaned over his plate and continued to eat. "Likely you misheard," he said without sparing her a glance.

"I see the nanny is awake."

As Tova's gaze swept over her, Gennie felt compelled to rise. "I'm terribly sorry," she said. "I had no idea I'd be sleeping past dinner."

"And breakfast," Tova muttered, hanging her cloak on the peg, then pointing at Gennie. "The apron, please."

Gennie looked down, then quickly shed the garment and handed it to Tova. Likely nothing she'd do would please the housekeeper.

Except leave, that is, which she planned to do in a month.

"So where is Charlotte now?" she asked, causing both Elias and Tova to stare.

"The girl is at school." Tova's sharp response and subsequent dismissal of her startled Gennie. Only the knowledge that Tova somehow saw her as a threat kept Gennie from taking offense as the older woman stormed from the kitchen in a huff.

Oblivious to the feminine battle of wills waging around him, Elias went back to his eggs. "You got a chill?" he asked.

"A chill?" Gennie looked down at the table scarf still knotted around her. "No. Just, well…" Proper description escaped her, so she decided to change the subject. "I wonder if I might be so bold as to inquire of something."

Elias set his fork down, the plate scraped clean. "Go ahead, but I don't promise an answer."

She nodded. "I'm of a mind to write to the girl's father to settle some things regarding his expectations of me, get some questions answered. Things of that nature."

"Go on," the old soldier said.

"And I wondered, if I posted such a letter, how long it would take for him to receive it."

He shrugged. "Depends. If you get lucky and catch a train headed to Leadville, he might be holding the letter before nightfall." Another shrug. "Then again, it might not get there at all. You never know about these things."

Gennie straightened her back and turned toward the door. "If there's nothing else for me to do while Charlotte is at school, I'll go and write that letter. Might you have pen and ink I could use?"

"All of that's in Daniel's office, and you're free to take and use whatever you need." Elias looked perplexed. "But aren't you forgetting something?" He pointed to the table and her plate.

"Oh," she said, hurrying to explain the food remaining there, "I'm not one to eat a big breakfast. I assure you, however, it was quite delicious."

"I do thank you," Elias said, "but what you're forgetting is to wash your plate and mug." He shrugged. "That's part of your duties, what with Tova busy cleaning and me doing all the cooking. Unless Charlotte's home, you're to do whatever Tova or I need done." The oddly dressed man rose and shoved his plate toward her. "And right now all I can think that needs doing is the dishes. Be sure and scrub that pan extra. An iron skillet doesn't need dish soap. Just clean it the usual way."

"The usual way." She paused and let the dish slide from her hands into the sink with a clatter. "Yes, of course."

And with that, he was off, leaving Gennie to decipher what the "usual way" might be. For that matter, leaving her to figure out exactly how dishes were washed.

At least she knew what she would say in her letter to Daniel Beck. In plain terms, she would tell him his daughter needed a father who did not stray so far from the home fires. She would add, of course, that while his daughter was not completely a lost cause, she did have quite a road to travel to become a young lady.

And finally, Gennie would have to tell Daniel Beck that while the job was not beyond her abilities, she would not be staying for the extended period of time it would take to accomplish it.

In short, the brief but exciting adventures of Gennie Cooper would soon mirror the ongoing adventure of Mae Winslow.

But first, she had to figure out the puzzle that was dish washing.

9

Had Ed been given the moment to do over, he likely would have wished for both eyes to be operational. As it was, Mae caught him unaware, and rather than dispatch him to kingdom come, she hobbled him to be sent there via the good marshal and a sturdy rope.

The rope he'd used on her, Mae kept as a souvenir, along with the horse the formerly fortunate felon rode in on. Renamed Lucky, the mare became her means of returning to Deadwood and Henry, both of which had found a dear place in her heart.

If only she'd watched where she was going and sent Lucky around the coiled rattler instead of over it.

☙❧

Gennie awaited Charlotte's return from school with a mixture of anticipation and trepidation. The dish washing proved short yet eventful, and she'd only have to replace a few broken plates to make things right.

In spite of—or perhaps because of—Gennie's skills at dish washing, Tova stood at the kitchen door, regarding her with what appeared to be great curiosity. "Did the girl return?"

"The girl?" Gennie shook her head. "Do you mean Charlotte? I thought she was at school."

"It just looks like she and not you…" Tova shook her head. "Never mind."

Seizing her opportunity, Gennie let the dishcloth fall to the floor, and smiled. "As you and Elias—that is, Mr. Howe—have said I'm to be at your bidding when Charlotte is in school." She propped up her grin with an enthusiasm she did not feel. "How can I help you?"

"Remove the towel from the floor," Tova said, turning up her nose.

"Fine." Gennie snagged the dishcloth and tossed it onto the table, then pressed past the housekeeper. "If that's all, I'll go find Elias and see if he would like me to do anything for him."

"Wait," Tova commanded.

Gennie turned. "Yes?" she asked, sweet as cream. "Did you think of something?"

"Mr. Beck's study needs a thorough cleaning. Come. I'll show you."

Gennie followed the housekeeper's straight back through a narrow hallway that opened into a foyer of similar size and construction to her family home in Newport. While the Cooper home had been decorated with one of Mama's priceless papers depicting the English countryside, this space bore no such adornment. What it lost in wall décor, it more than adequately made up in the ornamentation that had been tacked to walls and set on every available space, like so much gilded debris.

A woman's touch was sorely needed to make what was sadly garish into something grand. Perhaps during her short stay, Gennie might offer some assistance.

She ducked just in time to miss an oversized statue of what looked like a plucked chicken. Likely the artist had intended a different effect, possibly an ostrich or other exotic bird, but the featherless metal fowl looked exactly like the pompous rooster that populated the servants' chicken yard in Newport.

"It's beautiful, yes?" Tova asked as she gazed at the statue with something akin to wonder.

"Truly like nothing I've seen," Gennie said, touching its bejeweled beak.

Other items of décor were less overdone and obviously well chosen, though Gennie couldn't find more than a few. Then the housekeeper opened the doors to a room that changed her mind about the home's owner.

Gennie walked into Daniel Beck's private sanctum and felt as if she'd stepped into another time and place. The carpet beneath her feet was a lovely cinnamon-colored Sarouk, and the walls bore wainscoting in a dark wood that sent her mind reeling back to visits to the English country home of Papa's second cousin, the Marquis of Something-or-Other.

Volumes of Shakespeare and Dumas shared space with titles by Aristotle and Voltaire. Upturned on an Empire table beside a leather chair was a copy of *A Tale of Two Cities* with what appeared to be a railroad schedule marking a place midway through the novel. Next to it was *Aesop's Fables,* open to the beginning of a story called "The Fawn and His Mother."

The room smelled of leather and Morocco varnish, and made her miss Papa terribly. She spied the desk, with its sheaves of fresh paper stacked beside a filled inkwell, and debated whether her first letter would be to Mr. Beck or her father.

Both could bring trouble, but writing Papa might be an exercise in understanding what brought her to Denver in the first place. Not that she'd mention she'd gone any farther than Boston.

"Are you listening?" Tova inquired.

"Yes, yes, please do continue."

Gennie turned from the desk to see the housekeeper had fetched some sort of cleaning equipment and was brandishing it with great excitement. In terms that sounded more like a foreign language than plain English, Tova explained the proper procedure for everything from dusting to winding the Viennese eagle clock.

"Which must be done daily to keep it running," Gennie said. Noting Tova's raised eyebrows, she added, "Mama loves the sound of ours, though I find the chiming every fifteen minutes quite annoying. And as the thing is set in the belly of the eagle, I always wondered why it chimed rather than chirped. Chirping would be the appropriate sound for a bird-shaped clock, don't you think?" She paused. "Of course, I always preferred the Empire style to the later Biedermeier pieces."

Tova responded by leaving the room without comment.

When the door shut, Gennie turned to her task, stepping over the cleaning equipment to seat herself at the oversized mahogany desk. "Likely Mr. Beck's never here long enough to notice the dust," she said under her breath as she reached for the writing paper.

Before the clock chimed the quarter hour, Gennie had completed a firm letter insisting the absent father of Charlotte Beck present himself to be accountable for the child, and she decided not to write her own father.

"Now to post it." Gennie rose and slipped the door open a notch. The coast clear, she slid past the horrid bejeweled bird and edged her way into the kitchen. There she found Tova and Elias at the kitchen table, discussing something related to a pie.

Leaving the pair to their culinary pursuits, Gennie backed quietly into the hall and slipped off her shoes. In a moment, she found the front door and escaped.

The air was brisk and bracing, a shock after the warmth of the home's interior. Ducking to pass beneath the kitchen window, Gennie returned her shoes to their rightful place then found Isak in the carriage house, mucking a stall.

"Might I post a letter?" she inquired. "It's rather urgent."

Tova's son paused his work. "Is it now?"

"Mr. Howe told me I might be able to get this to Mr. Beck via the train to Leadville."

"Well, now." Isak tossed the pitchfork aside and dusted off his hands. "Why didn't you say so? I'll hitch up the buggy."

In what seemed like no time, Gennie found herself riding through town beside the Scandinavian fellow. "Is it always this chilly in July?" she asked.

"Sometimes." He shrugged. "I say if you don't like the weather, give it a day, and it'll change."

Gennie grinned as she shivered. The buggy soon stopped in front of Union Station. A train whistle caught her attention, reminding Gennie of just how far she'd come since leaving Manhattan.

Far in distance, perhaps, but what had she accomplished? Washing dishes and cleaning an office were hardly what she'd come west to do. A train edged past the station, picking up speed as it rolled away.

With nothing to lose and only an adventure worthy of Mae Winslow to gain, Gennie considered climbing from the buggy and walking into Union Station to purchase a ticket for points west or north. Anywhere an adventure might be had.

"Miss?" Isak nudged her. "Post office is over there." He pointed away from the trains.

"All right." Gennie started to climb down, but Isak scampered around to lift her off the buggy. "Thank you," she said. "You're very kind."

Isak grinned and his cheeks went red beneath his pale hair. When she made no move to walk toward the post office, Isak shook his head. "Might I post it for you?"

"Yes, please." She handed him the letter with a smile, then looked back toward the station. When she returned her attention to Isak, she found he'd not yet made an effort to head to the post office. "Something wrong?"

The pink in his cheeks deepened. "Mailing a letter costs," he said without meeting her stare. "I'd offer to do it for you, but I didn't think to bring money." His gaze met hers. "I'm awful sorry."

She asked him the cost of posting a letter to Leadville in the fastest manner, and when he told her, her grin faded. At this rate, she'd have nothing left of her meager savings. "How much if I were to send it a bit slower?"

"Hold on," Isak said. "It appears this may be your lucky day."

Gennie watched the young man dart across the crowded platform and catch a well-dressed man by the sleeve. After a few moments of conversation, Isak handed the gentleman the letter and loped back to the wagon.

"That's Mr. August Meyer," Isak said as he helped Gennie back into the wagon. "He's an associate of Mr. Beck from over in Leadville. I've often driven him about Denver when he's visiting."

"Oh?"

Isak took his place on the seat beside Gennie and reached for the reins. "He's heading home to Leadville now and will see that Mr. Beck gets the letter."

"Wonderful."

The buggy returned to the Beck home without—as far as she could tell, anyway—being missed, and Gennie quickly climbed the stairs to her room and closed the door. Isak had informed her that while Charlotte completed her lessons at the same time each day, she'd always been allowed to return home at her own discretion.

This appalled Gennie, though she held her tongue. How much the son told the mother was not yet evident, and Gennie had yet to figure out whether Tova was jealous or merely disliked her on principle.

Whatever the reason, Gennie decided to stay out of the woman's way and keep to her room. The more she thought on it, dining alone with Elias Howe was likely enough to land one on the housekeeper's list of troublemakers.

As was making any changes to the staid routine of Beck Manor, which she found out later in the evening when she suggested Charlotte might benefit from instruction in decorum rather than being allowed to run free with the neighborhood children. She was a Beck, Gennie argued, and thus held to a higher standard. Tova disagreed, and Charlotte disappeared until well after the dinner bell had rung.

Oddly, the child had a pie in hand when she deigned to ring the front bell and make a grand entrance befitting a queen, just as the stars appeared over the Rockies.

Gennie had nothing to do but sit in her room all evening and wonder whether Mr. Meyer had delivered her letter to Daniel Beck.

That, and daydream of what Mae Winslow might do in a similar situation. Mae would certainly never hide while chaos reigned.

Falling asleep with this thought, Gennie decided that, like Mae, exile no longer suited her. Tomorrow she would begin the adventure she'd come to seek, and like it or not, Charlotte Beck would be coming along.

ல

The handwriting on the letter was exquisite, like the engraved invitations that too often graced his hall table. The ones Daniel ignored whenever possible and suffered through when he could no longer pretend to be away or otherwise occupied.

This, however, was no summons for supper or call to attend someone's charity ball. Daniel slammed the letter on the desk, then picked it up again, still unable to believe the impudence of the author.

"Something wrong, sir?" Hiram asked, stopping in the doorway.

"What?" Daniel said. "No, nothing." He held the letter up, then let it fall once more to the desk. "Yes, actually, there is something. I've received a demand from Charlotte's governess that I return to Denver. Can you believe the audacity?"

He thought he saw a smile cross Hiram's expression for a brief moment. "Audacity? Sir, I'm not sure to what you're referring. Might it be her decision to speak up, or her lack of decorum on what she said?"

"Oh, for goodness' sake, Hiram. A woman who does not know Charlotte has written to tell me how to parent. What right has she?"

"Perhaps she felt she was—"

"Was what?" He continued without allowing Hiram to answer. "This woman is an *employee*. A governess, of all things. How dare she question my abilities as a father to my daughter? How dare she question me at all? Not a single man in my employ would dare do such a thing, and yet this woman…this…*governess*…"

Blood pulsed in his temples. He clenched his fists and longed for something to slam them into. The one thing he'd not tolerate was being judged and found inadequate. He'd throttle the man who tried. And fire the woman.

"Hiram," he said, storming toward the door, then doubling back to snatch up the offending document. "Get me a train ticket."

"For Denver, sir?" Hiram backed away from the door to allow Daniel to pass.

"Yes, Denver," he tossed behind him as he ran down the stairs. He could hear Hiram following. "Where did you think I'd be going? I've got a situation to handle, and it can't wait. I want to be on today's train when it leaves, which, according to my watch, is in less than an hour. See to it."

"Yes sir," Hiram called. "But, sir?"

Daniel stopped and whirled around. "What?"

"You've got meetings all afternoon and dinner with Lieutenant Governor Tabor and his wife tonight. They're hosting the governor, you know."

He did. Barely had the storm of controversy lifted over the recent miners' strike when Daniel had been inundated by correspondence from the state's top politician. Thus far he'd avoided any discussions of a political nature, and had dreaded the evening ahead for that very reason. The governor was shopping for underlings, and the last thing Daniel needed was to add another responsibility to his growing list.

Hiram put on his determined look. "The governor's aide expressly requested your presence."

"I don't care what he requested. This takes precedence."

Hiram opened his mouth to respond, then wisely clamped it shut again.

"Cancel them all," Daniel said. "This woman called me an irresponsible parent, and I'll not stand for it."

"But, sir!"

"Hiram, do not join my governess in questioning my authority. It would be immediate grounds for dismissal."

The color drained from Hiram's face, and, for a moment, he looked as if he'd been rendered immobile.

"Look," Daniel said in what he hoped was a gentler tone, "I've known Tabor for some time. If you explain to Horace that I've been called home on a family emergency, I'm certain all will be forgiven." He paused to think. "Much as I hate to make this offer, tell him I'd be happy to host a gathering of some sort in his honor the next time he's in Denver."

"Yes sir," Hiram said, looking slightly less fearful. "And the miners?"

"I trust you," Daniel said. "You've got good sense and will handle anything that comes up." He turned on his heels and headed for the exit, attempting to modulate both his voice and his temper. "Those people will still have their jobs when I return. The author of this letter will not. Now, if you'll excuse me, I must pack."

Mae always hoped the rattle she heard would be in the hands of a baby and not attached to a creature the size of her arm and three times the length. With Lucky galloping off for parts unknown, she realized the rattler wasn't going away, and neither was she.

Any other helpless woman faced with deadly peril would reach for her lace handkerchief and soak it with tears. Mae, however, was neither helpless nor in possession of a handkerchief, lace or otherwise.

She did, however, have her trusty Colt revolver, which she slowly grasped even as the demon played its castanets double time. Unlike One-Eyed Ed, this varmint had better-than-average vision and no blind spots.

Whatever she did, she would have to do fast and with no margin for error. Her fingers met the cold steel of her weapon just as Lucky decided to return.

᳹

After what little Gennie had observed of the Beck girl's bad behavior, she realized it was likely as much attributed to the adults who allowed her free rein as it was to Charlotte, obviously a girl of high aptitude and even higher spirits. As Gennie ran the borrowed brush through her hair, she couldn't help recalling the events of last evening.

Last night, Tova and Elias were the only ones allowed near the child. Gennie's approach at bath time caused shrieking, as did her suggestion that she might see to the girl's bedtime routine. It was all most improper and, Gennie decided, most theatrical.

There was nothing wrong with Charlotte Beck that a firm hand and a good dose of prayer wouldn't handle. For a moment, she thought about giving the challenge a go. A few weeks under her tutelage and Charlotte would be a different child.

Then reality and good sense returned. A task this size would take months, and her time with the girl was limited to weeks. One month at best.

She paused, the brush gripped tightly in her hand. One month to tame Charlotte Beck. She smiled. She'd wanted a Wild West adventure, and the prospect of turning that girl into a young lady certainly qualified.

Of course, there was the distinct possibility that when Daniel Beck returned, her month might be cut short. "That could be a blessing," she whispered as the brush slid through the last of her tangles, "or I might just regret leaving so soon."

Still, she intended to leave her mark, even if it meant finding a way to let these people know she would do her job until her replacement arrived.

Gennie set the brush on the dresser and reached for the horrid frock. The Beck household might run fine without her, but she'd taken on the job of governess, and until Daniel Beck returned, she intended to do it.

She repeated this statement to herself three times before gathering the courage to take up the table scarf and make her way down to the kitchen. There she found Elias at the stove and Charlotte finishing her breakfast.

"Good morning, Mr. Howe," she said. "Breakfast smells delicious."

Rather than wait to be invited, Gennie took her place across the table from Charlotte and reached for a spoonful of eggs scrambled with some sort of meat. As she silently blessed the food, Gennie also prayed that the Lord and not her feelings would lead the coming conversation. Surely the former would have a much better result than the latter.

"Good morning, Charlotte."

The girl didn't respond.

"You're not deaf, child," Elias chided. "Else there'd be an excuse for your rude behavior."

Eyes narrowed to menacing slits met Gennie's unwavering gaze. She thought she heard the words, "Good Morning," though it sounded more like a hiss than a hello.

Choosing to ignore the child's atrocious response as well as her outfit of overalls, cap, and boots, Gennie focused on the lovely face that held such potential. Charlotte appeared to be concentrating on a book, though the girl's attention seemed to waver from Gennie to the page and back again.

On the table next to the egg concoction sat a pie, likely the same one the girl had brought home last night. Gennie watched Charlotte cut a large slice and slop it onto her plate, leaving a mess on the tablecloth.

"Pie for breakfast?" Gennie said as much to the adult in the room as to the child.

"I can have what I want," the girl replied.

Gennie looked at Elias, whose face told her the child likely spoke the truth.

"Charlotte," Gennie said firmly, "while I disagree that any breakfast is sufficient for a growing child, there's nothing to be done for it this morning. But you'll need a cloth to remove the stain."

The girl looked at Gennie as if she'd grown a third eye. Willfully, she stabbed her fork into the pie, then went back to reading her book. Behind her, Elias watched with interest until he saw Gennie's pointed stare. Then, suddenly, something on the stove seemed to catch his attention, and he turned his back.

Tova stepped into the room, a basket of clean laundry in her arms. While Elias greeted the housekeeper, Gennie kept her attention focused on the girl.

When it became apparent that a showdown was not likely to produce a winner, Gennie decided to try a different means of reaching the child. She'd already thought of several possible activities—china painting, embroidery, and a lesson in the care and braiding of hair, among them—for the hours between school's end and dinner's beginning, all of which would be beneficial for a girl's upbringing.

On second thought, perhaps embroidery wasn't such a good idea. The thought of Charlotte Beck in possession of sharp objects made Gennie shiver.

"After school today, I've an afternoon of adventure planned for us, Charlotte," Gennie said with as much enthusiasm as she could muster.

The girl continued to turn pages in her book, though Gennie noted a brief look of interest.

"Then it's settled," Gennie said. "I'll fetch you from school myself."

"I think that's a grand idea," Elias said. "Isak can fetch you wherever the two of you would like to go."

Tova's inelegant snort caught Gennie off guard. Rather than argue, Gennie rose and nodded before escaping. She was a coward, true, but some battles were better fought in small skirmishes, and she intended to meet Charlotte Beck on the battlefield immediately after school. There was no need to do the same with Tova.

A visit to the carriage house kept Gennie well away from the perturbed Scandinavian housekeeper. The horses, a bay and a well-matched pair of chestnut mares, were exquisite. She stepped carefully across the straw-covered floor to rub her hand over the muzzle of the bay. As she did, the makeshift shawl slipped, and Gennie reached to adjust it.

"She's a spirited one."

Gennie turned toward the voice and found Isak watching her.

"That one's Mr. Beck's favorite."

"She's exquisite. They all are."

Isak ducked his head as he stepped past her and opened the stall. Gennie watched as he led first one chestnut then the other out and harnessed them to a waiting wagon.

"A moment of your time," Tova called, exiting the house and walking toward them. The housekeeper thrust a folded piece of paper in Gennie's direction and gave her a look that dared her to complain. "Isak," Tova said without taking her eyes off Gennie, "your other duties will wait until after the governess has completed her errand."

Before Gennie could form a question, Tova dismissed them both and stalked back inside. She turned to Isak, who seemed amused.

"It appears I'm to fetch you to the grocer's," he said.

"More than just the grocer's, it seems." Gennie consulted the paper and discovered the list of destinations was much longer than a mere trip for foodstuffs. "Perhaps you should have this." She handed him the paper.

"My mother wishes you to be out of the house for an extended period, I think."

"Her wish is my command." The sarcastic statement slipped out before Gennie could stop it. "Oh my, I'm terribly sorry. That was an awful thing to say. It's just that she seems to have taken a dislike to me."

"I wouldn't be so worried," Isak said. "I'm sure she likes you just fine."

"She picked out the dress."

"Ah, I see." His laughter was contagious.

"Miss McTaggart."

Gennie froze at the sound of Tova's reproving voice. Isak's merriment ceased, though his smile was only barely tamed.

"I require my tablecloth to remain here," Tova said as she approached.

Isak made it his business to be occupied with securing the horses by the time his mother reached Gennie. He did, however, send her a most impudent wink.

"The tablecloth," Tova said, her arm outstretched.

Gennie gathered the makeshift scarf closer. "I need it."

"Likely to sell," Tova snapped. "I'll not have Mr. Beck's things go missing."

"Sell?" Gennie straightened her spine and eyed the woman with what she hoped was something akin to superiority. "I'll have you know the only reason I need this thing is because you chose this horrid dress for me."

The housekeeper's face flamed bright red. Behind her, Gennie heard Isak's footsteps retreating into the carriage house.

"And furthermore…" Gennie caught her breath as well as the expression on Tova's face. "Never mind."

"Turn around," Tova said, her voice hard as steel.

Gennie turned and slid the table scarf off her shoulders to reveal the gap in her dress. For a moment, nothing happened. Then, quickly, Tova finished the job of buttoning her in and yanked away the scarf.

"Isak!"

A moment later, Gennie was lifted onto the wagon seat as Tova bustled back toward the house. To Gennie's surprise, the housekeeper paused at the door to call to her.

"Add one more thing to the list."

Isak handed Gennie the list and a pencil. "All right. What is it?"

Tova straightened her spine and gave Gennie a look of distaste. "See that you find an outfit that does not cause me this sort of trouble. Mr. Beck keeps an account at Fisher's."

Gennie nodded, her smile concealed behind her hand. Perhaps she and the stern housekeeper might become friends after all.

Isak made short work of negotiating the distance to downtown Denver, though finding a place to park the wagon took some doing. The city appeared no different than Manhattan, Gennie decided. A definite disappointment.

Before Isak took the list and went about collecting the needed items, he pointed Gennie toward Fisher's Dry Goods. She went willingly. Never had a shopping trip been so needed.

As she stepped inside the store, Gennie paused to allow her eyes to adjust to the dim light. What she saw when her vision cleared was truly a disappointment. Instead of row upon row of beautiful dresses, she found precious few garments among the items for sale.

"Careful," a bespectacled young man said as he climbed off a ladder in the rear of the store. "The floor's been freshly waxed."

"Thank you." She picked her way toward the clothing section.

"Are you looking for anything in particular?" he called.

"I'm in need of dresses," she said. "And all that goes with them, actually."

The clerk gestured to his left, where bolts of calico were piled nearly to the ceiling. "We've enough fabric to make any housewife smile."

Calico. Housewife. Smile. Where she came from, those three things did not go together.

"Actually," she said, turning from the mountain of cloth, "I'd hoped to find something already made."

He nodded as he adjusted his spectacles. "I shoulda pegged you for a store-bought gal."

"A store-bought gal," she said in her best attempt to be serious. "Yes, that's me."

"Then come this way," he said. "Fisher's Dry Goods has the broadest selection of ready-made clothing this side of the Rockies."

"Indeed." Gennie fell in step beside him, pausing only when she passed a display of jewelry items made from bear teeth, or so the sign boasted.

"Over here," he called. "Might I show you anything in particular?"

"I'll browse, thank you," she said, though she held out little hope she might actually find anything among the slim choices the lone clothing rack held.

Somehow, she pulled together a decently constructed dress in a lovely shade of blue, and a hat that matched. While it was nothing near her usual mode of dress, Gennie felt sure she could endure her short time in Denver clothed in such a manner. A smart pair of shoes in something approximating Denver's version of the latest Paris fashions was added to the stack on the counter. When she returned to New York, she'd have a check sent to Mr. Beck as reimbursement.

She could do with this for a few days, but one good dress was not enough. The hideous garment she wore notwithstanding, she would need a second set of clothing. This she found in a mint-colored ensemble, which she decided to wear out of the store.

The surprised clerk pointed her to a back room, where she shed the saffron dress and tossed it into a rubbish bin. Gennie donned the mint gown and tied a ribbon sash around her waist, already feeling more like herself. And more like an adventurer. Perhaps she'd find someone to take her on a tour of Denver. If Mr. Beck released her from her duties, she'd have plenty of time to see the sights.

For that, she would need a proper riding outfit. She found a jacket in a lovely buckskin with fringe on the sleeves. Holding the supple leather to her nose, she inhaled what she knew immediately to be the fragrance of the Wild West.

As Gennie slipped it on over her new dress, she instantly felt transported to the pages of last month's novel. In it, Mae had worn a jacket much like this one while rescuing three small children from a mountain lion's attack.

A pair of boots beckoned, and she reached for them. Sliding out of her shoes, Gennie stepped into what could have passed for a pair of Mae Winslow's own footwear. They were big enough to share and flopped when she attempted a step, but she didn't mind. The store was empty except for the clerk, who had returned to whatever called him up on the ladder.

Boots and a jacket with fringe on it. All she needed was a buckskin skirt and the appropriate hat, and she'd be as close to a Wild West adventure as she'd been since arriving in Denver.

Then she spied the section reserved for reading materials. There, prominently displayed on a shelf near the store's entrance, was the latest edition of Mae Winslow's adventures.

Her heart skipped a beat, and she couldn't move fast enough to fetch the slim volume from its resting place. The oversized boots slowed her down, but she managed a decent pace as she crossed the store.

Just as she reached for the novel, the store's door opened, hitting her squarely on the backside and sending her sprawling. She landed in a most unladylike heap, and volume XXVII of Mae's adventures came to a stop against a pair of well-worn boots.

Following them upward, Gennie's gaze slid past long legs, broad shoulders, and an even broader smile set between a pair of deep dimples. A fringe of sandy hair nearly hid eyes the color of a stormy afternoon as he leaned over her.

"What have we here?" he said in a dreamy combination of slow drawl and British aristocracy. "George," he called to the clerk, "it appears Mae Winslow has stepped off the pages of her latest penny dreadful and landed in your store."

11

Mae urged Lucky to a trot and left what remained of the shot-up snake baking in the afternoon sun. The skin would make Henry a lovely belt, and the rattles, well, maybe they'd entertain a little Henry Jr. someday.

"Henry Jr." She laughed as she spurred the horse to a full gallop. "Wouldn't that just be the dandiest thing? And maybe a little Mae, as well."

The Bible said a man with a quiver full of young 'uns was a man well blessed. Not that Henry's quiver would be full anytime soon. Even if they were married, she hadn't seen soap and water in a week. Likely he'd prefer she kept to the trail than start keeping house for him.

And for today, that suited her just fine. Especially with a dark cloud looming on the horizon. Mae stood in the stirrups and pushed her hat back, letting the wind do the job of brushing the tangles from her hair. She'd ride for the caves and wait out whatever storm was blowing in.

Then tomorrow she'd see Deadwood and dear Henry.

◦◦◦

Daniel could have stared at the woman sprawled before him until forced to stop, but propriety required he help her to her feet. How best to accomplish the trick eluded him, however, as the woman seemed incapable of helping in the process.

He offered his hand, but she merely stared. A question as to how he might assist went unanswered.

She seemed stunned into a complete stupor. Being a man, and a poor example of gentlemanly virtues on occasion, he took the opportunity to stare. And it was quite the opportunity.

Hair the color of honey and the texture of silk tumbled over the too-broad shoulders of the buckskin jacket and teased the collar of a prim and proper frock the shade of pistachio ice cream. Her cheeks had pinked to match her lips, forming a contrast that set his mind reeling.

Then he spied the boots.

While he'd never manage to wedge his feet into them, they were obviously far too large for this make-believe cowgirl. They also proved a great hindrance when she attempted to scramble to her feet, for the overlong soles merely slid along the polished floorboards like sleds on the North Slope. With nothing to hold her feet to the floor, the boots skidded and slipped but did not allow her to stand. Asking her to remove them would be most improper, as would questioning why she wore them in the first place.

Yet despite the oddness of her ensemble, she did look quite fetching in it.

"You're staring," she said, and unless he misunderstood, she'd added a saucy tone to the chastisement.

"I am," he said, "though no man with a pulse would fault me for it."

"And you have me at a disadvantage," she said, "for should I find fault with you, I've no recourse but to endure it."

Daniel grinned. Had this creature just crossed the delicate line between being a damsel in distress and being a damsel who was interested?

"Then I shall remedy the situation," he said, "though I might have to resort to extraordinary measures. Your ensemble, well, presents a bit of a problem."

"Yes, about that—"

He held up his hand to silence her. "No, don't tell me. You've gone missing from the Wild West show."

"Not exactly."

"You're a western version of Little Bo Peep, only instead of sheep, you've lost your cattle. I'm quite handy at finding things, so perhaps I might be of assistance."

"Indeed, you might," she said. "Though the assistance I most sorely need is likely not something you can help with. Now if you will excuse me, I'll gather my dignity."

"I beg to protest," he said. "I find your dignity quite intact."

"And yet I am sprawled on the floor like a wanton woman. Which I am decidedly not," she added quickly and with great emphasis.

"Ah, I do see the dilemma."

There was nothing to do but haul her upright, which he did. She landed on both feet, or rather both boots, and began sputtering some sort of nonsense that Daniel waved away even as he held tight to keep her from pitching forward.

She was a beauty, this odd combination of cowgirl and lady, and Daniel was reluctant to let go. "Are you steady on your feet now?" he asked, hoping she might say no.

"I am." Eyes of columbine blue fringed with thick dark lashes rose to meet his stare, and he felt the impact to his toes.

Her answer disappointed him, though he'd never liked a helpless woman. "You're sure?" His words came out half an octave lower than he expected. She didn't seem to notice as she stared at him with a look he'd seen on women much less interesting than this one. An odd thrill surged through him as he realized they were flirting. He'd indulged in his share of it before, but never had he enjoyed it quite as much as now. Emboldened, he continued. "Because I could stand here holding you up all afternoon if need be."

"And I could let you," he thought he heard, though it might have been wishful thinking on his part.

When she said no more, Daniel rushed to fill the silence, afraid she'd notice he still held her. "Perhaps we could wait until the rest of the Wild West show returns for you. Surely you're the star attraction."

"In my dreams," she said with a wistful grin, seeming to study a spot somewhere behind him.

"No," he said, recognizing he was acting as foolish as a boy barely out of knee pants but unable to stop himself, "not in *your* dreams."

Blue Eyes jerked her attention back to him. "No?"

"No," he said gently as he leaned toward her. "More likely in mine."

When she formed the word *oh,* her lips pursed, and Daniel stared. What was happening to him? A perfect stranger had captured his attention like no practiced belle of the ball had ever managed. All save one, that is.

The reminder almost caused him to let go. Almost made him look away from the lips he inexplicably wanted to remember tonight when he laid his head on his pillow.

"Everything all right over here, folks?" George called.

Out of the corner of his eye, Daniel saw the clerk approach. He released Blue Eyes and took a step backward. "Just fine," he said, forcing his attention onto the clerk.

"Thank you," the woman said as she moved away, shrugging out of the buckskin jacket and disappearing behind a display of handbags.

Daniel itched to follow and at least inquire as to her name, but wisely stood his ground, even when he heard the thud of boots hitting the floor. A woman like that could get under a man's skin, and he couldn't allow such a thing.

Not anymore.

"Something I can help you with, Daniel?" George inquired.

It took a moment to remember exactly why he'd come into Fisher's at all. "A surprise for my daughter," he finally said. "Something to make her forgive me for my absence."

"I've got just the thing." George scampered away, leaving Daniel to search the store for Blue Eyes.

He found her near the front again, this time with a fresh copy of Mae Winslow's adventures in hand. Boldness overtook him, and he sauntered her way. Perhaps he too would take up reading the penny dreadfuls. He picked up the first one he saw.

"That Mae Winslow's quite a character," he said as casually as he could manage. "Always one adventure after another."

She held a copy of the same book against her chest, one hand shielding the cover. "What?" she asked as if she'd not heard him. "Oh, yes, I suppose. At least, I've heard." Her cheeks grew a shade closer to scarlet. "That is, I've known people who've purchased the books and told me her adventures are quite…"

"Adventuresome?" he supplied.

"Yes." She carefully replaced the book on the shelf, then turned to study a display of shaving cups.

Daniel set his book beside hers, then slid up next to the woman who'd well and truly entranced him. "Please tell me you're not in the market for one of these for your husband."

Just before she ducked her head, Daniel thought he saw her smile. "No," she said.

Interesting. But did that mean no husband or just no, she wasn't buying something for him? How to find out? If only he had more practice in this area. His skills were more than rusty.

"Your brother, perhaps?"

This time she met his gaze with what appeared to be a twinkle in her eyes. Long lashes swept cheekbones set high under porcelain skin. "No, I rather doubt Connor is in need of one at present."

"A pity," he said, brushing her sleeve as he reached past her and took up one of the ridiculous mugs. Instead of regarding the crockery cup, he never broke his eye contact with her. "It's possibly the finest example I've seen in a very long time. Just beautiful, with the kind of lines that would make a man happy to reach for it every morning."

"Sir," she said softly, with just the right combination of outrage and interest to make a man grin, "are we still talking about the shaving mug?"

"No." He spoke slowly, deliberately. "I'm not certain we are, and I do apologize."

"Were I to accept your apology," she said, stepping away just slow enough to allow him to replace the mug and follow, "then I would also have to accept the fact that you are not a gentleman." She paused in her motion and he did the same. "And I'm reluctant to do that. Surely you understand."

He did. A bead of perspiration trickled down the back of his neck and disappeared inside his collar.

"I think you'll be quite happy with what I've found, sir," George called, his mission accomplished far too soon.

"Thank you, George," Daniel said, but when he turned back to the woman, she was nowhere to be found. He reluctantly returned to the counter and paid for the gift, waiting while George wrapped it, not realizing until he'd left the store that he didn't even know what he'd bought.

Out on the sidewalk, he consulted his watch and thought of finding his way to Charlotte's school rather than the office. Only the need to send out several telegrams and finalize his plans to fire the governess sent him up the street toward his workplace, though not without a last glance toward the store, in case the blue-eyed woman reappeared.

Gennie stumbled toward the counter on wobbling knees, careful to note the direction the intriguing man had departed. "I'll pay for the novel," she told the clerk, "and the rest will go on Mr. Beck's household account."

"Is that so?" the fellow said, raising an eyebrow in surprise. "I wonder why he didn't tell me himself. You're sure he'll approve?"

"Actually, it was Tova. She's the—"

"Housekeeper." He nodded. "Yes, I know. Now that you mention it, I recognized the dress you came in with as one she bought for you." The clerk leaned closer. "So," he said with what seemed like quite a bit of innuendo, "you're the gal who's been hired to tame Charlotte Beck."

"I am."

His laughter grated on her, but she maintained her dignity and her silence.

"You're an awfully pretty woman to be going about such ugly business." He slapped his palm on the counter, and Gennie jumped. "For all I respect Daniel, I sure don't understand why he doesn't turn that girl over his knee and—" He shook his head. "Well, I can't judge, and goodness knows he's had his share of difficulty that goes beyond a misbehaving child. Poor man's been hounded mercilessly by the local women ever since he lost his wife, you know."

An interesting fact. Not that it was any business of hers. An adventure of the Wild West variety did not depend in the least on Daniel Beck's domestic situation.

"I couldn't help noticing you've attracted a bit of interest, but I've got to warn you, lassoing that one's a lost cause."

Her brows shot up in outrage, but she quickly tamed them. Loath to discuss her personal business with a shopkeeper, Gennie withdrew the appropriate amount of money from her reticule and pushed the coins toward him. "If you'll excuse me, I'd prefer to settle my account now."

"I see." He looked toward the door, then slowly back to her. A strange look crossed his face as he regarded her in an odd way.

"Is there a problem?" she asked, adjusting her collar and straightening her cuffs.

"Problem? No, miss. Just speculating on something I ought not speculate on." He went back to tallying the amounts with his pencil. "Should I have these items delivered, or will you be taking them with you?"

Gennie decided to ignore the man's poor behavior in favor of taking the high road. "I'll have them now, please."

Just then, the door opened and Isak stuck his head inside. "I've finished my errands, miss," he called. "Just want to let you know I had to leave the wagon around the corner. Too much traffic out front. So turn left when you come out the door and go around the corner in the opposite direction from Mr. Beck's office."

"I don't know where his office is," she said, "but I'm sure I can find the wagon."

The clerk never looked up. He wrapped her purchases, then without comment offered a slip of paper for her to sign. As she gathered the packages and made her way to the door, she heard the clerk make a *tsk*-ing sound.

She froze, then glanced over her shoulder to see the man regarding her openly. "What?" she demanded.

He shrugged. "Can't say as I blame him. 'Course, once Anna Finch hears tell of this, you can expect she'll not like it one bit."

Gennie opened her mouth to speak, but the words refused to come. "I am not that kind of woman," she finally managed. "And anyone who takes issue with my employment is advised to lodge a complaint with Mr. Beck himself."

"Oh, I doubt he'd put up with anyone telling him a pretty thing like you doesn't belong under his roof."

Gennie drew herself up to her full height, ire coursing through her veins. This man was insufferable, his insinuations intolerable. "I repeat," she said, "I am not the type of woman to entertain the advances of a man with whom I am not betrothed." And yet she'd just stood in broad daylight in full view of the front window of Fisher's and flirted shamelessly with a total stranger. "And I demand an apology, sir," she added with more bravado than she felt.

"Of course you're not," he said, though his tone and expression betrayed his words. "And I do beg your pardon."

To stay and fight the clerk's impression of her bore hard on Gennie, but she reminded herself this was a man with whom she would likely never have any further contact. She squared her shoulders and turned away, not sparing the awful man even the briefest of parting words. As she huffed around the corner to the wagon, Isak took her packages, then lifted her onto the seat.

"Something wrong, miss?"

"No," she said as she tried to still her shaking limbs. "Everything is fine. Wonderful, in fact."

But as Isak pulled the wagon around and turned in front of the store, she couldn't resist giving the place one last look of disgust, even as her knees continued quaking. How dare that awful shopkeeper think she might be carrying on with Daniel Beck. A man who couldn't even stay home long enough to raise his child certainly held no appeal for her. That nice man with the lovely accent, on the other hand, that was another story altogether, one she might have pursued under different circumstances. Indeed, had she not had a perfectly wonderful man waiting for her back in Manhattan, she might have…might have what?

Gennie sighed and banished the thought. She did have a perfectly wonderful man waiting for her back in Manhattan, and in less than a month she'd be seeing him again. And perhaps she'd be brazen enough to ask for another of the banker's wonderful kisses. Gennie touched her lips, then felt shame rise inside her.

When had she turned into such a brazen hussy? First she'd practically fallen at the feet of that gentleman in Fisher's, and now she sat in a wagon on a public street, imagining a man's kisses.

Mama would be shocked and disappointed, wondering what had happened to her well-heeled debutante daughter.

Gennie smiled behind her gloved hand. Perhaps some of the Wild West had already rubbed off on her, just enough to make life interesting.

Unfortunately, it got more interesting when Isak pulled the wagon to a stop near Charlotte's school.

"I'll wait while you fetch her," he said nonchalantly.

"All right." Gennie climbed from the wagon and strolled toward the schoolhouse. How difficult could this be?

"Miss?" Isak called. "There's fresh mud in the street. I'd be careful if I were you."

She was about to ask why when the first volley hit her squarely in the jaw. Swiping at the splattered mess of mud, Gennie looked up to see Charlotte Beck standing at the edge of the schoolyard, a wicked gleam on her face and several children egging her on.

Gennie took a deep breath and walked toward the Beck child. It would never do to allow the heathen to know she'd hit her mark not only with the mud, but also with her attempt to rile her governess.

Her hands thick with mud, Gennie reached Charlotte and grasped her firmly by the wrist, staring down the onlookers and daring them to comment. No one moved or spoke.

"Eww," Charlotte said. "You're getting me dirty."

"Come along. I'm sure your friends have places to be as well." Gennie gave the assembled crowd a pointed look that sent them scattering. "Or perhaps I should go in and have a visit with your teacher."

Charlotte's eyes widened. "You wouldn't."

"I would," Gennie said, "though I don't think it will be necessary today. After all, we're headed home."

Charlotte seemed surprised. "You said we were going to have an adventure."

"That was before you chose to pelt me with mud." She paused to consider her words. "Now the adventure shall be a bath, with soap and shampoo. Then we shall address your wardrobe and attempt to do something with that hair of yours. Into the wagon with you."

The menacing look from breakfast returned. "I don't want to. I want Tova to come and fetch me later." She made a decent attempt to yank her arm from Gennie's grip, but failed.

Gennie swiped the last of the mud from her jaw and shook it from her free hand, even as she tightened her grip on the girl. "You'll come now, Charlotte Beck, or I'll know the reason why."

"The reason why is, I don't like you, and I'm too old to have a governess."

Charlotte paused to reach down, ostensibly for more mud. Gennie countered by picking up her pace even as the girl dug in her heels. By the time the pair reached the wagon, Gennie's skirts were sodden with mud, as were Charlotte's overalls.

To his credit, Isak only quirked a pale brow as they approached, then quickly recovered to hand first Charlotte then Gennie up into the wagon. "Home?" he asked cautiously.

"Yes," Gennie said. "Please."

They rode in silence, Charlotte wedged between her and Isak. Gennie kept a close watch on the girl lest she bolt and run, something more likely than the possibility she might ride quietly home without further complaint.

And yet she did, much to Gennie's surprise. As the wagon turned a corner and the Beck home came into view, Gennie had only one thought: *Thank You, Lord, that this is only temporary.*

As soon as the wagon rolled to a stop, Charlotte scrambled over Isak and ran into the waiting arms of Tova.

While Isak slipped off into the stables, Gennie gathered her packages. With the same care she'd taken the first time she was introduced to Mama's dear friend and the inspiration for her name, Empress Eugenia, Gennie straightened her spine and walked with her head held high.

"What is the meaning of this?" the housekeeper demanded as she held the girl at arm's length.

"Ask Charlotte," Gennie said. "And don't have Isak bother with preparing the bath. I can see to it myself." She paused to look down at the Beck girl. "Come with me."

"No." She tightened her grip around Tova, who looked none too pleased to be tarred with the same mud that covered the child. "Tova won't make me. She's not mean like you."

"I must say the child is a bit upset." The housekeeper gave Gennie a severe look. "Perhaps you've been too hard on her."

"Tova," Gennie said as firmly as she could manage without giving her rising temper free rein, "until I am replaced, I am the child's caregiver. I do not tell you how to carry out your duties, and I would appreciate it greatly if you gave me the same consideration."

While the housekeeper stood open-mouthed, Gennie grasped the wrist of her charge and led her inside.

12

Fat raindrops pelted the ground and spotted Mae's best buckskin jacket, so she decided to see if Lucky could ride between them. It was a theory tried and tested back home when she was a barefoot girl and Papa knew more than all the books in the library. She'd asked him if it were possible to run fast enough to stay dry, and he'd told her there was one way to find out and that was to try. If it didn't work today, maybe next time it would.

She was still trying, and it still wasn't working. Same could be said for catching criminals. One day she'd figure out how to do that and stay where it was warm and dry.

Until then, however, she'd still be trying to outrun the wind and ride between the raindrops.

⬡⬡

Having left Hiram behind in Leadville to manage things, the duty of purchasing Miss McTaggart's train ticket and banishing her from Denver fell solely to Daniel. The irritation he worked up each time he read the brazen woman's letter was enough to fuel the flames of outrage and ready him for the task.

As Daniel settled behind his desk, however, his thoughts refused to remain on the recalcitrant nanny or the apologies he must wire to the governor and to Lieutenant Governor Horace Tabor. He saw instead blue eyes, boots, and buckskin instead of train tickets and telegrams, and he preferred it that way.

Failing any success at redirecting his thoughts, Daniel packed up his work and shoved it into a desk drawer. Today he would take only his gift to Charlotte home with him.

And perhaps tonight, once the issue of the governess was handled, he might even initiate a game of charades with the imp. She did love the game, though he rarely took the time to play it with her. Maybe he'd even convince Tova to stay and team up with Elias. The old coot would likely not complain. The thought of Elias's finding love this late in life made Daniel smile.

If only there was a woman who looked at him like Tova regarded Elias, one who cared for his heart more than his wallet or last name. The thought brought him full circle to Blue Eyes, which sent him out into the Denver afternoon with nothing to show for his time spent in the office.

The walk home would do him good, Daniel decided, though instead of turning toward home, he found his boots walking in the direction of the dry goods store. George greeted him with a concerned look.

"Something wrong with the order?" the clerk asked.

"Order?" Daniel asked as the door closed behind him with a clang.

George nodded. "Yes, the clothes your employee signed for."

He shook his head. "I've no idea what you're talking about," he said as he headed for the back of the store, "but I'm sure Tova was acting within her purview."

"Wasn't Tova." George skittered to catch up. "Though she was with Isak, so I figured it was all right."

Daniel stopped short and the clerk nearly slammed into him. "Oh, you must mean Charlotte's new governess."

"Yes," George said, "I suppose I do."

Spying what he came for, Daniel turned on his heels. "Does this come in a smaller size?"

George lifted the buckskin jacket from its resting place and frowned. "I believe so, but it'd be real small. It's been a popular item. I've only got boys' sizes left, and a sparse few at that."

"Would a boy's size fit a woman?"

"Likely so." The clerk gave Daniel a sideways look. "Depends on the size of the woman. Who've you got in mind?"

He almost answered, then decided to be discreet. "Oh, I don't know. A woman of average size, I suppose." Daniel pretended to think on the subject a moment. "What about that woman who was in here earlier? Would you have something that would fit a person of her size?"

To his credit, the clerk didn't seem surprised. "I'll check."

While George scurried off to the back room, Daniel meandered through the aisles and ended up at the book rack. Bypassing a copy of the *New York Times* and several other venerable publications, he lifted a copy of the latest issue of *Mae Winslow, Woman of the West* and smiled. As an afterthought, he picked up one more for himself.

"Here it is," George said as he emerged from the back. "Just one left. You're a lucky man, Mr. Beck."

"I'm hoping to be," he said under his breath. "Say, do you have any notepaper, George?"

"I do."

By the time Daniel reached the counter, George had both paper and ink ready. "You wanting to add a note to this gift?" He paused. "I'm just assuming it's a gift," he added quickly.

"I am." Daniel pointed to the display of footwear in the far corner before dipping the pen in the inkwell. "Remember those boots the young lady was wearing?"

George's ears pinked and he ducked his head. "I do," he said. "Would you like me to fetch a pair in her size? That I know I've got."

Daniel looked up from his writing. "How do you know her size?" He shook his head. "Never mind. I don't need to know. I suppose you know her address as well."

The clerk looked confused. "Sure I do. Is that a trick question?"

Waving away a response, Daniel scribbled a note, then shook the page to dry the ink. "Put this inside the book and wrap it all up for delivery to the young lady with my compliments."

Greater confusion showed in the clerk's face. "You're sure you don't want to take it with you?"

Irritation flared. With the situation that awaited him at home, the last thing he needed to deal with was a clerk who fancied himself a comedian. "Just handle it, George," he said as he turned and headed for the door. "Today."

"Yes sir, Mr. Beck," he called. "Today it is."

As the door closed with a jangle, Daniel thought he heard George's complaining about the odd ways of the wealthy, but with all the traffic clogging the Denver streets, he couldn't ever be sure. It certainly wasn't like the old days, when a man could walk down the middle of any street in town and not fear death under the wheels of a streetcar. He'd bunked in far more meager quarters back then. Not that he felt completely comfortable in the grand home. Some days he wondered if building the overblown castle had been for his own comfort or to somehow show the earl that he, too, could live like royalty even though his inheritance had been gladly signed away.

The best deal he'd ever made.

He waited for the streetcar to come to a stop at the curb, then smiled as he stepped in and handed his fare to the driver. Though trouble awaited at home in the form of an impudent governess, he took solace in the fact that once Miss McTaggart had been dispatched to New York, he could concentrate on finding the infinitely interesting Miss Blue Eyes.

He'd long since given up on the thrill of the chase, but now he looked forward to it, especially when the one he'd be chasing had a penchant for buckskin and boots.

A thought teased the edge of belief, and he allowed it only a second of his time: perhaps she might be the one to put the smile back on his face. The smile that reached all the way to his heart.

Ridiculous. She was a moment's amusement and nothing more. Of the few women who'd kept his attention more than a week or two, only Georgiana had found the key to his heart.

As the streetcar jerked forward, Daniel turned to look out the window. George stood in the doorway of the store. It occurred to him that the clerk was the only witness to Daniel's foolishly smitten behavior. His grin broadened. What man could resist a woman in oversized boots and buckskins?

The streetcar soon reached the end of the line, as did thoughts of the woman whose name he'd foolishly forgotten to ask. With each step toward home, his mind turned over the reasons why yet another governess would be leaving. Other than the last Miss McTaggart, none had lasted longer than six months. One resigned after less than a week.

He sighed. While all logical evidence pointed to Charlotte as the culprit, Daniel could not fathom the reason. In his presence, she was a lovely — if imperfect — young lady. She was a bit willful, and she needed a great deal of improvement in the social graces, but he would defy anyone to call her anything less than delightful.

"Good afternoon, Mr. Beck."

Daniel stifled a groan as he saw Anna Finch and her mother strolling arm in arm toward him, looking more like plumed birds than the cream of Denver's social crop. The Finch women carried umbrellas to shield ensembles burdened with enough baubles and lace to empty the notions department at Fisher's.

"Ladies," he said as he tipped his hat. "Nice day for a stroll. It appears the Lord is blessing us with unseasonably cool weather."

"Indeed, it does," the older Finch woman said, "though I must wonder why you're out walking when you've a lovely buggy and that handsome driver to take you where you want to go."

"Mama." Anna patted her mother's gloved hand. "It's none of our business what Mr. Beck's doing afoot." She regarded him with wide eyes. "Please excuse my mother. She can be quite forward. Really, we're not interested in the least."

The look she gave him said exactly the opposite.

"Well then, I won't keep you ladies." Daniel replaced his hat atop his head and moved past the women, a difficult proposition considering the width of their skirts and the narrowness of the walkway. "Do enjoy your evening."

"Wait!"

Miss Finch spoke the word with such force that Daniel had no choice but to turn and see the cause. He found one shocked older woman and one coy yet determined former debutante.

"Yes?" he asked, though he knew the question held the key to a door he'd rather keep locked.

"I was wondering…" A flush came to Miss Finch's cheeks that Daniel guessed had nothing to do with the temperature.

"Yes?"

"Well, that is, the Millers are hosting an evening with that actor." She turned to her mother. "What was his name?"

The women tossed names about while Daniel considered an exit strategy. Before he could figure out how to quickly take his leave, Anna came up with the name.

"Yes," she said, her enthusiasm higher than necessary, "that's the fellow. I know it was mentioned you'd possibly be in attendance if you weren't detained elsewhere. And it appears you're right here."

Daniel tamed his grin. "Yes, it appears so."

"Yes, it does." She looked away and bit her lip.

"And as for the event tonight…" He paused to consider his words. "While I would be pleased to be in such lovely company as your mother and yourself, I fear I must put another woman's wishes ahead of yours."

"Oh."

He allowed her crestfallen look to remain for a moment. "Indeed, my daughter will be my focus this evening. I believe a rousing game of charades is planned."

Anna's giggle was not altogether unpleasant, even if it put him in mind of a girl rather than a grown woman. Seizing the chance to leave on a happy note, Daniel once again bade them a good evening and turned toward home.

"Wait!"

This time, he turned without speaking.

"The blond woman," Anna said, her gloved hands worrying the handle of her umbrella. "She's lovely."

Daniel felt the heat rise to his temples. Had the Finch women witnessed his shameless flirting back at the dry goods store?

"Blond woman?" he said as innocently as he could manage.

"Yes, dear," Mrs. Finch chimed in. "Might she be dear Miss McTaggart's replacement, or have you gone and betrothed yourself without giving my daughter a chance at you?"

"Mother!"

"I'm merely stating the obvious, Anna," she said before turning her unblinking gaze back to meet Daniel's stare. "Well, have you?"

The squeal of his estate gates opening caught Daniel's attention, as did the clattering of hoofs as a buggy turned onto the street. At the reins sat Elias, putting Daniel in mind of another long-ago escape. While that one had taken place in time of war and under heavy enemy fire, this one felt just as dangerous. And just as welcome.

Elias slowed the buggy as he approached, and Daniel climbed aboard and waved to the womenfolk. "You saved me, old friend," he said when the Finch women were safely out of earshot.

"I did, indeed," Elias said, "and I am about to save you some more."

Rather than argue the semantics of the statement, Daniel merely nodded and awaited what he expected to be an interesting explanation. Anything that sent the buggy careening down the street and turning corners practically on two wheels had to be worth the wait.

∞

"You can't make me take a bath. I'll not do it."

Gennie ignored the child's protests as well as the complaints of Tova, who lagged a few steps behind. With one hand firmly on the girl's overalls strap, she opened the door to the nursery with the other.

"I said I won't take a bath, and I don't have to." Charlotte tugged against Gennie's grip. "Besides, there's no bathing closet in the nursery. Anyone who isn't stupid knows that."

Gennie looked back at Tova, who had ceased following and stood at the top of the steps. "Is that true?"

The housekeeper nodded. "Mr. Beck was afraid she might be harmed should she get into the water without supervision."

"No danger of that today." Gennie swiped at the flaking mud on her cheeks. "She will have plenty of supervision."

"I won't," Charlotte protested.

Gennie turned the corner and found her own bedroom door. "Fetch the child's bedclothes," she called to Tova. "But take your time. This chore will likely not be done quickly or easily."

The battle that ensued was nearly lost several times when Charlotte tried to escape. First she attempted to slip out the door while Gennie filled the tub. Then, when Tova knocked, Charlotte opened the window and nearly made it all the way out onto the ledge, where a tree limb the size of a man's arm could have easily accommodated her exit.

Or given way and allowed her to fall to the ground in a heap.

Gennie shuddered at the thought and turned the key to lock them both inside the bathing closet. Setting the key on the windowsill, she reached for the cake of soap. "All right, let's get started. Your filthy overalls first, please."

"No."

"I did not ask, Charlotte. The overalls need washing, and so do you."

Charlotte walked toward her, a repentant look on her face. For a moment, Gennie entertained the hope that the child might actually have given up the fight.

Then the girl lunged for the key and raced to the door. Before she could fit it into the lock, Gennie wrenched it away. Through the window out of the corner of her eye, she saw Isak washing down the bay mare. At the sound of his name, Tova's son came running.

"Catch this and give it to your mother." Gennie tossed the key out the window, then snapped the curtains shut. Slowly pivoting, she noted with more than a little glee the shock on Charlotte's face.

"You threw the key out the window," the girl said.

"I did."

"I hate baths."

"I didn't ask," Gennie responded in as calm a tone as she could manage. "If you're shy, I'll turn my head, but you must get into the tub before the water gets cold. I'll not have your father returning to find his only daughter has caught a chill on my watch."

"Papa's returning?"

Only two words, and yet their hopeful tone threatened to break Gennie's heart. "I've certainly written to tell him he must."

"Do you think he will?"

"Yes," she said slowly, "I think he will." Rather than look directly at the girl, Gennie tested the temperature of the water, then stirred in a healthy measure of the rose-scented bath salts she'd found in the back of the cupboard this morning.

For a moment, Charlotte's defiance seemed to disappear. Then she took a long look at the water. "I won't do it."

"Very well." Gennie reached into the cabinet and withdrew a hairbrush. "Then we shall deal with the tangles first. The bath can come after."

"You're serious."

Gennie took a step toward her. "I am, though in my experience, it's much easier to comb through wet hair than dry."

"But you're covered in mud," Charlotte said in a suspiciously sweet voice. "Shouldn't you go before me? I promise I'll play quietly in my room until it's my turn." When Gennie only stared, the girl sighed loudly. "Oh, all right, but I'll wash my own hair."

"We shall see about that," Gennie said. "I'm not convinced you know how."

That did it. In a flash, the girl shed her overalls along with the rest of her clothing and dove into the tub with a splash. She came up for air, sputtering. "It smells horrible. What did you put in here?"

"Never mind." Gennie piled the filthy clothing beside the door. "Just see that you come out smelling like it."

Mae rode the horse into the cave at a trot, reining her in when darkness meant she could no longer find sure footing on the sandy ground. Turning the horse around proved impossible, so she left the stubborn mare to her own devices.

A lit match revealed nothing spectacular about the cave, nor were there any other occupants. Warm and dry, with just enough jerky to silence her growling gut, Mae settled into a sleep the likes of which she hadn't had in days. Weeks, maybe.

She dreamed of dear Henry, then woke blushing. "I need to get myself married up, and soon."

☙❧

Daniel rode next to Elias in silence, occasionally tipping his hat to those he recognized. And saying a prayer for others who nearly missed landing between the buggy wheels and the road.

He loved his friend, but Elias's driving had never been something Daniel could claim he liked. Thankfully, hiring Isak had all but eliminated the situation Daniel found himself in.

Already they'd circled downtown once. Another lap—or another close call—and Daniel knew he'd have to say something. Elias slowed the mare to a trot as they turned down Eighteenth and headed past the Windsor Hotel.

The doorman waved, and Daniel returned the gesture, remembering the last time he'd walked through those doors. It seemed as though every dignitary in the state had been in attendance. It also seemed as though the evening would never end. But then, most nights that he was coerced to don his formal wear turned out the same: dodging single females, talking business, and watching the clock until he could make an exit without offending his host.

Elias came to the end of Eighteenth and turned left, indicating the next lap of downtown Denver was about to begin.

"All right," Daniel said, "I'm getting dizzy making these circles, I haven't seen my daughter in a week, and I've got pressing business to discuss with her new governess. What say we go home now?"

His old friend gave Daniel a sideways look. "I'm not a hundred percent sure that's a good idea, Daniel."

"Look," Daniel said, "either you're going to tell me what's going on back at my home, or I'm going to take over the reins. At this rate, Charlotte will be in bed before I get out of this buggy."

Elias urged the mare to a stop just past Union Station. "It all started right here, Daniel." He pointed to the train station. "I'll not give you the details. One of the womenfolk can do that. Let's just say Charlie and her new nanny didn't exactly hit it off from the beginning."

Daniel laughed. "Is that all?"

"I fail to see why that's funny." Elias leaned forward and grasped the reins tighter. "You have no idea the female fiasco you're about to land in the middle of."

Daniel clamped a hand on Elias's shoulder and gave him a good-natured shake. This time his old friend had protected him from an enemy that obviously did not exist. "What say we do as we have on too many occasions to count, Elias? Let's go face that female fiasco together."

Elias laughed, then slapped the reins and turned the buggy toward home. "I'm a brave man, Daniel," he said. "I faced down General Sherman himself, but this time you're on your own."

As soon as the buggy stopped in front of the carriage house, Daniel climbed down. Elias, however, took his time.

Daniel got all the way to the house before turning to challenge the old coot. "Are you intent on letting me do this alone?"

Elias lifted his hat to scratch his head. "You know I'll not be thought of as a coward, Daniel," he said as he caught up, "but I promise, you could bring ten of me and we'd still be outgunned."

"Oh, it can't be as bad as all that." He paused just inside the house. "Besides, if it's the governess that's caused all this fuss, rest assured she will be gone as soon as I speak to her." The look on Elias's face surprised him. "What?"

"You might want to wait on that."

"Not fire the woman for impertinence and telling me how to parent to my child?" He froze, then pivoted. "Why?"

Elias yanked at his collar but didn't answer.

"All right, then." Daniel stepped into the kitchen and inhaled the familiar scent of baking bread. "Much as I tire of the leaving, I never tire of the homecoming. Where's my Charlie?"

He got as far as the stairs before Tova blocked his way. "I'd advise you not to go any farther just yet, sir."

"You too, Tova?"

He pressed past the housekeeper to take the stairs two at a time. With each step, Daniel cursed the fact he'd insisted on building such a grand mansion. Tova and Elias trailed behind him.

The sound of a scuffle upstairs caught his attention, as did the squeal that followed. "What's going on up there?"

"A bath, sir," Tova said.

"A bath?" Daniel froze as another squeal pierced the silence. "That sounded like my daughter."

"I reckon it is," Elias said. "Last I heard, the nanny was intent on seeing at least the top layer of mud removed."

"Top layer of mud?" Daniel looked to Elias and then Tova. Neither seemed interested in elaborating. "Charlotte was playing in the mud? That seems a bit childish."

"Actually, sir," Tova said, "I believe the nanny got the worst of it. The girl only seemed to be wearing whatever rubbed off."

He shook his head. None of this made sense, but asking for details from these two seemed futile. Another squeal, followed by a definite yelp, sent him hurrying up the rest of the stairs.

"Where is she?" he called.

"The nanny's bathing closet," Tova called, "but I wouldn't try to go in there if I were you, sir."

"Yes, well, you're not me, Tova. If someone were torturing your child, I doubt you'd be ignoring it." He ran to the room on the opposite side of Charlotte's parlor, his resolve to fire the woman he'd mistakenly trusted with his daughter growing stronger with every step. As soon as he saw the woman, he'd order her out of his home. Whatever things she'd brought would be mailed to her forwarding address.

He halted at the door to her bedchamber. Old habits died hard, and he'd been taught to be a gentleman. A gentleman did not step into a lady's bedchamber uninvited. Another squeal, however, caused him to throw propriety out the window. He turned the knob and stormed into the room. Finding it empty, he followed the sounds of splashing to the closed door of the bathing closet.

A trickle of water leaked from beneath a door that was, to his surprise, locked. Outrage and yet another shriek from inside the bathing closet sent his shoulder crashing into the door. How dare anyone lock him out of a room of his home, especially when his daughter was on the other side?

Anger warred with concern as he prepared to break down the door.

"Sir?" Tova called from somewhere behind him. "Perhaps the key would help."

∽∾

While getting Charlotte into the tub had been relatively easy, washing her hair was just the opposite. Charlotte Beck did not like to get her face wet. This Gennie discovered while getting soaked from head to toe, despite the fact she was still fully clothed.

"All right, then," Gennie had declared as she used the towel to wipe the water from her face. "We'll manage, but you'll not splash me again or I'll be forced to go for help."

For a moment, it appeared Charlotte would not give up the fight, so Gennie made good on her threat by walking to the window and throwing open the curtains. To her surprise, though the buggy was gone, Isak had remained behind.

"Isak," she called as she raised the window sash, "might it be possible to come and help me up here? Charlotte's being a bit of a problem, but the shampoo must come out."

"I don't know, miss," he said, then realized she was playacting. "Oh yes, of course. Should I fetch Mr. Howe, as well?"

"Don't you dare bring those boys in here!" Charlotte squealed.

Boys? Gennie tried not to laugh as she called a quick, "Never mind," and closed the window and curtains. Likely neither of the men had been called boys in a very long time, but the empty threat worked.

With a little cooperation on the girl's part, the soaping of her long tresses was done. Each time Gennie came too close to her head with the pitcher of water to rinse it, however, the girl made enough noise to wake the dead. To remove the soap from Charlotte's hair, Gennie borrowed a memory from her own past and encouraged the girl to dive for pennies.

Any penny she found, while keeping her eyes and nose covered with a washcloth, she kept to be spent on a future shopping trip. It worked, and most of the soap was rinsed away. With the last three cents in her reticule, Gennie had managed to purchase compliance, however temporary.

Gennie heard footsteps approaching and dove for the door. While her clothing, albeit soaked, still rendered her decent, the mud once caked on her cheeks now ran down the front of her frock in slimy ribbons. She was, in short, a wretched mess.

"Tova, please wait," she called as the key scraped against the lock. "A few more minutes, and we'll be finished." She pressed her shoulder into the door. With the task nearly complete, she feared any disruption might cause the girl's obedient state to disappear.

To her surprise, the door thumped hard against her shoulder.

"I demand you open this door at once," came a deep and slightly familiar voice.

Charlotte bobbed to the surface, the final penny in her hand. "Papa?"

"Yes, Buttercup, it's me."

Buttercup? Gennie shook her head and pressed harder against the door. Of all the terms one might use to describe the girl, *buttercup* was not one of them.

"I've learned to dive for pennies, Papa," Charlotte said as she shimmied out of the tub and into a towel. "I got all three, and I put my face under water."

"Mr. Beck, might I have a few more minutes with Charlotte? She's not yet had her hair combed."

"I don't care. Come out here and speak to me."

"I'm not decent, Mr. Beck. Would you have me come out and speak to you in a less-than-proper state?"

Silence.

Charlotte shook the water from her hair much like a dog might dry his shaggy coat. Fat water drops landed on Gennie's already stained frock and splattered back into the once-clear bath water.

"I insist you stop that at once, Charlotte Beck. You're making a mess."

"See here," the girl's father said through the door. "I'll not have you speaking to my daughter that way. Get yourself decent, then come out and explain yourself."

"No." Gennie turned to glare at the girl, who stopped her antics immediately. "Someone must take this child in hand. Since you and the others in this house are unwilling or unable, the task has fallen to me. I will speak to you when my job here is done."

"Oh, your job's done here, all right," he said.

Gennie blinked back her astonishment at the words she'd just spoken and the response they had garnered. If the child's father fired her, that just gave her the chance to escape and have her adventure. Why did she care if the girl went to bed with tangles and soapsuds?

Stepping away from the door, Gennie was about to tell the man just that, when Charlotte snatched Gennie's wrapper from the hook behind the tub and threw it on over her towel. Before Gennie could voice a protest, the girl bounded out the door for what sounded like a gleeful reunion with her father.

To his credit, the man slammed the door shut with himself and his daughter on the other side. The confrontation would obviously happen later rather than sooner. That she would be summarily dismissed was clear.

Beyond caring, Gennie flopped down on the window seat and stared at the formerly rose-scented bath water, now the color of the

Hudson River after a hard rain. The effort to drain and clean the tub then refill it was beyond her, both in energy and ability, and the likelihood that Tova would accommodate the request was slim to none.

It was all too much. While the celebration continued on the other side of the door, Gennie rested her head on the windowsill and fought back tears. *Lord, how did I get myself into this mess?*

Downstairs, the bell rang. The commotion outside her door moved away, presumably to greet whoever had arrived to join the party. Had she the strength, Gennie would have seized the opportunity to gather her wits, her copy of *Mae Winslow, Woman of the West* and her nearly empty reticule and escape down the back stairs.

But that would involve changing clothes, cleaning up, and possibly coercing Isak into dropping her off at the Windsor Hotel. Surely from there she could discreetly have some funds wired to supplement the meager amount she still held in her possession. She'd have to plead her case well, lest Papa's banker tell the men in her life—Papa and Chandler—where she'd gone off to. That would require either the truth, which would get her fetched home before she could blink twice, or a lie, which she'd not do.

Then a brilliant thought occurred. "Hester," she said as she rose. "Hester Vanowen!"

She'd send a telegram, and by morning her oldest and dearest friend would have come through. Of course, she'd have to explain to Hester why she'd gone off, but that was easily accomplished. She'd plead temporary insanity by reason of dime novels. Hester also fancied the adventures of Mae Winslow. She, of all people, would understand.

Her course of action secured, Gennie went about draining the filthy bath water. Now what? With no towel or wrapper, bathing would be difficult. She walked to the washstand and cupped her hands in the cool water, then splashed her face. After a few repeats of the process, all traces of the mud were gone from her face and neck. Her dress, however, looked to be a total loss. Good thing she had thought to buy two outfits at the store that morning. She still had the blue dress to wear.

She crept through her bedchamber and peered out the door. The long hallway was empty, though sounds of people laughing and talking filtered up from below, reminding her she was not alone.

In a few minutes' time, she'd changed her dress, collected her reticule, and slipped down the back stairs. Finding the kitchen empty, she quickly made her way to the stable. It too was empty. So much for asking Isak to see her into town.

She raced toward the street, not slowing down until she'd left sight of the Beck home. Only then did she realize she'd forgotten to leave a note. Rather than risk changing her mind if she returned, Gennie picked up her pace. She had a telegram to send and a bath to take. Then, perhaps, she'd have a message delivered.

Likely no one would miss her until morning, anyway. By then, she'd be on her way to the real reason she got on the train in New York: a Wild West adventure.

14

A woman is either in want of a husband or wanting to rid herself of one. That had been Mae's opinion until Henry crashed into her life on the back of a runaway mustang. He'd been a cowboy and a daring man who feared nothing but the boredom that came when one no longer rode the trail.

He'd been her kind of man, her kind of adventure. And then the law got him—literally—and he settled into life as a respectable lawyer. Where she spent her days wasn't something they talked about until he started counting the nights she was gone.

That's when the trouble started.

☙❧

The Windsor Hotel bustled with activity, but after her walk into town, Gennie was too tired to appreciate anything other than the warm bath and soft mattress her room would surely offer. She marched across the elegant lobby, hoping she wasn't tracking mud all over its beautiful marble floor.

"One room for the night, please," she said when her turn before the clerk arrived.

He was tall and thin, putting her in mind of a scarecrow with spectacles as he looked over the gold rims and down at her. "Next," he said to the person behind her.

"Excuse me?" She shouldered back in front of the well-dressed couple and placed her palms on the counter. "Perhaps you misunderstood. I am here to secure a room for the night."

"There's no misunderstanding," he said in a less-than-polite tone. "We're a reputable hotel and you—alone, with no luggage—obviously are not."

"I beg your pardon?"

Once again, he looked beyond Gennie. His eyes narrowed, and he gestured for a porter. "Remove that man at once."

The porter's face paled, and he whispered something to the clerk. Gennie looked around to see a cowboy ambling toward them.

"I don't care who he is. Tell him he can start his own hotel, but he certainly isn't welcome in this one dressed like that." The clerk returned his attention to Gennie. "And you, miss—"

She squared her shoulders. "Sir, in all my travels, I've never come upon such a rude hotelier."

His eyes narrowed. "What did you call me?"

"You heard me." Gennie pointed her finger at the loathsome man, then took what she hoped would be a calming breath. It did not work. "I learned early on to be civil to those in the trade. However, you are making it most difficult."

"Is that so?"

"Yes," she said slowly, "that is so."

The clerk put on a wide smile and rested his hands on his hips. "Perhaps I can make it simpler for you." He summoned the porter again. "Escort this woman out, please. If she attempts to return, see that she suffers the same fate as the cowboy." He looked past her yet again. "Next!"

Gennie stumbled away, stung, and with each step she took toward the exit, her anger grew. By the time she reached the lovely front doors, she was ready to go back to the desk and confront the imperious autocrat.

"Don't bother, hon."

She turned to see the fellow in rugged western gear standing just outside the door. Crossing the threshold, she emerged onto the street and into the jovial company of a man who identified himself only as Brown.

"One of these days there'll be a place for people like us."

Gennie decided that whatever "people" he referred to, they must be much nicer than the ones who populated the registration desk at the Windsor Hotel.

"He's not a bad fellow," Brown said, "nor is this a bad place. The opposite, actually."

She looked back at the lovely awnings, the inviting shops, and the beautiful interior, and imagined the guest rooms were just as wonderful. Her tired body sagged.

The man adjusted his Stetson and offered a firm handshake of farewell. "When I open my hotel, I'll send you an engraved invitation."

Gennie couldn't help but smile at the absurd statement. "Yes, please do."

He pulled a pad of paper from his shirt pocket. "What's your name, miss, and how do I find you?"

"Eugenia Flora Cooper. How to find me? That's a bit more complicated."

"She's currently staying at the Beck mansion as governess. That is correct, isn't it? You're Charlotte Beck's new governess?"

Turning to see who spoke, Gennie saw a lovely brunette standing a few feet away. With her was an older lady who must have been her mother. The pair exchanged words, and with a flutter of her gloved hand, the older woman disappeared inside the Windsor.

"I am," Gennie answered, "at least temporarily."

"I'm Anna Finch," the woman said as she approached. "I live next door to Mr. Beck."

Brown looked up from his notepad. "Anna Finch," he said. "Yes, I know your pa. Fine man. On the list for sure." And with that, he bade them good-bye and ambled away.

"Interesting fellow," Gennie said when the man disappeared around the corner. "And a very nice man."

"Yes. Papa speaks highly of Mr. Brown. He's quite the entrepreneur." The dark-haired woman smiled. "Eugenia, it's so nice to meet you."

"Please call me Gennie. Only the empress calls me Eugenia, and I suspect she's teasing me when she does."

Anna Finch looked at her as if she'd grown a third eye in the middle of her forehead.

"She's a family friend," Gennie explained. "Mama and Papa visited her often, and when I was born...well, they liked the name, I suppose."

Anna shook her head. "Gennie, are you referring to Empress Eugenia, the wife of Napoleon III?"

"Yes. Do you know her?"

"Not exactly, though who hasn't heard of her?" Anna paused to give Gennie an odd look. "How does a woman whose parents know royalty end up as a nanny in Denver?"

"The truth?" Gennie leaned close. "I wanted a Wild West adventure."

Anna laughed. "You'll certainly have that at the Beck house."

Gennie shrugged. "I'd hoped for more." And then she thought of the man at the dry goods store. Flirting with a stranger certainly wasn't like her, so perhaps her Wild West adventure had already begun. By degrees, she became aware of the Finch woman speaking.

"I'm sorry. What were you saying?"

"Ours is the house on the left on the other side of the shrubs. The big house with the..." Anna shook her head. "Oh, it doesn't matter. Suffice it to say I'm so close to Daniel's house, I can see his window from mine." Immediately her hand covered her gaping mouth, and her cheeks blazed bright red. "Oh, I didn't mean it that way. What I meant was—"

The poor woman seemed truly distressed. "It's all right, truly." Gennie touched her sleeve. "I knew what you meant."

"You did?" The relief in Anna's voice was unmistakable. "Honestly? Because people rarely understand me. That is," she quickly corrected, "I rarely seem to make myself understandable."

Gennie's smile was genuine. "Perhaps that's just the way of things." She shrugged. "I've found that it is often when we try the least, we are understood the most."

Anna's brown eyes widened. "Goodness, you're quite profound for a governess." Again embarrassment etched itself across her lovely features. "Oh, there I go again. There's nothing wrong with being a governess. It's just that one rarely expects a person in that profession to…" She paused and looked ready to cry. "Oh, I'm just hopeless."

Comforting a stranger on a public street seemed a bit odd, but after only a few minutes, Gennie felt as though she'd known Anna Finch all her life. In fact, she'd spent much of her life being just like her.

"Thank you," Anna said as she dabbed at her eyes with a lovely handkerchief, obviously grateful for someone who understood. "I'm very glad to have made your acquaintance."

"As am I," Gennie said.

The hotel doors opened and Mrs. Finch appeared. "Do come inside, Anna," she said. "We must take our chairs for the oratorical performance."

"Coming, Mother." Anna turned to Gennie. "Oh my, I didn't ask. Are you here with Daniel—I mean, Mr. Beck? He mentioned he'd be otherwise detained with his daughter, but I had hoped, that is…"

"I'm quite alone," Gennie said.

"Do come and sit with Mother and me, then. I understand the performance will be riveting."

Gennie noticed the porter staring through the open door and imagined what might happen should she dare to return to the Windsor's lobby, even in the company of Anna Finch. "Much as I appreciate the invitation, I'm afraid I must decline."

"Oh, I see. You must have promised to play charades with Mr. Beck and Charlotte."

"Charades?" She already felt as if she'd been playing the game of hidden identity since she set foot on Colorado soil.

Anna giggled. "Oh, I have the best idea. Wait here."

She disappeared inside to carry on a somewhat spirited conversation with her mother, who'd drifted near the doorway. After much nodding and speaking behind gloved hands, Anna turned on her heels and marched back outside, the pink in her cheeks flaming bright.

"Everything all right?" Gennie asked as she watched the older woman storm off in what was obviously a huff.

"Yes," Anna said, "everything's fine." She put on a smile that didn't quite reach her eyes. "I'll have my driver drop us at the Beck home. I haven't played charades in ever so long."

Torn between the quick and easy ride back to the Becks' and the need to send Hester's telegram, Gennie froze. Her absence might have been noticed by now, and that would require an explanation. At least she hadn't left the note she'd thought about leaving. It made returning, even temporarily, much easier than begging for a job she'd abandoned.

She was still thinking when Anna touched her shoulder.

"I've already told you I'm hopeless when it comes to saying the right thing, Gennie, so please don't take offense."

"I won't."

"Your dress," Anna said. "It's a bit, well, I wonder if perhaps you'd... That is, we're much the same size and I have extra..." An exasperated look crossed her face. "Oh, what I'm trying to say is that the dress doesn't fit that well, and you're much too pretty to walk around like that. Maybe I could help."

Gennie looked down at the store-bought dress. It didn't fit as well as her tailored gowns, of course, but it was the best she could find in Fisher's. "Oh no, I couldn't ask that of you."

"You're not asking," she said. "I'm offering."

Gennie tried not to be horrified that she was considering accepting a stranger's charity. Mama would be horrified enough for the both of them. Slowly, she warmed to the idea, however. "You see, my trunk was left behind in New York, so I've only got the clothes I wore on the train." She shook her head. "That's not true. Those seem to have gone missing."

"You poor dear."

"And then Tova shopped for me." Gennie paused. "Suffice it to say our tastes differ. I managed to find this in the dry goods store."

"I see." Anna waved her hand, and a liveried man jumped to attention. In a matter of minutes, Gennie found herself transported to the Finch home by way of the telegraph office, where Anna's closet practically emptied itself at her feet.

"I couldn't, honestly," Gennie said as yet another lovely gown was offered up.

Anna turned, a silk Shantung wrap dangling from her right hand. "Oh goodness, I've done it again. I never intended to embarrass you." She let the lovely garment fall to the floor. "I only meant to help. Forgive me. I tend to be a bit, well, overenthusiastic."

Gennie retrieved the Shantung wrap and handed it back to Anna. "Truly, you are an answer to prayer. I'm waiting for a telegram from my friend in New York, and then hopefully I can pay you for some of the beautiful things you've offered."

"Pay? Oh, pish posh. You'll do nothing of the sort." Anna waved away Gennie's offer with a sweep of her hand. "I'm the youngest of five girls. Even though all my sisters are married, Papa's still budgeting for five wardrobes every season." She pointed to the room-sized closet that would have been a luxury even in Manhattan. "You see the results."

"I do." Gennie grinned. "And as your new friend, I'm happy to help you with this problem."

Anna flopped down on the nearest chair, her grin slipping. "If only my other problem were so simple to repair."

Gennie shrugged into a pink-striped dress very much like one she'd left hanging in her closet back home. "I'll help if I can."

"Oh, Gennie, I'm going to be totally honest with you." Anna scooped up a ruffled and lace-covered ball gown and held it to her chest. Her fingers worried with the hemline, then abruptly stopped. "There's no help for this. You see, I'm hopelessly in love with Daniel Beck. When I found you standing outside the Windsor, I recognized you immediately. I'm ashamed to admit I thought to befriend you in order to get closer to him."

"Anna," Gennie said gently, "does he return this affection you have for him?"

Anna's brown eyes glistened as they met Gennie's gaze. "He barely notices I'm alive."

A plan began to form, and it was all Gennie could do not to smile despite her new friend's sad state. "Do you like children?" she asked, plotting her course.

"Oh yes. I love children."

"Even if they are, at times, difficult?"

Her new friend smiled. "You're referring to Charlotte."

"I am."

"I know she's a challenge, but I wish you could have known her when she and her mother first came to live with Daniel. She was no bigger than a minute. Cook said she might have been five, though she looked much younger."

Gennie's interest piqued. "What happened to her mother?"

"Oh, that's such a sad story." Anna rose and walked to the window. True to her statement, Gennie could see the Beck house above the hedges. "I never knew for sure, but Mr. Beck's housekeeper told our cook that Mrs. Beck had been living in England but came to Denver to take the air."

"Take the air?"

Anna turned and nodded. "It is believed the Colorado air has curative properties. Charlotte's mother was quite ill when she arrived here, and she lasted less than a year. Daniel was devastated."

"She went back to England?"

"No," Anna said, her voice cracking. "She died. Charlotte had only just met her father, and suddenly he was all she had. Well, him and Elias. Soon after, I believe, they brought Tova and Isak in to help."

"That poor child." It went a long way toward explaining why Charlotte was so difficult, a motherless child in a strange land. "That sort of trauma must be hard to overcome."

"For both of them, I'm sure," Anna said. "I've always wondered how it must have felt for Daniel when a long-lost wife and a child he didn't know he had suddenly arrived on his doorstep. Cook says he had no idea Georgiana was with child when he left England. Something about a mysterious falling out between him and his father and brother."

"Really?" Gennie longed to ask more but held her tongue.

Anna nodded, then gestured to the door. "I'll have Thames drop off a trunk full of clothing with Tova in the morning. The others you can put in this satchel." Anna lifted a small traveling case from beneath a pile of clothing in the corner of her closet and handed it to Gennie. "For now, I should get you back to the Becks. I'm sure they're wondering where you went." She shook her head. "Wait, of course they're not. You were at the Windsor and changed your mind about attending the performance. They'll likely not expect you for another hour or so."

"All the better to surprise them," Gennie said with an enthusiasm she did not feel.

Truthfully, she was not looking forward to the confrontation with Charlotte's absent father, but Anna seemed quite anxious to pay a visit to the Beck home. So much so that she had the driver drop them at the curb in front of the Beck home on his way back to the Windsor rather than spend the extra few minutes it would take to walk.

It might have been amusing had Anna's excitement not turned to abject terror the moment her well-shod foot landed on Beck turf. "You go ahead," she said, thrusting Gennie toward the massive front doors. "I've changed my mind."

Gennie linked arms with the reluctant neighbor and urged her forward. Anna took three steps, then froze.

"Come on, Anna."

Stricken, the Finch woman could only shake her head. When she finally found her voice, she'd managed to worry herself into a panic. "I'm not good at this. I want to be, but I'm not."

"Good at what?" Gennie patted her new friend on the shoulder. "I don't understand."

"Well, of course you don't," Anna said with vehemence. "It's likely you've never been in love with a man like Daniel Beck. Oh, Gennie, I know you work for him and probably are immune to his charms, but I swear every time I come near him, I turn into a puddle and start saying the most idiotic things." She paused to take a long breath. "I'm hopeless. That's the long and short of it. Have you ever felt like that? Unable to speak anything but nonsense while your heart's doing this silly fluttering and your mind's gone totally blank?"

Gennie thought of the man she'd met only briefly at Fisher's. "Yes," she said, "I think I know exactly what you mean."

And then that very man opened the door of Daniel Beck's house.

The trouble Mae dreamed up was nothing compared to the wind blowing away everything that wasn't nailed down outside the cave. The sky went from gray to black to green, and balls of ice pelted the ground and rolled inside, confusing poor Lucky into thinking someone was aiming at her.

The fair female knew a fire might prove disastrous, so she remained in the dim light and waited. She might have been there until the sun shone again, for she could have happily slept once more even with the threat of marriageable dreams, and in fact had settled down for just that, when the hordes were released.

Bats.

✺

The last person Daniel expected to find standing on his doorstep was Blue Eyes herself. George must have given her his address. He smiled. He owed old George a substantial tip the next time he traded at Fisher's.

"Well, look who's here," he said. Then he spied Anna Finch. "And look who else is here." His voice faltered a bit before he found it again. "Please, both of you, do come in."

"It's terribly late," Anna said, "and I'm sure we're imposing." Her soft brown eyes darted toward the blonde, then back to Daniel. "Well, I am, anyway."

Instead of wasting time trying to decipher the Finch woman's statement, Daniel allowed his attention to fall on Blue Eyes. He had no name for her. As he offered her his arm to lead her inside, he made what he hoped would be an offhand comment. "I'm sorry, but I'm at a loss, Miss…"

"Cooper," Anna supplied from where she still held the door frame. "Really, Mr. Beck. Her name is Eugenia Cooper, and she's named after the wife of Napoleon III. Stop teasing us."

Miss Cooper seemed as much at a loss as he. She'd been easily led to the parlor, but would she remain? She looked ready to flee at a moment's notice. Unlike Anna, who never seemed comfortable around him, she just seemed confused. Or perhaps she was wary of him for some unknown reason.

He was generally good at reading people, but Eugenia Cooper stumped him. At Fisher's she'd shown more than adequate interest, but here she seemed as though she'd changed her mind. Still, she'd convinced his neighbor to accompany her on a late-evening social call. That alone spoke volumes.

If only he could figure out what it said.

"Really, Anna," Blue Eyes said, seeming flustered, "it's just Gennie."

"Just Gennie." Daniel offered a place on the settee to the blonde, then watched while she settled there. "Gennie is a lovely name."

"It suffices," she said stiffly.

"But I wonder," he said slowly, "whether you've had your Wild West adventure yet, Gennie."

"No, actually, not yet." She glanced at Anna, who still stood frozen at the front door. "But it's going to happen very soon. I can feel it. Do come and join us, Anna."

"Yes, do join us," Daniel said as he straightened and made for the chair nearest the settee, then watched Anna wedge herself between them.

For all her awkwardness, Anna Finch was a nice enough young woman who might be a great beauty should she learn to relax. Other than her insistence on openly pursuing him and her inability to complete an intelligible sentence in his presence, she was decent company. She'd certainly earned his respect a few years ago, when she befriended a grieving Charlotte and allowed the little girl to tag along to tea parties and other innocuous events.

If only his daughter still wished to play the part of a well-heeled debutante. He'd hoped the new Miss McTaggart could accomplish this, but the combination of the letter and tonight's bathing fiasco had dashed all chances of such a thing.

But he'd not think of the irritating woman likely hiding in her room and praying his ire would pass. He'd been about ready to fire her through the door, when this vision of loveliness landed on his doorstep. The Lord had presented him with a rare and lovely gift in the form of Eugenia Cooper, and he'd not miss a moment of getting to know her.

"So," Daniel said as casually as he could manage, "what brings you here tonight?"

Anna's giggle surprised him. "Don't you recall mentioning you'd be spending an evening with your daughter playing charades?"

"She's upstairs, asleep." He shrugged. "I did hope to spend the evening with her, as I'll likely not be in Denver long, but she was exhausted and fell asleep in the middle of dinner." He tempered his words. "I blame the torturous scrubbing she endured this afternoon."

"Torturous scrubbing?" Miss Cooper let out an inelegant snort that stunned and delighted him in equal measure. "I hardly think a bath will ruin a child. What do you think, Anna?"

"A bath?" Miss Finch sought his gaze and seemed to be attempting to formulate a response. "Yes, well, I'm for them, of course. I do enjoy a bath, though I've been known to stay too long in the water and cause my skin to prune up."

"Is that so?" Daniel replied, trying not to smile. "It must be something of a problem for you, Miss Finch."

"Oh, it is," she said. "Why, you'd be surprised that even my toes are affected."

That was not an image he cared to have in his mind. Gennie Cooper's wide blue eyes, however, were quite another matter. "So, Miss Cooper, are you thus afflicted as well?"

"Afflicted?" She leaned toward him. "Actually, I find bath time to be the best hour of the day. I do love a hot bath, and if rose bath salts are available, I partake liberally. And daily. Always torturously scrubbing every inch of me. And," she added, seemingly to torture him, "I wash and comb my hair. Daily. Torturously. Without fail."

The scent of roses would never again conjure the same image. Daniel tugged at his collar and cleared his throat. "Where are my manners? Might I offer you ladies something to drink? Perhaps a treat from Elias's kitchen?"

"My, but you're quite the host tonight, Mr. Beck," Anna said.

"Am I?" He never took his eyes off Miss Cooper.

Anna shook her head. "Yes, you're acting like you don't even know who—"

"Actually," Miss Cooper interrupted, "I am a bit parched."

"Coffee." He shook his head. "No, lemonade perhaps. Or tea. Oh, I'll see what I find. How's that?"

Daniel left his chair so fast he didn't bother to ask what she'd like or even extend the courtesy to Anna. He retreated to the kitchen, where he wondered what he'd done to have the Lord reduce him to the state of a blathering schoolboy.

"He's acting very odd," Anna said. "And I should know. I'm usually the one making a fool of myself." She gave Gennie a sideways look. "What's going on here, really?"

Gennie sighed. "I'm still trying to figure it out."

Daniel Beck could not possibly be the horrid ogre who regularly abandoned his daughter and bullied governesses from the other side of bathroom doors. He also could not possibly be the man who'd swept her off her feet in the Fisher's Dry Goods Store.

And he certainly couldn't be the man she'd just decided to match up with her new friend Anna Finch.

Gennie leaned against the back of the settee and closed her eyes. How could one man possibly be two?

She bolted upright, her eyes opening to see Anna's shocked expression as she grasped her friend's hands. "Anna, please tell me Daniel Beck has a brother."

Anna smiled. "Yes, actually, he does. Remember, I mentioned him just a bit ago?"

"I knew it!" She let go of Anna, then rose, only to fall back into the settee again and slap her knees with her palms. "I knew he couldn't be the same man I met. He just couldn't. Oh, the voice was the same, and he certainly looks like him, but that man and Daniel Beck absolutely cannot be one and the same."

"What are you talking about, Gennie?"

How to explain to her new friend that she'd shamelessly flirted with a stranger, then actually entertained romantic thoughts of him? Even someone who'd known her for years would likely not understand. For that matter, Gennie didn't understand.

And yet there was no denying her meeting with the stranger in Fisher's would remain forever etched in her memory. At least until she accepted Chandler Dodd's offer of marriage.

But that had not yet happened.

"Gennie?"

"It's all very complicated." She turned to Anna. "Mr. Beck's brother, they're twins, right?"

"Twins?" Anna laughed as she shook her head. "I don't know. I've never met him."

"But he's here in Denver, and it's possible they could pass for twins?"

"No, and no. From what I understand, Daniel and his brother had some sort of falling out years ago. Something to do with the family business Daniel built, then gave to his brother to run. Cook surmised a woman must have come between them. I always wondered if it might have been Charlotte's mother, but I was never brave enough to ask."

"And there's no possibility of a recent reunion? Perhaps a mending of the ways?"

Anna looked confused and then, by degrees, thoughtful. "I'm just going to admit this to you, Gennie. I've got my spies, and I know almost everything that happens over here. If some kind of long-lost reunion had happened with Daniel and his brother, I would have heard about it." She looked away. "And, yes, I am that pathetic. I can't explain why, but Daniel Beck has always fascinated me."

"I understand completely." And then it hit her. First the realization, then a sinking feeling that began in her gut and traveled quickly to her brain. "Oh, no, no, no. I flirted shamelessly with a man I abhor, detest, and despise. The man I couldn't stop thinking about is the man I'm plotting to make my escape from."

Anna grasped Gennie by the shoulders. "What is going on, Gennie? You're babbling on and not making a lick of sense. In fact, *you* sound like *me*."

"That's because it makes no sense. I actually liked him, Anna. I *liked* him." Gennie leaned back once again and closed her eyes. "I'm such an idiot. A Wild West adventure does not include donning buckskins and boots and playing the coquette with Daniel Beck, no matter how much I enjoyed it."

"Wait a minute." Anna's grip on Gennie's arm caused her eyes to fly open. "You flirted with Daniel Beck?"

"Yes. No. Oh, I don't know."

Anna's eyes narrowed. "Explain yourself."

"I can't. I don't know what happened. I was at Fisher's, and then he was at Fisher's, and then there was the Mae Winslow novel and a pair of boots and the fringed jacket that looked and smelled just as I imagined the Wild West to look and smell. Well, not the West but the people who populated it." She paused to take a breath. "I'm not making a lick of sense, am I?"

All poor Anna seemed capable of was shaking her head.

"Look, here's the thing," Gennie quickly said. "I don't even like Daniel Beck. He's an absent father and a complete autocrat who undermines my authority as governess. And while I'm on the topic, I never intended to be a governess at all. I only traded train tickets with the real governess so she could get married. She and her husband are expected in a few weeks, and then the jig's up and I'm gone."

Anna rose and backed away from the settee, nearly upsetting an awful beaded floor lamp in the process. She caught it before it—and she—hit the floor, but neither appeared to have the ability to remain upright much longer.

"I'm leaving, Gennie. It's late and there's obviously something wrong between you and Daniel that Daniel has no idea about. I might be a goose-headed fool, but I notice things, and I've seen how he looks at you." Dissolving into tears, she made short work of retracing her steps to the door.

"No, wait!" Gennie scrambled to catch Anna. "I've got a plan, and it won't work without you."

Her new friend paused, one hand on the doorknob and the other swiping at fresh tears. "What plan? To steal my chance of having Daniel Beck notice me? Well, congratulations. It looks like your plan's working."

She yanked at the door and ran out into the night. Gennie chased after her and caught her hand.

"Listen to me," she said in a tone just harsh enough to get the sensitive woman's attention. "I do not have any interest in Daniel Beck. Yes, I admit I felt a temporary attraction to him at the dry goods store, but only temporary, and only because I had no idea who he was. I am a soon-to-be-betrothed woman from Manhattan who has no intention of remaining in Denver beyond the end of the month."

Anna said nothing.

"Are you listening?" Gennie continued. "When you saw me at the Windsor, I'd left my job and was trying to get a room there until my friend Hester wired money."

Anna shook her head. "Why should I believe you?"

"I don't suppose you have any reason to." Gennie released her grip. "If someone had told me two weeks ago I would be standing in front of a silver baron's mansion in Denver explaining why I flirted shamelessly with someone I now find an atrocious excuse for a man, I'd have called them crazy. And if I were told I'd finally be given the chance to have a Wild West adventure only to waste precious time trying to find a mother for a child who detests me, I would have, well…"

Gennie ran out of words. She looked up at the clear night sky and took a deep, long breath of Wild West air. To her surprise, Anna began to giggle.

Gennie reluctantly swung her gaze from Orion and the North Star to Anna Finch. "I fail to see what's so funny."

"That's just it," Anna said. "It's not funny. And yet, it's so—well, I don't know—remarkable."

"Remarkable." Gennie shrugged. "Well, I suppose one could make an argument for the use of that term. I can think of a few others, however."

"No," Anna said, "don't you see? I've been praying for a wife for Daniel and a mother for Charlotte since Georgiana's funeral. Somehow over time, that wife and mother became me."

"And that's what I want too." Gennie pointed back to the house, every window save one lit up like Christmas. "That's a house in dire need of a woman's touch. Would you believe there's a jungle-themed guest room upstairs? And have you *seen* the jeweled chicken?"

Anna doubled over laughing, even as she continued to swipe at her tears. "I think it's supposed to be an ostrich. Tova is quite proud of it, though I understand Daniel refers to it in less-than-glowing terms when his housekeeper's not in earshot."

"Well, imagine poor Charlotte growing up in a house where she must face the jeweled chicken every time she walks up the staircase."

"I heard that!"

Gennie looked up to see the object of their discussion hanging halfway out of the nursery window. "Go back inside this instant, Charlotte Beck, or you'll fall."

"I'm going to tell my papa you were laughing at his chicken."

"Say what you want," Gennie called, "but you'll have better luck telling him if you're inside and not lying on the ground in a heap."

The girl seemed to ponder the point only a moment before disappearing back into the nursery.

"Well," Gennie said with a sigh, "I've won that battle but will likely lose the war. Do you see why she needs a mother? I'm hopeless at this."

"You did keep her from landing on her head." Anna shrugged. "I'd say you're not completely hopeless."

"That may be true, but I never set out to do this, Anna. I want an adventure." She wrapped her hands around her midsection. "Does it look like I'd find a Wild West adventure here?"

The door opened, spilling a golden light that reached just beyond where Gennie stood.

"Ladies?" Daniel called.

"I should go," Anna said.

"No, don't." Gennie caught her friend's arm. "I'd feel better if we talked about the plans I have. I want you and Daniel to be wed so Charlotte can have a suitable woman's influence."

"I want that too, Gennie, but I just don't see how it will happen."

"Oh, believe me, it will. And soon, for my time in Denver is limited."

"But it's been so many years and he's never indicated the slightest— oh no. Here he comes."

Gennie glanced back at the house, completely unprepared for the flip her stomach did when she saw Daniel Beck's silhouette in the doorway.

Think of Chandler. Think of what an awful father this man is. Think of anything else…

Daniel moved toward them in long strides, and Anna backed up at the same rate. "It's been lovely seeing you again, Mr. Beck," she called. "And Gennie, I'll see that the trunk is delivered first thing tomorrow."

"Thank you," Gennie replied, "and don't forget we have plans. I'd like it very much if we get together soon to discuss them."

She barely finished her sentence before her new friend disappeared behind the thick hedges that divided the property from the Finch home, leaving her alone with Daniel Beck.

Alone with Daniel Beck. Gennie swallowed and tried to muster enough good sense to either walk back up to the open front door or out the open front gate.

Think of Chandler.

Chandler Dodd was a fine man, a man not given to bad behavior or, likely, lax parental duties. A man who, for a moment, paled in comparison to the one she'd met at the dry goods store.

Think of what an awful father this man is.

Spending time with a child was essential to proper development. It should be no surprise that Charlotte was so unruly.

But the moon showed off his sandy hair to its best, and behind the shadows covering his face were eyes she remembered as kind, yet teasing. She glanced up at the sky and searched for any constellation she might identify, but her gaze drifted earthward to the man headed down the path toward her.

Think of anything else…

Like how she felt when she wrote the letter demanding he return and take charge of his child. Gennie tried to work up enough anger over who he was to forget who he used to be, but all she saw was the charming man from Fisher's who played the gentleman and the rogue in equal measure.

When he stepped from the shadows, moonlight played over features that wore concern. He reached to touch her sleeve, then seemed to reconsider and let his arm fall to his side.

"Miss Cooper," he whispered, leaning close enough for her to see the stubble of a day's beard on his chin, "what are you doing on my lawn?"

The voice. The… No.

The plan. Think of the plan.

"Anna Finch is lovely, isn't she?" Gennie said.

"Anna Finch is a beautiful young woman." His smile gave her hope he might play along with the diversion. "As," he said slowly, softly, "are you. And *you* are here."

Gennie straightened her spine and her resolve. She'd not be cowed into soppy sentiment by a man with whom she had nothing in common nor held any respect for.

"How did you find me?" he said with the slightest chuckle in his lovely Cambridge-meets-Charleston accent.

Not that anything about this man was lovely. Not in the least. He was a poor example of a parent and a—

"I see you've been rendered mute. You found me, and that's all that matters." He moved closer. "I don't know what it is about you, Miss Cooper, but I find myself acting like, well, I'm not myself."

She took a step back and collided with something sharp. Shock propelled her forward, and Daniel Beck caught her.

"The hedge," he said against her ear. "You bumped it."

Her heart hammered furiously as she scrambled to right herself. While Daniel assisted in her finding safe footing, he kept his arms firmly around her.

"I'm fine," she said, though she felt anything but. She met his unwavering gaze.

Think of the plan.

"As I was saying," Gennie began, averting her eyes, "Anna Finch is a lovely woman."

"Lovely," he echoed.

"And she's quite clever, actually."

"Clever," slipped from his lips as his hand moved from her shoulder to the small of her back.

Don't look at him.

She did.

Swayed by his half-closed eyes, Gennie felt her strength ebb. Perhaps just for a moment she might enjoy the attention. Enjoy a bit of harmless flirtation. Enjoy the night air and the…

The plan.

"Mr. Beck, please—"

"All right. I will." He grinned and pressed his palm against her back to move her deeper into his arms.

"Mr. Beck, really," she whispered, though she angled her face toward him.

"Miss Cooper," he said, his voice a ragged breath against her cheek, "really."

And beneath all the stars in the Denver sky, the silver baron traced his thumb across her lower lip, then followed its path with a kiss that curled her toes. And then another.

Reeling, Gennie pressed her palms against Daniel's chest in a careful balance between keeping propriety and losing control. Her fingers curled around a handful of Daniel's shirt and held on tight.

A door slammed somewhere in the vast distance outside their embrace.

"Miss Cooper," he whispered against her ear. "You should know I don't make a habit of this sort of behavior."

"A pity, for you're quite good at it," she said, scandalizing herself with the delicious boldness of her wit.

"Is that so?" His attention darted past her, and he stiffened. "Buttercup?" He nearly dropped her in his haste to part ways.

Gennie straightened her hair as she followed his gaze. "Charlotte?"

"Papa, why are you kissing my governess?" The girl stepped between them to point at her father and then back at Gennie. "You *said* you were going to fire her."

"Fire her?" The man who'd only just kissed her within an inch of insanity stared at Gennie as if she'd grown a second nose. "But I…your *governess*?" Daniel shook his head, looking as though he'd just been struck by a carriage. "Who are you?"

Still reeling from the kiss, Gennie latched on to the first words that registered in her addled mind. "You were going to fire me?" she demanded, letting indignation carry her past the whirl of emotions. "If anyone needs to be relieved of duty, sir, it should be you. Fire me, indeed." She straightened her backbone, ignored her quaking insides, and stormed toward the house.

She got three steps away before turning to stride back into the circle of his arms. This time she kissed him. Soundly.

"What was that for?" he called when she once again headed for the door.

"Something to remember me by, Mr. Beck," She glanced over her shoulder to give him a look she hoped punctuated her statement.. "You've just lost not only a governess but likely the only woman you didn't sweep off her feet."

A lie, but she'd be over him by morning.

16

Her father said bats kept mosquitoes at bay. Mama, however, likened them to rodents with wings. Mae was a firm believer in the latter.

Wings whipped overhead and horrid squeals mimicked the sound of the devil and his throng as they emerged in a cloud so thick a person couldn't see if there were hundreds or thousands of the evil creatures. Never one to shy from a fight, Mae found her rifle and swung it around her head.

Lucky decided to escape and fight another day. She forgot, however, to let Mae in on the plan.

☙❧

Things began to move slowly, as if the world continued to turn but the spot where Daniel stood whirled in the opposite direction. Charlotte's crying ceased when Gennie Cooper—or Miss McTaggart, or whoever she was—stalked inside and up the stairs.

"Enough of this, Buttercup," he said in a poor attempt to placate the child.

"But you were *kissing* her, Papa." She placed her hands on either side of his face and forced his attention away from the open door. "*Kissing* her."

Daniel sighed. "It appears I was."

"Appears?" She turned to walk away in much the same manner as her governess, and Daniel followed, dazed. By the time she reached the stairs, Charlotte had added the occasional loud sigh to her performance.

At the top step, she whirled to face him. "Traitor!" she shouted before storming into the nursery and slamming the door.

"Daniel, what in tarnation's gotten into the womenfolk around here?" Elias called as he trudged out of the kitchen. "I made a full pot of coffee, and there's nobody here but you and me to drink it. Was that a door I heard slamming?"

"Two of them, actually."

"Two? You mean you aggravated Miss Finch too? I thought that one was so slap-fool in love with you, she'd never find a heart for irritation where you're concerned."

Daniel sunk onto the sofa and stretched his legs in front of him. "No, she left before I could affect her. My charm was only used to send Charlotte and Miss Cooper into a tizzy."

Elias joined him and helped himself to a cup of coffee. "Who's Miss Cooper?"

"Ah, now that's quite a story."

His old friend lifted the cup in salute. "Leave it to Daniel Beck to take a perfectly quiet evening and make a story out of it. What's happened this time?"

"It's simple, really," Daniel said as he settled deeper into the cushions. "Our Miss McTaggart is not Miss McTaggart at all. She's Miss Cooper. Eugenia Cooper. Named after Napoleon III's wife."

Elias lifted a shaggy brow. "Go on."

"I'm not altogether clear how it happened, but it appears you went to the train station to fetch a governess and came home with a blue-eyed blonde looking for a Wild West adventure."

The old soldier set down his coffee mug and started a chuckle that soon blossomed into a full-blown belly laugh. "Tell the truth, Daniel. Given the choice, don't you think I picked the right one?"

Daniel lifted his mug and shook his head. "It all sounds good in theory, but the reality of it is another matter."

"You can't kiss a theory," Elias said as he rose and removed the mug from Daniel's hand. "And, yes, I admit to spying on you just a bit, but if I don't, who'll be around to rescue you when the need arises?"

"You could've rescued me before I kissed the woman I came home to fire."

"Well, now, that is a story, my boy." Another chuckle, this time shaking the tray until the mugs slid to one side. "How does it end?"

"I wish I knew, Elias." Daniel laced his hands behind his head and closed his eyes. "I honestly wish I knew."

∽∾

Gennie undressed and fell onto the bed without bothering to turn on the lights. As she rolled onto her side, something crackled beneath her. She reached over and lit the bedside lamp and found a paper-wrapped package marked Fisher's Dry Goods.

"Where did this come from?"

She made short work of the string binding the parcel, tossing it aside and unfolding the paper to reveal a buckskin jacket and a pair of boots. Her heart sank even as she smiled.

She lifted the boots first and held them to the light. Chocolate brown leather stitched in white with toes as pointed as her Turkish slippers, they looked to be just her size. She set them aside and reached for the jacket. Somehow, it appeared the sender had found it in her size as well.

When she pulled the jacket toward her, a book fell to the floor with a thud. *Mae Winslow, Woman of the West*. The most current volume.

Then she spied the slip of paper wedged between the pages.

She pulled out the folded note and opened it. *To Blue Eyes. Here's hoping I can play some part in your Wild West adventure.* It was signed *DB.*

Her fingers let the paper fall, and it made two circles before landing somewhere beneath the bed. "DB," she said, "for Daniel Beck. Oh, I'm so stupid. Why did I ever think it was the least bit appropriate to flirt with him?"

She'd created quite the mess, something she might have avoided had she listened to Mama's words of warning. Flirting with the same man you criticize for being a horrible father was one thing, but kissing him? And then another thought occurred to her: she'd kissed not one, but two men since deciding to leave home.

What sort of hussy was she becoming?

Gennie leaned back against the quilt, the jacket spread across her. Inhaling the scent of leather, she reached to put out the light. Tomorrow she would march downstairs and offer her formal notice as well as return the gifts. Likely Mr. Beck no longer wished her to have them, anyway. Surely by then Hester would have responded by wiring the funds and maybe even written a note in support of her adventure. Perhaps she'd bring Hester back a buckskin jacket and a pair of boots.

As for the grand plan to forge a marriage between Anna Finch and Daniel Beck, she'd have to do some serious thinking as to whether Miss Finch was better off not becoming Charlotte's new stepmother, though it would break the dear woman's heart to hear it.

"Well, that is your fault, Daniel Beck," she said as she allowed her eyes to slide shut. "If you weren't such an awful man, there would be no need for any of this."

That statement did nothing to stop her racing thoughts. Daniel Beck could not possibly be as awful as she'd once assumed. How could he be, when she'd not only allowed him to kiss her but also shamelessly enjoyed it?

That, she decided as sleep overtook her, was the worst part of all.

She dreamed of cowboys and Indians, of Anna Finch and the scarecrow clerk at the Windsor. But most of all, she dreamed of Chandler and Daniel.

They met on a field and marched off fifty paces, then turned as if to shoot. Instead of pistols, they carried old-fashioned muskets, and rather than merely fire at each other, they each hopped onto racing stallions and bounded across the field like players in a Wild West show. Then came Anna, the crack shot who aimed her six-shooters at the apple atop the head of the clerk from the Windsor Hotel.

Gennie stood in the center of the field, holding a much younger Charlotte Beck in her arms. Chandler and Daniel made circles around her, shooting at each other and missing over her head. Anna rode sidesaddle, the apple between her teeth.

Abruptly everything changed, and all three stopped to stare at Gennie and Charlotte. Slowly, as if God Himself had slowed life to a fraction of its normal speed, each of them took aim.

And then they all fired at once.

Gennie awoke in a sweat and realized the buckskin jacket still lay atop her. She threw it off and rose, despite the fact the sun was nothing more than the beginnings of an orange glow in the eastern sky. A bath and a freshly borrowed dress in a cornflower blue did little to calm her jangled nerves.

It wasn't the dream, however, that continued to replay itself in her mind. It was the kiss.

Daniel Beck's kiss.

Her fumbling fingers managed to force her hair into some semblance of decency, but Gennie found herself unable to look into the eyes of the woman in the mirror. She'd behaved shamefully, and she'd done so right out in full view of anyone passing down the street.

Despite her good intentions, the plan to match Anna Finch with Charlotte's father would have to be carried out by someone else. There was nothing left to do but quit. That is, if she had a job to leave.

She walked down the back stairs, her head held high. The sounds of Elias and Tova's genial bantering ceased when she opened the kitchen door and stepped into the bacon-scented room. Neither Charlotte nor her father were in attendance. Likely, Gennie realized, they took their breakfast in the formal dining room.

All the better.

Without comment, she retrieved a plate from the drainboard and went about ladling eggs and choosing slices of bacon, then slathering butter on a steaming biscuit. As the butter melted down the side of the biscuit, her courage faded.

"Go ahead," she said as she laid her napkin atop the untouched food. "You've surely got questions. Ask them."

She braved a look at Elias, who stood with his back to her. Rather than his usual Confederate grays, today the older man wore a starched white shirt missing its collar. Atop his curls sat a gray infantry slouch hat with a smart cavalry cord banding its brim. When Tova looked his direction, he began to whistle Dixie.

How appropriate, as she felt she too was marching toward defeat. Gennie shook her head and made to stand.

"I have questions," Tova said. She set a glass of milk in front of Gennie, then lifted the napkin from the plate and handed her a fresh one. "And you have breakfast. Eat."

Gennie shook her head but did as the housekeeper asked, jabbing her fork into the eggs. Three bites later, she still waited for the questions.

"All right. It's a long story," she said. "Would you like to hear it from the beginning?"

⊙⊙

Daniel listened from the door, just out of sight, while Miss Cooper told a tale of exchanged train tickets and a life back in New York that included a solid banker-type who would likely be proposing marriage upon her return. He'd been about to storm through the door and fire her on the spot when he heard that last part.

Somehow, the fact that sending her away meant sending her into the arms of another man made firing Miss Cooper more difficult than expected. Much as he wanted her gone, especially after last night's unfortunate lapse on his part, he foolishly hoped she'd miss him just a little.

"So you can see I'm going to have to tender my resignation," Miss Cooper said.

Uh-oh.

"Don't be so hasty, Miss McTaggart," Elias said.

"Cooper," she corrected. "Eugenia Cooper, though I prefer Gennie. And I don't believe I am acting in haste. I've deceived all of you, Charlotte despises me, and Mr. Beck, well, he's likely going to fire me, anyway. I don't think I endeared myself to him when I demanded he come home and be a father to his daughter."

From his vantage point, Daniel could see none of them, so the silence that followed baffled him. Did his best friend and housekeeper agree or disagree with the soon-to-be-former governess?

"I think I can speak for the both of us," Elias said. "Tova and me, that is." Daniel heard the housekeeper's murmur of agreement. "And we've been watching you. Our Charlotte's a pill, but we feel like she's as much ours as she is Daniel's, and we're not going to stand for some stranger coming in and causing disruption."

"And I've done just that."

"No," Tova said. "Well, perhaps a little, but in a good way, I think. What do you say, Elias?"

Daniel leaned in, trying to catch sight of the one man he'd go to his death for. The adjustment in location only allowed him a glimpse of one sleeve. Not exactly enough to judge a reaction, though he did note that the old soldier's fingers formed a fist.

"I reckon this house needed a little disruption. I didn't read what you wrote to Daniel, but I know it set his feathers to ruffling."

To say the least.

"And I don't doubt there's truth to be had on both sides of that issue." Elias paused. "But as much as that girl bucks your authority, I can see she's warming to you."

Miss Cooper's chuckle lacked humor. "Pelting me with mud in the school yard is a fine way to show it."

Pelting her with mud in the school yard? Daniel made a note to further investigate this. Surely his daughter had done nothing of the kind.

"But you didn't let her get away with it, and that makes you more than suitable for helping us raise her."

Another murmur of agreement from Tova.

Miss Cooper protested. "All I did was cancel an outing I'd planned for her, then enter into an exercise in futility when I attempted to wash the mud off her."

Elias laughed. "You really don't understand what you've done already, do you? Tova here's been with us four years, and—"

"Five, Elias," Tova interjected.

"Five years," the old soldier corrected, "and in all those five years, have you ever managed to get that girl to put her face in the water?"

"I have not."

"Any of those other gals Daniel hired manage it that you know of, Tova?"

"Only the last Miss McTaggart could even swab the girl's face without sending her into a fit of howling." A pause. "She's quite high strung when it comes to her baths."

"I noticed," Miss Cooper said, punctuating the sentence with another humorless laugh. "In fact, she's quite high strung, period."

"You could say that," Elias said, "but you've not walked a mile in her moccasins."

"I don't follow," Miss Cooper said.

"Her papa's all she's got," Elias said. "I don't reckon you've been told this, but she lost her mama while she was still a little tot. Daniel, he loves her more than life itself. Too much, maybe."

Too much? Daniel frowned. He'd never heard this from Elias.

"He intends the best for his little girl. That means he's often away, seeing to the mines so's she'll want for nothing." He paused and Daniel saw him shake his fingers, then place them flat on the table. "I'm not saying you shouldn't have called Daniel out on being away so much, but I think maybe you need to better understand the why of it."

Silence and then the creaking of a chair, likely from someone shifting positions.

"I suppose a case can be made for what you're saying, Mr. Howe," Miss Cooper said, "but I thought to point out to Mr. Beck that his daughter might be better served should he focus on her rather than the business."

"Fair enough, and now you've told him." Elias paused. "Looks like he listened, 'cause he sure hot-footed it back home, didn't he?"

"I suppose," she said in a tone that offered little enthusiasm.

"So let's look at this," Elias continued. "You've been here three days. In that time you've managed to get Charlotte bathed and Daniel home. I'd say that's no small thing."

"But Mr. Beck—"

"Mr. Beck would like to speak to you privately," Daniel said as he pushed the door open. "When you're finished here, of course."

Tova scrambled to her feet, but Elias stood firm. Something in his expression told Daniel his friend might not be as surprised as the ladies that Daniel had joined them.

Miss Cooper rose, her back ramrod straight, and gave him a look that told him nothing of what she must be feeling. "Now is fine," she said, "unless Mr. Howe or Tova need me to—"

"No!" they said in unison.

"Very well, then," Daniel said, his gaze landing on Elias, who dared to offer an insolent wink. "Follow me, please."

17

"Bats, rats, it's all the same." Mae knew she made little sense, but the frustrated female had been walking the better part of the night with nothing to lead her but the North Star and a keen instinct for finding trouble.

Making a bed and falling into it tempted her, as did leaving the heavy rifle behind. Neither would happen, for she knew well the dangers a lone woman faced.

What must Henry be thinking now? Might he suspect she was about to walk through the soles of her best boots—her only boots—just because the horse was misnamed?

"Lord, I know You're up there. Might I trouble You to send…"

She almost said it. Almost asked for help.

"That is," she corrected, "I'd be much obliged if You'd send me an idea on what I need to do next."

&⊙&

With each step Daniel took toward the library, his brain ticked off a few reasons to keep Miss Cooper in his employ, along with a multitude of reasons to send her back to Manhattan and the banker. He'd hoped—prayed—that by the time he ushered the woman into his private domain, he might have a clear winner between the two options.

Unfortunately, he did not.

"Sit down, Miss Cooper." He pointed to one chair only for her to blithely sit in another.

Add one more reason to fire her.

"Thank you for the boots and jacket," she said as she smoothed her skirt over her knees. "It was a lovely gesture."

And another reason for keeping her.

"You're most welcome."

He settled behind the desk and pushed a stack of letters aside. The gesture reminded him of the correspondence from his father, which further reminded him of the dire need to tame Charlotte before she was introduced to her grandfather.

Daniel had decided to set aside the past in cautious optimism of a future for Charlotte. He made the choice out of love for his daughter and not any obligation or desire to mend the frayed edges of his own relationship with his father. He didn't need the old man's money or his blessings. The latter was worth nothing, and the former had already been signed away to the one who most deserved it. He cared little for the old man's opinion of him, but he'd not have his daughter's heart broken should her grandfather judge her and find her wanting.

In order to be presented to the earl in the most positive light, Charlotte would need to be polished just a bit. Sadly, Elias and Tova were right. The refined Miss Cooper was the most likely candidate—other than Anna Finch, whose constant presence in his home would surely drive him to distraction. Yet another reason for keeping Miss Cooper on the payroll.

Then there was their kiss beneath the stars. That one fit both categories.

"I can't keep them, of course."

Daniel shook his head. "I'm sorry. What were you saying?"

"The gifts." Miss Cooper's blue eyes barely blinked. "Much as I appreciate the gesture, I cannot keep them."

Daniel paused, his decision hanging in the balance. "You'll need them where we're going, Miss Cooper, so don't think of the jacket and boots as gifts." He leaned back in his chair. "The book, now, that was clearly a gift, though I venture to guess you'll work off the cost of it in the additional duties I'm about to assign you."

She stood. "But, sir, in light of——" Her cheeks pinked and she looked away. "In light of last night's…well, you know…," she said in a voice just above a whisper, "I think my hasty departure would benefit all parties."

Daniel stood and walked around to rest his hip on the edge of the desk. "While I would agree that removing you from my home would allow me to sleep easier at night, I can also say that doing so is quite impossible just now."

"Impossible?" Her lips formed a pout that became a worried look. "Are you insinuating that you will not accept my resignation?"

He crossed his arms over his chest and ignored the strong desire to grin. "I don't insinuate, Miss Cooper. I'm far too busy for such silliness."

She tapped her chin. "But you said——"

"I said you cannot yet resign." He leaned forward. "I've need of you."

The words hung between them, though Miss Cooper thankfully did not acknowledge any possible double meaning. She did, however, seem to be preparing to argue.

"Look," Daniel said, "I should explain. I've need of a woman of culture and refinement who can pass those traits on to Charlotte in a short period of time. A very short period of time, actually."

"Then I'm definitely not your girl, Mr. Beck." She leaned forward, daring him to argue. "Or perhaps you've already forgotten the bathing and shampooing debacle. If I recall, you used the term 'torturous scrubbing.'"

Daniel winced. He'd been a bit harsh with Miss Cooper, though to be fair, she'd been more than harsh in her letter to him regarding his ability to parent Charlotte.

"I might have misjudged the incident slightly," he said, though each syllable was excruciating to admit. "And perhaps I might have misjudged you, as well."

He waited for Miss Cooper's admission of her own misjudgment, then realized none was forthcoming. "Might have?" she said instead.

"That's the best I can offer. I have observed you to be a woman of some manners and breeding," he said as a brilliant strategy occurred to him, "though I am not altogether certain you're up to the task. In fact, now that I think on it, I've probably made a mistake in asking this of you." Daniel looked away. "Of course, I welcome the opportunity for you to prove me wrong." He met her eyes. "I dare you."

The taunt worked. Miss Cooper sank back into the chair, her spine straight and her eyes narrowed. "You dare me?"

Daniel's nod was slow, his gaze unwavering. "My daughter will be presented to a member of the royal family some weeks from now."

"And?"

There was no sympathy in her response, nor did she seem to care to whom Charlotte would be presented. In short, the mention of royalty seemed to evoke none of the awe that he'd seen in others. Another reason to fire her.

Or was it a reason to keep her?

Too late to debate. He'd already put all his cards on the table. All that remained was to see whether his bet would pay off.

He knew he'd have to offer the woman something she'd have trouble turning down, lest she walk out the door and leave him with only Anna Finch to tutor Charlotte.

"I would like to strike a bargain with you. One that involves the very thing you came here to find."

Was it his imagination or did he now have Eugenia Cooper's attention?

"I cannot possibly imagine what you could offer that would be of interest to me."

Her words belied what he'd learned last night. Though they might never even tolerate each other, there was no denying what passed between them when they kissed. He'd have to walk a fine line with this one. What he wanted for Charlotte had to take precedence over what he wanted for himself.

"Miss Cooper," he said slowly, "would you help me with my problem if I promised to help with yours?"

"Mr. Beck, I cannot imagine you would trust me to take your daughter in hand when you did not trust me to do something as simple as supervise a bath and shampoo." She held up her hand to silence his protest. "However, I am amenable to any apologies you might want to offer, though I cannot imagine what problem of mine you think you might possibly be able to solve."

His grin was impossible to hide. "Your Wild West adventure. You tame Charlotte, and I'll see that you have your chance to tame the West as well." Her stunned look broadened his smile. "What say you?"

What could she say? The man was certifiable. First he stormed around like a bull in a china closet, then had the nerve to coerce her into a kiss.

Well, perhaps *coerce* wasn't the correct term, but she neither expected it nor planned to allow it to happen again. And now he dared try and convince her to stay by promising the very thing she'd already decided she'd have to leave to find?

It was a lure she'd not take.

"A Wild West adventure in exchange for teaching your daughter to behave properly?" Gennie shook her head and took a step toward the door. "Impossible. Now if you'll excuse me, I'll pack my—"

Mr. Beck stepped between Gennie and the door. "Yes, do pack," he said. "We leave tomorrow morning for Leadville."

"Leadville?"

"You've heard of it, perhaps?"

Leadville was one of Mae Winslow's favorites. The dime-novel heroine often chased bad guys through the streets of the city in the clouds and saved hapless miners from certain doom in places such as California Gulch and Beggars Alley.

"You've been made the offer," he said. "I'll also not promise you free rein with Charlotte. She's my daughter—my only child—and I will guard her heart and her safety with my life. Do you understand?"

She did.

"In exchange for your cooperation, I will agree to allow you to take charge of Charlotte during those times when you are offering instruction or seeing to her daily routine."

"You're ignoring the fact that I've turned you down."

Daniel Beck's slow grin started with his eyes. "As I recall, you did not turn *me* down, Miss Cooper. And as for the job, you'll accept."

Heat rose in her cheeks. "You're awfully confident, Mr. Beck."

"I've reason to be," he said, seemingly without shame. "Now, about this bargain."

Her traitorous knees began to quake. "You'll not interfere?" she asked as she attempted to stand straighter, taller, without giving evidence of her shaky foundation.

"I cannot promise."

Gennie shrugged and pressed past him. "Then neither can I."

He caught her wrist and hauled her back against him, then abruptly released her. "Perhaps you're right. I can't even be in the same room with you without—"

"Without?"

"Never mind." Mr. Beck stepped back to allow her to walk out the door if she so chose. "I'll not be reduced to begging, Miss Cooper. There are any number of young women who would love to take the position I've offered you. Sadly, they would be more interested in capturing me than tutoring Charlotte."

"I cannot imagine why."

He looked down at her, but she could not meet his stare. "Of course you can, Miss Cooper."

Gennie let the statement hang between them, hoping her expression indicated an outrage she did not feel. He was right.

"While you do offer certain"—he paused—"temptations, I am not a man given to imposing myself on women who do not appreciate my advances. Though, I must point out, you've given ample evidence to support both sides of that case." She opened her mouth to respond, but he held his hand up to silence her. "I am, however, a man who greatly dislikes the ridiculous cat-and-mouse game that is Denver society. Give me a horse and saddle over a biddy and a book reading any day. This is why I need a woman who will help my daughter navigate the treacherous waters of society in general and Denver specifically. Her debut will be in a few weeks. At that time, you are free to leave."

"All of this I am to perform for merely the promise of a Wild West adventure?" Gennie looked around the library, then back to the silver baron. "Forgive me, but other than the outrageous décor in most of the rooms, this looks very much like what I left. How can you possibly offer an authentic Wild West adventure when you obviously have no idea what one would entail?"

Rather than evoke his ire, Gennie's question seemed to amuse him. "Try me," he said in a voice so husky and low it might have been a growl.

"Now who is daring whom?"

He took her hand in his, and Gennie's heart began to pound. She feared another kiss, then, when he made no move to do so, felt disappointment.

"Mr. Beck, you're making this decision easy for me."

"I am?" He looked perplexed as he turned her hand over and seemed to study her palm. "How so?"

She remembered her plan to bring Anna into the Beck family and marveled at how well this proposition of Daniel Beck's fit with it. "I've a plan of my own," she said, struggling to maintain a calm facade, "and because of that, I am going to agree to yours."

"And this plan of yours, should I be concerned?"

"Of course." Gennie pulled her fingers from his grip and turned to step out into the hallway. "One more thing." She paused beneath the jeweled bird statue and looked over her shoulder at Mr. Beck. "How serious are you about cultivating culture and breeding in your daughter?"

The silver baron had moved to the door frame, leaning against it as if he had nowhere to be but that very spot. "Very."

"Then I shall require a budget for purchasing suitable clothing for your daughter, which you and the rest of the staff *will* join me in requiring she wear."

He moved toward her, stopping mere inches away. "If you think it's necessary."

"It is." She stared up at him a moment in an attempt to emphasize her point, as well as to be certain her knees would not buckle. When she felt she'd accomplished the feat, Gennie headed for the stairs and the sanctity of her room.

She'd almost reached the top step when she turned to see him staring up at her. Emboldened, Gennie smiled. "Mr. Beck?"

He rested both hands on the carved and gilded newel post. "Call me Daniel."

Gennie gripped the rail but did not let her smile slip. "No, that would be most improper."

The man had the audacity to laugh. "As you wish."

"There's just one more thing. A requirement, if you will."

"And what might that be?"

She pointed to the horrid bird. "It's me or that bejeweled poultry. One of us stays and the other goes."

This time his laugh might have shaken the chandeliers back home in Manhattan. "Do be serious."

"I *am* serious." She wasn't, of course, but it gave her—and him— one last opportunity for an exit.

"Done." He took the steps two at a time, stopping just below her and placing his eyes at the same level as hers. They were gray, with the most interesting circle of gold at the center. "Permit me to observe that you're serious far too much of the time, Miss Cooper."

"And you, Mr. Beck, are far too observant. Dispose of the chicken before the rooster crows."

With that, she managed to find her door and close it before collapsing onto the nearest chair. The Bible on the bedside table beckoned, but she hadn't the strength in her trembling arms to reach for such a heavy volume.

"Oh my," she whispered as she fanned herself with the copy of Mae Winslow's adventures Mr. Beck had given her. "Lord, what in the world have I done? And if it please You, might You advise me on how to undo it?"

A rap at the door startled her. "Miss Cooper?"

She rose but could not manage the trek to the door. "Yes?"

"The bird is gone," Mr. Beck said. "You may come out now."

Gennie reached for the mantel and held on tight, her gaze moving to the open window and the expanse of green lawn beyond. Without much difficulty, she could once again escape across that lawn and find her way back to town. By now Hester had surely wired enough money to get her home.

Or on a train headed to Deadwood or Dodge City.

"Miss Cooper?"

She forced herself to look away from freedom. "Yes?"

"The Wild West adventure I promised?"

Sinking onto the chair once more, Gennie sighed. "Yes."

"It begins in precisely fifteen minutes at the carriage house. It's a bit warm for the jacket today, but don't forget your boots."

His own boots rang a staccato rhythm out on the floorboards that faded away to an uneasy silence. Gennie set the dime novel aside and reached for the more exciting of the two adventure books—the Bible.

Evidently God wanted Mae to take a bath, because the very next thing she did was stumble into a creek. The water was brown, but her clothes didn't mind, and neither did she. It took some doing, but she managed to climb from the water fresh as a daisy and ready to take on the next problem that came her way.

She changed her mind when she stepped onto the bank and saw One-Eyed Ed aiming his pistol at the middle of her forehead.

ᗿ

Gennie nodded to Isak as she entered the carriage house. The sweet smell of hay mingled with the earthy scent of horses to remind her of the carriage house back in Newport. There she and Hester had whiled away the hours, playing in the empty stalls, then enduring the torturous removal of straw from their hair before going in to take afternoon tea and biscuits with Mama.

"Good. You're prompt." She turned to see Daniel Beck at the opposite end of the long breezeway. "I assume you can ride."

"Ride? A *horse*?"

He strode toward her, and she noticed the hamper in his hand. "Yes, a horse, Miss Cooper."

"Actually, no."

"No?" He gave her a sideways look as he set the hamper down. "But a woman of your quality must surely have had lessons at some point."

"While I appreciate the endorsement of my quality," she said, "I was not a willing participant in lessons of that sort."

A warm breeze lifted a strand of his hair and set it back against his forehead. "Is that so?" He shook his head. "Don't tell me you were a fearful child. I'll not believe it."

"I don't suppose it's too late for me to learn." She lifted her gaze in time to see him look away, smiling. "I'm a quick study, and I've read many books on the subject." Mae Winslow rode her pony in nearly every episode. Surely Gennie had absorbed enough of the mechanics of the procedure to translate to performing it herself. "As I understand it, the horse does the work, and I merely maintain my balance and steer."

"It's never too late, Miss Cooper." He gestured to the stall across from where she stood. A massive horse of chocolate brown eyed her suspiciously. "Why don't we start with that one? Think you can 'balance and steer' her?"

The animal's nostrils flared, and it pawed the ground.

"Do you have anything smaller?" Gennie asked sheepishly.

"Smaller?" The corners of his eyes crinkled when he smiled. "You mean like a pony?"

"Yes," she said with what she hoped would be a good measure of enthusiasm, "a pony would be grand. I do love ponies."

He scratched his head and seemed to ponder her statement. "We had a pony once, but Charlotte outgrew her."

"Oh." She gave the giant horse another look. "If he's all you've got, then—"

"She," he corrected. "Blossom's a mare."

"Blossom." Gennie pushed her fear aside and stepped forward to stroke the horse's muzzle. "Hello, Blossom."

"See, she's not so bad." Mr. Beck reached past her to pat the horse. "Especially now that I've brought her home. I think she much prefers it over the livery."

Gennie backed away to watch the bonding of man and beast. The horse looked at Daniel Beck like a puppy regarded its master. "Why keep a horse at the livery when you have a perfectly lovely place for her here?"

"Until my operations in Leadville expanded, I was based here in Denver. Spent most of my time in the office downtown." He looked away as if remembering. "I'd often come to a point in the day when I couldn't stand being inside another second, so I'd go down the street and fetch Blossom. She and I logged plenty of miles together."

She inched closer and once again felt the horse's muzzle. Wild brown eyes looked at her as if recognizing an old friend—or was it an enemy? Blossom made a whinnying sound, followed by a shuddering move. Gennie jumped.

Daniel Beck placed his palm on her shoulder as if to comfort her. "You really are afraid, aren't you?" he said without a bit of sympathy evident in his voice. "She can sense it, so try to calm down a bit before you touch her again."

"All right." Gennie took a deep breath, then let it out slowly. If Mae Winslow could do this, so could she. "I'm ready to try again."

The silver baron looked skeptical. "Are you suddenly over your skittishness?"

"I am."

"Give me your hand."

He placed her palm atop the horse's muzzle again, then put his over hers. After a moment, he pulled away and stepped back.

The horse's eyes moved from Mr. Beck to Gennie, regarding her impassively. By degrees, Gennie felt herself—and the horse—relax. She moved her palm up to scratch the horse behind her ear, then ran her hand down the side of her muzzle to feel the velvet softness of her nose. To her credit, Blossom endured it all without complaint or sudden movement.

Mr. Beck stepped closer and offered his palm to the horse. On it lay a carrot, which the animal plucked up and ate.

"See? She's gentle as a lamb. Charlotte rides her."

A horse that could be ridden by a child and ate carrots from the hand of a man, and Gennie was afraid to ride her? "If Charlotte can ride her, I want to as well."

Mr. Beck shook his head. "You don't have to, Miss Cooper. I can have Isak ready the buggy."

"No," Gennie said, "I want to ride this horse."

"All right, but first you'll go with me. Then we'll see if you're ready to ride alone."

Gennie gave him a relieved smile. "Yes, I would rather that, if you please."

Mr. Beck called to Isak, who quickly removed the sidesaddle from Blossom and placed a man's saddle on the mare. The silver baron easily climbed up and seated himself, but Gennie had no idea how to join him.

Isak fetched a stool, and a moment later, she found herself sideways in the saddle with Daniel Beck holding tight to her midsection. She froze, unsure how she'd remain atop the horse, and even more unsure she wanted to.

"Calm, Miss Cooper," he whispered. "Remember, a horse can sense fear."

But the harder she tried not to be afraid, the more fear set in. "I'm not sure this is a good idea."

"Hold on a minute." He made a clicking sound, and the horse moved forward.

Gennie squealed, then covered her mouth with the back of her hand. "We're moving."

"That's right," he said. "Now hold tight to the saddle horn." He paused. "Or to me. Whichever you prefer."

She grasped what she figured to be the saddle horn and held on for dear life while Mr. Beck urged the horse in a tight circle around the carriage house. When they'd completed their lap around the small structure, Gennie called the ride a success.

"Now I can say I've ridden a horse," she said when the silver baron reined the beast to a halt.

"Not yet," he said with a chuckle. "Now hold on."

"No," she said with a squeal when the horse bolted forward at Mr. Beck's command. "You hold on — to me! I'll not fall off this monster!"

By the time they'd made a full circle around the house, Gennie almost thought she was having fun. On the second circuit, she knew she was. The third time around, she glanced at Mr. Beck over her shoulder and said, "Can you make this thing run?"

"Run?" His chuckle tickled her ear. "Of course, but I'll have to hold you tighter." He paused. "I wouldn't want you to fall off this monster."

"Yes, of course," she said.

"If you're sure."

"Do stop trying to talk me out of this, Mr. Beck."

He sighed. "All right, but I'll have to move you closer."

Gennie nodded and tightened her grip on the saddle horn. "Do what you must."

Do what you must?

Daniel groaned and hauled the blonde against him, anchoring her there with his free hand. Her slim waist made holding her as easy as when he and Charlotte rode this way, but this was decidedly *not* Charlotte.

He looked down and noted she'd indeed worn the boots he bought for her. Unlike the last pair he'd seen on her feet, these appeared to fit. A memory of her sprawled at his feet tried to intrude on his mind, but he would not allow it.

What had begun as an innocent exercise in mending fences with the governess had quickly spiraled out of his control and into something quite different. The scent of roses and the feel of her back against his chest put Daniel in mind of more than a morning spent riding with his daughter's governess. Without much provocation, he could easily repeat the kiss of last night.

He put the thought out of his mind and pressed Blossom forward. They reached a good solid trot in no time, and he felt the mare straining to burst into her favored gallop.

"Not yet, girl," he said to the horse. "This isn't Charlotte."

Miss Cooper leaned against him as they rounded the turn on the south end of the house. "Have you any idea how humiliating it is to have one's horsemanship skills compared to those of a ten-year-old?"

"That ten-year-old's been in a saddle half her life," he quipped as they hit the straightaway. He allowed Blossom a bit more rein, and she quickly complied with a burst of speed.

The governess squealed but held on tight. Two more times around the house and he called a halt to the exercise.

"Has Blossom tired of the running?" Miss Cooper asked.

The mare could've gone all day at that pace, but Daniel needed a diversion lest his thoughts head in a direction the Lord would not approve.

"Actually, I thought to graduate you to riding alone. What's your opinion on this, Miss Cooper?"

"Alone?" The word came out as a squeak.

Blossom sensed the woman's nervousness and began to fidget. "All right, I can see we may be ahead of ourselves on this." He motioned to Isak, who quickly came to his rescue. "Help Miss Cooper down, then fetch the rig and the basket."

The lad did as he was told, and soon the governess's booted feet stood on solid ground again. Daniel, however, required one more trip around the house at a full gallop before he was ready to call an end to the riding and climb aboard the more civil buggy.

"Give her an extra treat and take care in grooming her," he called to Isak as the young man led Blossom back into the stables.

"I will, sir," Isak said, "and enjoy your adventure. Mama said not to worry. She'd see that Charlotte was fetched home from school."

With a nod, Daniel headed out. Likely they'd be back well before time to fetch Charlotte from her lessons. A smart man would've waited and brought the child along.

When it came to Miss Eugenia Cooper, Daniel knew he could be accused of acting in a number of ways, but smart was not among them. This much became obvious when he turned the rig onto Eighteenth Street and merged with the traffic that plagued the growing city.

At every turn, he saw someone he knew. Each time, he tipped his hat, then wondered what they would say about the lovely, unknown blonde at his side. The word would likely be out before the next beer could be served over at John Asmussen's Saloon in Hop Alley.

For some reason, Daniel seemed doomed to continually be the focus of interest for mothers with daughters of marriageable age. It was a curse he tried to avoid at every turn. Only his time in Leadville seemed free from the plague that was Denver's social season. And unlike his native England, where the season was a brief moment in a year, it seemed here one could find diversion every night if so inclined.

Thus, Daniel kept to home when in Denver, and to arriving alone when events could not be missed. His ride down the middle of town would certainly set tongues wagging. It might also, however, give some the impression he was no longer on the marriage market. Daniel smiled. This buggy ride downtown might be the best move he hadn't intended to make.

"Oh, look." Miss Cooper touched his sleeve, then pointed to the sidewalk some distance away. "There's Anna Finch and her mother. We should stop and invite them to come with us. Why didn't I think of it before?"

"Why indeed?" Daniel said without enthusiasm as he negotiated the tangle of buggies and riders until he reached the curb. Miss Cooper leaned out to greet the Finch women and extend the invitation.

"Oh no, we couldn't," said Mrs. Finch.

"But, Mama, it's a lovely day, and we have no lunch plans that can't be easily canceled," Anna said.

A discussion ensued while Daniel sat mute, unable to discern which way to pray on the matter. If his time spent thus far with the governess was any indicator, a trip alone into the high desert could be fraught with dangers that paled in comparison to rattlesnakes and bobcats. For those things, he had a rifle under the buckboard and his Colt strapped to his thigh.

It was the other danger, that of a pretty woman looking for adventure, that tugged at his heart and made him glad the Finch women were now approaching.

"Are you certain you don't mind the intrusion?" Mrs. Finch asked as she helped herself to the spot beside him.

"You know you're always welcome, Mrs. Finch," he said. "And I warrant Elias has once again prepared a feast for ten rather than two, so there will be plenty for all."

"Oh, I do hope he's sent some of his roasted hen. I do love a good roasted hen. I've tried a dozen times to pry that recipe out of him, but he won't tell a living soul."

She paused, and Daniel opened his mouth to comment, but she immediately turned to another topic. He could but nod as the older woman prattled on.

Miss Cooper moved into his line of sight looking fresh as a daisy and twice as pretty. The remembrance of her straight back pressed against his chest bore hard on him, and for a moment, Daniel allowed it. She'd smelled like roses and felt like heaven in his arms.

He should've fired her when he had the chance instead of laying down the law to Charlotte over breakfast and threatening to send her to boarding school should she make the slightest misstep where the governess was concerned.

And now the one plotting missteps was Daniel himself.

Thank You, Lord, for saving me from certain disaster. And yet, as the balance in the buggy swung from one man and one woman to one man and three women, Daniel wondered whether he'd been saved from disaster or merely invited a different kind.

"My pleasure, ladies," he said, waiting until Anna and Miss Cooper were seated behind them. "Hold on to your hats. It's going to be a wild ride."

He urged the matched bays back into the slow-moving Denver traffic.

"Oh dear, my plumes are flying," Mrs. Finch called as she latched gloved hands to her feathered headgear. "Do slow down, Daniel. Where's the fire?"

A poor question to ask a man fresh from the torture of spending time with Gennie Cooper. "I don't know, Mrs. Finch," he said, sliding a grin to the woman beside him. "Though I'm bound to find it if I can just get this buggy moving faster."

He slapped the reins, and they were off. If Blue Eyes wanted a Wild West adventure, Daniel would show her what a carriage ride could be with a man who knew how to drive one.

Two turns and a near miss with a mule later, Daniel felt suitably chastised and a bit embarrassed at his poor behavior. They limped along the lane at a snail's pace until he reached the site he'd chosen for today's picnic.

Settling three ladies, a blanket, and Elias's food basket onto the prairie in full view of the snowcapped Rockies nearly did him in. To top it off, his spot next to Miss Cooper was taken by Anna's mother.

"I've got you over there," she said, gesturing to a place barely big enough for a lad in knee britches. "Anna, do help Daniel with his plate."

Before he could protest, half the winter's larder sat on the ridiculous china plates Elias had packed. He wedged himself into his assigned seat and stabbed at cold chicken with a gold fork. If he couldn't manage to enjoy the picnic, at least he could enjoy the food. While he chewed, he watched the ladies pick their portions as if the food was priced by the ounce.

Mrs. Finch gave up on her hat and flipped the feathered creation backward, where it fell onto the grass. Something about the awful thing reminded him of the priceless piece of art the governess required banished.

"A penny for your thoughts," Anna said. "You appear to be enjoying them."

Daniel slid his gaze past Anna to rest on Blue Eyes. "I am," he said.

And he was, preferring to entertain himself in the quiet enjoyment of the food while the ladies chatted.

"You must attend," he heard Mrs. Finch say to Gennie.

"Perhaps," was her coy response.

"I'm sure our Mr. Beck will accompany you."

He popped a slice of apple in his mouth and chewed slowly while the ladies stared at him.

"I'm afraid he'll be away that evening," Miss Cooper said after a moment. "Leadville, isn't it?"

"Leadville?" he managed as he swallowed. Then he realized the governess was saving his hide. "Oh, Leadville. Yes." He shrugged. "A pity, but I fear she's correct. Leadville. Yes, that's where I'll be."

And thus Miss Cooper went in one moment from the bane of his existence to the reason he wore a smile. Perhaps he should keep her around, if only to deflect the advances of the Finch women. An entertaining thought.

"Dear," Mrs. Finch said later as he helped her into the buggy, "your Miss Cooper is a delight."

He looked past the older woman to where Gennie and Anna stood together. Heads bent toward each other, the pair appeared thick as thieves.

"She is, isn't she?" he said. "Though I confess she vexes me at times."

The elder Finch adjusted her feathered hat, then placed her hand atop Daniel's. "Of course she does, dear. Though I wager she might not cause such turmoil should you elect to stop kissing her on your front lawn."

"Why, Mrs. Finch," he said with as wicked a grin as he could manage. "Are you jealous?"

To her credit, Mrs. Finch winked. "Dear, if I weren't old as the hills and happily married, I just might show you a thing or two about the art of wooing. However, as you've missed me by a generation, I'll leave you with this thought."

Anna and Gennie broke off their powwow and headed toward the carriage. "Please do."

She tapped his arm with her fan. "Sometimes what the Lord meant for you is right under your nose, and you're so close you miss it altogether."

19

"Didn't expect me, did you?" the ruffian asked.

"Actually, I did, Edward," Mae said as if she'd been planning a party and he'd shown up right on time. "Bad pennies, you know. They always turn up."

"That's not funny, Mae." He cocked the weapon. "Take it back."

She was about to when behind him she spied what might be her solution. Or, as things generally went with the horse named Lucky, her doom.

&

Charlotte was none too pleased when she returned home to find her governess still on the payroll. Isak broke the news to her on the way home, then had to chase the child half a block before putting her back in the buggy. This Gennie learned from Tova, who seemed to have changed her opinion of Gennie since that morning.

Gennie sat across the table from Charlotte, who glared at her. Elias and Tova observed from the other side of the kitchen. They gave the appearance they were busy, but neither seemed to accomplish anything other than taking turns looking over their shoulders at the silent war going on at the table.

"Aren't you excited your father is taking you to Leadville tomorrow?" Gennie finally asked.

Charlotte gave Gennie a sullen look. "Not if *you're* going."

Gennie decided to ignore the impertinence. "When you're finished, we'll go and pack your things."

The child never looked up as she said, "Tova can do that."

Looking past Charlotte to Tova, Gennie nodded. "Yes, unless Tova objects, I suppose she could."

"Of course," Tova said. "I'll have the new clothes washed and packed well before you leave."

"New clothes?" Charlotte jerked her head up. "What new clothes?"

"After your bath, I might be persuaded to show you what you'll be wearing on the train," Gennie said. "The rest are still being laundered."

"But I just took a bath yesterday."

"And you shall likely have another tomorrow." Gennie rose. "I'll prepare your bath. Do come up before the water gets cold."

The bath went much smoother than the fiasco of the night before, but when Charlotte got a glimpse of the dress she'd be wearing on the train the next morning, she was furious.

"Don't blame Miss Cooper," Elias said as he came to stand behind Gennie in the nursery door. "Your papa had a fancy dress shop drop a load of them by this afternoon, then picked through them himself."

Gennie smiled behind her hand as she recalled poor Mr. Beck summoning her to help him sort through the multiple hampers of clothing delivered to his library.

Charlotte stomped her feet like a child half her age. "Papa did not do any such thing. I'm going to ask him myself, and when he hears you've been lying to me to make me wear that awful dress, he's going to be mighty upset."

Elias allowed Charlotte a wide berth as she stormed out of the nursery. "Likely she won't be happy once Daniel gives her what for."

Gennie looked up, suddenly very tired. "Does he actually do that? Discipline her, I mean."

"In a fashion, I suppose he does," Elias said. "Though not nearly enough to my way of thinking." He paused. "Not that I judge him for it, mind you. Daniel's a good man who loves his own to a fault. Sometimes that can make a man a bit shortsighted."

"If that's a fault, then we should all be so afflicted." Gennie stifled a yawn as she closed the lid on the first of two trunks filled with Charlotte's things. "I wonder if I should wait up."

"How about I let Daniel know you're going to make an early night of it? I'm sure he won't minding putting Charlotte to bed once she's wound down enough to make the attempt."

"Yes, please."

Elias had only been gone a moment when he returned with word she could turn in for the night.

"Thank you," she told the older man. "I'm not anticipating an easy morning."

Elias chuckled. "I reckon if she's tired enough, the morning'll be fine. It's when Charlotte's got her sleep in that she's in fine form."

He was right. The next morning, Gennie dressed a nearly sleeping child without much complaint, and her father carried her down to the buggy. They boarded the train in near darkness, making Gennie wish she, like Charlotte, could doze with her head on a broad shoulder.

Their arrival in Leadville came just as Charlotte was rousing. While Daniel and his hired man picked out their luggage and supervised the loading of the wagon, Gennie played the dual roles of governess and tourist.

Charlotte ceased complaining when she noticed a man in buckskins and a tricorn hat leading a baby bear by a rope through the primitive train station. The girl gawked in a most unladylike fashion, but Gennie couldn't blame her.

While Denver could be almost any city in America, Leadville was unmistakably set in the Wild West. And set high. From her vantage point, Gennie could see the clouds dipping beyond the mountains as if they'd fallen behind them, and the air felt thinner, clearer. Gennie drew in a deep draft of it and marveled at how far she'd come from the train station in New York City.

"After you, ladies," Mr. Beck called. "Our hotel awaits."

The short ride from the station took them past numerous shops and dining establishments. It also brought them nearer to the mines and the various businesses related to the industry.

"What's that smell?" Charlotte asked. "It stinks here."

"That's smelt."

"Well, that's the truth," Charlotte said. "It definitely smells."

"No," her father said with a grin. "Smelt. It's part of the mining process."

She held her nose until the fellow Mr. Beck called Hiram announced their arrival at the Mountain Palace Hotel. Even then, the girl seemed more interested in complaining about the smell than noticing her surroundings.

Gennie, however, was fascinated with Leadville. From the crude shacks seemingly nailed together from whatever was found nearby, to the relatively modern downtown hotels and shops, Leadville appeared to come straight out of the pages of a dime novel. She expected some Mae Winslow look-alike to round the corner at every turn.

What she saw instead were dozens of women of seemingly high character, and three times that number who looked to be the opposite. It did not escape her attention that both types smiled and waved at the wagon when they rolled past.

Hiram handed the reins over to Daniel and jumped out. "I'll let them know you're here, Mr. Beck." He returned a short while later with news they'd been given the Presidential Suite along with the neighboring Governor's Suite.

"Wonderful," Gennie said as Daniel Beck lowered her from the wagon. His hands remained on her waist only a moment, and when he released her, she nearly stumbled.

"Careful." Hiram caught her hand and eased her onto the sidewalk while Daniel helped his daughter from the wagon. "This way to your rooms," he said. "I'll have the luggage brought up once you've approved the quarters." He turned to Gennie. "Mr. Beck usually stays at the Clarendon, but given the protests from the miners awhile back, he thought it better to find a less-traveled—"

"Hiram," Mr. Beck snapped. "Enough of that."

"Yes sir." Hiram moved forward, keys in hand, up two flights of stairs to the end of the third-floor hallway. "Ladies," he said as he turned the key in the door marked PS and swung it open, "this will be your quarters while in Leadville."

He moved on to the next door, Mr. Beck at his heels.

"Come on, now, Charlotte," Gennie said when she noticed the child standing sullenly against the far wall of the corridor.

"I won't share a room with you."

"Take your complaints to your father, Charlotte. I've no say in the matter."

Leaving the girl to pout alone, Gennie took three steps into the room and stopped short. If this was the Presidential Suite, then someone needed to call for a reelection.

What the chamber lacked in elegance, it made up for in size. That, unfortunately, was the room's only positive feature. Two beds of a size befitting two persons each were wedged in either corner of the sparsely furnished chamber, a window of considerable width between them. A table and two chairs were placed near the door, and a decently comfortable parlor set held court in the center of the room.

Curtains in a somber gray strewn with scarlet rosebuds had been left half open to allow the afternoon sun to stream in, while the window beyond remained shut tight. A coating of what appeared to be some sort of dust encrusted the outside of the frame. Mine dust, or some other such thing, Mr. Beck had called it on their drive in. A by-product of doing business in Leadville, and a hazard of daily life here, he'd explained, yet Gennie had not expected to see the city through a layer of it.

Charlotte paused to toss aside her summer hat before launching herself onto one of the two garishly covered beds.

"Careful," Gennie cautioned. "There could be any number of vermin there."

"I'll have you know we run a clean establishment."

Gennie turned to see a woman in what appeared to be a maid's uniform standing in the doorway, her arms loaded with towels and extra pillows. Two narrowed brown eyes peered over the teetering pile.

"I'm terribly sorry," Gennie said, "but it appears…that is, from the looks of things, I—"

"There's your trouble." The maid pressed past and dumped her bundles on the empty bed, then pivoted to stare at Gennie. "You never can tell from the looks of things what's underneath." She eyed Gennie as if the comment were about her and not the lumpy mattresses.

Gennie ran her hand over the cold iron filigree of the bedpost and worked up her most penitent expression. "Again, I do apologize."

The woman stood her ground. "Perhaps you should check those vermin-infested beds before you offer your apologies." She paused. "Go on there, child. Do be sure there won't be anything in your bed tonight but you."

Remorse bit hard, but Charlotte happily removed the quilt, then the sheets below. "Nothing here that I can see," Charlotte said.

Both child and maid stared at Gennie. "Well, then," Gennie said, "I do think this matter is settled." To emphasize the point, she perched on the edge of the empty bed, careful not to topple the linens and towels.

The woman seemed to consider further discussing the room for a moment, then bustled toward the door. At the door frame, she stopped and gave Gennie a firm look over her shoulder. "As I said, I run a clean establishment." Her brown eyes narrowed. "A place where none but those with high moral standards are allowed."

"And we are most grateful for that, aren't we, Charlotte?"

"You should be." She pointed at Gennie. "Mr. Beck being a single, eligible man and all, I don't like the idea of him having the room next door to such a pretty thing, even if she is his daughter's caretaker. It's lucky for you my husband, Ira, knows Mr. Beck from their association with the Greater Leadville Beautification and Improvement Society and can vouch for his sterling character." She laughed. "Sterling character. Silver. Get it?"

Taken aback by the stern woman's laughter, it took Gennie a moment to reply. "Yes, that's quite funny. I must remember to tell Mr. Beck. As for the other subject, I assure you there's nothing but a professional relationship between Charlotte's father and myself."

Charlotte's feet landed with a thump on the rug. "Don't believe her. My daddy kissed her, and I know it was her fault."

Gennie rose, heat flooding her cheeks. "Don't mind Charlotte. She does go on."

"Does she?" The woman held her basket to her chest as if trying to determine the truth.

"Ladies, do the accommodations meet your approval?" Daniel appeared in the door. "Well, how nice to see you again, Mrs. Stegman. Do tell Ira the new place is all he promised and more."

Mrs. Stegman's expression softened. "Yes, of course. Thank you, Mr. Beck." Before she made her exit, she turned to give Gennie one last direct look. "And do let me know if any difficulties occur during your stay. I'll be happy to handle them personally."

As soon as the woman left, Charlotte launched herself into her father's arms. "Papa, don't make me share a room with *her*."

Mr. Beck gently but firmly set his daughter down, then bent to meet her on eye level. "We had this discussion yesterday. Would you care to have it again in front of Miss Cooper?"

The girl's "no" was barely audible.

"Then what do you say to Miss Cooper regarding your impertinent behavior?"

"I'm sorry," she said, though her gaze never left the lovely kid boots that matched her yellow summer frock.

"Apology accepted," Gennie said as a porter arrived, bearing their trunks.

"Now, Buttercup, Mr. Stegman has sent two baskets of fruit to my room by mistake. Why don't you fetch one back here for you and Miss Cooper to enjoy later?"

When the girl showed little enthusiasm for the activity, Mr. Beck turned and pointed her out the door. She disappeared into the hall, her footsteps echoing as she stomped her way next door.

Mr. Beck pulled a key from his pocket and handed it to Gennie. "I took the liberty of locking your truck." His gaze met hers. "This isn't Denver, Miss Cooper. You'll find a pistol suitable for a lady packed inside. You *do* know how to use a pistol, don't you?"

She did. For all his insistence that ladies must act like ladies, Papa required both Gennie and Mama to know how to escape should they be faced with an intruder while he was away. So fearful was Gennie of awaking to some horrible criminal standing over her that she bought a pistol and paid the gunsmith handsomely to teach her how to use it. Unfortunately, Papa got wind of her escapade and confiscated the weapon. He did, however, begin a longstanding habit of taking her with him to practice shooting on their Long Island and Newport properties.

She didn't mention any of this to Mr. Beck, who waited for an answer. "Might I see the weapon to determine whether it's something I can operate?"

She handed the key back to him and watched while he retrieved a small pistol that looked very much like the one Papa had taken away from her. "Yes," she said as she held it, then handed it back, "I can use this if I must, but surely I won't need to."

Mr. Beck placed the weapon atop the other items in the trunk, then locked it and handed the key back to Gennie. "I hope not," he said, "but I will admit that though the town has grown, we still have a certain bad element. I'd prefer to know that my daughter—and you, of course—will be protected when I cannot do it myself."

Gennie nodded as Mr. Beck set the key atop the trunk. Charlotte raced in with a basket of fruit, nearly toppling the table in the process.

"Slow down, Buttercup," he said.

"I want to go back in your room." Charlotte stepped into the hallway.

"All right, but only until I have to leave for the office. Then you'll have to come back here to your own room. Understand?"

With Charlotte's reluctant nod, the Becks headed down the hall to the Governor's Suite, and Gennie began what, until now, had always been done for her: unpacking. While some of the things looked lovely pulled directly from the trunk, others would need wrinkles removed.

For that, she would have to rely on Mrs. Stegman for advice on a suitable laundress.

When she was done with her things, Gennie placed the pistol in the tray and closed her trunk, locking it before placing the key on top of the trunk and moving on to tackle Charlotte's trunk. The work went faster than she expected, and to her surprise, Gennie didn't mind that the menial labor had been left to her. She was, after all, the governess.

And she was in Leadville—the Wild West. It was all too exciting.

Gennie went to the window to try to open the sash. She succeeded on the third attempt and only coughed for a moment when the breeze blew in.

Three floors down, Gennie spied Mr. Beck and Hiram deep in conversation at the back of the wagon. Charlotte had wandered a few feet away and appeared to be watching a group of schoolchildren with some measure of interest.

Turning her attention away from those she knew, Gennie began to study those she did not. Across the way, a gentleman in a stained apron swept the street beneath a sign advertising a meat market. Next door, two men in broad-brimmed hats stepped out of what appeared to be the marshal's office, then paused to slap each other on the back. When they parted, one crossed the street to join Mr. Beck and Hiram, while the other headed north to disappear into the Lucky Lad and Lady Saloon.

Gennie leaned farther out the window to allow the cool breeze to play over the back of her neck. For a moment, she closed her eyes and imagined Mae Winslow bolting over the sill and sliding down the drainpipe to a waiting buckboard complete with her true love, Henry, holding the reins.

When she opened them again, she saw instead the empty wagon

where only a moment ago Mr. Beck and his associates had been conversing. Gone too was Charlotte. Likely they'd gone somewhere for a leisurely lunch and forgotten all about her. Not a terribly disappointing situation considering that in her sleep-deprived state, the lumpy mattress had begun to look appealing.

She elected to take the one nearest the door and leave the rumpled bed for Charlotte. She slipped out of her shoes and padded to the window to pull the curtains shut against the noonday sun.

That's when she spied Charlotte squatting behind the wagon along with two other children. Curious, Gennie watched while the trio huddled together. As Gennie was about to turn away, a squeal went up, and she saw Charlotte racing toward the hotel with something bouncing behind her, attached to a rope. The other two children disappeared in different directions.

"You there! Come back, you rascals!" a man called as he darted from behind the wagon and appeared to be trying to decide in which of the three directions to give chase.

"What in the world?" Gennie slipped back into her shoes and donned her hat, intending to head downstairs, confront the child, and get to the bottom of whatever had happened. She stormed past her trunk, then stopped and turned to stare at the key atop it. Perhaps a bit of caution should be exercised in this situation.

Gennie opened the trunk and quickly retrieved the pistol. Hiding it in her skirts was easily accomplished, as was leaving the room undetected. By the time she reached the lobby, however, a crowd had gathered, with Charlotte Beck at its center.

The criminal turned and smiled. "Nice of you to return my horse. I missed her."

"Well, I didn't," Mae said, the memory of bats and snakes still too tender. "And I've not missed you, either." She stuck the Colt in his gut, then shoved him to the ground and snatched up his pistol. Ed kicked like a mule, but she'd learned her mule taming from the best. Sidestepping his boots, the fair creature reached for her lariat and made short work of hog-tying the fellow at the ankles. Rather than waste a bullet, Mae used the business end of the Colt to knock Ed out cold.

This time when she climbed onto Lucky, she made sure she didn't look back. Ed wasn't about to give chase now, with her rope around his boots and a headache that wouldn't soon leave him.

Thus, with the villain dispatched, the race home began.

If only she weren't riding Lucky.

⸎

Jeb Sanders sat across the desk from Daniel, a tired expression on his unshaven face. "Mr. Beck, I know those boys are kin, but I didn't have nothing to do with the jailbreak or the accidents at the mine."

When Daniel said nothing, Jeb rolled up his sleeve and offered his arm as evidence. "See that there?" He pointed to a bandage, frayed and browned at the edges. "That's from trying to stop your mule team before they went over the cliff with the wagon."

Daniel nodded.

"And that there?" He gestured to his trouser leg, where a spot near the knee wore a sizable patch. "That's what I got for the trouble. I'm just now walking right, and it's been near to a week."

Only three days had passed, but Daniel didn't figure the fact was worth mentioning. He leaned back in his chair and let out a long breath. "What exactly can I do for you, then?"

Jeb seemed to think on the question, though Daniel suspected the man had planned his speech ever since he jumped on that wagon just before it went over the cliff. "I'm not fit for mining right now, sir," he said, "but I do need the work. Don't tell nobody this, but I'm not keeping much of what I earn. That goes back home to keep Mama and the little ones fed."

"I see."

The revelation was not particularly surprising in its content, as most miners posted their earnings back east or west or down south to family. Whether it was true in Jeb Sanders's case would remain to be seen. Finding the truth of it was a simple matter Hiram could handle in an afternoon.

"So's a job of some sort where I can earn an honest living until I'm not so stove-up would go far to getting me back on my feet." Jeb chuckled. "Didn't intend that, but that's right funny, ain't it? Asking for a change of job 'cause I can't walk good until I'm back on my feet."

Daniel tried to logic it out and failed. "Indeed."

Jeb sobered. "Look, I'm nervous, and when I'm nervous, I make jokes." He leaned forward. "Here's the honest truth, Mr. Beck. I know I got a long way to go to make up for the reputation I lost just by being related to those knuckleheads."

"As long as we're being honest," Daniel said, "I'll admit you're right. Other than the usual Saturday-night scuffles, your record's been clean since you came to Leadville. I know, because I talked to the marshal this morning." He paused to let the statement sink in. "That doesn't mean I trust you, Sanders. It means I want to. Do you understand?"

The miner looked Daniel straight in the eye. "I do, sir."

Daniel rose and Jeb followed suit, albeit a bit slower. "Sanders, I appreciate your coming here today." He pulled an envelope from his pocket and handed it to the miner.

"What's this?" Jeb weighed it in his hand. "Unless I miss my guess, that's money in there."

Daniel watched the man carefully as he spoke. "It is."

Sanders let the packet drop to the desk, then shoved his hat back onto his head. "Sir," he said slowly, "I don't mean no disrespect, but I don't want charity, nor did I ask for it."

"Excuse me, sir." Hiram stuck his head inside the office and gestured to Daniel. "There's an emergency at the hotel. You're needed right away."

"Emergency?" He yanked on his hat and pushed past Hiram. "What's happened? Is it Charlotte?"

By the time he reached the street, Hiram had told him snatches of the problem. Charlotte had been caught playing some sort of prank on a rough character, and he'd gone into the Mountain Palace after her. In the process of chasing the child around the lobby, several items had been damaged or broken. To make matters worse, her governess had actually aimed her pistol into the crowd. All three of them waited in the lobby for someone from the marshal's office to come and sort things out.

Daniel stormed through the doors of the Mountain Palace, and the crowd assembled in the lobby parted. Charlotte raced toward him and fell into his arms, babbling something about a mean man and a rope. Mrs. Stegman bounded toward him next, promising to evict the lot of them if the situation was not remedied. A few others, including a rough-looking character who appeared to have come straight from either the mine or the saloon, expressed opinions on what should take place.

"Quiet!" Daniel finally shouted. When the noise ceased, Daniel handed Charlotte over to Hiram and made his way to Miss Cooper, who sat on a brocade sofa with the pistol on her lap. "All right," he said, "what happened?"

Before the governess could open her mouth, several people around her began talking at once. Meanwhile, she stared up at him with eyes dampened by tears.

"Enough! Let the lady speak," Daniel said, and once again quiet reigned. "Miss Cooper?"

She gave a shuddering sigh, then handed Daniel the pistol. "Here, take this before I shoot that awful man."

"Now see here," the rough character said. "You'll not shoot me, gal, else the law'll take you in. 'Sides, I done nothing to be shot over."

Slowly the governess rose. "You, sir, are an awful man who chases innocent children and frightens them half to death." She took a step past Daniel toward the man. "And furthermore, you had no right to—"

"What's going on here?" Daniel turned to see the marshal making his way toward them. "You got this figured out yet, Beck? I heard tell your girlfriend's been threatening to shoot people."

"I am not his girlfriend," Miss Cooper said, "and if anyone needed shooting, it would be that awful man there."

The miner took a step forward. "Maybe you're the one who needs to be—"

"See here." Daniel shouldered his way between Miss Cooper and the man, blocking her path and, hopefully, a shooting. "Look, man," he said, "I'd not make her any more upset if I were you."

The marshal put his hand on the miner's chest. "Settle yourself down, Batson." When the fellow had calmed a bit, the marshal nodded. "Perhaps you'd like to tell me what's got her so angry."

Batson looked sheepish, though the veins in his thick neck still bulged. "Well, it all started with a pie."

"A pie?" The marshal looked more perturbed than amused. "You mean to tell me I got pulled away from a perfectly good nap because of a pie?" He looked beyond Daniel to Miss Cooper. "This better be good."

"I don't know about good," Miss Cooper said, "but I can tell you the truth." She pointed at Batson. "That man there was the victim of a practical joke by Miss Charlotte Beck and two local children. I saw it myself."

"What did you see, miss?" the marshal asked.

Miss Cooper related the story of watching Charlotte and two new friends hiding behind the wagon, then running in three directions. "I didn't know what was tied to the string. All I saw was Charlotte running back toward the hotel and that man chasing her, making all sorts of awful threats."

The governess came around Daniel to stand at his side. A second later, Charlotte broke free from Hiram to run toward them. To Daniel's surprise, she aimed herself at Miss Cooper.

"She saved me," Charlotte said. "That man was going to kill me!"

Daniel glared at the miner, his fists itching to connect with Batson's smug face. If the marshal hadn't restrained him, he might have done just that.

"Don't make me add you to the list of folks going to jail, Daniel," he said.

"I don't want to go to jail," Charlotte wailed as she held on to Miss Cooper, "and I don't want her to go, either. She didn't steal the pie. I did."

The marshal exchanged glances with Daniel before releasing him to focus on Charlotte. "Miss Beck, maybe we ought to hear the rest of this story." He leaned toward Daniel. "We could handle this in a more private place if you'd like."

When Daniel nodded, the marshal called to Mrs. Stegman, who led them to a dining room off the lobby.

"All right now," the marshal said to those left grumbling in the lobby. "You can all go home now. If anyone's got any statement to make, stop on over to my office and leave it with one of my deputies." He gestured for Daniel to follow him. "I'll need her gun."

Daniel handed over the pistol, then watched as the marshal checked to see if it had been fired. When he was done, he dropped the pistol into Daniel's palm, then gave him a sideways look. "This weapon has no ammunition in it."

Daniel nodded. "I didn't think she'd have need of it. At least not the first hour we were in town."

The marshal shook his head, then shrugged. "Lesson learned, and yet I'm awful glad that pretty girl didn't have anything she could cause damage with." He gave Miss Cooper an appreciative glance. "Well, at least nothing in the way of ammunition."

When Daniel didn't respond, the marshal elbowed him. "Pretty and full of spunk too. You're a lucky man, Beck."

"No," he quickly said, "she's just the governess."

The marshal's eyes narrowed. "A woman of that caliber is never just the governess, son. If you haven't figured it out yet, you will."

Before Daniel could offer an opposing viewpoint, the marshal walked over to Charlotte, Miss Cooper, and Batson, and pointed to the dining room. "Let's get this over with so I can go back to my nap."

When the last one had filed in, the marshal closed the doors and gestured toward Charlotte. "All right, now. Let's hear about this pie thievery you've been up to, Miss Beck."

Charlotte's lower lip trembled as she climbed into Daniel's arms. "I wasn't trying to be bad, Papa," she said. "It just happened."

"What just happened?" the marshal asked.

"It was supposed to be a trick."

"What kind of trick, Buttercup?" Daniel pulled his handkerchief from his pocket and wiped away his daughter's tears. "Tell the marshal the truth, now."

His daughter nodded slowly. "See, my papa was having a meeting, so I had to behave myself because I didn't want to go upstairs. I saw these children who looked like they were having fun with a rope and some other stuff, so I went over and talked to them. At first they called me names because of how I was wearing this dress and all." She gave Miss Cooper a pointed look. "I told them it was my new dress that my governess made me wear, and then they laughed at me some more."

She paused to swipe at her eyes.

"And then what happened?" the marshal asked gently.

"Well, they told me if I wanted to play with them I had to take a dare, so I told them I would take any old dare they wanted because I'm not afraid of nothing."

"Of anything," Miss Cooper corrected.

"Of anything," Charlotte said. "So then I did it."

"Did what?" Daniel asked. "You must tell the officer what you've done."

"She tricked me, that's what she did," Batson said.

"You'll have your turn." The marshal pointed at Charlotte. "Exactly what was your dare?"

Charlotte seemed reluctant to speak again. "There was this pie on the windowsill in the house behind the hotel. Those children told me if I took it for them and got away with it, they'd be my friends. It was easy, 'cause I've done it—" She stopped short and put her hands over her mouth.

"Before?" the marshal supplied.

Charlotte nodded slowly.

Daniel stood transfixed. "You've stolen pies before? You mean to tell me you've committed—"

"Better we stick to the topic at hand," the marshal urged. "I'm sure you and your daughter can discuss her other criminal infractions out of earshot of a lawman."

"Indeed we will," Daniel said, biting back the rest of the things he would say in the privacy of their rooms.

"So you stole the pie," the marshal offered. "Then what happened?"

"They still wouldn't be my friends." She bit her lower lip and appeared ready to cry again. "They wanted me to do one more dare, then they promised they would be my friends."

"And what was that dare?" he asked.

Charlotte gave Daniel a sheepish look, then regarded the marshal with tear-filled eyes. "I had to tie a rope around the pie and set it where someone would find it. When they stopped to pick up the pie, I had to yank it back under the wagon. I didn't think the mean man would fall and land on his face. And I didn't mean to laugh at him, because even though it was funny, it wasn't really funny at all. That's what Miss Cooper said, and she was right. And then when she told the man he shouldn't have been so mad, he told Miss Cooper she had soup for brains."

Daniel could tell the lawman was having a hard time keeping a straight face. "Is that right?" the marshal said.

Daniel, however, was still stunned over his daughter's admission. If he'd missed Charlotte's tendency toward theft, what else had he missed?

"Is that all, Miss Beck? Or is there more to the story?"

Charlotte shook her head. "No, that's all, except he chased me back to the hotel, yelling and saying bad words my papa would whip me for and telling me I wasn't going to get away with anything just because I was Daniel Beck's brat."

Again her tears spilled over, and Daniel caught them with his shirt sleeve since the handkerchief had long since seen its limit. "Shh," he whispered as he cradled his daughter, "Papa won't let the man hurt you."

"And neither will the city of Leadville. We have laws against hurting innocent children." The marshal looked at Charlotte again. "Did he say anything else?"

She nodded as she stepped away from Daniel to entwine her hand with Miss Cooper's.

The governess patted Charlotte's shoulder. "I heard him say there were miners in this town waiting for a way to get back at Charlotte's father. He told her they'd be glad to see that Charlotte suffered just as they had."

Outrage filled Daniel, and then dread. He looked at Hiram, who was already making notes.

"I never said any such thing," the miner sputtered.

"You did," Miss Cooper said. "I heard it."

"And that's when she pulled out her gun and saved me." Charlotte looked up at her governess. "Isn't that right, Miss Cooper?"

"Yes." The governess patted the girl's back and soothed away a tear.

The marshal seemed to consider the statement a minute before turning to the miner. "Batson, you're lucky that woman didn't have any bullets in her gun."

"She didn't?" The miner seemed surprised and then, by degrees, embarrassed. "Well, it doesn't matter whether she had bullets or not.

She ought not to be waving that weapon around and frightening people like that."

"Me frightening people?" Miss Cooper let go of Charlotte's hand and moved toward the miner.

She might have reached him had Daniel not cut her off. "Hold on there," he whispered against her ear. "Let's allow the marshal to do his job."

"Let me go, Mr. Beck. That man's got to stop saying things that aren't true."

"Well now," the marshal said with obvious amusement. "How do you plan to stop him?"

"I don't know," Miss Cooper replied, "but I'll figure out a way if I have to."

The marshal frowned. "That's what I'm here for, Miss Cooper. So just calm yourself."

She looked as if she might bolt after the miner, so Daniel kept a tight grip on her. At least that's what he told himself as he held her against him much the same way he had during their horseback riding lesson just yesterday.

If the marshal noticed, he didn't say so. Rather, he looked past the miner to Hiram. "Would you mind running across the street to fetch my deputy? I'd like to get all these statements down before the facts get jumbled up. I could do it, but nobody'd be able to read what I wrote."

When the deputy returned, the marshal ordered him to take Batson over to the jail to get his statement. "And let him cool his heels in a cell for a few hours until he learns how to treat a lady." He winked at Charlotte. "My mistake. I should have said two ladies."

After Batson was gone, Daniel released Gennie. "If you're done with the ladies, might they be allowed to go back upstairs to their room?"

"I don't see why not." The marshal shrugged. "Long as nobody skips town until this matter's settled, you're free to do whatever you want." With a nod, Miss Cooper led Charlotte out of the room. The marshal watched them go, then turned to wink at Daniel. "Just don't let the beautification folks catch you."

Daniel shook his head. "I don't know what you mean."

"Oh, that committee of do-gooders who meet over at the opera house on occasion. Aren't you one of 'em?"

Daniel made a face. "I admit I got roped into going to a meeting, but it was out of obligation to Horace."

"Well, even Horace Tabor didn't intend for the vigilantes in that group to do what they've been attempting." The marshal looked aggrieved. "Would you believe they're trying to close down the saloons and send the houses of negotiable affection into bankruptcy?"

"I visit neither," Daniel said, truthfully, "and as far as I can tell, you'd have a whole lot less work to do without them."

The marshal tipped back his Stetson and scratched his forehead. "Hadn't thought of it like that. Most of the guests in my jail do either booze it up, then go and get robbed over at the cathouse, or rob someone at the cathouse, then go and booze it up."

Daniel nodded. "So maybe you ought to join the committee."

"Nope." The marshal replaced his hat on his head just right and stepped out into the hotel lobby. "I'm not a joiner. Besides, the women in that group scare me."

"Speaking of scared," Daniel said, ushering the topic back to more urgent ground, "what do you make of this Batson fellow's threat?"

"Normally I'd not fret too much. A man who's been embarrassed by a woman and a child's not going to be the most rational fellow in the room." The lawman paused. "However, I know he's got connections to that fellow who started all the fuss with the miners' strike."

"Should I be concerned for my daughter's safety?"

"Excuse me, Mr. Beck, Marshal. Might I have a word with you?" Daniel turned to see Jeb Sanders coming toward them. "Marshal, you ought to know that Mr. Beck's little girl has gone and played a trick on the wrong man."

The marshal waved away Jeb's comment. "I told anyone with information to go and talk to my deputy."

"I did," Jeb countered, "but considering who I am, I doubt he believed me."

"Well, now that you mention it, why should I believe you? What with those cousins of yours—"

"Marshal, I am blood kin to those two, but that doesn't mean we were cut from the same cloth." Jeb paused to give Daniel an even stare. "I got myself dunked in Casper Creek last summer, and I'm a different man. A changed man."

"One swim in the creek and you're different?" The marshal snorted. "That's a good one, Sanders."

"You go ahead and laugh, Marshal, but the Lord and me are fast friends now, and He'll bear out what I can't prove."

"You sound like you mean it," Daniel said. "So maybe you could tell me what you think the deputy didn't believe. After all, I'm responsible for Charlotte and Miss Cooper's being here in the first place."

Sanders nodded. "What they told you about wanting to get back at you and other mine owners for what they didn't accomplish in the strike. I've heard the same, sir, and not just from him."

"That's just grumbling," the marshal said. "Nobody's got any proof."

"He chased my daughter and threatened her, and I intend to press charges," Daniel said. "So there's your proof."

The marshal paused a second before nodding. "It'll do for now, but I can't hold Batson forever. Eventually, he'll serve his time and go free."

"That's fine," Daniel said. "When that happens, my daughter and her governess will be back in Denver, where that man and his kind can't get to them."

"All right, then," the marshal said. He tipped his hat and strode out of the hotel.

"What're you going to do until then?" Sanders asked after the marshal took his leave.

"Do?" Daniel paused. "I hadn't thought of it. Post some guards, I guess."

"That's a good idea. You got anybody in mind?"

"I suppose one or two of the officers might be persuaded to take on an extra job working for me while we're here."

The miner shook his head. "Don't see how that's possible, sir. They're still down a man. Until a replacement's hired for the man my sorry cousins killed, they're likely not going to find extra time to work for anybody."

"You said you're a believing man, am I right?"

Sanders grinned. "I am, sir. Almost a year now."

Daniel placed his hand on Jeb's shoulder. "Then I'd appreciate it if you'd say a prayer for our safety. I'm not minimizing the risk, but if the Lord wants us to leave here unscathed, there's nothing Batson and his men can do about it."

But as he parted company with Sanders and headed upstairs, Daniel struggled with believing what he knew in his heart to be true. Or perhaps, he decided as he reached the doors of the Governor's Suite, his faith just hadn't been stretched quite that far yet.

How Abraham had done it, Daniel would never know.

21

There are times when things are going so well that one cannot help
but wonder when they will take a turn down the wrong path. Such,
it seemed, was the fate of Mae Winslow, Woman of the West. And
yet, when she spied Deadwood up ahead, she knew she'd finally
found the trail that led home.

A quick check above showed only blue skies, and there were no
snakes below. Nor did it appear she'd be picking the remains of any
bats from her hair.

All was well and home loomed ahead, as did the thought of seeing dear Henry.

Suddenly terror gripped the fair maiden, the likes of which
she'd not felt since the train upon which she rode experienced a
broken brake line going down Kimbles Mountain.

ᏦᏯ

Hiram arranged for a deputy to stay outside the Presidential Suite until
his shift started at five. After that, another deputy came on but could
only remain until ten. As he left, Daniel took up his place outside the
door.

He'd just settled into his chair when Ira Stegman ambled up, a worried look on his face. "You can't stay out here, Daniel."

"Don't be ridiculous."

"No," Ira said. "You've got to go back to your room. It's not proper."
He paused. "I've told my wife I'll see to it, so please do as I ask."

Daniel thought to argue but instead decided to strike a deal. "I'll go back to my room if you'll provide protection for my daughter and her governess in there."

"Done." Ira smiled. "Now, go to your room so I can go to mine."

Daniel crossed his arms over his chest and shook his head. "Not so fast, Ira. Exactly what will you be doing to protect them?"

"We've got a full house tonight," the hotel owner said, "and my brother's visiting from Central City."

"I fail to understand how either of these things will keep Charlotte and Miss Cooper safe."

"The full house means plenty of ears to hear if there's trouble."

"And your brother from Central City?"

Ira laughed. "He's a prizefighter."

Daniel leaned forward. "But is he any good?"

Ira shrugged. "He's undefeated."

"All right, then," Daniel said. "I'll leave this chair when your brother comes to sit in it. Tell him to name his price."

Another laugh. "You're serious?"

"I am."

Five minutes later, a man of considerable girth and muscles bounded up the stairs. The price for a night's worth of guarding was high, but Daniel didn't care. He would have gladly paid twice that, not that he intended to let Ira's brother know.

"Good night," Daniel said. To his surprise, the fellow picked up his chair and moved it over beside the staircase. "What are you doing?"

"Mary told me it wasn't proper to sit outside the door."

Daniel slapped his forehead and took two long, deep breaths before finding his voice. "What is your name?"

"Sam," the monster of a man said. "Sam Stegman."

"Pleased to make your acquaintance." He paused to shake the big fellow's hand and found his grip like iron. "All right, Sam, I paid good money for you to keep watch over my daughter and her governess. Please tell me what's improper about that."

"Oh, I don't have to understand it," Sam said. "My brother's been hitched to Mary Stegman more than ten years, and not once can I remember him winning a fight with her." He shrugged. "I guess Ira told you I'm a prizefighter." When Daniel nodded, he continued. "Well, I didn't learn to win without calculating the odds."

"I see."

"Yeah, and the odds of going against Mary Stegman and winning are just about zero." He paused. "So when she tells me I can watch over your gals from the stairs, I just say, 'Yes ma'am.' Now, I understand if you want to lower the price or find someone else, but I've got to tell you, I don't think that would suit Mary at all."

"I can see your point." Daniel gestured to the door of the Presidential Suite. "But understand mine. The least little sound comes from that room, and you're to treat it like the battle of your life. Understand?"

Sam nodded. "Mary fixed me up with strong coffee, so I'll be awake. You go on to sleep and don't worry about a thing."

The idea sounded plausible in theory, Daniel sleeping while the prizefighter stood guard, but it proved impossible in practice. Despite the cool nighttime temperatures in Leadville, his room felt stifling. When he opened his window, he heard every sound going on three floors below.

In either case, sleep was impossible.

He lay on his back, his fingers laced behind his head, and chastised himself as a fool while the heat gathered in the room. He should have known it was too soon after the strike to bring Charlotte to Leadville.

Further, he should never have left her on her own to return upstairs. He should have watched her go inside and waited for her to wave through the window.

Daniel rolled over onto his stomach and punched his pillow twice. *God, why didn't You warn me she was like this?*

But as he lay his head on the pillow, Daniel knew He had. More than once. Through things Elias, Tova, Miss Cooper, and others had told him. He'd loved the child too much to believe her capable of the things she'd been accused of.

All of this he would have to address back home in Denver. Tonight, however, his prayers centered on protection for those he loved. Indeed, God had sent him not just one bodyguard, but three: two police officers and a prizefighter. For that, Daniel gave thanks. And He'd also seen fit that Miss Cooper knew how to use a firearm. Again, he professed his heartfelt thanks.

Continuing in this way, Daniel soon figured the blessings in his life far outweighed all else. By degrees, he felt himself relax.

And then he heard a muffled scream.

Gennie woke at the sound of a scream to find Charlotte sitting upright. Even in the moonlight, she could tell the child was barely awake. She reached for her wrapper.

"Did you have a nightmare?"

Charlotte nodded, whimpering, and Gennie climbed out of bed to go to her. Someone knocked, likely Mr. Beck.

"We're fine," she called. "Charlotte had a bad dream."

"All right." It was the girl's father. "Might I help her to sleep again?"

"Sir," an unfamiliar voice said, "Mary won't allow you to go in there."

"Charlotte, let me check who's out there with your father." Gennie went to the door and opened it just enough to see Daniel and a man of massive size standing nearby. "Who are you?" she asked the giant.

"That's Sam," Mr. Beck said. "He's Ira's brother. He's a prizefighter."

She turned to repeat the information to Charlotte.

"Tonight I'm guarding your door." Sam pointed to the stairs. "From there, because it's not proper to sit outside."

Again Gennie relayed the information to her charge. "Well, good night, then," she said when Charlotte called her name.

Gennie went to the girl and sat on the edge of her bed. "Do you think you could sleep if I were to sit with you for a bit?"

"Maybe," Charlotte said, though a few minutes later the child once again slept soundly.

Tiptoeing back toward her bed, Gennie paused at the window. Even at this time of night, the streets of Leadville were filled with people. Men fell in and out of saloons, assisted or lured by women dressed in silks and satins.

Gennie shut the curtain and shed her wrapper, then climbed back into bed. Today had been a long one, fraught with excitement. At the thought of aiming a pistol at anyone, she shuddered. What had come over her? When she saw that man chasing Charlotte, all she could think of was saving the child. If that meant shooting a man, then she would have.

She let out a long breath. "Thank You, Lord, that there were no bullets in the pistol."

Continuing in that vein, she offered prayers until her thoughts began to scatter. Finally, she managed to close both eyes and keep them closed.

Sleep overtook her in moments, or at least it felt like sleep. Her body heavy and her mind slow as molasses, she barely reacted when someone in the room below banged on the wall. Waiting for more, she heard no further noise. Then came heavy footsteps. Sam.

"Miss Cooper?"

"We're fine, Sam."

"Very well." His paces took him away from the door.

She'd almost fallen back to sleep when Charlotte let out a loud scream. Gennie bounded from the bed without bothering to throw on her wrapper. Unless the child was quieted quickly, the entire floor would be awake.

This time, however, Charlotte refused to be consoled. Her screams split the night and almost covered the sound of Sam's knocking at the door.

"We're fine," she called. "Just a bad dream. No need to worry."

"Open the door," she thought she heard someone say, but with Charlotte screaming in her ear, there was little she could discern.

Someone pounded again on the door, or at least it seemed that way from the changes in light she could see beneath the door. Perhaps it was Sam pacing. Or, given the volume of the girl's shrieks, it might be any or all of the folks unlucky enough to be staying on the third floor tonight.

Gennie opened her mouth to respond, but before she could, the door flew open and a man covered in some sort of cloak rushed inside. In the dark, all she knew was this did not look anything like the monster assigned to guard them from down the hall.

Her screams joined Charlotte's. She called for help and Daniel Beck, caring not that she hadn't thought to slip back into her wrapper.

Then the gaslights came on, and Daniel Beck stood in front of her.

He reached her before she could flee to him. He embraced her quickly, then flew to Charlotte's side and took his daughter in his arms. "Are you hurt?"

Gennie looked down at her state of undress, then over at Charlotte, who had finally awakened and now regarded them with curiosity. Reaching for a blanket to cover up only made things worse, for the bed covers had been tucked in so tight by the efficient Mrs. Stegman that it was nearly impossible to remove them.

She finally managed it, just as she realized the noise had brought not only Daniel Beck, but also most of the occupants of the third floor, along with Mr. and Mrs. Stegman. The only person she didn't immediately see was the bodyguard. He appeared a few seconds later, out of breath and looking as if he'd just wakened from a deep sleep.

Mr. Beck stood and grasped her by the elbows. "What happened?"

"Screams," she managed as she pulled away. Her breath came in gasps, the words unable to form despite her best efforts. By degrees, she realized Mr. Beck wore not a cloak but a bed sheet. It slipped off, revealing an expanse of bare chest he quickly hid by tying the fabric on like a toga.

"Try again," he said. "Was someone in here? Have you or Charlotte been harmed?"

"Then more screams, and I couldn't hear the knock. And then the door opened, and without telling me who it was, the man…you…" She gasped for breath, then pointed to the door. "Hurt? I don't think so," she finally managed.

Slowly Mr. Beck turned to greet their audience. His ears turned red, and he cleared his throat. "It's really quite humorous how this happened," he said as he adjusted his toga.

"Out of the room at once, Mr. Beck," Mr. Stegman said, nothing in his voice even suggesting humor.

"But my daughter…" He pointed to Charlotte, who looked no worse for the fright she'd given them all.

"Your daughter looks fine," Mary Stegman said. "Your governess, however, looks as if she might have just climbed from the bed."

A stunned murmur rolled forward from the back of the crowd assembled in the hallway. By the time it reached Mary, she'd obviously become immune.

"Leave my establishment at once," she said.

"But…" Mr. Beck stammered on about payments and friendships, then began again to protest his innocence. As an afterthought, he also added that Gennie too was unsoiled.

Before long, Gennie had heard quite enough. "Excuse me," she said, but Daniel and Mrs. Stegman continued to argue. "Excuse me," she repeated, but only Charlotte seemed to hear. She'd absolutely had enough. "Would you all just stop talking and listen to me?"

The room fell into stunned silence, and Gennie realized she had no words of brilliance at the ready.

"This is not what it appears," she said. "You see, I am certain the events of the day were just too much for Charlotte. She had a nightmare and could not wake from it."

"An excellent theory," Mrs. Stegman said, "and yet you're standing here with no shame whatsoever wearing my bed quilt over what looks to be quite an expensive nightgown. I told you today that things are not always as they seem." She gave Gennie a disgusted look. "I believe you've proved this fact, Miss Cooper."

"No, honestly," Gennie continued. "There's nothing going on between Charlotte's father and me."

"Then why would that child say you kissed her father?" When Gennie had no immediate words of rebuttal, the innkeeper shook her head. "I think what we have here is two people who couldn't control themselves even though there is an impressionable girl right under their noses."

"Look now," Mr. Beck said. "Come on, Ira. You know me. You

know I'm not that kind of man." When Mr. Stegman looked away, Gennie's employer turned to Mrs. Stegman. "Mary, listen to reason. You've got a wrong impression of us. I vow I'll not let you down if you'll just brew a pot of coffee and let us all talk about this downstairs in the kitchen."

"All of us?" She glanced behind her, then returned her gaze to Mr. Beck. "I don't think the occupants of the entire third floor would fit in my kitchen. For that gathering, you'll need a bigger venue." She laughed, but the sound held no humor. "What say we wake up your friend Horace Tabor and borrow his opera house? Indeed, that might hold all the people who have been forced to witness your cavorting about in your unmentionables with a woman in her nightgown." She paused to take a breath. "An unmarried woman you have already kissed."

Another pause, and then Charlotte ran to Gennie and began to wail.

"Everything's going to be fine, Buttercup," Daniel said.

But from the looks on the faces staring at him, it would not. The situation was ludicrous at best and downright irritating. He'd put too much money and time into the town of Leadville to have their citizenry accusing him of such outrageous acts.

He adjusted his toga and attempted a glare. When the president of the Greater Leadville Beautification and Improvement Society looked away, Mr. Beck turned to its first lady. "You know me, Mary. I set you and Ira up with this establishment because I believed in what you wanted to accomplish. You're good people, and this is an upstanding establishment."

"Exactly the reason we can't tolerate lewd behavior." Mary looked down her nose at his costume, then back up at his face. "There are any number of other places where this kind of behavior is not only allowed, but encouraged. Go there and leave us be."

Anger flared and Daniel clenched his fists. "Would someone just listen?"

"Go right ahead," Ira said. "Deny it all, please, or explain it away, so I can get some sleep."

Daniel looked to Ira's brother. "Sam," he said, "you've been outside the door all night. Tell them this is not what it looks like. Tell them I've been in my own room until just now, like the rest of you."

Sam looked sheepish. "Well, actually, the first thing I saw was you here in the room. You must've been awfully quiet when you snuck in to see the lady."

"But I didn't sneak—"

"I've heard enough, Daniel Beck, and I'll not have you and your kind corrupting anyone else. Out of my hotel!" Mary Stegman shouted. "The whole lot of you, and don't come back until you've made a decent woman of this, this...tart!"

"Now, see here," Daniel said, "Miss Cooper is a fine, upstanding woman who would never corrupt anyone." He glanced over his shoulder to see the governess huddled beneath a blanket in a condition that certainly belied his statement. "Why not ask Charlotte what happened? She is innocent in all this and should be able to give an honest accounting of the events."

Mary looked doubtful, but Ira stepped forward and nodded. "Yes, all right. Let's hear what the girl has to say."

"Charlotte, honey," Daniel said as gently as he could manage, "would you tell them what happened tonight?"

His daughter nodded and nestled closer to Miss Cooper. "I heard scary-people noises."

Daniel took note of the crowd at the door, then focused on Mary

Stegman. Irritation still rode high, but he'd not let his reputation or that of Miss Cooper be ruined over a misunderstanding.

"Charlotte, could you tell the nice people about how you screamed, and then Miss Cooper and I came to your rescue?"

"Oh yes," she said. "When I opened my eyes, both of you were here. You hugged us, just like the day when you hugged Miss Cooper, only this time I was there too."

"When your papa hugged Miss Cooper?" Ira Stegman asked.

Charlotte nodded. "I was watching from the window that time, and they were right out in front of the house, so it wasn't really like spying because anyone could have seen them when my papa kissed her."

"Out!" Mary Stegman said, then turned to her husband. "And if you don't see to it, I will."

Ira caught Daniel's gaze and shrugged. "Mary's right. How can we change this town if we on the committee don't live up to the moral standards we voted in, Daniel?"

"Standards?"

Ira shook his head. "You were there when we took the vote. In fact, if memory serves me correctly, you seconded the motion."

Had he? So much had happened since he'd joined the committee in the opera house. Perhaps he had voted something in without completely understanding what he'd agreed to.

The sheet began to slip, and he gripped it tighter. "So exactly what rule did I agree to that you now think I've broken?"

Ira looked him up and down, then raked his gaze over Miss Cooper as if she were a prize heifer up at auction. "A code of general moral decency, Daniel. While it may be fine for others to go out and frequent the sporting women, the Lord says it's not fine, and so does the committee. And that's just one of the rules you've broken here tonight."

"Are you calling Miss Cooper a—"

"I'm saying she was paid for something, Daniel. And from the looks of it, watching your daughter is just one of her duties."

Daniel took a step forward, rage blurring his vision. And yet his daughter was watching, which meant he must temper not only his words, but also his behavior. "I will not have you refer to Miss Cooper in such a way, nor will I tolerate your insinuations."

Ira's gaze didn't waver. "I'll not make you pack up, but you can't stay with us the rest of the night. Take the woman and your daughter and go. You can send someone to get your things tomorrow." He paused. "And per the terms of the agreement you've broken, there are penalties. I'll have to review the wording and get back to you on exactly what those are, so you can count on a visit from me tomorrow at your office." Ira swept his gaze over Miss Cooper in a less-than-gentlemanly fashion. "Likely you'll sleep through breakfast, so let's say a quarter to ten."

From the back of the crowd, Hiram elbowed his way through. One look at him and Daniel knew he'd slept through all but the last few minutes of the fiasco.

"What's going on here?" he asked. "And where in the world are your pants, Mr. Beck?"

22

And yet terror was a companion she could easily shed, even when it threatened to stay far longer than it was welcome. Mae took a deep breath and remembered who she was: Mae Winslow, Woman of the West. Domesticity was nothing to fear.

Slipping back into the lace-curtained cottage with furniture from back East and needlepoint pillows on the settee was accomplished easily enough. Remembering how to act like she lived here was not nearly as simple.

Oh, it was her home, bought and paid for with the countless bounties she'd collected over the years, but tatting lace doilies when she attempted it was fraught with more danger than killing snakes.

Still, her respectable lawyer awaited, and Mae would make tea and cookies and welcome him into her parlor if it killed her.

And given the face on the other side of the back door, it might.

&oc;

Daniel leaned his elbows on his desk and tried in vain to stretch out the kinks in his back. With only one room left at the Clarendon, he'd cajoled Sam into guarding the women at that hotel, then slept on the floor of Hiram's room back at the Mountain Palace.

And he'd practically had to beg to be allowed to do that.

With each twinge of his back, his anger increased. The fact that a law-abiding father couldn't see to the welfare of his daughter chafed at him.

"I'm all for this campaign to run the seedier side of the community out of the city limits," he told Hiram, "but I'm not sure what to make of it when I'm tarred with the same brush as people who actually deserve it."

Hiram didn't look up, though he did pause in his scribbling.

"And then there are these ridiculous sanctions Ira prattled on about." He stood and began to pace. "I'm a businessman, Hiram, and a good one. I've had more than my share of opportunities to indulge in ill-mannered behavior, but have I?"

He waited until it became apparent his second-in-command did not plan to respond. Of course Hiram knew the answer.

"That's right. I haven't. And why?" This time he didn't bother to wait. "Because I am a man of honor. Of character. Of..." Daniel once again sank into his chair. "I'm in big trouble, aren't I?"

His assistant nodded, setting aside his notes. "It appears so. I've had a chance to see this resolution you and the other members of the committee drafted."

"And?"

Hiram sighed. "And the moral turpitude clause is a concern."

"A concern?" Daniel shook his head. "How so?"

"It appears last night's lapse in judgment may actually have actionable consequences." Hiram steepled his hands. "The question is whether Mr. Stegman will let this debacle die a quiet death or choose to make an example out of you."

Daniel picked up his pen, then set it back against the inkwell. "You've met Mary Stegman. Which do you think will happen?"

Checking his watch, Hiram shrugged. "You're about to find out. What say I go and fetch the trunks? The clerk over at the Clarendon promised there would be another room vacant for us tonight."

The idea of sharing a room with Hiram irked him, but not as much as the reason for it. He nodded and sent the man on his way. While he awaited Ira's arrival, Daniel bypassed the stack of documents needing his attention and reached into the drawer for the Bible he kept there.

A ribbon held his place in Isaiah, and he opened to that spot. "'Behold, I have refined thee, but not with silver; I have chosen thee in the furnace of affliction.'" He sighed. "Isn't that the truth?"

Daniel turned to see Ira Stegman entering his office, and rose, setting his Bible aside. He gestured to the seat across from him, then remained standing until the hotel owner had made himself comfortable.

"Well, now," Stegman said, "I'd like to think you're actually reading that Bible rather than just hoping I'd catch you looking at it."

Giving in to his temper would serve no purpose. As a businessman, he knew this. As a man falsely accused and royally aggrieved, he strongly wished otherwise. He resisted the urge to pound his fists on the desk and demand an apology.

For now.

"I can see you're a man of few words this morning, Daniel, so I'll be brief as well."

Daniel lifted a brow but kept his hands hidden.

"This morning we called an emergency meeting of the committee," Ira said, "and a vote was taken on the meaning of the rules we all agreed to, you included."

"Funny," Daniel said with what he hoped would be deadly calm. "I don't recall an invitation to that meeting." He paused to let the words settle hard on the man he'd sat beside in church and worked beside in the mines before he bankrolled the man's hotel venture. "Any reason why all the members weren't called in? Or was it to be sure I'd be hung out to dry without opposition?"

Ira exhaled a long breath and his features relaxed. "Look, Daniel," he said, "if it were up to me, I'd turn my back on the whole thing and pretend it never happened. Likely every man standing in the hallway last night feels the same way, and let me tell you, we had a long list of important men staying with us last night."

Daniel nodded. He'd recognized more than a few faces among the crowd—not that any of them had looked him in the eye.

"And here's the thing," Ira continued. "I took a poll—an informal one, mind you—before the meeting started, and not a man there was willing to say a word against you."

For the first time since last night, Daniel felt his temper subside a notch. "I'm glad to hear it, Ira."

The other man shifted positions. "Well, don't be too glad. That's the good news. The bad news is our wives don't share our opinion."

"I see." Daniel stifled a smile though he should have felt outrage. "So the womenfolk would have me hanged?"

"No," Ira said slowly, "I believe talk of hanging was reserved for the pretty governess of yours. You they preferred to see tarred and feathered and run out of town on a rail."

"Comforting." Daniel regarded Stegman a moment. "I'm a businessman, Ira. I've enough concern just keeping my daughter and her governess safe until we can return to Denver. I don't have the time nor the inclination to worry about what a gaggle of housewives think." He paused. "Though I am sure your wife's opinion would be of the greatest value to me."

Ira chuckled. "Don't be so certain, though I do believe I have a solution for the issue of the womenfolk's safety."

"Oh?" Daniel leaned forward. "What's that?"

"My brother's taken a liking to the two of them. Said Miss Cooper's a real lady, and your daughter, she's quite the charmer."

Daniel smiled in spite of himself. "Indeed."

"He's willing to act as bodyguard as long as you'll have him." Ira paused to shift positions. "I told him to hold off talking to you about it until I had a chance to give you my spiel. Chances are you might not want anything to do with me and my family after you hear the rest of what I've got to say."

"Go on."

"A few of us have been pondering this." He studied the ceiling a minute before returning his attention to Daniel. "I think there's a way out of this mess that will make everyone happy. Well, maybe 'happy's' not the right word, but at least you won't be forced to sell off the Beck mines and leave town."

"Sell off the mines!" Daniel scrambled to his feet. "You and that idiotic committee for the beautification of whatever it is are absolutely certifiable."

"The Greater Leadville Beautification and Improvement Society," Ira said with a calmness that did not befit the situation. "And if you'll just hear me out, I think you'll agree the mayor and I have come up with a whopper of a fix for this."

"The mayor?"

Ira nodded. "Well, and the marshal. Pastor Kent's in on it too, but he didn't actually come up with the plan. Come to think of it, he never did officially approve of it, but I think that's just a formality."

"Ira," Daniel said carefully, "if you don't tell me what you're talking about pretty soon, I'm going to lose my temper." He paused. "You don't want that, trust me."

∞

Gennie held tight to the buggy seat with one hand and held her hand-kerchief over her nose with the other. Between the dust and the altitude, she'd decided this part of the Wild West was nothing at all like the place portrayed in Mae's stories.

"Where are we going?" she asked when the worst of the dust cloud, along with the crowd of buildings downtown, was behind them.

Daniel gestured toward the foothills where, he claimed, a decent view of Leadville awaited. "I thought to have a picnic, though I don't know if it will compare to the one we shared with the Finch ladies."

The reminder caused Gennie to wince. While she'd hoped the event might be an opportunity to draw Daniel and Anna closer together, quite the opposite seemed to have happened. Anna's mother went on and on about every conceivable topic under the sun while Anna nibbled on the contents of the food basket and looked longingly at Daniel Beck.

It was all highly frustrating. Perhaps she'd find a way to make the situation right today.

But first, she should mention the other situation, the one that caused them to be banished from the Mountain Palace Hotel. Daniel hadn't said a word about the incident, though Gennie could do nothing but think of the humiliation it must have brought him.

She'd certainly been horrified at the entire mess. What would her mother think if she knew?

But then, Mama would have been good and truly appalled long before last night. The incident at the Mountain Palace would have been just one more reason for the socially adept Mrs. Cooper to swoon.

Still, Gennie realized, as she held tight and watched the city slip behind her, she'd be leaving Colorado soon enough, while Mr. Beck would not. Long after last night was a distant memory for her, Daniel Beck would still have to see these people at church and do business with them. The poor man.

Then there was poor Charlotte. That she'd practically changed her entire opinion of Gennie since that horrible miner terrorized her was tempered by the fact that Charlotte would be left without her when Gennie returned to New York City.

It was a problem with no good solution.

"You're awful pensive," Mr. Beck said.

Gennie offered her employer a smile, though the butterflies in her stomach threatened to take flight at the distance they'd come up the mountain. "I suppose I am."

Their gazes collided. "Is Charlotte misbehaving?"

"The opposite, actually." She gave him a sideways glance and found he'd gone back to concentrating on the road ahead. "Though she was not pleased to be left with Sam today."

As she had a man waiting back in Manhattan, Gennie knew she shouldn't think such thoughts, but Daniel Beck was quite a handsome man. Not handsome in the conventional sense, for there was nothing pretty about him. Rather, he had a pleasant combination of features that made him easy on the eye, yet altogether interesting.

Were there enough days left in her stay, Gennie might have asked him how a man of British descent came about having a touch of southern accent and a houseman given to wearing Confederate regalia. Then there was the issue of his late wife. How did a man come to be presented with a five-year-old he didn't know he had by a woman he'd made his wife, then left behind in England? It was all so confusing, and yet so interesting.

There was that word again. Gennie sighed. If there was one term she could use to describe Daniel Beck, it would be *interesting*.

He cracked the reins, and the buggy jolted forward as they began their ascent into the green hills. Soon the remains of the dust filtered away, and the air became clear and crisp.

"I'd hoped to make good on my offer of a Wild West adventure," he said after a while, "but unfortunately, it appears safety has become an issue. For that, I apologize."

"There's no need," she said. "I'm sure you wouldn't have brought us here if you'd suspected there might be a problem."

"Indeed." His attention never veered from the road ahead, yet Gennie felt as if he were somehow observing her.

The buggy wheels came close to the edge of the road, and the incline became steeper. With each turn, the clouds came nearer, and Gennie's fears rose.

While she'd never been particularly afraid of heights, she'd never had to traverse a mountain road in an open buggy. Add in the lack of conversation, and she felt the urge to jump off the contraption and race back to town just to find level ground.

To her surprise, Daniel's hand covered hers. "I should have asked if you minded that we'd be going up into the mountains." He lifted his hand to grasp the reins and halt the horse's ascent. "I can take you back if you're uncomfortable."

"I am," she said with a nervous laugh, "but I think it's good for me, so get this buggy moving before I change my mind." She braved another look at Mr. Beck and found him smiling. "What?"

He shrugged and set the buggy in motion. "Miss Cooper, I can honestly say you are the most interesting woman I've ever met."

Her laughter came from pure amusement. "Mr. Beck, I can't decide whether or not that's the nicest thing a man's ever said to me."

"You let me know when you've decided," he said. "In the meantime, I want you to know I've got Hiram working on tickets back to Denver for tomorrow or the day after. I wish it were sooner, but there's just so few spots on that narrow-gauge line and too many folks wanting them."

"I understand." She paused to inhale more of the crisp air. "I know

I should be after last night, but I'm honestly in no hurry to leave Leadville. It's just so"—Gennie caught her breath as they turned a corner and the whole of Leadville lay before her—"beautiful."

"Beautiful? I suppose one who doesn't spend much time here would think so." He shrugged and urged the horses on. "Me? I see the smelters and the mines, and I know what it looked like before."

Gennie heard the wistfulness in his voice. "What did it look like?"

He laughed. "It was green. Not much else here, except the mining shacks and a few places in town where a man could get…"

She glanced over and saw his ears had turned red. "Mr. Beck," she said, "are you blushing?"

"No," he said as he returned her stare, "but if I finish that sentence, I guarantee I'd make you blush."

Surely he heard her gasp, but as the color faded from his face, the intensity did not diminish from his stare. Neither did the heat she felt building where moments ago butterflies had taken flight.

Gennie cleared her throat and looked away, trying to find another subject upon which to converse. When nothing came to mind save those topics fraught with danger, she elected to say nothing.

"Sam told us the marshal thought that awful man's claims were a bunch of hooey," she said when she could stand the silence no longer. "A few men wanting to make out like there was something when there's nothing." She shrugged. "I don't know what all of that means, but Sam says it's good."

Though he continued to concentrate on guiding the horses up the ever-narrowing road, Daniel Beck looked relieved. The buggy pitched and leaned, but the horses stayed surefooted and evenly paced.

Then the road became a path that leaned into the mountain. In order to keep from sliding against Mr. Beck, Gennie had to hold on to the buggy seat with both hands. At first, she accomplished this without difficulty. Then the heat of the afternoon, which had already warmed her shoulders and back, took its toll on her palms.

"Let go." Mr. Beck's voice was nearly a growl, so low and soft did he speak. "I'll catch you."

And he did, grasping her around the waist with one hand while expertly guiding the horses with the other. By the time they reached a grassy spot within view of the summit, Gennie decided she rather liked the mountains after all.

In fact, she could have remained right there, gazing over the distant landscape indefinitely, such was the beauty of the view. Her companion had not yet moved, either.

Her shoulder brushing his, Gennie sighed. "It's all so lovely."

"Lovely, yes," he said softly. "It is indeed."

Abruptly, Mr. Beck climbed down from the buggy, then helped her do the same. He handed her the basket and pointed to a rock outcropping a few yards away. "I'll tend to the horses if you want to go have a better look at the valley."

She wandered that direction but found more interest in looking back at Daniel Beck than she did in looking down at Leadville. "Where's your mine, Mr. Beck?" she asked when he joined her.

"There." He gestured toward a massive collection of buildings, some with smoke billowing from tall stacks and others looking much like the storefronts downtown. He pointed out the smelter and the mine shafts, then grew silent.

"What?" she asked when she caught him looking pensive.

He shook his head. "I was just thinking how one stupid mistake almost cost me all this."

Gennie turned away from the forests of aspen and blue spruce to lean her back on the rocks and look up at a sky so blue it hurt to stare at it. She closed her eyes and let the sun bathe her face, not caring if she developed freckles. Each one, she decided, would carry a memory of her Wild West adventure. Of today, high in the foothills above Leadville.

The warmth of the rough granite seeped through the thin cotton of her frock to heat her back. When she lifted her eyelids a tiny bit, she could observe Daniel Beck without being noticed.

He seemed deep in thought, the corners of his eyes crinkled against the glare of the noonday sun. When he glanced down at her, she remained very still, hoping he would not know she'd been peering up at him from beneath her lashes. Slowly, his gaze washed over her, and it was all she could do not to open her eyes. Was it the sun or her close proximity to Daniel Beck that bathed her in such warmth?

He leaned onto his elbows, looking away. Disappointment set in, but then his attention returned to her.

"Miss Cooper," he whispered. "Open your eyes."

She did, and the sight of him took her breath away. She'd seen long-ing on the faces of too many fresh-faced schoolboys and attentive sons of family friends not to recognize the emotion. On Daniel Beck, how-ever, the look was no safe wishing-for-a-kiss expression. The look was more than a promise and slightly less than a demand. She felt fear and anticipation in equal measure as she waited for the moment he would fit his lips to hers.

He ran a callused finger over her lower lip, reached for her hands and grasped them in his, then pulled her toward him. The abrupt change in position combined with the thin air to make her head spin.

She crumpled at his feet. For a moment, the world went black.

She blinked and all was right again, though she now lay in what felt to be soft grass. "I feel like such a ninny," Gennie said. She attempted to rise up on one elbow, only to have the mountain move and knock her back to the ground.

"Altitude sickness," someone said as her eyes closed and strong arms wrapped around her. "Miss Cooper," she heard through a wave of something that felt like exhaustion. "Open your eyes, Miss Cooper."

She tried, but couldn't accomplish the feat. She preferred to snuggle against this warmth she'd found.

"Eugenia." Pause. "Gennie."

A palm cradled her jaw. She leaned into it.

Then came the kiss. Soft, tender, and just as warm as the sunshine she'd enjoyed only a moment ago. Or was it longer? She had no idea.

With regret, she opened her eyes.

"Welcome back, Sleeping Beauty," Daniel Beck said. "It appears you've got a case of altitude sickness."

"Is that what it was?" She looked deep into his eyes. "Did you kiss me?"

"Don't you remember?"

She blinked and nearly allowed herself to give in to sleep once more. "I thought I was dreaming."

"So," he said softly, "did I."

23

Ed shot at her through the door's small glass window, but such were her finely honed instincts that Mae ducked as the bullet whizzed by. She rolled to the floor and found she'd missed a spot while mopping. "The better to catch it with my lace handkerchief," she said, handling the stain while keeping a watch for Ed.

When the shadow fell across the steaming teapot, she knew she had him. Now she only had to dispatch the criminal before dear Henry came for tea. It was a difficult job, but not above the exceptional skills of Mae Winslow, Woman of the West.

First, however, she must check on the cookies.

GG

The ride back to Leadville was much less memorable. When Mr. Beck pulled the buggy to a halt in front of the Clarendon, Gennie felt as if she'd walked up the mountain and back, rather than ridden.

Leaning on Mr. Beck's arm, Gennie allowed him to help her inside and seat her at a table in the dining room he'd chosen for them. A uniformed waiter soon brought a glass of water.

"No, thank you," Gennie said, resting her elbows on the table. As she cradled her chin to keep her head up, she had the absurd thought that Mama would be horrified that she'd committed yet another breach of manners.

"Drink it," Daniel countered in a surprisingly no-nonsense tone. "You'll feel better."

A beautiful young woman with stunning eyes and exquisite taste in clothing moved toward them through the maze of tables. She leaned toward Mr. Beck with what Gennie recognized as the practiced air of a coquette.

"You get her drunk too early in the evening, Danny Boy?"

"Mind your manners," he said with a chuckle that jolted Gennie wide awake. "It's altitude sickness."

"Isn't that funny?" The powdered and pampered female helped herself to the seat next to Mr. Beck, then leaned toward him, her expensive fur—a ludicrous garment to wear in July—slipping to reveal a nearly bare shoulder. "I thought she might have Daniel Beck disease. All the bad girls get it."

"Behave." One word, yet Gennie couldn't decide if it was a dare or a demand.

"Me? Misbehave?" The woman offered Mr. Beck a dazzling smile, then bumped shoulders with him. "Not in public."

"That's enough, Mrs. Doe."

"Call me Baby," she said.

Baby? Of all the nerve. What sort of man flirted with a beautiful woman in front of his...

His daughter's governess. That's all she was, and all she should be.

After all, she had a perfectly suitable and reliable banker awaiting her return. Likely he'd already made a trip to Tiffany and Company for a diamond solitaire in that new style that was all the rage.

Except that when she looked at Mr. Beck, she forgot all about aqua-colored boxes and glittering diamonds. For the first time since stepping onto Colorado soil, Gennie wondered if Daniel Beck just might be her Wild West adventure.

She tried not to frown, but exhaustion kept her from succeeding.

"Look there," the woman said in a singsong voice. "Your girl's waking up."

"I'm not his girl," Gennie said as she attempted to stand. She got four steps from the table before returning to land in her chair once more. "I just don't feel so well." She looked at the beautiful woman, beyond caring about propriety. "You can have him, you know. I'm just the governess."

The woman's attention darted to the lone male at the table, who seemed aggravatingly smug at the jousting going on between the females. "What are you smiling at, Daniel Beck? Are you going to let this woman continue to believe she's just the governess?"

Mr. Beck's smile disappeared, and he suddenly looked as if he might bolt and run at any moment. Meanwhile, Gennie wished she could.

"Don't worry, Governess. I don't want your man." She rose with a wink. "I've already got one. I would love to get to know you better. You look like you'd be a lot of fun." She paused. "Well, after you kick this altitude sickness, that is."

Gennie managed a smile. Maybe this woman wasn't so bad, after all. "I'm Gennie," she said. "Gennie Cooper."

"Pleased to meet you, Gennie Cooper." The woman leaned over to shake her hand. "My friends call me Baby. Baby Doe. It's been a pleasure, Gennie. Danny Boy."

Taking a sip of water, Gennie watched Baby Doe glide from the room. Mr. Beck, however, was watching Gennie.

"I'm fine," she said.

He offered a weak smile. "I don't suppose the two of us will ever manage a picnic."

"We don't have much luck at that, do we?"

His expression grew serious. "It's probably for the best. I'm not certain being alone with you is a good idea." Before Gennie could comment, he continued. "Look, I must confess the real purpose for taking that buggy ride today was not to have a picnic." He paused. "I've spoken to Ira Stegman."

Another sip of water, and Gennie began to feel closer to normal. "Oh?" She set the glass down. "Why?"

"He thinks this whole thing will blow over if you promise never to return to Leadville."

"Never? That's so" — she paused — "permanent."

Mr. Beck shrugged. "I doubt they'd enforce it after a few years if you decided to come back for a visit."

Gennie tried to imagine returning to Leadville with Chandler, but the image wouldn't come.

"No," she said, "I don't think that would be much of a hardship. How and to whom do I make this promise?"

He looked a bit sheepish. "There's more."

"More?" She gave him a sideways look. "How much more?"

"Ira seems to think that if you admit you staged everything to try and trap me..." He froze. "No, I'll not have a woman take the fall for me."

He pushed away from the table and stalked out of the dining room. Still somewhat unsteady on her feet, Gennie nonetheless managed to catch up to him before he reached the street. "Where are you going?"

"To call a meeting of the Greater Leadville Beautification and Improvement Society." He stopped on the sidewalk to shake his head. "No, wait."

"What?"

"I'm not going to dignify their petty complaints. Until we get on that train back to Denver, it's business as usual." He started walking again and glanced at her over his shoulder. "If you need me, I'll be at the mine office."

Gennie watched him for a moment, then turned to go back inside. She'd almost made it to the lobby stairs when someone called her name. Turning, she saw a group of women waiting near the door, and her heart sank. The only one she recognized was Mary Stegman.

"Might we have a moment of your time, Miss Cooper?" Mrs. Stegman said. "We'd like to speak to you regarding last night's incident."

Squaring her shoulders, Gennie exhaled slowly. "Anything you want to say to me, you can say here."

Another woman stepped forward. "I don't think you want us to do that, dear." She gave the lobby a cursory glance. "What with the Clarendon being such a busy place."

"All right, then," Gennie said. "I'll invite you upstairs, but I warn you I've charge of a ten-year-old girl. I don't want her to overhear something she doesn't need to know about."

"I'd say it's too late for that," a woman in a blue dress said. Several others snickered.

Without bothering to respond, Gennie led the women upstairs. The group stepped into the hotel room she shared with Charlotte, and Sam quickly slipped out.

As soon as Charlotte had been given a book to read, Gennie addressed the group. "I'm willing to listen," she said, "but please understand I am just the governess."

And only a temporary one, at that.

"Then I'll get right to the point," Mary Stegman said. "If Daniel Beck doesn't do right by you, then we've got a serious problem in Leadville."

"Mrs. Stegman," Gennie said carefully, "any action Mr. Beck does or does not take will hardly affect the city of Leadville." She stopped to turn her attention to each of the women in turn before continuing. "I am his employee, nothing more. I'm certainly not looking to capture him for a husband." Out of the corner of her eye, she saw Charlotte take notice. "If you'll excuse me, I'd like to get back to doing my job."

"I'm not satisfied that this has been handled properly," said a woman in a green summer frock and matching hat. "I saw her walk inside looking faint. How do we know she's not, well, *you know?*"

Gennie recoiled in horror at the woman's insinuations. "I demand an apology," she said. "You're not only making an unsubstantiated accusation, but you are doing so in a public forum. Were I back home in New York, you would certainly be hearing from my lawyers."

A twitter of laughter rippled across the well-dressed crowd.

"You know what you are?" Gennie continued, her anger building. "You're a bunch of bullies. Neither Daniel nor I have done anything wrong, unless perhaps you would fault us both for caring for Charlotte too much."

"'Daniel,' is it?" someone toward the back said.

"Of course she's on a first-name basis with the man," another said. "After all, they're—"

"Hush now," Mrs. Stegman said, "and mind there's an innocent child present."

Having heard her name, Charlotte set the book aside and came to stand by Gennie. "Is Papa in trouble?"

Gennie gathered the girl into her arms. "No. Your papa's a good man who is doing the right thing."

"Why don't we let him decide that." Mrs. Stegman said.

"Decide what?" Gennie asked.

"Let him decide if he will do the right thing." The older woman's eyes narrowed. "Is there a reason you wouldn't want to come with us to pay a visit to Mr. Beck and settle this once and for all?"

"If it will end this silly situation, then yes, I'll come." She squeezed Charlotte's hand. "You stay and finish your book, and I'll have Sam come back and stay with you."

In no time, Gennie found herself in a wagon with half a dozen smirking women. Along the way to the Beck mine, their party was joined by a handful of men, some of whom she recognized, who appeared even less happy to be in the parade than she.

By the time the wagon rolled to a stop in front of the mine, Gennie had begun to wonder whether agreeing to come here with them was a good idea after all.

"Uh-oh." Hiram looked out the window of the mine's small front office, then back at Daniel. "I knew the women were on the warpath, but I didn't expect they'd come all the way out here." He paused. "And they've got Miss Cooper with them."

"They do?" Daniel stalked to the window, then bit back the choice words he longed to say. "Well, it had to come to this, I suppose. Go and let them in."

Hiram barely managed to sidestep the stampede as the doors opened. Calico and cross looks seemed the order of the day, though Miss Cooper did her best to stand away from the crowd. That is, until Ira's wife took her by the elbow and thrust her forward.

"Mr. Beck, I trust you know why we've come to see you today."

Daniel looked past the riled-up females to the five or six shame-faced men leaning against the back wall. "Ira, you letting your wife speak for you today?" he called.

"I reckon I'll wait my turn," the other man responded.

"Fair enough." Daniel nodded to Mrs. Stegman. "To answer your question, ma'am, I figure I'm going to hear about it anyway, so why don't you tell me why you're here."

"I'm here because you've violated a sacred oath, Mr. Beck." Mrs. Stegman's voice rose an octave as she said his name. "And as such I...no, *we* demand you right this wrong and make this girl an honest woman."

He allowed his gaze to slide across the crowd to collide with the blue eyes of the woman in question. "An honest woman?" Daniel pretended to think as he scratched his head. "Miss Cooper, what have you been telling these ladies about me?"

Before she could respond, Mary stepped between them and pointed her finger at Daniel. "Don't you make light of these proceedings. You've a serious charge leveled against you, sir."

"A serious charge?" He shook his head. "Oh, my dear Mrs. Stegman. There's been nothing serious about Eugenia Cooper since she moved into my home. Lest you think me wrong, ask her about her ultimatum to remove herself or my chicken." His chuckle was carefully scripted to punctuate the jest without causing offense.

It failed miserably.

A moment later, all six women were shouting at once. Only Gennie Cooper and the men kept their silence. The commotion continued until a shrill whistle pierced the air.

In an instant, silence reigned. Ira stepped to the front of the stunned crowd.

"Daniel, while I'm not saying the ladies don't have a point, I will admit you've not shown me anything other than that you're a good man." He studied his palms, then swung his attention back to Daniel. "You signed the same declaration we did," he continued, "and I thought you shared the same purpose we had in clearing Leadville of undesirables."

"Of course I do, Ira," Daniel said. "And in our conversation of yesterday afternoon we agreed this was an issue that had run its course and would be considered no longer. Am I mistaken in believing you're satisfied with my explanation of the unfortunate series of events?"

Ira seemed to consider his statement. "All right, then. Ladies, I believe your work here is done."

"But it's not done at all," Mrs. Stegman said. "It won't be done until this man—"

"It's my turn now," Ira said firmly. "And I'd appreciate it if you'd not interrupt." He turned to Daniel. "If you don't mind, I'd like to consult with the rest of the committee and get back to you on what we think would be the best solution to this problem." He paused. "I would hate to see Beck Mines suffer for what appears to be a simply repaired situation."

"I beg your pardon?" For the first time since the females barged in, concern replaced Daniel's irritation. "Ira, are you threatening me?"

Ira met his stare. "I don't threaten, though I'll tell you right now there's a list of things you should be concerned about."

"Such as?"

"Such as the decency proclamation we all agreed to over at the opera house. I'm just as bound by it as you," he added. "Were I to participate in any unsavory activities, my business could be taken, just like yours."

"Now see here. No one's taking Beck Mines from me, so banish that thought from your heads."

Ira shook his head. "Daniel, I'm going to give you a chance here and now to explain yourself."

Daniel straightened his spine and narrowed his eyes. "Ira," he said slowly, "I am a man of honor. You know this." When Ira did not respond, Daniel began to get worried. "Ira?"

"Look," the other man continued, "we've said what we came to say. Now it's up to you to do the right thing and clear this mess up once and for all."

"How can I do that?"

"You can start by formally answering to the committee for the charges against you, then pledging to correct them."

Daniel looked past the men to Hiram, who stood ashen faced in the corner. "Fine. Level your charges so that I might answer them."

"Moral laxness and contributing to the delinquency of a child," Ira said. "I believe that about covers it."

Daniel sagged against his desk. A glance at Hiram told him the poor man had done the same. Only Miss Cooper still stood, and from the look on her face, she was fighting mad.

"You bullies!" she said. "This is a good man. How dare you accuse him of such things?"

"He wore nothing but a sheet," a woman from the back called out. "Saw it for myself."

Daniel itched to ask just what a married woman was doing in a hotel in her own town in the middle of the night, but he kept his peace. Instead, he took a deep breath and let it out slowly. "Will there be a trial for this, Ira, or shall you string me up without one?"

Ira appeared duly shamed at the question. "I know you're a God-fearin' man. I'll take this up with the committee at the next meeting and get back to you."

"Why wait?" one of the fellows at the back asked. "Let's take a vote right now."

Ira gestured to the door. "Outside, the lot of you. If we're going to take a vote, we'll not do it in front of Daniel."

While the men filed out, the women remained in place, their glares divided equally between Daniel and Miss Cooper.

"You too," Ira called to the women. "I'll not leave Daniel in the lion's den." With that poor attempt at humor, Ira followed the last of the females out onto the sidewalk, where a debate commenced.

"Any progress on trading in those train tickets, Hiram?" Daniel asked as he watched the animated discussion between the men and women.

"Not yet, sir."

Daniel looked at Miss Cooper, who now slumped in a chair near the door. She seemed to be having difficulty in two areas: remaining upright and not looking out at the folks likely debating her future.

"Still feeling poorly?" he asked.

"What? No, I'm fine now," she claimed, though she looked anything but.

"I'm sorry I've brought you here to be treated this way." He shrugged. "I know they mean well. This town could use cleaning up. It's just that I don't take kindly to vigilantes of any kind." He gestured toward the window. "From where I sit, I can't tell the difference between the ones who string men from trees and the ones standing outside my office."

"Vigilantes." She nodded. "Yes, that's it exactly."

Daniel turned to his assistant. "Hiram, would you see that Miss Cooper gets back to the Clarendon without the good ladies of Leadville stringing her up with their apron strings?"

"If you don't mind, I prefer to stay here," the governess said.

"I do mind," he responded with as little emotion as possible. "If you're here, how can you be adequately supervising Charlotte?"

His comment found its mark, and a few seconds later, she allowed Hiram to lead her past the silently accusing women. Daniel busied himself at his desk, or at least kept up the pretense of it, until his door opened once more.

"We're ready if you are," Ira Stegman said.

Daniel looked past the men to where their womenfolk stood glaring at him from the street. "Of course," he said, praying this time only the men would partake of the opportunity. He got his wish when Ira closed the door and only half a dozen of Leadville's leading male citizens remained inside—one of which, Daniel noted, was the mayor. The women, no longer clustered at the door, gathered across the street.

Ira looked uncomfortable, though the others seemed to be enjoying themselves. "I thought we had a plan that would work, Daniel," Ira said, "but it appears our wives are bound and determined to make an example out of you and Miss Cooper."

"Then let them," Daniel said, his temper barely holding. "Aren't you all men? Act like it!"

"Spoken like a true bachelor," the mayor said.

"Not for long, if things go as my wife would like," Ira said. "A marriage appears to be the simplest solution."

"What are you talking about?" Daniel shook his head. "Don't tell me they plan to see Miss Cooper and me wed?" When no one answered, Daniel's temper finally got the best of him. "Well, I won't have it. I'll not be made an example of. You've chosen the wrong man to do this to."

Ira stepped forward. "Much as I hate this, Daniel, there's nothing we can do. Our wives won't rest until—"

"I don't care," he thundered. "Handle your wives, and I'll handle my business. Now, if you'll excuse me, I need to get back to it."

"Daniel, it's not that simple," the mayor said. "If you don't agree to make this situation right, there could be all sorts of trouble."

"What kind of trouble, Mayor? Surely you're not going to hold me to some silly proclamation I agreed to while trying to remain awake." He paused to search their faces. "We all know there's no basis in law for a company to be seized because its owner has committed some act the townspeople disapprove of."

"True, but we do have to live with these women." The mayor looked uneasy. "There are permits. Lots of them. They come through my offices as a matter of course, and I generally don't find fault with them. However, if I'm catching grief at home, that might make me cranky enough to take a second look at some of the paperwork coming into and going out of Beck Mines."

Daniel could barely restrain himself. "Are you trying to blackmail me, Mayor?"

"Oh, no," he said. "There's plenty of that going on at my house. I certainly wouldn't want to pass it on to you."

A few others mumbled in agreement. Each of them, Daniel knew, was involved in the Beck Mines in some way. To ignore their demands would be equivalent to putting a Closed sign on the company's front door.

"I'm not going to marry the woman, and that's final," he said. "So if that's the only solution you see to this problem, I'll go ahead and close the mine today."

"Actually, Daniel," Ira said, "I think I've got a solution that might work for everyone. That is, if you can get Miss Cooper to agree to it."

"And you don't tell our wives," the mayor added.

24

The cookies burned, and the bullet she used to shoot One-Eyed Ed shattered her best teapot, but according to Henry, she looked lovely in her new yellow dress.

"Marry up with me, Mae," he said for the hundredth time, "and you'll not regret it."

She dropped a lump of sugar in his tea and prayed the hog-tied criminal in her basement wouldn't come to before her beau left for choir practice. If he did, Mae would have to explain her secret life.

And she was not yet brave enough to do that.

"Terribly sorry about the cookies, Henry," she said as she heard an unmistakable thump and knew her cover was about to be blown.

⬦

"I'm not going to do it, Mr. Beck," Gennie said. "I cannot believe you even considered it."

Mr. Beck looked around the room at the men assembled there, then back at her. "Under the circumstances," he said, "perhaps you should call me Daniel."

"All right, Daniel, but I refuse to take wedding vows with a man I barely know. This is not the Dark Ages."

"Actually," the mayor said, "you've not heard the entire plan."

Gennie looked at Daniel, her heart sinking. "There's more?"

"Ira came up with a plan that, I'm sad to say, just might work." He shook his head. "Though I must tell you, I can't recall when I've been more furious at being railroaded into something."

She could tell by looking at Daniel Beck that he spoke the truth. "I'm listening," she said.

"It's brilliant, actually," Mr. Stegman said. "Daniel will marry you right here in this office, and then all our troubles are solved."

"And mine are just beginning." She shook her head. "No offense, Daniel, but I'd prefer to pick out my own husband, thank you very much."

She turned to head for the door, but the mayor cleared his throat. "It wouldn't be a real wedding, Miss Cooper."

"Now how can that be?" she asked. "Where I come from, a wedding is a wedding. What's going to be different about this one?"

Ira scratched his head, then looked over at the mayor, who nodded. "We've done a little research into this, and a wedding's only legal if you turn in the paperwork for it. All we've got to do is lose the papers, and the wedding never happened."

"Never happened," the mayor echoed.

She looked at Daniel, who appeared thoroughly miserable. "I don't know, gentlemen. Might I have a moment with the groom-to-be?"

When the office had cleared of all but Daniel Beck, Gennie took a deep breath. "I'm not going to do it."

He shrugged. "Then don't."

His response stunned her. "All right." She paused. "But what will happen if I don't?"

"To you? Nothing. You'll go back to New York and marry that banker and live happily ever after."

"So you know about Chandler Dodd?"

"I overheard some of it," he said, "though I've got to say in my limited experience, a woman in love doesn't make a habit of kissing another man." He paused. "Especially not more than once." He paused again. "And with such enthusiasm."

"I didn't have enthusiasm."

His grin grew despite the gravity of the situation. "If that wasn't enthusiasm, then that Dodd fellow's a lucky man."

A knock ended the argument she was about to make.

"What's the verdict, folks?" the mayor called.

Daniel looked at Gennie but said nothing.

"Do I have your assurance we are just going through the motions? It's not a real marriage?" She looked at Daniel. "My father will have your hide made into pillows if this isn't the case. He's a very powerful man, you know."

"And yet powerless to control his daughter," Daniel muttered.

"I heard that," she said.

"As I understand it, that is correct." Daniel called Ira and the mayor into the room. "She's agreed, though the thought of an actual marriage to me does not make her enthusiastic."

He punctuated the word with a wink, which Gennie ignored.

"So," Daniel continued, "if we can be assured the paperwork for this will never be filed, then we've agreed to go forward with what I must say is possibly the most idiotic plan I've ever had the misfortune to be a part of."

"I'll take that as a yes." Ira stuck his head out the office door. "Good news, honey," he called to his wife. "Daniel and Miss Cooper are getting hitched."

Daniel kept his expression unreadable. "Might I have another moment alone with my bride-to-be?"

Ira herded the mayor out with a promise to go fetch a parson. "Don't you go running off now," he said jovially as he closed the door.

Gennie leaned against the wall and tried to take in what was happening. Daniel, however, had begun to pace.

"You need to know that I find this situation abominable," he said. "The thought of marrying you like this makes me absolutely furious."

"Well," Gennie said with as much sarcasm as she could muster, "I suppose I don't have to worry about a wedding night."

Daniel moved toward her, then stopped. "That, Miss Cooper, is the biggest regret I have in this whole mess."

Hiram's voice rang out on the other side of the door, and Daniel called to him. In a modicum of words, he explained the situation.

"Then I suppose you'll be happy to know I've managed to book tickets on tomorrow's train to Denver," Hiram said.

"Good work, though I'd have preferred to be gone before sunset."

"I tried, sir," Hiram said, "but it wasn't to be."

Gennie took a seat near the window and pointedly ignored the men until the parson arrived. In less than three minutes' time, and in full view of the good folks of the Greater Leadville Beautification and Improvement Society and their wives, she became a married woman.

The only person who seemed less enthusiastic than Gennie was the groom.

"What would you like me to tell Charlotte?" Gennie asked once the crowd of Leadville citizens, finally satisfied, had left.

"Tell her we're going back to Denver tomorrow," Daniel replied without looking up from the stack of papers on his desk.

When Gennie returned to the Clarendon, she found that news of her midday nuptials had spread quickly. After fending off congratulations and questions, she entered the solace of her chamber only to find Sam and Charlotte had been busy in her absence.

In bold letters, Sam had helped Charlotte decorate and hang a sign that said "Congratulations, Papa and Miss Cooper."

"Oh, no." Gennie sank onto the nearest chair. "What have we done?"

They'd done nothing, of course, except possibly lie to an entire town and one little girl who looked more than pleased to have Gennie as her new mama.

Daniel attempted to explain the situation to Charlotte upon his arrival at the Clarendon an hour later, but her ten-year-old mind couldn't get past the fact they'd said vows in front of the preacher.

"It's exactly like I prayed it would be," she said. "I'm so happy."

"Now, Buttercup," Daniel said, "we're just pretending."

Her eyes wide, Charlotte shook her head. "I don't understand, Papa. If the preacher says you're married, then aren't you?"

"It's complicated." Daniel looked to Gennie for assistance.

She turned away, leaving him to answer his daughter's questions alone. It was, after all, because of him that she'd perpetrated this fraud.

And yet, she could've said no.

That thought followed her through the afternoon until, as she stepped into the hotel dining room at the usual dinner hour, she found she'd walked into what appeared to be a celebration. "What's this?" she asked Hiram, who had planted himself near the exit.

Daniel's assistant leaned toward her. "It appears Leadville's elite have gathered with the purpose of having an intimate supper with the celebrities of the moment."

Gennie frowned. "Stop being sarcastic, Hiram. There are easily a hundred people in this room, and I don't see a single celebrity." She slid him a sideways look as Daniel moved toward her through the crowd. "Though the president himself could be in here, and I'd never find him."

She gestured discreetly toward a table where an inordinate amount of attention was being placed on an older man and a lovely young woman with fair hair and curls. Gennie recognized the woman at once as the friendly person who'd introduced herself as Baby. "Who is that man with Mrs. Doe? He looks familiar. Is he her father?"

Hiram's brows rose. "That's Mr. Tabor. And he should look familiar. He's our lieutenant governor."

"I see." She returned Mrs. Doe's wave. "Are they friends?"

"Yes, well, that's not exactly..." Hiram seemed at a loss, though his expression told the rest of the tale.

"Ah." She met the woman's gaze and exchanged smiles.

"Gennie, dear," Daniel called when he'd nearly reached her. "Come and meet a few of my friends."

"Really, I don't think—"

"Good idea." Daniel grasped her wrist and leaned in close. "Don't think, Miss Cooper, or you'll ruin our ruse."

Firmly extricating herself from his grip, Gennie shook her head. "This will never work."

"It must."

"Look at those two," said a man with too much hair oil as he pressed through the crowd to slap Daniel on the back. "Give your blushing bride a kiss, you lucky man."

"In good time, Fenton." Daniel slid Gennie a sideways glance. "Dear, this is Ike Fenton. Do say hello."

Gennie shook his hand, only to find he wore as much oil on his fingers as on his head. She looked at her now-spotted gloves with dismay.

"Fetching thing," Fenton said. "You got a sister back home who might want to marry up with a rich man, honey?"

Several responses occurred to her, but Daniel excused himself from the loathsome man's company, taking Gennie with him. "A moment of your time, dear," he said, though his expression was far more tender than his grip.

Leading her out the nearest exit took more than a moment, and by the time he'd accomplished the feat, Gennie was glad for the respite. Her conscience was beginning to plague her worse than the store-bought slippers she wore.

"You're doing great, Miss Cooper," he said when he'd slipped with her into an alcove off the lobby. "I appreciate your willingness to—"

"Willingness?" Her temper flared. "Did I really have a choice? Willingness indicates a choice."

"Keep your voice down."

"Keep my voice down?" Her blood boiled. "'Keep your voice down, Miss Cooper. I appreciate your willingness, Miss Cooper. Do tell the parson you agree to be my wife, Miss Cooper.'" Gennie stomped her foot. "No, Mr. Beck, I do not recall any sort of—"

Daniel pulled her against him and kissed her. "That was for your own good as well as mine."

"My own good?" She wiped her mouth with the back of her shaking hand. "Now I've positively heard it all."

"Trouble in paradise?" Ira Stegman paused at the alcove, his wife at his side.

"It appears my bride is reluctant to remain downstairs," Daniel said. "I've explained to her I'll not take her up to the bridal suite until we've done our social duties at the reception." He looked past Ira. "Much obliged for the hasty response to our nuptials, ma'am."

Mrs. Stegman nodded, and the feathers on her bonnet swayed. "Nonsense, Daniel. You're practically family. It was the least the Ladies' Society could do." She reached past her husband to grasp Gennie's arm. "Let's discuss what sort of position you'd like in the society."

"I...well, that is..." Gennie looked to Daniel for help. Thankfully, he did not miss her plea.

"Now, Mrs. Stegman," he said, yanking Gennie back into his arms. "Don't you think her social duties might be put on hold for now?" He nuzzled Gennie's neck. "After all, she is only just married."

The older woman's giggle took Gennie by surprise. "What was I thinking? Of course your wifely duties would take precedence."

"That's exactly what I told her."

Wifely duties? Gennie elbowed Daniel, who quietly coughed. "Perhaps we should go in and thank our guests for this lovely reception, then, dear."

His pained look turned genial as soon as he led her into the crowd. Gennie endured the congratulations of nearly every soul in the room before stopping at a table opposite the exit, where Charlotte sat.

The girl grasped her hand. "I thought you said it was pretend," she whispered.

"I thought so too," Gennie said with a sigh. "I suppose someone should tell them that."

Charlotte shook her head. "I think you're just teasing me."

"Buttercup, can we continue this conversation later?" Daniel gestured to a table decked out in wedding finery. "Go and sit with Miss Cooper—that is, Gennie—and we will discuss it later."

"I want to know now. Are you married or not?"

A couple nearby turned to look at them, and Daniel shrugged. "She's new to the idea," he said, engaging the husband in conversation and gesturing to Gennie behind his back to take Charlotte to the table.

Gennie groaned and linked arms with the girl. Somehow she managed to move the child to the table and get her seated. "Now, dear," she said when the girl refused to stop staring at her, "your father and I have explained it all to you. It's just a little game…"

The words sounded as false as the other excuses she'd told Charlotte. As false as the ones she'd told herself.

She could have said no.

The meal began, and Daniel came to sit beside her. "I didn't expect this," he said to Gennie as he gathered Charlotte into his lap, "or I'd have warned you."

"So you say." Gennie's gaze surveyed the room. "Interesting how the same people practicing vigilante justice on us mere hours ago are now falling over one another to wish us the best." She returned her attention to Daniel and caught him staring. "What? Have I spilled the soup on myself?" Gennie looked down at the front of her gown, then back up at Daniel. "Stop looking at me like that."

Daniel's brows rose and he dabbed at the corner of his mouth. "Miss Cooper, I have no idea what you're talking about."

"That's Mrs. Beck, dear," she reminded him in a less-than-sweet tone.

Lieutenant Governor Tabor stood and raised his glass. "A toast to the happy couple."

Daniel rose slowly and deposited Charlotte in the chair beside him. "Thank you, Horace," he said as he lifted his glass.

Gennie remained seated. Her knocking knees could never have supported her. If only she could find a way to make an exit from the forced festivities. Thankfully, Charlotte gave her a reason.

"Your daughter is exhausted," she said to Daniel when he sat once more. She gestured to the child, who rested her elbows on the table. "I'll see she gets to bed. No need for you to leave the party."

"Are you certain?" Was that regret she saw on his face?

"Very." She rose, and Daniel joined her. "Do make my apologies to your friends."

Gennie swept Charlotte from the room and headed upstairs to the bridal suite, where she made sure the door was locked tight.

"See?" she said as she turned to tackle the job of preparing Charlotte for bed. "If your papa and I were really married, it would be him, not you, in that monstrosity of a bed tonight, so be thankful."

Charlotte giggled, and Gennie admonished her for racing over to climb beneath the massive curtains.

"You're filthy, child," she said, "and your bath is drawn, so into it you go."

The girl stood her ground.

"Fine, then," Gennie said. "I'll sleep in the bed, and you can have the pallet on the floor over there."

Charlotte dashed toward the tub.

Some time later, heavy footsteps paused outside in the hall, but only for a moment before continuing on. Gennie punched the lumpy pillow and rolled onto her back on the makeshift pallet before gathering the blanket to her chin.

I could have said no.

⌘

That thought followed Gennie all the way to Denver and echoed in her mind as she boarded the streetcar for the downtown area and the telegraph office. Fully expecting a response from Hester Vanowen to have languished there until she returned, she was surprised to find nothing waiting for her. Gennie peered into her near-empty reticule and extracted enough coins to pay for a brief telegram reminding her old friend of the prior request.

With nothing left to do but go back to the Beck home, she climbed aboard the streetcar and rode all the way back to the end of the line, wondering why she'd not heard from Hester. That concern faded when she spied Anna Finch waiting for her on the sidewalk.

"How was Leadville?" she asked as she fell into step with Gennie.

"Interesting" was the best answer Gennie could give.

They walked in silence for a full block before Anna stopped. "You've fallen in love with him. I can tell."

Gennie shook her head. "No, of course not. We did spend a bit of time together, and there were some interesting developments while in Leadville, but love? Hardly. You're the one who loves Daniel Beck, not me."

Anna shook her head. "I'm not convinced."

"Then don't be," Gennie said as she stalked ahead. "My opinion in the matter of Daniel Beck doesn't seem to matter to anyone anyway."

She left Anna at the gate of the Beck house and stormed inside. Elias and Tova sat at the kitchen table.

"Your trunks have been unpacked," Tova said. "What would you like me to do with the pistol?"

"The pistol?" Gennie shook her head. "Considering the events of the last few days, I suggest you keep it as far away from me as you can."

She headed upstairs to see to Charlotte's bedtime routine. When one story was not enough, she went down to the library to fetch another. There, she walked in on Daniel, who sat at the desk, looking at a letter.

"I'm terribly sorry," she said, turning to leave.

He looked up as if he hadn't heard her come in. "No, it's fine. I'm guessing Charlotte asked for another book." When she nodded, he pointed out two of her favorites. "Take them both," he said. "She may want a third."

"She'll not have a third," Gennie said, "but I will give her a choice."

His nod dismissed her, and Gennie escaped upstairs feeling she'd somehow been judged and found lacking. That feeling intensified when she returned the books to the library awhile later and found Daniel still sitting at the desk.

"I'm sorry," she said again. "I'll just leave these outside and put them away in the morning."

"No." He looked up from his work. "Come in and sit, please."

"Perhaps tomorrow," she said. "I'm exhausted."

"No. Now, please." He sighed. "There's no need to put this off."

Daniel gestured to the empty chair, and she grudgingly sat in the one next to it. "All right, but is it impertinent of me to ask that, given the late hour, you be brief?"

"First, I would like to know what your plans are for preparing Charlotte to meet her grandfather."

Her grandfather? He was the royal personage to whom Charlotte would be presented? "Now that she's wearing socially appropriate attire, I thought to introduce her to events where she can use her manners and deportment."

"Charlotte has manners and deportment?"

Gennie nodded. "She began her lessons in Leadville, and they will continue until I leave." She recited one of Mama's favorite lines. "The end of learning is the end of knowledge, Mr. Beck."

"Daniel."

"Oh, of course," she said. "It wouldn't do to call one's husband by anything other than his given name."

"Speaking of Leadville." His gaze collided with hers. "Do you realize that had you not chosen to scream at the most inopportune time, none of this would have happened?"

Gennie blinked hard and shook her head. "Do I understand you correctly? Are you blaming *me*?"

"If you recall, the occupants of the third floor were summoned not when Charlotte had her nightmare, but when you screamed at my entrance into the room." He held his hand up to stop her protest. "And let me remind you, I knocked before I entered."

"You knocked, and therefore I should not have screamed when a man wearing what appeared to be some sort of strange traveling cloak barged into a hotel room already under guard due to threats by an awful miner who chased your daughter?"

Daniel seemed to let all of that sink in before slowly nodding.

Outrage of a depth she'd never felt before welled up in Gennie. "Look here, Daniel Beck. I will not accept responsibility for this."

"Stop it," a small voice demanded. Gennie turned to see Charlotte standing in the doorway.

"Did we wake you, Buttercup?" Daniel asked.

"Papa, why are you being so mean to Miss Cooper? She married you because you asked her to. That's how mommies and daddies get married."

"Yes," Daniel said, "that is the conventional way of doing things."

Charlotte rubbed her eyes. "Why didn't you and Miss Cooper do things the 'ventional way?"

Gennie rose and herded her charge into the hallway. "We can discuss this tomorrow, Charlotte. Tonight you need to sleep."

The girl offered no protest until they reached the stairs. "I forgot to tell him good night," she said as she raced back to the library.

Gennie waited at the bottom of the stairs. She couldn't see Charlotte or Daniel from her position, but she could hear their voices through the open door.

"We need Miss Cooper," Charlotte told her father, "and you should be nice to her."

"I am nice," he said.

"No, you're not," Charlotte replied in that insistent way she had. "You didn't marry her the 'ventional way, and now she's not a bona fide wife."

"Where did you hear that? About Gennie not being bona fide?"

"I heard Elias and Tova talking about it." She paused. "They said you only married her to keep your stupid mines from getting back-rupted."

"Back-rupted?" He chuckled. "You mean bankrupted. And what you need to understand is that we didn't actually get married."

"But people said you did."

"Yes," he said slowly.

"And Mr. Sam helped me make a sign for you."

Gennie crept closer, but still could see neither father nor daughter. *Please, Lord,* she prayed, *help Daniel handle this the right way.*

"You know, Buttercup," he said gently, "Miss Cooper's not planning to stay with us forever."

"But she has to. I like her."

"It's wonderful that you like her." He chuckled. "A miracle, even, but she has a mama and a papa in New York who would miss her terribly if she didn't go back to them."

Silence.

Gennie crept closer until she could see the back of Charlotte's head. "If she leaves, I'll run away."

"Don't you ever say that," Daniel snapped. "Never."

"I'm sorry, Papa, but I love Miss Cooper. She protected me from the bad man even though I was mean to her." She paused to sniffle. "You love her too, don't you?"

Gennie walked away before he responded. There was no need to eavesdrop on the answer when she already knew what he would say.

25

"Terribly sorry you've got to leave so suddenly," Mae said, practically pushing Henry out the door. "Might you be interested in a stroll later?"

"Can't commit," he said. "An interesting problem that rarely afflicts me."

She stared, not quite sure whether his meaning was intentional. With dear Henry, she never really knew.

Another thump and she slammed the door. Peering through the lace curtains, she saw Henry had already beat a path for home.

His home.

"Oh, Henry, someday we will find one that will be ours together," she whispered. "But for now, mine's got an angry criminal in the basement, and I must see to him."

&c.

"The invitations are on the silver tray in the foyer," Tova said when Gennie returned from delivering Charlotte to school.

"Invitations?"

Tova nodded. "Before I always threw them away, but I understand Mr. Beck will be going out again."

"He will?" Despite the fact their marriage was a sham and their kisses had all been mistakes, Gennie felt a twinge of jealousy not unlike the moment when Baby Doe called Daniel "Danny Boy."

"Likely Miss Finch's ball gowns will have to be taken in a bit at the waist if you're to wear them. If you have time this morning, perhaps I could do that for you."

Gennie shook her head. "I think you've misunderstood. I've not been invited to go to anywhere with Daniel."

Tova nodded. "Perhaps I misunderstood."

"No, Tova," Daniel said from the top of the stairs, "you did not misunderstand. If my daughter is to be accepted into society, it starts with me doing my part." He looked at Gennie. "And if I go alone, the matrons will trot out their marriageable daughters again. I can't tolerate that, and I won't."

Gennie thought of Anna next door. How would she manage to cause this stubborn man to change his thinking? *Lord,* she prayed, *I know You can do what I cannot, and changing Daniel Beck is something I certainly cannot do.*

But sticking close by him until she had a better plan was something she *could* do.

"Well, Tova," she said, "what's on the schedule for tonight? I'd like to be sure my ensemble is appropriate."

"The Millers are hosting a ball," she said.

"Likely a thinly veiled excuse for a suffragette rally," Daniel said.

"Actually, the invitation says to dress as an invention," Tova said.

"An invention?" Daniel shook his head. "What sort of frippery is that?"

"It sounds like an interesting challenge." Gennie grinned as she looked up at the ceiling.

Later in the privacy of her bedchamber, Gennie examined gown after gown until she found the one that best fit the invention she'd chosen. Only one item remained, and she enlisted Elias to comb the massive attic for just the right accessory.

When the knock came at her door, Gennie found uncharacteristic butterflies dancing in her stomach. She'd attended countless balls, soirees, and galas; tonight's event, a simple costume ball in a Denver home, should have been just another evening out.

"Mr. Beck's waiting." Tova slipped the door open a notch, then sucked in a deep breath. "Oh my," she said.

Gennie's heart sank. "I knew it. I look a fool." She reached for the glittering diamonds at her ears. "Tell Mr. Beck I'm staying in tonight."

"You'll do no such thing," came a booming voice from downstairs.

She gave Tova a beseeching look.

"Go now," Tova said. "You'll be the belle of the ball."

"The belle of the ball?" Gennie chuckled. "I hardly think so."

"Go," Tova repeated, "and enjoy yourself. Charlotte and I will have—"

"You're beautiful!" Charlotte slid around Tova and skidded to a stop inches from the toe of Gennie's slippered foot.

"Slow down, Charlotte," Gennie said. She took a deep breath and moved toward the door.

"You could learn a lesson from the speed at which my daughter moves," Daniel called as he stood in the foyer. He turned to Elias, who kept a safe distance at the parlor door. "I fail to understand what a woman does that takes…" Noting Elias's sudden change of expression, Daniel stopped. "What's wrong with you, Elias?"

His friend seemed unable to do anything but point toward the stairs. Daniel turned to follow Elias's stunned gaze.

Gennie made her way down the staircase. At least, he thought the vision in shimmering gold was his governess.

"She's a sight." Elias crossed the foyer to nudge Daniel. "Didn't expect that, now, did you?"

"What do you think?" she asked when she reached the bottom of the stairs.

Her hair had been piled atop her head in a fashionable style, then decorated with glittering gems. A second look told him those gems matched the ones attached to her dress at intervals. They also matched the crystals on the trio of chandeliers that once hung in his dining room.

As she moved from the stairs, her costume caught the new chandelier's light and sent prisms of color bouncing around the room. "Daniel?"

"I'm not sure what it is," Daniel said, his mouth suddenly dry. "I mean, I'm not sure what this represents."

"Daniel, you're not making any sense." Elias chuckled. "Not that I blame you."

Gennie's expression fell. "You don't like it, do you?"

She turned to go back up the stairs, but Daniel caught her by the wrist. A wrist encircled by a string of crystals that matched the ones at her ears and neck. "We're late," he said, his voice belying the fact she'd taken his breath away.

Gennie stepped out into the night air, and Daniel followed like a hapless pup. As he landed in the carriage beside her, he managed to form a question. "Gennie," he said carefully, "exactly what invention does your costume represent?"

"I might ask you the same." She looked him up and down. "I fail to see you've donned anything other than your customary evening suit. Where's your costume?"

Daniel leaned back and called to Isak to commence the drive to the Miller home. "My costume?" He gestured to his chest. "I'm wearing it, Gennie."

She gave him a sideways look. "What invention could you possibly be?"

"Isn't it obvious?" He put on his best grin. "I'm man, of course."

Her laughter filled the carriage. "That's ridiculous."

"Gennie," he said with mock horror. "Do you not think man is God's best invention?"

To her credit, the governess appeared to be considering it. "I suppose I never thought of it that way," she finally said as the carriage rolled out of the gates.

Reaching across the distance between them, Daniel lifted a curl of hair from her shoulder and watched the attached crystal catch the lamplight. "Your turn."

"My invention is fire." She lifted a crystal at her neck. "Can you feature it?"

He could. Easily. And likely would for quite some time.

ॐ

Indeed, she and Daniel Beck were quite different.

And yet when Gennie stepped into the Millers' ballroom on Daniel's arm, those differences faded away. For a man of decidedly frontier tastes, he was an accomplished dancer, gliding her around the room with such skill that she felt she might leave her dancing slippers behind and float away, her golden skirts billowing in the breeze.

While his costume was interesting and cheating in equal measure, Gennie found herself smiling at the thought of his daring choice. When Anna joined her, she almost felt guilty for the grin she wore.

"We must find a way for him to dance with you, Anna," she said to her friend, who wore a costume with numerous circles attached.

"Perhaps dressing as the wheel was not my best choice," Anna said. "I'll certainly not capture Daniel's attention in the same manner as your gown of fire."

Gennie shook her head and glanced across the room at Daniel, who seemed embroiled in an intense conversation with several business types. "He'll come to his senses, Anna."

"I'm not so sure," she said. "I think he took leave of them the minute you arrived."

Gennie denied it, of course, and added a promise to discuss Anna at length with Daniel on their drive home. This became difficult, however, when Daniel changed the subject each time she mentioned his neighbor's name.

Finally, she'd had enough. "Daniel, I must know what you find so uninteresting about Anna Finch. I think she's quite lovely."

"Yes, she's very lovely," he said as the carriage passed beneath a gaslight. "But what man would think of the wheel when he's faced with fire?" He leaned back and closed his eyes. "Explain this to me, Governess, for I am merely a man."

She could only laugh, though it appeared her plan to draw attention to Anna was in grave danger.

The following night, they attended an oratory lecture at the opera house. Halfway through the insufferable speaker's monologue, Daniel started snoring and had to be jabbed awake. Daniel repaid the favor several days later when an ambassador from a Central American country droned on in stilted English, and Gennie was forced to find respite behind her fan.

By the end of the week, their strained silence at home had given way to the easy camaraderie they'd shared on other occasions. Her only disappointment came in her failed attempts at bringing Daniel together with Anna. With her time in Denver drawing to a close, Gennie had almost decided that only a miracle would accomplish the feat. Anna, it seemed, had given up entirely.

"Tonight will be different," Gennie said as she finished pinning her hair and rose to take a look at the newly altered ball gown. The dress shimmered in a blue that Tova said complimented her eyes.

"You look lovely." Charlotte settled on the seat beside Gennie at the vanity.

"Thank you. Would you like your hair done up like mine?"

"Yes, please," the girl said. Half an hour later, Charlotte Beck looked ready to go to the ball as well.

"Your ball gown for the night is a nightgown," Gennie told her, "and you'll only be dreaming of dances with handsome princes. Someday, however, you will be the belle of the ball."

"Promise?"

"I do."

When Gennie swept down the stairs, she found Daniel gawking. "So Tova's repairs meet your approval?"

It seemed he could only nod as he handed her into their carriage, and they headed out into the night.

As yet another attempt to fuse the futures of Anna Finch and Daniel Beck failed, she wondered whether it was at all possible. Every time Anna drew near, he seemed to suddenly feel the urge to dance with Gennie.

How could he resist escorting Gennie around the dance floor when she was easily the loveliest woman in the room? Along with her beauty, she had tamed his daughter and gone far toward preparing her to meet the earl.

If only he were as prepared.

But that was a thought for another day. Tonight he held Gennie Cooper in his arms, and all of Denver society was reduced to merely watching.

He had not kissed her since their near-picnic, and keeping that record was an ongoing exercise in restraint. While he could not say he loved her, Daniel was painfully aware of just how very much he was smitten.

As he handed her into the buggy for the trip home, he made the mistake of looking into her eyes. For a moment, he recalled the day they met in Fisher's Dry Goods Store. "You never did wear that buckskin jacket," he said as he took his place beside her.

She gave him a sideways look, then giggled. "I don't suppose the mayor and his wife would have understood if I'd worn it tonight."

"Perhaps not," Daniel said, "but I would have."

"Oh?"

He leaned in, powerless to stop what he'd ignored for far too long. "Gennie, I promised you a Wild West adventure, and I fear I've let you down."

Her laughter held more than a little nervousness. "Didn't Miss Finch look lovely tonight?"

"She always does," he said. "But then, her father sees to that." He paused to gather his wits only to realize he'd lost them altogether. "Gennie, I don't want to talk about Anna Finch tonight."

"But she's ever so clever, and—"

He placed a finger over her lips. "Shh," he said. "Don't talk."

There was nothing left to do but kiss her.

"I'll be leaving soon," she said a moment later.

Daniel sat back and shook his head. "I've kissed my share of women, but this is the first time one of them said that afterward."

Gennie looked away. "Two weeks and a day. That's when my train leaves for New York."

"I see."

Her fingers captured his. "I'll never forget you, Daniel."

"No," he said, "it is I who will not forget you."

"I need to tell you who I am."

Daniel gestured for her to wait. They were only minutes from home. Home. The big house had come to feel that way since Gennie Cooper arrived, and not just because she'd done what he'd been unable to: get rid of that awful jeweled bird Tova loved so much.

"Leave us, Isak," he said when the buggy halted in the drive. When the boy had gone into the carriage house, Daniel turned to Gennie. "All right. Go ahead."

She leaned back against the cushions and looked up into the night sky. "It's a long story."

"And one you do not have to tell." He sat back too and stared up at God's creation overhead. "I'm content with today. We don't need anything else, do we?"

"I suppose not." The evening breeze carried her soft comment along with the fresh scent of impending rain.

He looked over at her. "That's not exactly a ringing endorsement."

Gennie shifted to look at him. "I've been thinking, Daniel. Denver, Leadville, it's all been something special. Charlotte has come to be like my own, and I'm not sure how that happened. It seems like just yesterday she was robbing me at the train station."

Daniel sat bolt upright. "She robbed you at the train station? Why am I just now hearing of this?"

She waved away the question. "She was a motherless girl seeking attention."

He took immediate exception to the statement. "What does that mean? She had me. Are you saying I was somehow deficient as a parent?" He remembered her letter. "Indeed, that is exactly what you told me, isn't it?"

"Daniel." Her fingers found his shoulder and then, by degrees, his jaw line. "A father is a precious part of a little girl's world, and I was wrong to insinuate you had failed in that area. But a girl needs a woman's influence." She sat back and let her hand fall into her lap. "Now Miss Finch, she would be—"

"Enough. Why do you insist on trying to throw me together with Anna Finch?" He swiveled to face her. "Can't you see it's you I've wanted since the first time I saw you at the dry goods store?"

His admission stunned them both. Daniel sat back and found Orion again, looking into the celestial heavens rather than at the heavenly creature beside him. He'd just bared his heart to a woman who not only had a train ticket to New York in two weeks, but also was practically betrothed to another.

What sort of idiot had he become since he'd fallen for the woman in boots and buckskins?

"Kiss me again, Daniel, so I'll have this memory to take back to New York."

He tore his attention from the sky. Kiss her? He could do that all night and die a happy man.

Throwing care to the summer breeze, Daniel pulled her onto his lap, then leaned away so he could look at her. She was stunning. No more beautiful woman took a breath. Thick lashes swept high cheekbones that, in the moonlight, seemed dusted with silver. Even his Georgiana paled in comparison, though to be fair, hers was a much-faded memory.

And Charlotte loved them both.

Had he every ounce of the silver that could be hauled up from beneath the Leadville mountains, he'd not come close to the value of this woman. Or of his daughter and his good friends.

The revelation stunned him, and his hands began to shake.

"Daniel? Is something wrong?"

When he did not answer, she started to sit up.

"No," he said through the lump in his throat. "Please stay there. The moonlight. You."

She reached for him, placing both hands behind his neck and pulling him to her. "There are memories to be made, Daniel," she said. "I'm not ready to leave you tonight."

Nor was he ready to leave her. If ever he wished that marriage license had been real, the vows they made true, now was the time. He could have happily lived out the Song of Solomon right here under God's stars.

But she'd told Tova and Elias that someone else held her heart. Another man would soon claim her.

All of her.

Daniel shuddered and nearly dropped her. Carefully, as if handling a precious and fragile thing, he settled her on the buggy cushion. Again those impossibly long lashes swept cheekbones sculpted by God.

He touched them, then cupped her cheeks, traced her jaw, found a tender spot on the back of her neck. "I could love you, Eugenia Flora Cooper."

Gennie's eyes flew open. "How do you know my full name?"

"I know more than you think," he said, "and I could still love you."

Her surprise gave way to impudence. "Well, I don't know a thing about you, Daniel Beck, except perhaps that you're a very secretive man."

"I am? I hadn't realized." He paused to draw in a deep breath of her rose-scented skin. "I am entranced, Gennie," he said softly. "Ask me anything."

She touched the tip of his nose. "Anything?"

"Anything."

"How did you come to live in Denver?" she asked. "Were you longing for a Wild West adventure too?"

He chuckled. "Hardly. Though I certainly found it. To tell this story, I must go to its beginning in England. The family lands in the shadow of Scafell Pike, to be exact." He paused to rest on his elbow. "We'd profited from the deposits beneath the mountains for generations, but until I took the company and made it something, we'd barely gotten by. Two years, Gennie, and I had the Beck name where it should have been two generations ago."

She said nothing, though he knew she listened intently.

"The Beck inheritance had finally come to mean something, though I cared less for it than I did the challenge of besting the land and bringing out what was hidden beneath it." He closed his eyes and saw it all. "I had everything, all before I turned five and twenty."

"It sounds wonderful," she said.

"Oh, it was. She was."

"Charlotte's mother?"

Daniel opened his eyes. "Yes."

To her credit, she said nothing, even though she surely wanted to know more. For a time, they remained in silence, with only the whisper of the wind through the aspens and junipers for company.

"Elias will tell you I saved his life," Daniel said, "and I warrant I've plucked the old coot from more than one scrape over the years. But it is he whom I credit for the life I now live."

Gennie smiled, and he longed to fit his lips to hers. But he'd embarked on this road, and stopping was not an option he'd take, lest he not return to it.

"I lost it all." He shook his head. "No, that's not right. I gave it all away. Willingly. Only Georgiana had value to me. The mines were not yet mine, nor yet my brother's, so my father was within his rights to deliver the ultimatum. What he did not expect was that I would choose Georgiana over him and his company. He thought her beneath me." Daniel sat back, unable to believe he'd said these things. And yet there was so much more to tell. He skipped ahead, unwilling to stop, yet unable to give a full accounting of things he'd not contemplated in a decade.

"Elias was a man without a country. His Confederacy had fallen and his ship, the *Bernadette,* which had sought refuge in British waters, was taken. I too had lost everything. He found a vessel, signed us on as crew, and we sailed from England, never to return."

"What happened next?"

Daniel shrugged. "A man with soldiering skills can always get by. The South was defeated, but not without need of men who could use their weapons. The West too."

"What happened to Georgiana? Did she come with you?"

"Georgiana." Funny how he remembered her as he last saw her on the doorstep of his father's home and not as she was when she returned to him five years later. "No," he said slowly, "she chose another."

"But Charlotte, your marriage."

He nodded, caught in the web of a memory he longed to forget. "I did marry her, though it proved my downfall. My father thought her common, and he was right, though only by birth and certainly not by character." Or so he thought.

"I won't ask anything further," she whispered. "Some things are private between a husband and wife."

Daniel smiled despite himself. "There are a substantial number of persons in Leadville who would argue that we are husband and wife."

"Ah," she said, "but what does God say? Is it not He who decides these things?"

Daniel remembered a mountain stream. A woman whose swollen belly would bear his brother's child. A wedding that cost him everything except his pride. That, he had already given away.

There was so much more to the story. A brother's betrayal. Two signatures on a document giving an innocent child both halves of an inheritance that would mean full control of the mines Daniel had returned to their glory. And a heart scarred by time and a woman, but healed by a Savior.

"Daniel?"

He looked down to see Gennie staring at him, felt her insistent tug on his neck. He knew she wanted a kiss, as did he. What he didn't know — couldn't be sure of — is whether this time the kiss would become more.

He gave in to the urge to kiss her but held at bay his want of more with her. "I fear we've come to the end of us, Gennie," he said. "To claim you as mine, I would have to steal you from another. This I now realize I cannot do."

26

Mae found only pieces of rope and an open window in her basement.

"Time to ride again," she said as she gladly retrieved her hidden buckskins and prepared to return to the trail that was her true home.

Turning the key in the lock, she left behind what would be the dream of most women, and disappeared into the sagebrush.

She didn't get a full mile from home before she realized she'd been followed.

ᘓᘔ

Charlotte had only just left for school when Gennie found herself alone in the big house. Elias and Tova were at the market, their trip together necessitated by a good-natured argument over the ingredients to some recipe.

With nothing to do but think on what happened—and what might have happened last night—Gennie went to the library to find something to read. A book on etiquette beckoned, and she pulled down the slim volume. This would make for good reading when Charlotte returned from school. With her departure looming, Gennie wanted to be sure she'd done as well as she could her job teaching Charlotte how to be a lady. She still marveled that the girl had taken to wearing dresses and enduring baths without screaming. Elias swore Gennie was a miracle worker, while Tova merely gave her silent approval.

A knock at the front door caused Gennie to set the book aside. She opened the latch and instantly regretted it.

The man who stood outside gave her a look that made her want to slam the door. "Is your mister about?"

She'd not say no. "He's unavailable. Perhaps you would like to come back another time."

"I'll wait," he said.

"Very well." She opened the door a bit wider, then cursed herself for a fool when he took the gesture as an invitation and came in.

He walked with a slight limp, favoring the leg with a fraying patch on the knee. When he worried with his rolled-up shirt sleeve, she noted a jagged pink scar that ran nearly from elbow to wrist.

Gennie put him in the parlor, then excused herself to go into the kitchen. She'd seen where Tova had hidden her pistol, and she retrieved it now from behind the potato bin. Placing the weapon in her skirt, Gennie returned to the parlor to make small talk.

"I didn't get your name," she said to the man, lowering herself on the settee.

"I didn't give it to you."

His response startled her. "I'm Gennie," she said.

"Yes," he responded.

They sat for what seemed like an eternity. Finally, the fellow made his excuses, then left without telling her his name. "Just tell him I'm an old friend."

She found it odd and mentioned the incident to Tova when she returned.

"I'll tell Elias and Isak to watch for him," the housekeeper said. "And you will no longer open the door when left alone, yes?"

"Yes," Gennie echoed. She gathered her volume on etiquette and climbed the stairs. If only the library carried books on the life of a woman torn between two worlds.

Then she realized she had that very book in her room—the latest episode of *Mae Winslow, Woman of the West.*

She might have happily finished the dime novel, then perhaps done some mending on Charlotte's wardrobe, a new skill she'd learned from Tova since returning from Leadville. The fact she could place thread in the eye of a needle, tie a knot, and accomplish something so rare as to let out a hem or take in a seam still made her smile. Perhaps Mama would cease her despair at the fact her daughter was hopeless at stitching. Embroidery could not be difficult to learn now that she'd mastered such skills.

Instead, while Charlotte practiced the pianoforte with her instructor, Gennie took pen and paper and prepared the text of a telegram to Hester Vanowen regarding the funds that must have gone missing. Someone in the Vanowen household was surely a thief, or perhaps it was that fellow down at the Western Union office. In either case, the monies were no longer needed as her visit neared its end.

As Charlotte continued her practicing, Gennie made her excuses to Tova and slipped out to take the streetcar downtown. Inside the Western Union office, she handed over the last of her funds, then watched the shifty-eyed fellow with care until the telegram was sent.

As she turned to leave, she almost ran over Elias Howe.

"Fancy meeting you here," he said as if he were greeting her at some social function instead of the telegraph office. "You on your way home?" When she nodded, he smiled. "Good, then we can ride together. Give me just a minute to send this to that Hiram fellow over in Leadville."

The ride back was brief and quiet. Elias did not ask the nature of her visit, nor did Gennie offer an explanation.

"Tova tells me you had a visitor earlier today," he said when they were almost home.

"A visitor?" She shook her head. "Oh, that strange man. Yes, he said he was a friend of Daniel's."

"Did he now?" Elias shrugged. "And he didn't leave a name?"

"No. Do you find that odd?"

"It is," Elias said. "Probably some fellow Daniel's done business with or, more likely, one who's been on the receiving end of his charity. In his line of work, it could be either." He paused and seemed to consider it a moment. "Likely the latter," he said as the buggy rolled up the drive. "That Daniel, he's got a soft heart."

"Yes," Gennie said, "he does."

Elias might have questioned her further, but Tova burst out of the back door, a dishtowel still in her hands. "Come and see who's here, Elias," she said. "You'll never guess."

Gennie followed the old soldier inside, then gasped at the familiar figure seated in the kitchen. "Sam?"

Sam Stegman rose to envelop Gennie in a bear hug, then shook Elias's hand. "Mr. Beck sent for me," he said to Gennie. "Said I'm to hire on permanently. Or at least until they catch the fellow who made the threats."

"I see we're all here," Daniel said from the doorway. "Sam, Elias, why don't you join me in the library? Tova, we'll need some strong coffee."

The others did as they were told, leaving Gennie alone in the kitchen with only the plinking sounds of Charlotte's pianoforte practice for company. Then Sam's words sunk in.

"Until they catch the fellow who made the threats."

Her heart sank. That awful miner from Leadville. What was his name? Bergman? No, Batson. She sucked in a shuddering breath as a thought occurred: the man she'd allowed in the house this morning might very well be one of them.

The conference in the library lasted over an hour, and when Daniel emerged, he seemed in no mood to speak to her.

"Please, Daniel," she said as he brushed past her on the stairs. "It's important."

He paused, one hand on the banister, and then turned to look down at her. "If it's about last night, don't bother. We both know that was a mistake neither of us will make again."

His flat, resigned words stunned her, as did his back as he climbed the stairs. A moment later, a door slammed.

Daniel stood behind the door he'd just slammed and cursed himself for a fool.

He'd begun his day with long-overdue morning prayers and a reading in Psalms, even though he'd had to thumb past Georgiana's obituary to do it. The Lord had met him there, and the result had been more disturbing than comforting.

There was much to think on, too much for one man to untangle in one day. The vows he'd pretended to make to a woman who belonged to another were foremost among the items that pierced his conscience. Then there was last night's near miss in the buggy. What was it about Gennie Cooper that made him feel like a young pup and an old worn-out dog at the same time?

It was a conundrum. No, she was a conundrum.

He paced the room, then returned to his spot at the door. It had occurred to him during the sleepless hours of last night that he only had to send one telegram and the wedding that had been engineered to deceive could become real.

They'd both signed documents in front of the parson and the mayor of Leadville. Those documents were now shredded and gone. Still, the smallest bit of doubt gave him pause to consider...

Consider what? Stealing a woman from the man she was supposed to marry? Daniel took up pacing again. That would make him no different than Edwin.

He stopped short, the situation suddenly clear. He and Eugenia Flora Cooper would be no more. There was nothing good to be had from considering anything but a swift end to a sordid situation.

This decided, he went to his writing table and began to draft a note to Hiram. While he'd entertained the idea that perhaps he'd turn over the Leadville operations to Hiram so Daniel could remain permanently in Denver, he now knew that would be folly.

Someone knocked on his door. "I must speak to you."

Daniel looked up. "Go away, Miss Cooper."

"I will not." She threw open the door and stepped inside. "If it is the last thing I do as your daughter's governess, I will make you listen to me. I know you're a hardheaded man, but I did not know until now that you would allow that stubborn streak of yours to put your daughter in danger."

He heard his pen clatter to the floor, unaware he'd still been holding it. "Do come in, Miss Cooper," he said, "though I warrant your reputation will be greatly compromised should you cross my threshold."

Daniel winced and looked away. Until now he'd been guilty of many things, but cruelty had not been among them. As a diversion, he retrieved his pen, hoping Miss Cooper would make the wise choice and flee.

He completed his mission to find she had not. She brought to his bedchamber a rose-scented presence that was impossible to ignore.

"All right," he said wearily, "what is it?"

"That Batson fellow? The one who chased Charlotte and made such a fuss?" When he nodded, she continued. "He was here."

"What?" Daniel rose so quickly that his chair toppled. "When?"

"No, wait," she said, touching her throat with her hand. "I misspoke. He was not actually here this morning, but I think one of his associates was."

He swallowed the words he wanted to say, then took a deep breath. "Sit," he said as he righted his chair, then pointed her toward it. When she complied, he bent to regard her at eye level, much as he would do with Charlotte. "Now, Miss Cooper—"

"Stop calling me that!" She rose and stabbed his shoulder with her index finger. "I have guarded your daughter with a pistol and my life, taken up sewing and mending, learned to wash dishes, and even gone through a marriage ceremony for you. And then there's last night and all those times before when I kissed you and you kissed me, and we could have—well, we didn't, and we shouldn't, because I still don't know what to do about Chandler, since I don't think I love him at all, but oh, how I did want to—"

"Miss Cooper!" He held his hands in front of him in case the vision in blue silk once again brandished her index finger in his direction. "Gennie."

Then he heard it. The very big thing she slipped in among all those other things.

"You don't think you love him?"

"I said that, didn't I?" She fell onto the chair with an inelegant flop, a stunned look on her face. "Oh my."

"Indeed." Much as he wanted to dwell on this fortuitous turn of events, Daniel shook his head. "You said something about an associate of Batson coming *here*? To Denver?"

Gennie shook her head. "Here. To our home. Your home," she corrected.

"Why do you think…?" He paused. "No, tell me what happened."

Gennie recounted her story of the man's early-morning visit and his refusal to identify himself.

"Did you notice anything unusual about him? Something for the authorities to go on?"

She told him about the limp and the scar on his arm, and Daniel strode to the hall. "Elias," he called. "Would you and Sam meet me in the library again? It appears our conversation regarding the threat to my family should be amended to add new information."

"Sure, boss," Elias said. "Should I have Isak fetch that Pinkerton fellow?"

"Yes, that would be a good idea."

Daniel went to Gennie and, against his better judgment, helped her to her feet. "Come tell Elias and Sam what you've told me."

She nodded, mute.

An overwhelming urge to protect her hit him. "It will be fine. I've taken every step to see to your safety and that of Charlotte."

"Oh, of course," she said blankly as she followed him downstairs to the library.

By the time she finished her story and answered Elias's questions, Isak had returned with Hank Thompson, the local Pinkerton agent. Gennie told her story yet again and answered the questions that followed.

The doorbell rang, and Elias disappeared down the hall, grumbling. He returned with a telegram for Gennie.

She looked at it and paled. "Might I be excused now?"

"I'm done with my questions, so there's no need for you to stay." Closing his notebook, Hank looked at Daniel. "You've got a man watching the ladies as we discussed?"

"Sam Stegman."

"The prizefighter?" The Pinkerton man grinned. "You rich folks sure do have connections."

Daniel saw Thompson out, then returned to the library to find Gennie gone. "Isak," he called as he stepped outside, "saddle up Blossom. I'm in the mood for a ride."

"Blossom?" Isak shook his head. "Can't do that, sir."

"You cannot saddle my horse for me? I'd best hear a good reason and fast." The sound of horse hoofs caught his attention. "Is that...?"

"Blossom? Yes sir. Miss Cooper asked for the sidesaddle but I didn't have it at the ready, so she said it wouldn't be too scandalous for her to ride like us menfolk, long as she kept to the side streets and avoided downtown."

Daniel tried to listen to the stable boy, but all he heard was the clip-clop of horse hoofs fading into the distance. "Is the buggy still ready?"

"Yes sir," Isak said. "I apologize, but I thought the Pinkerton man might need a ride back into town, so I—"

"Perfect!" Daniel headed to the other side of the carriage house and leaped into the buggy. He headed in the direction the obviously affected governess had gone.

He caught up to her easily, given the fact she was not only a novice horsewoman but also knew nothing about Denver. The street she'd taken dead-ended at the river, and having no way to cross, she'd been forced to double back.

"Get off that horse immediately," he shouted.

"Leave me alone," she called. "I'm having a Wild West adventure."

27

Circling back toward Deadwood proved futile, for the prairie was flat and visibility stretched for miles. Mae had two choices: either race for the hills or face whoever had the nerve to tail her, and fight it out.

She chose the latter, not because she was a woman with a death wish, but because she was a woman who never backed down. Loading her weapons in the open might prove disastrous should the stranger spur his mount and try to overtake her. The horse she rode was untried, and for the price she paid, likely not the best she could be riding.

⊗

Gennie ignored Daniel and spurred the horse on. She could thank Isak for the assistance in learning to ride what she discovered was quite a gentle animal. Indeed, the aptly named Blossom was a flower among horses. The thought made her laugh even as Daniel Beck made her frown.

"If you persist in following me, I shall be forced to ride into town and report you to the authorities."

His laughter held no humor. "Go right ahead, Gennie," he shouted over the sound of the horses' hoofs, "and while we're there, I will report you as a horse thief."

The statement deflated her, and Gennie reined the horse to a slow trot. "Have it your way, then," she said. "Men always do."

He looked surprised. "What does that mean?"

The telegram in her pocket was explanation enough, but he was the last one to whom she'd show it. "I'm leaving soon, Daniel," she said. "Won't you let me have this one last ride?"

Another laugh. "You are a dramatic woman, Gennie. You act as if you're going away today."

"Tomorrow," she corrected as she directed the animal off the road and onto a narrow path that lead along a tributary of the river, praying Daniel would not try to follow on foot. To be certain of it, she spurred Blossom to a canter. She heard Daniel shout her name a few times, but the horse easily outpaced him. When she felt she'd put enough distance between them, Gennie slowed the horse to a trot, then, where the river flowed under the railroad trestle, dismounted.

While the horse drank, she held the reins and tried to remember how to walk. Unaccustomed to the jostling of even the slowest of rides, Gennie decided she may have caused some sort of permanent damage. She couldn't walk more than a few steps without wincing from the effort. Thankfully, Blossom would take her all the way home. After that, a warm bath should do the trick.

A shot rang out and the horse startled, yanking the reins from Gennie's fingers. Another shot, and the horse bolted, disappearing in the direction they'd come.

"Wonderful. Now I'm in a fix." She sighed.

"Miss Cooper?" a decidedly male and somewhat familiar voice said.

Gennie turned to see Isak standing behind her, his hand on the gun at his hip. His face held no humor. "Isak? What's wrong? Did Daniel send you?"

Isak shrugged off his frown and gestured to the thicket. "Yeah, Mr. Beck sent me. Let's go home."

She followed with difficulty, wincing with every step. "How far are we going?" she asked after a few minutes. "Even though you've been a great teacher, I've not got the stamina I should."

"Not much farther," he said. "You can make it."

They emerged into a clearing, a coach parked at its center.

"Oh good," Gennie said. "I was afraid I'd have to walk all the way home. At the rate I'm going, that would take all day."

"After you." Isak handed her inside the darkened interior.

Gennie reached to raise the shade, and a hand went over her mouth. Another covered her eyes. She kicked against the dark form and heard a grunt.

The hand disappeared from her mouth, and she tried to scream. Before she could, however, something that tasted like sweat and bitter medicine filled her mouth.

☙❧

"Daniel," Elias called. "The horse is back, but Miss Cooper's not."

He tore out of the house to meet Elias. "I knew I shouldn't have left her alone." He caught his breath. "Surely she's with Isak."

"Isak?"

"You didn't think I would leave her without a bodyguard, did you? I sent the lad to watch her." He paused. "She certainly didn't want me around."

"About that," Elias said. "I've been meaning to ask—"

Isak raced toward the carriage house, his face red and his breath coming in gasps. "Mr. Beck, Mr. Howe," he managed, "they got her. Those men, they got her and took her away."

"What men?" Daniel shook the lad to get his attention. "Where is she now?"

"Didn't recognize them." He shrugged. "Last I saw her, she was over by the train trestle north of the city. You know, the one that's over Jackrabbit Creek?"

"Take me there," Daniel demanded as he practically threw the young man in the buggy. "Elias, you take the wagon and go fetch the law. You know where that trestle is?"

"I do," Elias said.

"What's going on here?" Tova stepped outside, a dishcloth over one shoulder.

Daniel turned to her. "Send Sam over to the school and tell him to take Charlotte to the Finch place until Elias or I come for them. It's important you tell him exactly that. Do you understand?"

Tova nodded. "Sam goes to the school and brings Charlotte to the Finch home until you come for him. Anything else?"

Daniel looked from Tova to Elias, who wore a worried look. "Yes," he added. "You go with Sam. I'm not taking any chances with those I love."

The old soldier gave a nod of approval, then turned to Tova. "Hurry yourself up. I don't take chances with those I love, either."

Daniel circled the drive and turned the buggy toward Jackrabbit Creek, unable to even look at the lad beside him. As the road narrowed to a path, he urged the horses on.

"I didn't know she'd leave with them," Isak said. "I really didn't know. He said he was a friend of hers."

"All right, kid." Daniel urged the horses forward, knowing he trod a fine line between speed and running the buggy into the river.

When they reached the trestle, Daniel pulled the horses to a halt. A dry wind blew the heat off the packed ground and circled the buggy like a dust devil. Daniel shielded his eyes against the glare of the sun and tried to see something, anything, that might tell him where they went.

If only last night's rain had touched Denver. Instead, the ground remained hard, a poor surface for discerning the direction of any traveler.

Direction. Daniel slapped his thigh.

"When you helped her into the coach, which way were the horses pointing?"

Isak gestured to the west.

"All right, then," Daniel said. "Let's go."

He pointed the horses north until he reached a place in the river where they could cross. There, in the wet dirt on the opposite bank, he found tracks.

"What now?" Isak asked.

"Now we pray!" Daniel urged the horses to a gallop. "This pair won't go much farther at this pace."

"What's that?" Isak pointed to a black spot in the distance.

"Looks like a coach." Daniel pointed the buggy toward the horizon.

The coach moved at quite a clip, but Daniel's horses were faster. As he closed the distance, Daniel saw the coach's team had no driver, and one door hung open.

As he moved within range, he saw that the coach did, however, have a passenger. Lying half on the floor and half on the seat was Gennie Cooper. He'd know that blond hair and cornflower blue dress anywhere.

Daniel began to pray. Then he devised a plan.

"I'm going to need your help, Isak." Daniel regarded him with a quick but serious look. "If you're really a part of this, then I could die trying to save Gennie."

The young man shook his head furiously. "I'm telling the truth, Mr. Beck. You just tell me what to do and I will do it."

"All right." Daniel gestured to the runaway coach. "Take the reins and get us as close to it as you can. When I think I can, I'll jump over and see if I can't get the thing stopped."

The boy's eyes went wide, but he nodded and did as he was told. When they were close enough, Daniel shouted Gennie's name.

She turned toward him, still holding tight to the seat in front of her. "No," she said. There were more words, but the thundering hoofs kept them from being heard.

Daniel watched the distance become shorter, and his prayers became more fervent. With less than a foot between the coach and the buggy, he prepared to jump.

"Move out of the way," he shouted, and she did, crawling onto the seat opposite the open door.

A shot rang out, and Daniel almost landed on the prairie.

Gennie pointed to the roof and shouted something about a man. A second look showed a fellow lying prone on top of the carriage. A length of rope had been tied to the reins, giving him the ability to halt the carriage at will.

It was a setup. Odd that the man couldn't hit him from barely a foot away.

Daniel reached for his Colt, then decided it was foolish to jump with his weapon at the ready. He turned to Isak. "The minute I jump, you turn this rig around and get out of that man's range. I'll not have your blood on my hands."

"Yes sir," Isak said.

"I want you to fetch the Pinkerton. You remember Hank Thompson, don't you?"

"I do, sir. What should I do when I get him?"

"Bring him out here so he can investigate."

"Yes sir. I'll do it fast as this team'll take me there and back."

"All right, then." Daniel gave Isak another hard look, then jumped, landing with a rolling thud in the spot where Gennie had just been lying.

Another shot split a hole in the roof, and Daniel scooted out of the way. "Are you harmed?" he asked Gennie.

"No," she shouted over the noise, "but that man up there's got to be stopped."

"I'll get him."

Daniel made to leave, and Gennie grabbed his arm. "Don't get yourself killed, Daniel Beck."

"I promise. Now hold on and stay out of the way." He paused to check the ammunition in his Colt. "Whatever you do, stay away from the windows and door."

She nodded, then swiped at a tear. "For the record," she said as she let him go, "this is not the kind of Wild West adventure I was looking for."

He crawled to the door, wedging himself into the opening. With his boots on the seat, Daniel managed to swing up to take a closer look at the fellow atop the coach.

A bullet zinged past his ear.

All right, Lord, that didn't work. What now?

Daniel swung around to see if he could reach the driver's seat, and another bullet sounded, this one nowhere near him. He spied the rope and devised a plan.

The man on top had obviously rolled to the left, for the rope was shifted far to that side, as were the reins. Daniel slid back into the coach and climbed over Gennie's legs to peer out of the shade. The end of the rope hung just out of reach.

"I've got a plan," he told Gennie. "You sit still and this thing will be stopped in no time."

Her eyes wide and ringed with tears, Gennie managed a nod. "What can I do?"

"Your job is to stay alive!"

Daniel slid out the window and snagged the rope. A hard tug sent the horses into a turn that nearly sent him spiraling off onto the ground. Daniel held tight to the rope and prayed the horses would stop before he landed under them. The man above tried to aim his gun at Daniel and keep his grip on the reins while the carriage careened over rutted ground.

"Be careful!" Gennie called.

"Yes, dear," Daniel managed.

He tightened his grip on the coach window, trying to reach the driver's seat. In order to lunge forward and grab the reins, he'd have to give up his hold on the rope. Praying once again, Daniel counted to three, then hefted himself up onto the seat and gave the fellow on the roof a push. A bullet nicked his shoulder as the man disappeared over the other side of the coach and landed with a thud that was almost drowned out by the clattering of the horses' hoofs.

For a moment, Daniel could only hold on tight and try to catch his breath.

He leaned forward and swiped at the reins, but missed and nearly toppled from the seat. On the second attempt, he managed to lean forward enough to snag them. The spooked horses, however, refused to stop for another half mile.

When the coach rolled to a halt, Gennie fell out the open door, then scrambled to her feet.

She met him halfway, clinging to Daniel as soon as he jumped from the driver's seat. He wrapped the frightened woman in an embrace and rested his chin atop her head. By the time Isak swung back around to pick them up, Gennie had almost stopped crying.

"You're bleeding," she said, and the bawling began again.

"It's just a scratch." Daniel let out a long breath and waited until she quieted again. He lifted her chin. "I promised you a Wild West adventure, and even though we didn't get back to Leadville, I think I delivered."

She swatted him on the arm, then started crying again.

∽∾

Gennie allowed Daniel to help her toward the house, but drew the line at letting him carry her.

"I'm perfectly capable of walking," she said, "though the doctor better get here soon, or I'll be forced to stitch up that wound of yours myself."

"It's just a scratch." Daniel dabbed gingerly at his shoulder with her handkerchief. "Besides, I've seen your stitching. I'll take my chances." He paused and looked past her. "Is that Jeb Sanders? What in the world is he doing in Denver?"

Gennie grabbed Daniel's arm and pulled him back. "I've seen that man before."

"In Leadville," he said.

"No, here." She paused. "He's the one I told you about. I let him in because he said he was a friend of yours, but he wouldn't leave his name."

"Him? He's one of my miners." Daniel raised his hand to wave at the miner but made sure he walked in front of Gennie as he approached. "Sanders, what are you doing in Denver?"

Jeb waved and closed his notebook, then limped down to meet them. "Howdy, Mr. Beck. Miss Cooper." He shrugged. "I guess you'll find out soon enough. I'm with the Pinkertons. Have been for nearly a year."

"You? A Pinkerton?"

Sanders ducked his head, then gave Daniel a sheepish look. "I am. I hated not telling you what I was up to, Mr. Beck, but I needed to be able to stay undercover out at the mine. We didn't want any more trouble like you all had back in the spring. I always favored the Beck Mines because you're a good, honest man, so I asked to be assigned there."

"I had no idea."

"The boss decided an inside man was the way to handle things." Sanders shook his head. "I hated having to associate with my cousins, and I plan to go back to Leadville soon as we wrap this up and find out how those boys got out of jail and which low-down dog shot that deputy." He paused. "I wouldn't be surprised to discover they were behind today's events."

"Speaking of that, do you know why Miss Cooper was abducted?"

Sanders shook his head. "She was never the intended victim."

"What do you mean?" Daniel's eyes widened. "Charlotte? They didn't get her, did they?"

Jeb checked his notepad. "Safe and sound. Right now she's having tea and practicing manners with a Miss Anna Finch."

"Oh no," Gennie said. "I forgot I'd promised Charlotte a tea party today."

"Under the circumstances, it's better she wasn't here, Miss Cooper." Sanders paused. "Much as I'm sure you were scared to death, your ride on the runaway coach wasn't supposed to cause you harm. The real purpose was to draw you and Daniel out of the house in order to get to the girl. That was a smart thing, sending the bodyguard to keep watch on the child today."

"But why go to such extremes? Miss Cooper could have been killed."

Sanders shook his head. "Again, I doubt that would have happened."

"But how did they know she wanted an adventure, Jeb?"

"Telegraph officer," he said. "The fellow's kin to the man driving the coach. Didn't take much to figure that out."

"But I don't even know that man, Jeb," Daniel said. "What grudge could he have against me and my family?"

"You own a mine, sir. The strike might be over, but there's still bad feelings with some of these men." The Pinkerton shrugged. "Looks like you're the one they hated most. I guess it doesn't pay to be the man who refuses to back down."

"I'll not apologize for doing the right thing," Daniel said, "but I'll also not risk the safety of my family."

"I can't make a guarantee, but I can promise you'll have the best protection our office can provide," he said.

Daniel slapped the man on the back. "I'll do you one better, Sanders. How would you like to work for me? And I don't mean at the mines."

28

Mae cast about for another option and found none. "Here's the test of your mettle," she said as she realized she might truly meet her end here.

Had she mistaken her calling? Would she finally regret not giving in to the call of home and hearth?

Fair Mae considered the chubby cheeks of the baby she might not live to rock, then gave more than a passing thought to the possibility she might petition the Lord for a second chance. Then clarity arrived, along with the distant sound of a train whistle.

"Perhaps another day," she whispered as she instead thanked God for bringing her this far. To ask Him to carry her further seemed too much to request.

But she did.

⊙⊙

"Try again, Charlotte," Gennie said as she watched the girl practice her curtsy. "And this time go deeper. I want your nose to almost touch the ground." She smiled as her duckling-turned-beautiful-swan went through the motions one more time.

Faced with her impending return to New York City, Gennie had spent the whole of last evening, once the excitement from her abduction wore off, and this morning plotting how to stay longer. Unfortunately, the harder she prayed that Daniel Beck would somehow come to his senses and see that she just might, if asked, continue her adventure here indefinitely, the more distant he seemed. He'd hardly even looked at her today.

Perhaps it was the distraction of his estranged father's impending visit. Not one but two letters had arrived for him with his father's return address. And then there were the others from Leadville, including an odd one marked Urgent that had been sent by the pastor who'd performed their mock marriage.

Charlotte called her name, and Gennie grinned. Soon the young girl would be ready to meet the man who held such sway over the Beck family. A secret longing, never dared spoken, was that Gennie too could meet this man who'd caused Daniel Beck such pain.

She'd give him what for, that much she knew. How a man could find fault with a fellow like Daniel was beyond her. Though the man did have one fault she alone could air a grievance over: he couldn't see love when it was right in front of him.

Love. Odd how she always thought she knew what that was. In her world, love was akin to duty, a deep abiding, even if not heart stirring. She'd felt this for Chandler, and until here, until Daniel, she might have been happy with the solid permanence the Dodd name offered.

But when she thought of Daniel Beck dodging bullets while hanging off the side of a wildly careening coach just to save her, Gennie never failed to have that jolt-to-the-heart kind of feeling that curled her toes and turned her insides to jelly.

Of course, she'd been unable to tell Daniel this. Nor about the telegram burning a hole in her skirts, the one she'd received yesterday.

"Gennie, you're not watching."

"I'm sorry, sweetheart." She nodded and the girl performed an acceptable bow, then rose to await Gennie's response. "You're very good at this," Gennie said as she clapped. "If I didn't know better, I'd think you don't mind this a bit."

Charlotte laughed. "Maybe I don't, but I'll never tell you. Papa!" She squealed and picked up her skirts to run across the ballroom and into the arms of her father.

"Such decorum," he chided, then winked.

Gennie felt the stupid jolt when he looked her way. Gaining control of whatever had her in its grasp would be difficult, but if he didn't need her, she certainly would not present anything but a calm and detached exterior.

Thankfully, she had a moment to work on this, for Daniel's focus was on Charlotte.

"I've been watching you, Buttercup, and you're a natural at this. You may need to teach me a thing or two."

"Waltz with me, Papa," Charlotte said. "I've been practicing." She looked over at Gennie. "Would you play so I can show Papa what I've learned?"

Gennie rose and walked to the pianoforte without making eye contact with him. As she seated herself on the stool, she chided herself for acting like a silly love-struck girl rather than a mature woman of marriageable age.

Her fingers glided over Charlotte's favorite waltz while father and daughter did the same on the dance floor. Seizing the chance to observe the pair, Gennie noted the similarities in the two were mostly in temperament rather than looks. Charlotte must be the image of her mother.

"Faster, Gennie," Charlotte called, and Gennie picked up the tempo. They were laughing now, father and daughter, and Gennie couldn't help but smile.

"Your turn, Miss Cooper."

Gennie glanced up. "Oh, no, you don't, Charlotte Beck. You're the one who needs lessons, not me."

"No," the girl said, her face quite serious. "It's Papa who is in need. He's a bit, well, hopeless."

Gennie braved her first direct look into Daniel's eyes since he walked into the ballroom. "Is he?" she managed.

Daniel shrugged. "She seems to think I'm a bit rusty."

"That's because you don't practice enough." Charlotte poked him in the chest, then pointed to Gennie. "With someone your own size, I mean."

Charlotte broke away from her father, took three running steps, then slid in her stocking feet toward Gennie. She leaned close. "Work with me here, Gennie. My father is hopeless at this, so you're going to have to help him."

"Oh, I don't know," Gennie said in a voice she hoped only Charlotte could hear. "His dancing's not so bad."

"I'm not talking about his dancing." The girl had the audacity to wink. "He loves you, you know. Now get off that stool and go dance with my father."

He loves you, you know.

Gennie tried to respond. The girl couldn't possibly be correct. She rose on quaking legs but could not make herself cross the ballroom to where Daniel stood, watching them with open curiosity.

"Go," Charlotte urged.

She tried, but her feet wouldn't move. Had she not lost all ability to speak, Gennie might have made her excuses and left the two of them to have fun without her.

"Papa, come and fetch your dancing partner. It appears she's heard of your reputation for stepping on toes."

"Yes," he said, "I do have that reputation."

Daniel walked toward her. Gennie's urge to bolt and run was tempered by the inability to do so.

He reached her and held out his hand, but she could only stare. "Might I have this dance?" His smile didn't quite reach his eyes. "And then we've business of a rather urgent nature to discuss."

Business. Dare she hope this was some ill-phrased attempt at cleverness on his part?

She nodded stiffly and took his hand. Charlotte began to play, but Daniel made no attempt to move.

The music stopped. "Put your hand on her back, Papa, and stop acting goofy."

Acting goofy. Indeed, that was how he felt in the presence of Gennie Cooper. He always had, since the moment he met her, but there was no hope for it. Not as long as she was promised to another.

His hand spanned her back, and she stiffened. The fact she'd been obviously unwilling to dance with him chafed at his heart. Could she not see all he wanted was to take her in his arms and dance through the next fifty years with her?

Charlotte began to play, and he forced himself to move. After a few halting steps, they found a rhythm. Unfortunately, looking into her eyes caused him to stumble. He mumbled a word of apology and went back to dancing.

It was the scent of roses, he decided, that did him in. Or maybe it was the softness of her hands and how they felt so small against his.

Stop, idiot. You're a grown man and not some pimple-faced boy with his first crush. When he dared a look into her eyes, the thoughts he had were not those of a boy, but a man. Remembering her in the moonlight was nearly his undoing, and he faltered and stomped horribly on her foot.

"Terribly sorry," he muttered, though removing his foot from hers was much easier than pushing away thoughts he had no business recalling.

"Hold her closer, Papa, and you won't step on her toes."

He glared at Charlotte but did as she asked. Was it his imagination, or did Gennie gasp?

They moved as one, her cheek pressed against his shoulder. A longing began, and Daniel knew he'd likely never shake free of this memory. To punctuate the thought, he pressed his palm against her back and moved her imperceptibly closer. This time it was a sigh he heard.

His own.

The imp played the song at least twice through and had begun her third time when Gennie called a halt. With a few mumbled words about a prior appointment of some sort, she fled.

Charlotte watched her governess go, then turned to stare at him. Her expression was not pleased. "What did you say to her, Papa?"

"Nothing," he said. "We merely danced."

She rose and walked toward him, and his heart squeezed. Where had the impudent pie-stealer gone? Somehow, in the short weeks Gennie Cooper had been with them, she'd worked a change in Charlotte that went well beyond giving up overalls for chintz frocks and pie stealing for playing the pianoforte.

The governess-who-wasn't had changed them all.

"Are you going to let her get away?" Charlotte demanded.

Daniel shrugged. "What can I do?"

His daughter moved behind him and gave his back a solid push. "Go after her. Unless you do something, she'll be gone soon."

Soon. His heart sank. How could he possibly cause her to fall in love with him in such a short time?

"Go." Charlotte pushed him again, and this time he set his feet in motion. What he'd say when he found Gennie was beyond his knowing, but if the Lord could bring her to his home, perhaps He could keep her here too.

This thought carried him into the library where, against his nature, he bellowed for Tova. "Fetch Miss Cooper," he said as he found his chair and began to sort through the mail. "And tell her I *require* her presence, not *wish* it. Are you clear on the difference?"

"Yes sir. Right away, sir." Tova hurried away, no doubt offended by his brusque behavior.

He sighed. Amends could be made later.

The top two letters on the stack were from his father. Daniel moved them aside to read later, but pondered them nonetheless. An interesting phenomenon had occurred in the time since he accepted his father's request for a visit. They'd begun to correspond.

It started as defiance on his part. The first letter had been filled with pointed remarks about his business, his happiness with life in Colorado, and his joy at watching Charlotte grow to be a delightful young lady.

Ironically, when he penned the words, none of them were true.

The earl's response was brief but somewhat cordial, but the next letter was longer. He wrote of the mines, the mountains, and the kitchen garden where he puttered about in his old age. Daniel laughed even now at the idea of the imperious royal tilling the soil in hopes of providing a few carrots for the manor's table.

His smile faded when he saw the next letter, a fat envelope marked Urgent and posted from Leadville. The sender was the parson who'd been dragged from his dinner table to preside at the sham wedding that pleased everyone in Leadville except the two participants. Daniel opened the envelope and emptied its contents—a folded sheaf of papers and a news clipping—onto the desk. He reached for the clipping first and noted the date. Last Friday.

Then he saw the headline below, a banner that took up a good quarter of the page: BEAUTY AND THE SILVER BARON; DANIEL BECK TAKES A BRIDE.

Daniel shook his head. "What in the world?"

He scanned the article, a flowery piece centered on the wonders Daniel had performed since coming to Leadville some years prior. The column sang his praises and mentioned everything except where he'd gone to primary school and what color his socks were that day. It also included quotes from several of the members of the Greater Leadville Beautification and Improvement Society, including a particularly moving one from Ira Stegman: "He believed in me, and I am thrilled for him."

"Oh, for crying out loud." Daniel slammed the page onto the desk.

The final paragraph of the article caught his attention. "The bride, Miss Eugenia Flora Cooper of the Manhattan, Boston, and Newport Coopers, is of sterling character and stunning beauty and has found favor both at home and abroad for her quick wit and apt humor. One *New York Times* reporter, in Leadville to cover the recent miners' strike, commented that of all of New York society, the Coopers were his favorite to cover. 'The fact she's wed an earl's son does not surprise me,' the reporter quipped, 'for the family has ties to the royal families of several European countries.'"

The words swam in front of Daniel's eyes, and he took a deep breath. Damage control. He'd put Hiram on it immediately.

A simple story retracting the article as a mistake would suffice. Of course, the *Times* reporter would have to be a part of the retraction.

Daniel reached for pen and paper to jot a note of reminder. This must be handled today, before the story got any farther than Leadville.

Stuffing the newsprint back in the envelope was simple enough, but the folded papers simply would not go. He opened the top drawer and swept the whole pile inside. Just as it closed, he saw the official seal on the first page.

Thoughts fled as he lifted a signed and executed marriage license from the drawer. His heart sank, and breathing became difficult.

So he and the woman who plagued his days and nights were indeed husband and wife. How was this possible?

And yet the implications intrigued him. Had he known, perhaps his memories might be colored with more than regret. He contemplated that a moment, allowing the thought to take hold.

He thumbed through the pages of the legal document until he came to the last—a writ of annulment with a note stating his signature would make the document valid. He read this with disappointment. Would it be that easy to rid her from his life?

Impossible, he knew, and yet he held the legal pages in front of him. The good pastor, or one of the others on the committee, had indeed seen to everything.

As easily as he'd married, he'd be free again. They both would be.

Oh, Lord, what have I done? Daniel sank back in the chair, but a knock brought him forward again. Tova slid the door open just enough to peer at him.

"You've a visitor, sir."

A visitor? What an odd way to refer to Gennie. "Send her in, of course."

Tova shook her head. "It's a him, sir, not a her."

She opened the door and moved back to allow a man in expensive but rumpled garb to push past. His build put Daniel in mind of someone who might have played rugby or football at Yale or Harvard, while his expression told of a man unused to the trouble this visit was causing him.

Daniel rose. "Do I know you?"

"You should. My name is Chandler Dodd."

Mae decided to make do and call out the traveler with what she already had. The rifle had only been used for batting practice, not shooting, so she went to it first. Riding like the wind, the fair female crossed the prairie on the untried steed, all the while praying that the man who had trailed her was friend and not foe.

Her rifle at the ready, Mae pulled up short and aimed at the oncoming shadowy figure.

"Mister," she called, "you come any closer, and it'll cost you your life."

※

Gennie decided she'd make Daniel wait just a few more minutes before answering his summons. She'd also decided to forgo any pretense of playing the coquette with him. If the man was too dense to see how very much she cared for him, then she'd just have to make it clear.

How, she hadn't quite figured out. That detail she could handle when the time came.

She made one more trip to the mirror, pinching her cheeks to heighten their color and retraining a few curls to frame her face. That done, she added a touch of rosewater at her wrists and neck, then reached for the doorknob.

Somewhere between the first and third versions of their waltz, she'd made a decision. She'd stay in Denver until Daniel Beck realized the real treasure was not at the bottom of some stupid mine in Leadville.

The real treasure was right here in his own home.

Though it would not be proper to remain under his roof once Daniel declared his intentions—and he would—she would soon be back under this roof as his wife. And this time, theirs would be a real wedding and not some imagined affair attended by people she barely knew. Mama and Papa would see that this was the wedding of the century.

It was not the wedding she most had her mind on, however, but the honeymoon. Anticipation made her hands shake, and she pressed her palms against her skirt. What was it about Daniel Beck that made her think of days and nights of happiness that went on forever?

"He loves you, you know."

"Oh, Charlotte, sweetheart, I do hope you know what you're talking about."

Then she thought of Anna. How would she tell Anna Finch that she'd inexplicably fallen in love with Daniel Beck? She'd have to, and soon.

Tiptoeing down the stairs, she slipped past the partially open door of the library and outside without anyone's seeing her. A moment later, she slid between the hedges and arrived at Anna's front door.

Her friend expressed surprise and pleasure in equal measure at the visit, but quickly realized something was wrong. Bypassing the formality of offering up tea and snacks, she took Gennie by the wrist and practically dragged her upstairs.

"All right," Anna said when she'd closed the door, "let's hear it, Gennie. This is about Daniel, isn't it?"

Gennie nodded. "How did you know?"

Anna leaned forward and grasped Gennie's hands. "I'm not blind, Gennie. I've known for quite some time that he's in love with you."

"You have?" Gennie shook her head. "How? I didn't see it."

"Well, of course not." Anna smiled. "Sometimes that's how God works, right?"

"I suppose." Gennie sighed. "Still, I really thought you would be the perfect mother for Charlotte."

"I know," she said, "and she and I will always be close. I think it's because I understand her. We're very much alike."

Gennie laughed. "How so? Have you been a pie thief too?"

Anna gave Gennie a devilish grin. "Not specifically, though I did cover for one recently."

"Oh?"

Her friend laughed and walked into her closet, returning with a bundle. "I have a confession of my own. Open it."

"What is this?"

Another laugh. "That's the traveling outfit you wore the day you arrived in Denver."

Gennie looked up. "How did you come to have this?"

"I caught the little thief red-handed in it." Anna grinned. "It seems she'd been wearing the outfit when she went out to steal pies off unsuspecting folks' kitchen windows."

Outrage was tempered by amusement. "Why my clothing?"

"Charlotte figured people would think it was you stealing those pies." Anna shrugged. "I confiscated it and told her I'd tattle unless she gave up her ways and learned to bake pies instead of steal them. I don't know how she managed to get around in it, what with the difference in your sizes."

Gennie handed the bundle back to Anna. "I don't think I'll be needing this anymore."

Anna pulled her to her feet and embraced her. "I just have one request."

"What's that?"

"Can I be your maid of honor?"

꤯

Gennie turned the knob of the front door and bounded inside, pausing only to collect herself before reaching the library. Through the closed door, she heard raised voices.

"You ought to go back on upstairs," she heard Elias say.

Gennie turned to find the old soldier dressed in full regalia despite the July heat. "He summoned me," she said.

"Since when does that matter?" he asked, though the chuckle she expected did not seem forthcoming.

The voices became louder, and she heard her name. "I should see what's going on."

"Don't," Elias called, but it was too late. She'd already opened the door.

She saw Daniel first, his face red and his expression sour. His gaze collided with hers, and she recoiled. She did not see love there.

Slowly the other man came into focus, and with it the reason for Daniel's obvious anger.

Gennie's mouth went dry. "Chandler."

No, Lord. Not yet. I just needed a little more time.

"Sweetheart!" The banker whisked her into an embrace she did not reciprocate.

"Chandler, what are you doing here?" she asked when she could manage it.

The banker seemed not to notice her discomfort. "Didn't you get my telegram? I came to bring you home."

Her fingers went to her throat, which felt like the Sahara. "But h-how did you find me?"

He took her hand and held it against his lips. "Hester was worried. She came to me with the telegram you sent." Chandler tossed the folded paper onto the desk, and Daniel picked it up. The words she wrote, so innocent then, looked damning now.

Need loan for quick exit. Wild West insufferable and so is Daniel Beck. Will repay upon return.

"Insufferable?" The word hung between them as Daniel waited for her to deny the validity of the document.

"You don't understand," she said, looking away. "I was angry. I wanted to go home."

"That's why I'm here," Chandler said. "Go pack your things. We've a train to catch." He shook his head. "No, on second thought, leave it all here. You'll want for nothing when we return."

I'll want for Daniel Beck. Do something, Lord. Please.

"I need to speak to Daniel alone."

Chandler pulled his ridiculously expensive watch from his pocket, then shook his head. "There's no time."

"Make the time, Chandler," she said. "You're an important man. I'm certain you can manage to delay a train for five minutes."

Her desperation must have shown, but Gennie didn't care. All she could think of was how close she'd come to a love she might very well be about to lose.

The only reason she would walk away from a man who made her feel wholly and completely alive was if he did not want her to stay.

While Daniel stared at her, Chandler began issuing orders, treating her like a child in need of instruction on the proper way to leave a home and board a train. The only instructions she needed at this point were the ones that would tell her how to reach through the shell she could see building around Daniel Beck. Surely the Lord had heard her groanings by now. Why hadn't He acted?

"Chandler, please," she interrupted. "Go wait in whatever conveyance brought you here."

"Darling, I—"

"Go. Now. Please." She used the authoritative tone she'd learned with Charlotte, and Chandler, surprised by her force, obeyed.

Until she heard Chandler's footsteps fade and the front door slam, she barely managed a breath. Woodenly, she went to the library door and shut it, then, in her final act of defiance, turned the key.

She loves you, Papa. Go after her.

The child was obviously deluded.

"Five minutes?" Daniel said. "Do we need even that?"

Gennie did not move from the door, nor did she turn around. His gaze went to the narrow span of her waist, to the spot where his palm had fit so nicely only an hour before.

It seemed like days.

No matter what the banker said about his hold on Gennie, Daniel knew his was stronger. He'd seen it. Felt it.

She was, after all, his wife.

The thought settled heavily on him, along with the realization that the door was locked. He could go to her now. Spin her around and kiss her until she forgot all about the banker. Until he forgot all about having the debacle that was getting their unintentional wedding annulled.

Before good sense could prevail, Daniel went to her. He stood close enough to touch her, though he dared not.

"Turn around."

She did, looking up with tears coursing down her cheeks. His fingers itched to wipe them away.

Daniel held out his hand. "The key, please."

She threw it, never removing her eyes from his as it clattered to the floor somewhere behind him.

A moment's indecision, and he gave in. She kissed him first but he did not protest. In her presence, he was a weak man. And what fault could be found? For today, for now, she was his wife.

Daniel lifted her into his arms and carried her to the settee. He pulled her to him, caring not that her hairpins scattered and her curls tumbled down around them. Not caring for propriety or common sense.

Not even caring an angry banker waited at the curb to take her away. She was his wife.

Legally.

His.

"No." The word welled from deep within, salting the wound where his heart had been previously broken. Upon Georgiana's death, he'd promised God never to repeat the sins of his past. Now he stood poised to once more take another man's woman.

Gennie moved to kiss him again, but he placed his finger on her lips. "Charlotte is Edwin's child. Edwin," he said carefully, "is my brother. I took Georgiana from him."

Gennie's curls shone like spun gold in the sunlight. "Why are you telling me this?"

"Because you need to know why I'm sending you back to the man you promised to marry."

"I made no such promise."

"Your father thinks otherwise. I've seen the letter." Daniel left her to retrieve the key and fit it into the lock, freeing himself from the temptation of tossing it out the window and forgetting the proof he'd seen with his own eyes.

He would forget her. A lie, but maybe God would make it true.

"You've not asked me if I wish to go back to him." Her voice wavered, as did his resolve. "If you had, I would tell you—"

"I'm not asking, Miss Cooper," he said before she could find the words to change his mind.

Gennie moved closer to him. Too close. "It's 'Mrs. Beck' to you."

Daniel stopped her, taking her gently by the shoulders lest she land in his arms. "No," he said. "It's not."

"But, Daniel…"

He allowed himself to gather her close, savoring the feel of her in his arms though he knew it meant more danger to him than any angry miner might cause. Hands that ignored his good sense moved up her spine to slip beneath her curls and find the warmth of her skin. He cupped her jaw, then slid his thumb across her lips.

"I want to stay," he thought she said, though her voice was low, quiet even through the tears that threatened.

"You belong to another." He lifted her palm to his lips. "That means you cannot be mine."

"But I—"

"No," came out much firmer than it felt.

She stared at him for a long moment, without blinking. Just as he felt the urge to relent, to spend the rest of their lives changing his mind—and hers—Gennie gave him a curt nod.

"You mean it. Very well." Wiping away her tears, she straightened her spine. "Good—good-bye, Daniel." She seemed to choke on the words.

Then she burst into tears again and fled.

Try as he might to move, Daniel could only watch in silence.

Long after she left, Daniel remained at his desk, reading every detail of the marriage and soon-to-be annulment. Explaining it all to Charlotte was not something he looked forward to doing. Perhaps he could ask Anna Finch for advice. She'd always had a way with the girl.

Daniel wrote a note and called for Tova. Elias came instead.

"You're a blame fool," his old friend said as he took the note and turned away. "An idiotic, hardheaded blame fool who ought to get on that horse Isak's already got saddled up and waiting for you and head that woman off before she gets away. Not that I have an opinion on it, of course." Elias slammed the door, then promptly reopened it. "And if I were you, which I'm not because I'd not be in this fix if I were, then I'd be sure and hunt up any lost hairpins before Tova finds them. You wouldn't want to set the gossips to talking."

All right, Lord. Unless You've got an objection, I'm going to take care of this right now.

He snatched up the annulment papers and reached for his pen, but the inkwell was dry.

"Of all the…" Daniel set the pen aside. "All right, then, Lord, I'll go get her, but I don't have any idea what You're up to."

Just as Elias said, Isak waited outside with Blossom saddled and ready. The horse practically flew over the dusty streets to Union Station, where Daniel leaped from her back and raced inside.

"Which one's headed for New York City?" he shouted to the ticket seller.

"New York City?" The clerk shrugged. "That'd be the 405, but she's pulling out right now."

Daniel's heart pounded and his breath came in short gasps, but he'd not quit now. "Where? Which one?"

The man pointed to the far end of the station where a Denver and Pacific engine sounded its warning.

"Over there? I'll never make it."

Then a thought occurred to him, and Daniel raced to find Blossom and aim her toward Jackrabbit Creek. "Lord, do you want me to catch her or just try?" he called over the pounding of the mare's hoofs. "I can do the trying, but You're going to have to cause me to catch her. That's the only way it'll happen."

He arrived at the trestle and tied up Blossom, then climbed to the edge of the tracks. "This is the craziest thing I've ever done," he muttered, waiting for the 405 to make the turn, then slow down to cross Jackrabbit Creek.

Daniel didn't have to wait long. The engine rumbled past, and he said one last prayer as the string of passenger cars slid by. Finally came the caboose, which he ran to catch.

Both hands grasped the rail, and Daniel felt the momentum haul him toward the platform, where he caught his boot on the step. He just needed to roll forward and he'd be on.

The July wind caught his shirt and whipped it about, and his hat went flying. Beneath him, the ground disappeared and the rocky banks of Jackrabbit Creek came into view. He tried to lunge forward, but his shirt caught on the rail and held him in place.

Yanking free, he made another attempt and felt the edge of the platform under his boots. The 405's whistle screamed as the train began to pick up speed.

Daniel's arms burned with the effort, but he held on. Then his foot slipped.

He skidded and clawed but found nothing to stop his fall except the cold waters of Jackrabbit Creek.

Gennie looked away as the train crossed Jackrabbit Creek. Too many memories threatened, each with a hundred tears to go along with it.

"Gennie?"

She turned her attention to the banker who'd come to fetch her. "I'm sorry," she said. "Please forgive my inattentiveness."

Chandler stretched his hand across the distance between them to entwine his fingers with hers. "I hold nothing against you," he said. "Nor shall we speak of this again."

"This?"

"Denver." He moved to join her. "You've had your visit, and now we're going home. To New York."

She almost smiled, but the effort exhausted her before she completed it. "I'd like to sleep now, Chandler," she managed.

The truth. When she slept, she could go where she wanted.

When she slept, her Wild West adventure did not have to end.

30

"Good, because that's what I've come for, Mae. I'm ready to give up my life."

"Henry?" Mae stuffed her rifle into her saddlebag and spurred the horse toward dear Henry. "How did you find me?" She gave the object of her dreams a surprised look. "And what is that you're wearing?"

He tipped his hat and adjusted his buckskin jacket. "I've got a secret life, Mae, and it's time you knew about it. But first, I've got an appointment with the parson, and this time I'm not taking no for an answer. You're going to marry me, Mae Winslow, and then we're hitting the trail together. I'm after a fellow named One-Eyed Ed. Ever heard of him?"

They lived happily ever after.

The furious felons and cagey criminals from Dodge City to Deadwood, Bozeman to Butte, however, did not.

⊖⊙

London, August 15

Daniel stepped off the ship with Charlotte at his side. The crossing had been accomplished with little trouble, and now he stood back where he started so many years before: on the docks at London.

Around him were the familiar sights and sounds, the smells of seawater and rotting fish a reminder Denver was far behind him. Leadville even farther.

His gaze scanned the crowd, though he had no idea what—or whom—he was looking for.

"Mr. Beck?" Daniel whirled around to find a man watching him. "Daniel Beck?"

"I am."

"Then you'll want to come with me."

He did and found his trunks had already been loaded on a carriage emblazoned with the Beck family crest. "After you, Buttercup," he said as he helped Charlotte inside.

The trip was not a brief one, but he found it far too short for his liking. Too soon the carriage clattered to a stop. There was no need to look out the carriage window to see where he'd been delivered.

"Papa, what are we waiting for?"

"What indeed?" Daniel threw open the carriage door and climbed out, then reached back to set Charlotte on her feet. Stepping onto the cobblestones sent him back a decade to a time when he'd found pleasure in walking across them. Perhaps this was something he could recover as readily as he could recall it. "We're here, Buttercup," he said with more bravado than he felt.

"I thought he lived in the mountains like we do," she said, looking up and down the London street.

"This is his city home," Daniel said. "Perhaps someday I'll take you to see Beck Manor." *But not as long as my brother still lives there.* "Now remember, your grandfather's not feeling well, so it's possible you'll not get to meet him on this trip."

The words he'd chosen and practiced, both for the truth they held and the protection they offered should his father cling to the belief that both he and Charlotte should remain in exile.

"Papa." Charlotte tugged on his sleeve. "Who is that man?"

Daniel followed the direction of his daughter's gaze, and his heart tumbled to the cobblestones. "That," he said, swallowing the lump in his throat, "is the Earl of… That's your grandfather."

New York City, September 21

The engraved invitation to tonight's soiree at the Vanowens sat atop two dozen others in the silver tray on Gennie's writing desk. The event marked the return of the Vanowen family from their extended visit to London and celebrated the visit of the Earl of Something-or-Other.

If Mama hadn't insisted, Gennie would've tossed it away like the other invitations she'd received since she returned. She hadn't spoken a word to Hester Vanowen since her betrayal. Tonight she would not only have to spend several hours in the traitor's presence, but she would also likely have to listen to a thousand and one excuses why it was perfectly appropriate to tell Chandler Dodd her secret.

At least Chandler seemed to have kept the trip just that—secret. Surely if Mama or Papa knew, they would've given away some hint of it by now. But then, Chandler was likely afraid he'd lose her if he told. What he didn't realize was he'd lost her the moment the door of Fisher's knocked her on the floor.

Gennie blinked hard as the ever-present tears threatened again. Some days she missed Denver and those she loved so much it hurt to breathe. Other days, it was merely excruciating.

To make matters worse, she highly expected Chandler would use tonight's event to announce their engagement. He'd been more than accommodating when she put him off each time he tried to discuss the matter, but just yesterday afternoon, he and Papa spent an inordinate amount of time closeted away in Papa's library. Then they left together, only to return some hours later, chattering uncharacteristically.

Something was in the works. The thought of it made her positively sick. And yet, what could she say? She couldn't marry him because she was still in love with Daniel Beck?

Gennie threw open the windows to let fresh air in, and along with it came the sounds and smells of Manhattan. While the sun was setting, there was no sunset to be seen beyond the buildings and no trees to sway in the breeze, save the few sparse ones planted on the esplanade.

It made her miss Colorado even more.

But she'd had her Wild West adventure, and now it was time to do the next thing. The dutiful thing.

Daniel, you idiot. Where are you tonight?

"It's time to get dressed, miss," her maid said. "Might you need assistance with your gown?"

Gennie nodded at Fiona, then allowed the maid to do the work of preparing her for yet another night out in Manhattan. She stared at the stranger in the mirror, watching her be painted, powdered, and primped into the woman who would surely be asked to join the Dodd family tonight.

When Fiona was done, Gennie reached past the more expensive perfumes to retrieve a small, nearly empty bottle. While the maid disappeared into the closet, she dabbed the rose-scented fragrance on her wrists, behind her ears, and at the base of her throat.

"Now for the dress," Fiona said with more enthusiasm than necessary. She brought out the frock, a freshly arrived House of Worth creation designed by Charles Frederick Worth himself and accompanied by a note stating the creation was sent with highest regards from their mutual friend Empress Eugenia.

"And it's silver." Gennie's laugh sounded hollow, even to herself. "How ironic."

Though the party was just across the street, Chandler insisted he escort her. "I assure you I'll not get lost," Gennie told him as he offered her his arm to cross the street. Instantly she regretted her ill humor. It wasn't Chandler's fault she was thus affected.

Gennie swung him a sideways glance. "Actually, it is."

"Is what?"

"Never mind." She shook her head and offered her wrap to the Vanowens' houseman. "Do forgive me, Chandler. I'm being insufferable tonight."

Chandler pulled her to a stop in an alcove beneath the wide staircase. *Oh no. Not now. Not here.*

"Miss Cooper, I've respected your request not to discuss what happened in Denver."

She looked around, certain someone would hear.

"Look at me." When she complied, he continued. "As you know, I've spent a considerable amount of time with your father of late." A group of partygoers climbed the stairs behind them, and Chandler grew silent until they were gone. "It has not escaped his attention that you've been a bit, well, subdued since their return from the Continent."

He paused and looked at her as if he expected some sort of acknowledgment, or perhaps an explanation. She gave him a nod and nothing else.

"I just want to say that I hope tonight will change all of that. It may be hard for you to believe, but your happiness is paramount to me." He paused. "That's why I've done what I could to facilitate the events of this evening."

"I see." Her heart sank. So tonight was indeed the night.

He ducked his head. "Just remember, it is because I love you that I've helped with certain things." He paused. "Know your happiness will always be my priority."

"Thank you," she managed, and she had no doubt he spoke the truth. Indeed, the man had been attentive to a fault, as well as kind and patient.

He just wasn't someone she could love.

Now all she had to do was figure out how to turn him down when he asked for her hand.

The sound of music and voices drew near, and Gennie fought the urge to turn and go home. Fiona had just fetched the latest adventures of Mae Winslow—rumored to be the last—and she longed to climb under her blankets and live through the Woman of the West just one more time.

Gennie paused at the top of the stairs to await the announcement of her name, then joined the others in a long receiving line. She gave but a cursory greeting to Hester, then moved on to Mrs. Vanowen, who embraced her heartily, then held her at arm's length and perused her carefully over the top of her bejeweled spectacles.

"You look lovely, darling," she said. "That must be the Worth the empress wrote me about. I'd imagined it as beautiful, but on you it's absolutely stunning."

Nodding, Gennie participated in the inane chatter one expected in these situations until the line moved her on. Since childhood, Mr. Vanowen had put her in mind of a walrus. From his tusk-like mustache to his portly frame, he'd been the least of all adults she'd expected to hold such power. Rather, he seemed a genial and truly funny fellow.

"Might I present the seventh Earl of Framingham?" he said in an official-sounding voice.

Gennie turned to greet the nobleman, and her smile wavered. Sandy hair threaded with silver and busy brows of the same color framed a face that seemed at once familiar and kind. When he reached to take her hands in his, they trembled.

"So you are Eugenia," he said.

She nodded, unsure what else to say.

"We've called her Gennie as long as she's been old enough to answer," Mr. Vanowen said.

"Gennie, it is," the earl said, still holding tight to her hands. "Might we visit more later? I warrant there's much we could find to discuss."

"Yes, of course," Gennie said. "That would be lovely."

He smiled and released her to turn to Chandler. Rather than wait, Gennie made her way toward Mama and Papa, who sat at a table near the dais. Mama practically bubbled with happiness, likely at her inclusion on the lofty Vanowen guest list.

"All right, Papa," Gennie said as she seated herself beside her father. "What's going on? You look positively touched with the mysterious."

"Touched with the mysterious." He grinned. "From your favorite fairy tale."

"Gennie!" A child's squeal, and a familiar one at that.

Gennie turned to see Charlotte Beck racing toward her, and rose. "Oh, my baby girl!" She enveloped the girl in a hug as tears clouded her vision. "I've missed you so. But what are you doing here?"

By degrees, she became aware of the fact that if Charlotte were here, likely so was her father.

Or perhaps not. The girl was practically eleven, and she'd mentioned on more than one occasion that without a governess, she'd be sent to finishing school. Had Daniel sent her to New York, where she'd somehow ended up at the Vanowen soiree? There was only one way to find out.

She held the girl at arm's length. "You look absolutely grown up tonight, sweetheart. Are you here with friends?"

"Not exactly," said a male voice behind her.

Gennie froze. Daniel.

"Turn around."

She couldn't move. Couldn't think.

Charlotte giggled and did the work for her, turning Gennie until she faced Daniel Beck.

"Daniel," slipped from her tongue, but nothing else would come.

He went past her to where her parents sat, and greeted them. Papa rose to slap Daniel on the back like a long lost friend. The silver baron then kissed Mama's hand, making her blush.

"Do you know one another?" Gennie asked.

Chandler came to stand beside her. "I facilitated an introduction," he said. "I thought it best under the circumstances."

"What circumstances?"

Charlotte pulled Gennie down and whispered in her ear. "He loves you. Go get him."

Daniel moved toward her, and their gazes collided as he accepted a handshake from Chandler. Gennie felt Daniel capture her wrist. "I'd deserve it if you walked away."

"I couldn't if I tried," she responded.

His smile was glorious, even when he looked back to her parents. "Might I borrow your daughter for a moment, sir?" He winked at Charlotte. "Perhaps you should go and see what trouble Grandfather is getting into. When I left him, he was eying the pie."

The girl scampered away to wrap her arms around the Earl of Framingham.

"That's your father?" Gennie asked.

Daniel shrugged. "He hasn't been for many years, but I'm happy to say he is now." He lifted her hand to his lips and kissed her knuckles. "I've missed you, Gennie."

She wanted to tell him how very much she too had missed him, but this was information he'd neither wanted then nor needed now.

"What brings you to the Vanowen party tonight?" she asked instead.

"Among other things, you," he said. "You left a few things undone in Denver, and I thought now might be a good time to take care of them."

Business? He'd come to discuss business with her? She tried to hide her disappointment by greeting those whom she recognized as she followed Daniel from the room. At the edge of the crowd, her conscience plagued her and she called for Daniel to wait. Then she saw he was limping.

"What happened?" she asked.

"I fell off a train," was his ludicrous response.

He guided her away from the busy ballroom and out onto the roof terrace. The skies were fading from orange to purple, and the first stars twinkled above the silver crescent moon. The scent of roses from Mrs. Vanowen's expansive garden perfumed the night and carpeted both sides of a path lit with gaslights and paved in marble.

"Daniel, what sort of business are we possibly going to take care of out here?"

"The kind I was too stupid and proud to take care of back in Denver." He shook his head. "That's not completely true. I did try, but when I fell off that train, I figured the Lord was trying to tell me to leave you alone." He paused to touch a climbing rose. "Turns out He was just telling me to hang on tighter."

Daniel searched her face to see if Gennie caught the dual meaning. If she did, she gave no indication.

Instead, she walked to the railing and looked out over the buildings, her own home included. He knew where she lived, even knew which window was hers. He could thank Jeb Sanders for that information.

The Pinkerton was not only good at his job, but over the last two months, he'd become a friend. In his status as an undercover agent, he'd also proven to be a good right-hand man for Hiram, who'd taken over the Leadville mines. Sanders provided updates through his New York colleagues of the comings and goings of Gennie Cooper. When the Pinkerton informed him Chandler Dodd had made a purchase at Tiffany and Company, Daniel knew action was required.

What sort of action took a few weeks to decide. Elias claimed it was his hard head, but Daniel knew it was his wounded heart.

He hadn't counted on the fact that Chandler knew before he did that Gennie was not meant to be Chandler's wife. While he'd hoped for Mr. Cooper's blessing, he hadn't counted on Chandler's giving up so easily.

Daniel would have fought to the death to keep Gennie.

"You resemble your father," she said, jarring his attention.

"I suppose I do, a little."

She turned and the dying rays of the sun spun gold into her hair, putting him in mind of their last afternoon together in his library. "And it appears he and Charlotte get along fabulously."

"Yes, the trip to England was a blessing in disguise." He paused to take in the sight of her and cursed himself for letting her go.

"Oh?" She shook her head. "I thought he was coming to Denver."

"The plans changed when his health wouldn't permit him to make the voyage. Charlotte insisted I make the overture and offer to bring her there." He moved to stand beside her at the rail. "I don't want to talk about Charlotte or my father or anything other than the reason I asked for a few minutes of your time."

"Of course." She rested her arms on the rail and studied her nails. "I'm sorry."

"Gennie?" Daniel placed his palm on her back. It fit just as he remembered. She straightened and seemed to be holding her breath. He moved closer, sliding his palms around to flatten his hands across her waist. "Breathe, Gennie," he whispered against the back of her neck. "Just breathe." He waited until he felt her relax. "Now turn around," he said, his lips brushing the base of her neck. "I need you to be looking at me when I say this."

She turned in his arms and looked up at him, and he almost forgot how to speak.

"I love you. I think I've loved you since you landed on the floor of Fisher's. I know I loved you when I saw you clomping around in those boots."

Anger flashed in her eyes. "Then why didn't you stop me, Daniel? Why did you just let me leave?" She shook her head. "No, you *told* me to leave."

"I was wrong."

"That's it? That's the business you came to discuss with me? Two months after you ordered me out of your home, you want to tell me you love me?"

Daniel shook his head. "No, that's not all." He pulled an envelope from his pocket. "We're married."

"That's the marriage license from Leadville. It wasn't…"

The former governess let out a long breath and sagged against the rail. Much as Daniel wanted to scoop her into his arms and hold her, he let her think it through, let her logic it out and see if she came to the same conclusion he had.

While she did, he prayed.

"It was real."

He nodded. "Gennie, I tried to come after you. I rode Blossom all the way to Jackrabbit Creek just so I could catch that train. I'm lucky the water wasn't any lower in the creek, or you'd be a rich widow." He looked away. "All right, that was a bad joke."

She stared at him. He couldn't tell what she was thinking.

"Gennie, I can't propose because we're already married," he said. "But I can promise you a Wild West adventure every day of your life."

She shook her head. "No, thank you."

"No, thank you?"

Gennie rose up on her toes, her lips near his. "Not every day, please. I don't think I could stand it." She met his gaze. "Wait. We're married."

"Yes," he managed.

She came torturously closer. "Legally wed."

He could only nod.

"Husband and wife."

Daniel scooped her into his arms, ignoring the twinge in his wounded leg, and carried her back inside.

"No, Daniel, not through the ballroom," she cried as he stepped through the open doors.

"Oh my," Mrs. Vanowen said as Gennie's foot nearly connected with a suspiciously familiar jeweled bird in the center of the buffet table. "This is quite irregular."

"Bravo, Daniel. Well done!" Papa called while Mama fanned herself and Charlotte and the earl clapped.

"Gennie!" Hester Vanowen called. "Where are you going?"

"My honeymoon." Daniel's wife pressed her lips against his ear. "And hurry. We've got two months of marriage to catch up on."

Daniel grinned. "Technically it's two and a half, but who's counting?"

"I will be," she whispered.

He set her on her feet and stole a kiss. "More of that later." He nodded to the houseman, who brought out an elegantly wrapped package of large dimensions. "A wedding present."

"What have you done?" She shook her head and unwrapped the gift, then squealed when she revealed the buckskin jacket. "This looks exactly like—"

"It is." He helped her shrug into it. "I had a feeling you'd have need of it again someday."

She gasped. "And my boots."

Daniel swept up the package and ushered Gennie to the stairs. "Might I help you put these on?"

Gennie looked around. "Daniel, people are watching."

He tried not to wince as he bent to one knee and lifted the edge of his wife's House of Worth dress—the one he'd personally picked from the three drawings the empress had sent. Gennie's shoes, chosen for their ease of removal, he tossed behind him, much to the delight of the watching crowd.

One by one, he slipped her boots into place, then, with a flourish, helped her stand. He looked up at the gallery and caught Charlotte watching, her hand solidly entwined with her grandfather's. He winked at his daughter, and she blew him a kiss. His father nodded, then straightened his back and gave Daniel a smart salute.

If ever he'd been a man given to tears, now would have been the time to shed them. Perhaps someday, when he and Gennie recalled this moment to their children's children, but not now. "One more surprise."

"No more, Daniel. It's too much."

Another kiss, in full view of anyone still shameless enough to stare. "It will never be enough," he whispered. "Never."

"Daniel."

On her lips, his name was a word, a name, and an invitation of such promise that he cut short the speech he'd prepared for the occasion.

"Close your eyes and take my hand."

She did as he asked, and he led her forward until the grand front doors of the Vanowen mansion opened to reveal the best part of tonight's plan.

"Look."

Gennie laughed when she saw Blossom, her mane braided with roses and ribbons.

"I had to bribe her to do that," Daniel said, "so you'd better appreciate it. Cost me plenty of carrots, I don't mind telling you." He followed his wife through the doors, tipping his hat at the doorman. "Oh," he said as if he'd forgotten, "there's one more thing."

"Daniel, really! You're spoiling me."

"Hold that opinion for later, darling." He leaned close. "You know how we brand our wives out west, don't you?"

Her blue eyes widened, then narrowed. "You're teasing me again."

Daniel grasped her left hand and brought her fingers to his lips. From his pocket he pulled the ring he'd picked up this morning, the one Mr. Tiffany himself had designed from a unique and very out-of-the-ordinary piece of material: a hairpin.

The blush his wife wore as she allowed him to slip it on her finger was worth what it took to convince the jeweler his participation in the creation would be a secret both took to the grave. The exquisite diamond ring matched the silly bauble Mr. Tiffany proudly took credit for, but Gennie would not see that until she looked under her pillow.

"Darling, I mentioned something about making up for lost time?" Gennie asked.

Her slow smile almost made him change his honeymoon plans and carry her across the street to the chamber where she woke that morning. Instead, he climbed onto the horse, then hauled his wife on in front of him.

"Hold on, Mrs. Beck. You're about to have the adventure of your life."

With a flourish, he spurred the horse on, pointing her west toward home.

Manhattan Miss Flees Soiree on Horseback with Surprise

NEW YORK CITY, September 22, 1880—A large company of ladies and gentlemen of quality gathered in the home of our city's premier host and hostess for a night of entertainment that will likely not be forgotten for some time. None were more surprised at last evening's Vanowen soiree than those in attendance.

Thinking to be part of a gathering honoring visiting royalty, the Earl of Framingham, they were instead forced to watch one Eugenia Flora Cooper of Fifth Avenue Manhattan flee the festivities atop an oddly festooned horse along with one Daniel Beck of Denver, Colorado. Adorned in a gown of the most exquisite quality, Miss Cooper presented herself to society as a young woman of good breeding and refinement. Indeed her father, one John Abbot Cooper of our city, is very well thought of in banking circles. Her mother keeps excellent company and was, before her marriage, at home among the elite of Boston and Newport.

While neither Mrs. Vanowen or her husband would comment on the shocking turn of events visited upon their evening, it is an established fact that the music was furnished by Lander and the supper by Delmonico. The many invited guests included Ex-Mayor Wickham, Dr. and Mrs. Agnew, Mr. Latham Fish, Mr. and Mrs. Malcomb Graham, Mr. Chandler Dodd and his parents, the elder Dodds, as well as many other local, national, and international dignitaries.

In response to the debacle, Miss Cooper's father offered the news that indeed his daughter had been wed to Mr. Beck for some months. When asked why the marriage had been held in confidence, the banker had no comment on the matter. Nor could he offer any information on why someone formerly known as a docile and amenable woman would don what appeared to be boots and some sort of woodsman's jacket for her humiliating ride up Fifth Avenue.

Thankfully the couple will reside in the West, where they both obviously will be more at home. As an aside to this, it has been learned that the Earl of Framingham will amend his tour of New York to board the Cooper railcar tomorrow at dawn in order to visit Denver and Leadville, where his son has considerable mining interests.

Becks Return From Wedding Tour Back East

DENVER, October 1, 1880—Delightful news from our own British royal Daniel Beck, who has wed the lovely Miss Eugenia Flora Cooper of Manhattan, New York. While in Leadville on a trip formerly explained as business, the pair said their vows with Mr. Beck's daughter Charlotte and much of the better citizens of the city in attendance.

Indeed it appears the silver magnate and his wife will live happily ever after, as witnessed by the round of receptions, suppers, and parties already planned for them as news arrived of their wedding. When asked at the train station why their nuptials had been kept secret, Mr. Beck was mum on the matter. Mrs. Beck, however, expressed her happiness at returning to the city she once only dreamed of.

"Daniel is my husband and Denver is now my home," the blushing bride said, accompanied by her handsome spouse. "A happier ending to a story has not been written than ours."

Mae Winslow

The Curious Case of the Wrangled Ring

Of all the misadventures our fair heroine Mae Winslow had found herself a part of, today's was without question the most dangerous. The maiden stood unarmed and unable to defend herself, her very life in the gravest of danger.

For if the seamstress trying to make a wedding frock out of yards of satin and lace missed her target by the tiniest amount, the pointed weapon in her hand would surely plunge into Mae's heart and kill her on the spot. Her proper, Boston-born Mama offered no protection, as she had fallen into soft snores in the chair nearest the shuttered window.

As if she discerned the direction of Mae's thoughts, the designing damsel lifted a perfectly sculpted brow. "Something amiss, miss?" she inquired in a thick Irish brogue. Then, obviously thinking herself quite clever, she repeated the question before falling into a fit of giggles and going back to her murderous ways. "A few more tucks here and a seam there, and this masterpiece will be delivered to your hotel," she said. "Though I do wonder whether you ought to have one last fitting this afternoon once I complete the work."

The door knob rattled before Mae could offer a protest.

"A telegram for Miss Winslow," came a feeble voice that failed to awaken Mama or cease the seamstresses' pervasive pinning. Whether lad or aged lady, there seemed little to recommend whomever carried the telegram. Still, it seemed someone should respond.

Mae attempted to step toward the door, but felt a hand grasp her elbow with a steely grip.

"You'll ruin my work. Do not move." With distinct displeasure, the seamstress made her way to the door. "Why, there's no one here. Only this letter." She turned, eyes wide. "I was told you were a woman of some importance back East come to wed the new governor. But this says your name is..." She shook her head. "Are you really...?"

Mae sighed. This sort of reaction had become all too frequent. Perhaps it was time to forever leave the name of Mae Winslow behind.

"Mae Winslow. Yes, I'm afraid so," Mama said, having revived from her rest. "She never would answer to the name her papa and I gave her. Practically since birth, she's ignored the proper and taken up with whatever suited her. It's a wonder dear Henry is willing to be yoked to her tonight."

Our fair one might have protested had Mae not been consumed with reading what was, in actuality, not a telegram but a cry for help. While the women prattled on, Mae made good on her ability to escape even the most dangerous situation undetected.

By the time Mama and the seamstress noticed her absence, Mae Winslow, Woman of the West, had divested herself of the horrid gown and found her way out the back. Around the corner of the building, trouble awaited in the form of dear Henry's harried houseman.

"I knew I could count on you," he said. "You must find the ring."

Mae shook her head, looking around for Henry, who had likely planned the elaborate ruse. "Tell your employer I find great pleasure in being released from the clutches of that awful seamstress, but I'll not be made sport of."

"I jest not," said the poor man, whose wringing hands spoke of the truth. "I was sent to fetch the ring you're to be given tonight." He mustered up a tear as he told of a thump on the head followed by a galloping horse. "When I awoke, the ring was no longer in my pocket. The thief said to tell you it had been taken by Dakota Dan."

A name she knew all too well.

Mae formed a plan. Purloining a mare from those assembled in the livery plagued her conscience only for a moment. She'd return the beast along with a hefty payment once her deed was done.

For she knew where to find Dakota Dan.

Rounding the bend at Forked Trail, she came upon the man she sought. Her horse, while not tried and true, was brave and bore the upward rise of the treacherous trail with vigor. Atop the bluff, she found a better view of the valley and Dakota Dan, seemingly oblivious to her presence.

Lacking any way to hobble the mare, Mae led it along behind her. Better to have the means to escape should such an exit be required. That the animal might alert Dan to her proximity was a risk she would have to take. And yet the man from the Dakotas seemed too preoccupied with his endeavors to pay her any heed. He raised some sort of weapon, something that glinted in the sun as he lifted it, then brought it down against the hard-packed earth.

He was digging a hole. The rogue.

Creeping ever nearer, Mae reached for the pistol hidden in her skirts, only to realize she'd removed it, along with her knife, before the fitting.

"So be it," she whispered to the mare. "I've wit enough to accomplish this."

And wit she called upon as she used her heel to cut a green vine from the brush to tie up the horse. With a promise to return, she moved through the thicket, inching closer to her prey. Soon only the space of a few feet remained between her and the man who'd stolen her wedding ring.

Dan stood with his back to her. Under other circumstances, Mae might have admired the cut of his jacket and the breadth of his shoulders, or the strength in his arms as he wielded the shovel.

But not now. Her purpose was not admiration but justice.

Her finely tuned senses took her within reach of the site where Dakota Dan, his efforts complete, tossed a leather sack into the hole. That done, the outlaw hastened to remove all signs of having buried his loot.

And then he did the most dastardly thing of all. Right there, practically within reach of Mae, Dakota Dan sat on a rock and pulled out a box lunch and a book.

Sighing, Mae crouched in the brush until her knees quaked, and yet the man seemed in no hurry to vacate the scene of his crime. Without weapons, she could hardly subdue such a man, so she vowed to wait him out. Surely he would soon leave.

The sun traveled across the sky, and Dakota Dan showed no interest in moving. From the length of the shadows, Mae knew she would soon be missed at the chapel. She hoped dear Henry would forgive her for arriving late to her own wedding. She was, after all, the bride and surely entitled to such things.

Time continued to pass, and good intentions aside, she somehow allowed her eyelids to fall, for soon she jerked awake. Dakota Dan stood above her.

"Mae Winslow," he said with more than a little admiration. "I heard you promised to end your crime fighting once you married."

"I'm not married yet," she protested, shielding her eyes from the sun's glare.

He gave a deep chuckle that cut through her, then his face grew serious. "I've been wondering what was taking you so long to come after me," he said in a slow drawl that accompanied a sweep of her prone person with his gaze.

Accustomed to such impertinence in men like this one, Mae looked past him to the still-soft patch of earth. From where she sat, she could easily reach the ring's hiding place, but could she fetch the pouch and make good her escape without Dan catching her?

"It has always interested me," she said as a plan formed, "that some men assume they garner more attention from women than is truly theirs."

Mae scooted away from his shadow and slowly rose. As she expected, the overconfident Dan merely watched while she reached for the ribbon restraining her hair.

"Impossible," he said with an arrogance that surprised her. "For you surely have come for what you want."

"I have, at that." Her heart beating faster, Mae forced a smile. "Indeed, you've found me out." She inched forward. "For you see, I was watching you swing your shovel."

One dark eyebrow rose, as did the corner of his mouth. With it, a pair of dimples appeared. Her statement had the desired effect, as Dakota Dan showed a keen interest in her every move.

Behind her back, Mae coiled the ribbon around her hand and

prepared to make good on her brilliant plan. All she needed was a distraction.

But Dakota Dan moved first, capturing her in a most brazen embrace. Eyes as blue as the Colorado sky caught her attention as his face drew near. She could hear his breathing, smell the scent of soap and saddle leather, see his jaw clench, watch the vein at his temple pulse.

Then the rogue had the audacity to capture her lips with his. She'd shared the occasional kiss with dear Henry, but this was, well...impertinent. Impossibly impertinent.

But to push him away might foil her plan. Resigned to endure the kiss, Mae waited.

Just then, the mare nickered. Dakota Dan turned toward the sound, and Mae sprang into action. Before the outlaw could gather his wits, Mae had his ankles knotted together with the most lovely length of pink ribbon she owned.

"A pity to leave it behind with the likes of you," she said as she bolted over the confused man. She hoisted the shovel in her delicate hands and quickly unearthed the leather pouch.

A whistle, and the mare came racing through the brush, trailing the broken vine like an extra rein. Mae caught the saddle and slid into place, riding off toward town, Dakota Dan still fumbling at the ribbon binding his ankles behind her.

"Where have you been?" Mama called as Mae put on her most penitent look and pressed past her into the church. "At this rate, you've barely got enough time to don your gown. Oh, mercy, look at your hair. It's full of tree branches."

Drama was, indeed, Mama's strong suit, for at best she'd borne a few leaves back with her from her escapade. Surely the speed of the horse's gallop had removed all the rest.

Mae allowed but the briefest of attention to her toilette, including a mere sweep of a brush through her tangles. The pink ribbon gone, she settled for one the color of the Colorado sunset, then sent Mama off to join Papa at the church. One last look out the window toward the West, where she'd left Dakota Dan and her life of crime fighting behind, and she made for the door.

Long ago she'd promised the Lord to follow His lead. Today that path led to dear Henry and a long overdue wedding.

Some moments later, Mae Winslow slipped quietly into the vestibule just as the pastor called to the organist to begin the anthem. There she found dear Henry, who greeted her with a kiss more appropriate to the honeymoon than the wedding.

"I feared you'd not come, sweet flower," he whispered, his gaze traveling the length of her.

"Nothing would keep me from this appointment," she responded with the truest of hearts.

Dear Henry reached to pluck something—a twig—from her curls. "Not even your former career as a crime fighter?"

"No need to continue that career, Governor Daniels," she said with a sly smile as she noticed his watch chain had been replaced with a pink ribbon. A familiar pink ribbon. "It appears Dakota Dan has been caught."

"Permanently," dear Henry said as he linked arms and led her toward the pastor, where the ring was finally set upon the right hand.

Or, rather, the left.